D1180491

# THE COST OF LIVING

# THE COST OF LIVING
*Early and Uncollected Stories*

# MAVIS GALLANT

*Introduction by*
## JHUMPA LAHIRI

BLOOMSBURY
LONDON · BERLIN · NEW YORK

First published in Great Britain 2009

Copyright © 2009 by Mavis Gallant
Introduction copyright © 2009 by Jhumpa Lahiri

First published in the United States in 2009 by the New York Review of
Books, 435 Hudson Street, New York, NY 10014

Bloomsbury Publishing Plc
36 Soho Square
London W1D 3QY

www.bloomsbury.com

Bloomsbury Publishing, London, New York and Berlin
A CIP catalogue record for this book is available from the British Library

ISBN 978 1 4088 0610 4

10 9 8 7 6 5 4 3 2 1

Printed in Great Britain by Clays Limited, St Ives plc

# CONTENTS

# INTRODUCTION

I HAPPENED to have the privilege of interviewing Mavis Gallant while the present collection was being assembled. Sitting with her in February 2009 at the Village Voice Bookshop in Paris, I asked how she thought her stories, published over the course of half a century, had changed. "I don't compare," she replied. "It's just a straight line to me." To prove her point, she briefly lifted, with her fingers, an apricot-colored necklace that rested against her chest. "They're like the beads on this."

The twenty stories here were published during the first twenty years of Gallant's career, between 1951 and 1971. They were written prior to the age of fifty; she turned eighty-seven just as this volume went to press. Many are culled from her first two collections, *The Other Paris* (1956) and *My Heart Is Broken* (1964), and also from *In Transit*, which was published in the late Eighties but contains earlier work. One story, originally published in *The New Yorker*, is a chapter from her first novel, *Green Water, Green Sky* (1959). In fact, all but three of these stories initially appeared in *The New Yorker*. None were included in *The Collected Stories*, published in 1996, which compiled only a fraction of Gallant's work, and a good third of them have never been collected in a book at all. They are arranged in chronological order. The earliest, "Madeline's Birthday," was published in *The New Yorker* on September 1, 1951. It is among more than one hundred stories by Gallant that the magazine would accept.

"Madeline's Birthday" was the second story Gallant submitted to *The New Yorker*; the first was returned with the inquiry, "Do you have anything else you can show us?" At the time, she was a twenty-seven-year-old reporter at the *Standard* in Montreal. Gallant was born in Montreal in 1922, ten years after John Cheever, ten years before John Updike. Along with Cheever and Updike, she kept company, in the pages of *The New Yorker*, with Donald Barthelme, J. D. Salinger, Frank O'Connor, and Sylvia Townsend Warner, all of whom were publishing fiction there regularly during the Fifties and Sixties. Most of Gallant's *New Yorker* stories were edited by William Maxwell; *My Heart Is Broken* is dedicated to him. Before "Madeline's Birthday" was accepted, she had already resolved to move to Paris and was determined to make her living exclusively as a writer of fiction. The sheer bravado of this decision, particularly for a single woman of that period, is astonishing. Gallant simultaneously abandoned a reliable paycheck and her country of origin in exchange for an artist's life on foreign soil. *The New Yorker* remained her home across the ocean; the magazine's steady support through the years was crucial to her, just as the steady stream of stories she contributed were for the magazine.

Readers of Gallant's fiction tend to associate it with Canada and France, and Michael Ondaatje, Russell Banks, and Douglas Gibson have all made selections of her work that highlight those attachments. But between the ages of thirteen and eighteen, the years following her father's death and her mother's remarriage, Gallant lived in and around New York City, a place she told me she loves, while attending a series of schools, sometimes as a boarder. These were the years leading up to World War Two, of the Great Depression and FDR's second term as president; Duke Ellington and his orchestra were playing at the Cotton Club, and the Empire State Building had recently been completed. Many of Gallant's earliest stories reflect her encounter with the United States: the characters in "Going Ashore," "One Morning in May," "The Picnic," and "Autumn Day" are all Americans, and many of them are New Yorkers. "Thieves and Rascals" takes place entirely in Manhattan, in its apartments and on its sidewalks, with the Museum of Modern Art, Grand Central Station, and Columbia University contributing to the backdrop. "Madeline's Birthday" is set just outside New York, in Connecticut, but as in many suburban tales, the city and its ways are an implicit presence throughout.

Part of Madeline's predicament is that she is a city child stuck in the country. She is the by-product of a broken marriage; her mother lives in Europe, and her father has remarried a woman she's never met. She is consequently a vagabond: "The days of her lifetime had been spent in so many different places—in schools, in camps, in the houses of people she was or was not related to—that the first sight of day was, almost by habit, bewildering." A student at boarding school, Madeline ends up living alone in a Manhattan apartment for three weeks because her mother has forgotten to instruct her to go to the home of Mrs. Tracy, a family friend, for the summer. Once the oversight is rectified and Madeline is safely installed in Connecticut, Mrs. Tracy believes she's saved Madeline from neglect, while Madeline, accustomed to her independence, feels like she's been taken hostage. Madeline is half girl, half woman, a creature at once precocious and vulnerable. She is neither a child, like Mrs. Tracy's six-year-old daughter, Allie, nor an adult, like Mrs. Tracy, whose husband works in the city and comes home only on weekends. On the morning of her seventeenth birthday, Madeline dreams of receiving a dollhouse, but her stepmother sends an unsuitable evening gown instead. Along with Madeline, Mrs. Tracy has taken in a German student named Paul, a boy orphaned by the war. Rounding out the cast of characters is Doris the maid, running an electric blender in the kitchen, and finally, offstage but central to the drama, there is Edward, the part-time patriarch of the household.

The maiden publication of any major writer is of interest, but "Madeline's Birthday" introduces a voice that is preternaturally mature. For a relatively fleet, satirical tale that isolates only an hour or two of human drama, it is surprisingly capacious, and also unsettling. It is a double portrait of adolescent angst and alienation on the one hand, and the false order and forced cheer of domesticity on the other. Part of its complexity is due to the fact that we have access not just to one or two but several points of view. This is the narrative equivalent of what acrobats do as they leap from one swinging bar to another—a feat ambitious enough in a novel, forbidding in the restricted confines of short fiction. The startling precision of Gallant's language, her agility as a storyteller, and her uncanny ability to distill, in a handful of words, the inner states of her characters—all are amply evident in this striking debut. Of Madeline's intolerance for Paul, with whom she must share a bathroom, Gallant writes, "They did not even have a cake of soap in common."

Thematically, "Madeline's Birthday" sets a precedent for a great deal that followed. It is about characters juxtaposed but estranged, about children living without parents, about women living without husbands. It is about attitudes toward foreigners (Mrs. Tracy is disappointed in Paul, who is dark, bespectacled, and "anything but arrogant," for not corresponding to her notion of Germans), and about the repercussions of history on personal lives. It is essentially about a denial of the truth; for Mrs. Tracy, who believes fervently in the healing powers of summers spent in her country house, who identifies wholly with its breezes and hinges and coverlets, has only the dimmest perception of the people surrounding her. Nonetheless, Mrs. Tracy makes a single observation that redeems her. "They're both adrift, in a way," she says of Madeline and Paul. Here Mrs. Tracy names a condition that is central to Gallant's writing. Her characters (including, as we shall see, Mrs. Tracy herself) are all adrift, either cut loose from their origins or caught between currents that are personal, temporal, political, sometimes a combination of all three. Bringing that drift into focus is the essence of Gallant's art.

With the prospect of publication in *The New Yorker*, Gallant moved to Europe in October 1950. After a brief stay in London, she went to Paris and lived in a hotel populated by expatriates. The experience provided a seed, perhaps, for the brilliant title

story in this volume, "The Cost of Living," which was published
in 1962, about a decade after "Madeline's Birthday." Compared
to the single narrative arc of "Madeline's Birthday," the plot of
"The Cost of Living" is involuted, told through the murky prism
of memory, its force accumulating like a series of waves. It is a
denser and more challenging story, virtually impossible, in my
opinion, to digest properly in a single reading; it is thus a story
that reveals a new level of technical mastery and sophistication in
Gallant's development. We leave behind the domestic comforts of
an eighteenth-century house in Connecticut for a hotel—a favorite setting in Gallant's work—on the Left Bank of Paris, claustro-
phobic and squalid, with silverfish and dusty claret hangings. We
travel from the bourgeois landscape to the bohemian, from a suburban American summer to an urban European winter. In the
opening paragraph, the unforgiving atmosphere is rendered with
Dickensian flourish: "dark with the season, dark with the cold,
dark with the dark air of cities." The lack of natural light is absolute: "The only light on the street was the blue neon sign of a
snack bar."

The story is narrated in the first person by an Australian
woman named Patricia, or Puss, who runs away to Paris at
twenty-seven and scrapes by giving piano lessons. Her older sister,
Louise, prudent and parsimonious, follows "wisely, calmly," with
money inherited after their parents' death, and though she can
afford better, stays with Puss at the same shabby hotel. Louise is
disappointed by Paris, a recurring dilemma in Gallant's world.
She arrives "thinking that Paris would be an easy, dreamy city,
full of trees and full of time...angelic children sailing boats in
the fountains, and calm summer streets." Instead, the parks are
"full of brats and quarreling mothers." Louise is one of the many
industrious tourists in Gallant's fiction who, having invested in a
journey to Europe, seeks to reap cultural gain: "Once she had
visited all the museums, and cycled around the famous squares,
and read what was written on the monuments, she felt she was
wasting her opportunities." Among the other residents at the

hotel are two aspiring, impoverished French actors—Sylvie (who lives in an unheated linen cupboard and whose indiscretions "spread like the track of a snail" across Paris), and Patrick, who is awaiting a visa and strives to get to America.

Two sisters, two actors; two Anglo-Saxons, two French; three women, one man. The permutations are many, and Gallant choreographs these four principal characters in a dance of shifting alliances and betrayals, a knotting together and an unraveling of familial, cultural, and sexual ties. The walls of the hotel are thin, so that conversations are easily overheard, private moments routinely glimpsed. But there is little comfort in all this closeness. Instead there is a disconcerting lack of solidarity, as well as honesty, among the characters. Puss, Louise, Sylvie, and Patrick live a communal life in which things are borrowed, passed back and forth, exchanged: books, bathtubs, lovers, viruses. And money. In fact, the fifth character driving this story is money: the need for it, the ebb and flow of it, the unequivocal way it dictates our lives. But unlike books and bathtubs, money is seldom successfully shared. As Puss reflects, "Friendship in bohemia meant money borrowed, recriminations, complaints, tears, theft, and deceit." The lingering effect of the story is as dark as the Paris winter, laying bare the precariousness of expatriate life, and a ruthless calculus of human relationships.

Following a stay of a few months in the hotel, Gallant moved in with a Parisian family; during our interview, she told me that she soon tired of living with expatriates, wanting instead to observe the French. She said that initially, as in "The Cost of Living," she described the French through the eyes of foreigners. But even in an early story like "The Picnic" (1952), she begins to enter the mind of French characters in the description of Madame Pégurin, an elderly woman who loves her pets more than her own children, rattles the pages of *Le Figaro*, and tells the American children living in her house that she dislikes foreigners. The subtleties of how we perceive each other and ourselves are never lost on Gallant; of these children, at once innocent and ignorant, she writes, "But they, fortunately, did not consider themselves foreign, and had pictured instead dark men with curling beards."

Though Gallant has lived in Paris now for nearly sixty years, she has remained attuned in her fiction to the shock of arrival, the discomfiture of the new, and alongside it, the eternal restlessness of human nature. She creates characters who yearn to live life abroad, as well as characters who must. There are women who follow their husbands to Europe, and those who flee them. There are children sent away to edify and find themselves, and children dragged along by their parents. Certain characters gladly jettison the past, considering their non-European upbringings a disease, while others cling stubbornly to food, language, and other customs. Louise, in "The Cost of Living," goes out of her way to procure soda biscuits in Paris, convinced that they are necessary for nursing the grippe. As is frequently the case among expatriate communities, cultural affinities trump class distinctions, making for strange bedfellows in unfamiliar surroundings. In "Acceptance of Their Ways," Mrs. Freeport, who cannot stand Italy "without the sound of an English voice in the house," takes in an English paying guest: "In the hush of the dead season, Mrs. Freeport preferred Lily's ironed-out Bayswater to no English at all."

Gallant's stories teem with characters unwilling fully to adjust, unable to take such things as family and homeland for granted. Instead there are makeshift families, adopted languages, improvised ways. But being foreign is not just a matter of crossing borders. The sense of being adrift, the absence of terra firma, is existential—perhaps not in the manner of Beckett or Camus, but with an impact that is nevertheless profound. Reality is vertiginous, these stories tell us, no matter where and how experienced. "Night and Day," about a man emerging from anesthesia following an accident, hovers in the interstices of consciousness: the character, suffering from amnesia, is rootless in the most basic of ways. Bound to a hospital bed and lacking a past, he observes, "This is what it means to be free."

Compounding the dislocation experienced by many of Gallant's characters is World War Two, the legacy of which permeates almost all of these stories, so much so that the war often serves as their unwritten prologues. The scars of war are fresh enough so that being Jewish in Europe remains shameful; children have lost their fathers in battle, and the American military is still present on European soil. The collective posture is one of frugality, of deprivation, and of doing without. Softening cauliflowers are salvaged from garbage cans, coffee grounds used more than once, chicken cooked in vinegar instead of wine. People have been forced to flee their homes, leaving everything behind: "all the tablecloths, the little coffee spoons!" This is the fate of Frau Stengel in "A Day Like Any Other," a *Volksdeutsche* refugee from Prague who keeps a picture of Hitler pressed between two magazines. Others must open up their homes to boarders in order to make ends meet. The result is a thrusting together of people from mismatched worlds, a mis-en-scène Gallant exploits to stunning effect again and again. In addition to the devastation of history's recent past, the stories allude to the politics of France in the Fifties and Sixties: the country's diminishing status as a colonial power, beginning with Indochina's independence in 1954 and followed by the Algerian War of 1954–62. The student uprisings of 1968 (which Gallant writes about in her book of nonfiction, *Paris Journals*), occur toward the end of this collection's timeline.

Two stories, "Willi" and "One Aspect of a Rainy Day," are about German characters in postwar Europe, a subject which Gallant would explore more extensively in the 1973 collection, *The Pegnitz Junction*. The characters dream of home but cannot return, and are not made to feel at home in France, where they live. They exist without resident permits, without legitimacy, with little but memories of a previous life. Willi, a former prisoner of war, now serves as a consultant on films made about the Occupation; twenty years on, the horrors of the Holocaust are already material for the movies. "One Aspect of a Rainy Day," about a German scholarship student, concerns a general strike and a political demonstration. Because of rain and an absent mayor, the demonstration is futile. "They might have been coming from anywhere—a cinema, or a funeral," the narrator observes when the desultory group breaks apart. The story was published in 1962, the year after the Paris Massacre, when French police attacked roughly thirty thousand unarmed peaceful Algerian demonstrators. "Sunday Afternoon" also takes place during the Algerian conflict. Veronica, a nineteen-year-old girl from London, sits in her apartment in curlers and a bathrobe while her American boyfriend, Jim, who has forgotten why he fell in love with her, talks to a Tunisian friend about whether Algeria will go to the Communists. Veronica is excluded from the conversation, expected only to pour the coffee; the story is less about politics than about the chauvinistic world of men. Veronica resists autonomy, crying when Jim tells her that she's free. We know he will never marry her: "She was the homeless, desperate girl in Paris against whom he might secretly measure, one future day, a plain but confident wife."

Veronica and Jim's casual cohabitation is an exception in this collection. Most of the couples are married, most of them unhappily. Infidelity runs through the stories as a matter of course. A wedding ring is flung, unforgettably, into the twilight. A number of the characters are either divorced or in overburdened, disillusioned relationships. Wives declare to their husbands that they do not like men. "Bernadette" is a particularly damning instance of a loveless marriage, and is also an indictment of domestic life in Fifties suburbia. The couple, Nora and Robbie, had once been campus liberals, writing plays, drinking beer out of old pickle jars, hoping to change the world. Now they live in a large pseudo-Tudor home outside Montreal, with a lawyer's salary, a live-in maid, and two daughters in boarding school. Nora's activism takes the form of cocktail parties, and Robbie, who serially seduces other women and is serially forgiven, is also seduced by sentimental literary images of the working class. Curious about the kitchen in which their maid, Bernadette, grew up, he asks her to describe it to him, and is told, simply, "It's big." The reality—

the table "masked with oilcloth...always set between meals, the thick plates turned upside down, the spoons in a glass jar...butter, vinegar, canned jam with the lid of the can half opened and wrenched back, ketchup, a tin of molasses glued to its saucer"—is impossible for Bernadette to articulate, or for her employer to comprehend.

Women of my generation, born after the mid-Sixties, were raised to believe that having a career and raising a family were not mutually exclusive pursuits, but for the women in Gallant's early stories, they almost always are. "You'll probably get married sometime, anyway, so what does it matter what you learn?" Mike asks Barbara, a teenaged girl who has failed out of one of New York City's best schools, in "One Morning in May." His remark "strike[s] her into silence," but moments later Barbara wonders if Mike might be the solution: "It had occurred to her many times in this lonely winter that only marriage would save her from disgrace, from growing up with no skills and no profession." This was a time before the pill, before the fight for the Equal Rights Amendment and *Roe versus Wade*. Gilles, in "The Burgundy Weekend," remembers the women of the generation just prior to those landmark struggles and reforms:

> "They were made out of butter. They had round faces and dimples and curly hair. Bright lipstick...They could have fallen in the Seine and never drowned—they'd have floated downstream on their petticoats. They wore Italian shoes that were a disaster. All those girls have ruined feet now. They looked like children dressed up—too much skirt, mother's shoes. They smiled and smiled and wanted to get married. They were infantile, underdeveloped. Retarded."

His brutal condescension shocks our ears, revealing a misogyny that has since become less socially acceptable. Though marriage tended to be a girl's only option for establishing herself in adulthood, it was often a premature one. Nineteen-year-old Cissy, in "Autumn Day," is an example of this: unsure of herself, fuzzy about the facts of life, dressed in Peter Pan collars and drinking sugary alcoholic drinks. Her husband, ten years older, is more of a parent than a sexual partner, telling her what to do and how to behave: "Don't talk war. Avoid people on farm. Meet Army wives. Go for walks." True to their time, in most of these marriages the husband works and the wife stays home to raise the family (the fashion model in "Thieves and Rascals," afraid to cry because she has a photo shoot the next morning and does not want puffy eyes, is an exception). Alongside economic dependence for women in traditional marriages, there are women who depend on other women ("The Cost of Living" and "Acceptance of Their Ways") and men who depend on women ("Travelers Must Be Content"). The dependency in these relationships is not so much emotional as literal, and it frequently turns parasitic. Characters in these stories may not connect to each other, but they need each other to survive.

Human dependency is at its most basic when it comes to children, and this book is filled with them. Only they have little to count on. Children are deemed a nuisance, a burden, "a remote, alarming race." This was an era when people began families young, when they were still essentially children themselves. Mothers resent their offspring for turning them ugly and spoiling their figures. Chaperones are typical, children left in the care of friends, extended family, and hired help. Or they are shipped off to boarding school (Nora, the wife in "Bernadette," sends away her daughters because she "didn't trust herself to bring them up"). There is a refusal, on the part of parents, to accept their children as they are. In "Thieves and Rascals," the father is annoyed that his daughter is "gauche and untidy," and that her Swiss governess has not groomed "a model little girl, clean and silent as a watch." Between mothers and daughters, there is often competition— mothers wanting to be mistaken for their daughters' sisters, for example—and there is also some meanness. In "The Wedding Ring," the mother tells her brunette daughter to cover her head with a hat lest the sun turn her hair into a "rusty old stove lid."

Perhaps these parents are feckless, perhaps they are too young or self-centered to care for offspring, perhaps they are simply undeserving of them. Whatever the reason, parents maintain a distance from their children, physical as well as emotional, relinquishing their responsibilities, or regarding them as an afterthought. Even when aware of their shortcomings, parents have little motivation to change. "We can't lie here and discuss her character and all her little ways," the mother in "Thieves and Rascals" says to her husband, after their daughter has been expelled from boarding school for spending a weekend in a hotel with a young man. "Evidently neither of us knows anything about them. We can talk about what lousy parents we are. That won't help either. We might as well sleep, if we can."

While this was not an era when mothers chose to raise children without partners, as they are free to do today, there is a significant number of single mothers in these pages. Two are women of lesser economic means, and both happen to be Canadian. Bea, in "Malcolm and Bea," who lives with her father and sisters in a house "behind a dried-up garden" with "seven Dwarfs on the fake chimneypiece," bears a child out of wedlock, having slept with its father "only the once." Bernadette, who does not even know the name of the man who impregnates her, is a maid. The rest are single because they are widows, or divorced, or because their husbands are fundamentally absent. "The Rejection" turns the tables on the single-mother theme; here we see a divorced father and his daughter, utterly estranged. For the most part, though, the spouseless parents are women, both young and middle-aged. Mrs. Tracy in "Madeline's Birthday," who only sees her husband on weekends, presents a relatively quotidian version, while Laure, in "The Burgundy Weekend," mother to two daughters in Paris, only sees her husband, who lives in New Haven, two months out of the year. In "Travelers Must Be Content," Bonnie is divorced and living in Europe with her teenaged daughter, Flor. In "A Day Like Any Other," Mrs. Kennedy's husband is convalescent, indulging "an obscure stomach complaint and a touchy liver" (and meanwhile smuggling wine to his bedside). He forces his family into a peripatetic lifestyle, retreating from one nursing home to the next, and hardly interacting with his daughters:

> The rules of the private clinics he frequented were all in his favor. In any case, he seldom asked to see the girls, for he felt that they were not at an interesting age. Wistfully, his wife sometimes wondered when their interesting age would begin—when they were old enough to be sent away to school, perhaps, or better still, safely disposed of in the handsome marriages that gave her so much concern.

Both Bonnie and Mrs. Kennedy, stranded by the men in their own lives, are nevertheless obsessed with their daughters' matrimonial destinies. Mrs. Kennedy repeatedly and grandiosely envisions the wedding ceremony of her daughters ("Chartres would be nice, though damp"); it is only hypothetically, and also at the ritual moment when they are no longer in her charge, that she feels closest to them.

"Going Ashore" is about a widowed mother and daughter literally adrift, on a cruise, seeking new horizons after the mother's latest romance has soured. The mother, Mrs. Ellenger, is distraught to be without male companionship. She is at once a defensive and delinquent parent, drinking brandy and reading old issues of *Vogue* instead of entertaining her daughter, Emma. At the end of the story, in a desperate plea, Mrs. Ellenger warns Emma never to marry. "Don't have anything to do with men," she says, lying with her daughter in bed. "We should always stick together, you and I. Promise me we'll always stay together." For Mrs. Ellenger, Emma becomes a substitute spouse; the child she resents is the only person who will not abandon her—at least, for as long as Emma has no choice in the matter. Perhaps due to the very lack of attention, Gallant's children are a flinty, self-sufficient breed. Madeline is perfectly content on her own in Manhattan, living off liverwurst sandwiches and going to the movies every day. And twelve-year-old Emma, whose mother retreats to her cabin, spends much of the cruise befriending the bartender and conversing with other adults. The children, in other words, learn to fend for themselves; throughout these stories, it's the adults who need taking care of.

"The Burgundy Weekend," the last, novella-like piece in this collection, was published in 1971, a year after Gallant's second novel, *A Fairly Good Time*. The story, which has not been reprinted since it appeared in *The Tamarack Review*, is written in five chapter-like sections, with the amplitude of a writer now accustomed to greater distance and range. Lucie and Jérôme Girard, a Canadian couple, are visiting France, and travel one weekend to see Madame Arrieu, a former acquaintance of Jérôme's. Madame Arrieu's granddaughter, Nadine, is a French version of Madeline, a solitary and disaffected teenager whose parents are cruising around the coast of Yugoslavia. Lucie is unlike many women in the preceding stories. She waits until her late twenties to marry Jérôme, who is an unemployed, neurotic intellectual dwelling in a self-concocted world. Because Jérôme has squandered his money, she continues working after marriage, as a nurse. It is Lucie who is the breadwinner, and the caretaker. In spite of the challenges of being married to Jérôme, she takes pride in being the only one able to understand and manage him: "She had a special ear for him, as a person conscious of mice can detect the faintest rustling." Though made to feel unwelcome by Nadine, who proceeds to flirt with Jérôme, Lucie holds her own during the weekend. Capable and grounded, she is not only a woman of her times but an indication that times have changed.

The story's central subject, in fact, is the passage of time, and it straddles the chronological sweep of this collection—looking back at the Fifties, taking place at the start of the Seventies, with the Sixties sandwiched in between. It encompasses three generations and numerous layers of history—layers at once living and dying. Members of the Resistance are literally dying off; Madame Arrieu, a survivor of World War Two, is at a televised memorial service for war deportees when the Girards arrive in Burgundy. Jérôme, who was a student in Paris in the Fifties and for whom this journey marks a return in midlife to the same house he visited twenty years ago, is assaulted by a changed, modern France. He seeks shelter in memories, in a numbing hybrid of present and past: seeing de Gaulle in Quebec in 1943; his first winter in Paris; falling in with left-wing activists concerned with reform in Morocco and Algeria. He recalls police brutality at a protest: "A head hitting a curb made one sound, a stick on a head made another. In those days you still remembered the brain beneath the bone: no one ever thought of that now." What Madame Arrieu previously predicted—that one day France would lose her colonies—is now the case. Whereas servants once boiled sheets with wood ash, a task that bloodied their hands, and then spread them on the grass to dry, now they use washing machines. The Beatles have already become yesterday's band, and no one is going to church on Sundays.

Like her character Jérôme, Gallant would eventually circle back in her writing, revisiting the past in her later work. But most of these stories were written in the present moment, marching forward, composed looking time in the face. They form the straight line Gallant likened them to during our interview, emerging with rapid momentum and, though she refers to herself as a slow writer, often at lightning speed. Here, in these twenty stories from twenty years, is a young writer paving her way, who in fact knew exactly where she was going; a writer spreading her wings and finding herself in glorious flight. Take for example the cadenza that opens "Travelers Must Be Content," an extended, probing passage that reads like theater curtains majestically parting, offering up the flesh and blood of a character. The first sentence is pure poetry: "Dreams of chaos were Wishart's meat; he was proud of their diversity, and of his trick of emerging from mortal danger unscathed." This is a secure and seasoned writer at work, one still in her thirties, one who demands intelligence from her readers and who rewards them with nothing short of genius.

Certainly there is a broad spectrum here, from traditional scene- and dialogue-based fiction, to compressed dreamlike narratives, to virtuosic character studies that radically redefine our notion of the short story. As the years pass Gallant's work deepens, but her humor is never abandoned, the exemplary tension of her language, even in longer works, never compromised. The smallest details stick like burrs: a web of warm milk skimmed from coffee, the peppery scent of geraniums. In her vast and searching stories, images have the intimate resonance of still-life painting: a small church is "a pink and white room with an almond pastry ceiling"; two servants sit "at opposite ends of a scrubbed table plucking ducks." In this collection, Gallant journeys from the New World to the Old, arriving in a creative territory uniquely her own. In the process, she transforms from a writer breaking ground to one in full flower, earning her place as one of the greatest literary artists of her time. Never have characters so adrift been so effectively anchored.

—JHUMPA LAHIRI

# THE COST OF LIVING

To Angela Hughes

Imagine that
it were given back to me to be
the child who knew departure would be sweet,
the boy who drew square-rigged ships, the girl who knew
truck routes from Ottawa to Mexico,
the boy who found a door in Latin verse
and made a map out of hexameters.

—MARILYN HACKER
"A Sunday After Easter"

# MADELINE'S BIRTHDAY

THE MORNING of Madeline Farr's seventeenth birthday, Mrs. Tracy awoke remembering that she had forgotten to order a cake. It was doubtful if this would matter to Madeline, who would probably make a point of not caring. But it does matter to me, Mrs. Tracy thought. Observances are important and it is, after all, my house.

She did not spring up at once but lay in a wash of morning sunlight, surveying her tanned arms, stretched overhead, while her mind opened doors and went from room to room of the eighteenth-century Connecticut farmhouse. She knew exactly how the curtains blew into Madeline's room, which had once been hers, and why there was silence on one floor and sound on the other. It was a house, she told herself, in which she had never known an unhappy moment.

"I cannot cope with it here," Madeline had written to her father shortly after she arrived. "One at a time would be all right but not all the Tracys and this German." "Cope" was a word Madeline had learned from her mother, who had divorced Madeline's father because she could not cope with him, and then had fled to Europe because she could not cope with the idea of his remarriage. "Can you take Madeline for the summer?" she had written to Anna Tracy, who was a girlhood friend. "You are so much better able to cope."

In the kitchen, directly beneath Mrs. Tracy's bedroom, Doris, who came in every day from the village, had turned on the radio. "McIntoshes were lively yesterday," the announcer said, "but Roman Beauties were quiet." Propelled out of the house to the orchard by this statement, Mrs. Tracy brought herself back to hear Doris's deliberate tread across the kitchen. She heard the refrigerator door slam and then, together with a sharp bite of static, the whir of the electric mixer. That would be Madeline's cake, which must, after all, have been mentioned. Or else Doris, her imagination uncommonly fired, had decided to make waffles for breakfast. The cake was more probable. Satisfied, Mrs. Tracy turned her thoughts to the upper floor.

She skimmed quickly over her husband's bed, which was firmly made up with a starched coverlet across the pillow. Edward spent only weekends in the country. She did not dwell on his life in town five days of the week. When he spoke of what he did, it sounded dull, a mélange of dust and air-conditioning, a heat-stricken party somewhere, and So-and-So, who had called and wanted to have lunch and been put off.

In the next room, Allie Tracy, who was nearly six, stirred and murmured in her bed. In less than a minute, she would be wide awake, paddling across the hall to the bathroom she shared with her mother. She would run water on her washcloth and flick her toothbrush under the faucet. She would pick up yesterday's overalls, which Mrs. Tracy had forgotten to put in the laundry, and pull them on, muttering fretfully at the buttons. Hairbrush in hand, Allie would then begin her morning chant: "Isn't anybody going to do my hair? If nobody does it, I want it cut off. I'm the only one at the beach who still has braids."

Thinking of the overalls, Mrs. Tracy rose, put on her dressing gown and slippers, and went out into the hall, where she met Allie trotting to the bathroom.

"Madeline might do your hair," Mrs. Tracy said. "And don't forget to wish her a happy birthday. Birthdays are important."

"I hope she's in a good mood," Allie said.

Had Edward Tracy been there, the day could not have been started with such verbal economy. "How's my girl?" he would have asked Allie, even though it was plain she was quite well. "Sleep well?" he would have asked of his wife, requiring an answer in spite of the fact that he slept in the next bed and would certainly know if she had been ill or seized with a nightmare. Allie and Mrs. Tracy were fond of him, but his absence was sometimes a relief. It delivered them from "good morning"s and marking time in a number of similar fashions.

Through the two open doors came the morning sun and a wind that rattled the pictures in the hall. Near the staircase was another pair of doors, both of them firmly shut, and from this Mrs. Tracy inferred that half the household still slept. She found it depressing. The hall seemed weighted at one end—like a rowboat, she thought.

Actually, the German boy, Paul Lange, who was also a guest for the summer, was not asleep behind the closed door of his room but fully dressed and listening to Mrs. Tracy and Allie. His shyness, which Mrs. Tracy had stopped trying to understand, would not allow him to emerge as long as there was movement in the upper hall. Also, he slept with his shades drawn, even though there were no neighbors on his side of the house.

"It shuts out the air. Who on earth are you hiding from?" Mrs. Tracy had once asked him. At this, the poor boy had drawn up his brows and looked so distressed that she had added, "Of course, it's your own affair. But I always thought Germans were terribly healthy and went in for fresh air." Thus did she frequently and unconsciously remind him of his origin, although part of her purpose in inviting him to spend the summer had been to help him forget it.

Mrs. Tracy's connection with Paul was remote, dating back to a prewar friendship in Munich with one of his cousins, a maiden lady now living in New York. Paul had been half orphaned in the war, and when his mother died, a few years later, his cousin had adopted him as a means of getting him to America. Impulsively, and with mixed motives of kindness and curiosity, Mrs. Tracy had offered to take him for the summer. His cousin had a small apartment and was beginning to regret having to share it with a grown boy.

Paul had disappointed Mrs. Tracy. He never spoke of the war, which must surely have affected his childhood, and he had none of the characteristics Mrs. Tracy would have accepted as German. He was not fair; he was dark and wore glasses. He could not swim. He was anything but arrogant. He disliked the sun. He spent as much time as he could in his room, and his waking life was centered around a university extension course.

Paul might just as well have stayed in town, for all the pleasure he gets from the country, Mrs. Tracy thought for the fiftieth time. Passing the last door, on her way downstairs, she heard a dull banging in Madeline's room that was probably a hinged window swinging in the wind.

Madeline awoke at that instant and was unable to place the banging sound or determine where she was. The days of her lifetime had been spent in so many different places—in schools, in camps, in the houses of people she was or was not related to—that the first sight of day was, almost by habit, bewildering. Opening her eyes, she recognized the room and knew that she was spending the summer in the country with the Tracys.

Reaching out of bed, she slammed the window. The room was suddenly quiet, and through the hot-air register she could hear Mrs. Tracy downstairs, asking Doris if she had ever seen such a perfect morning. Doris's answer was lost in the whir of the electric mixer.

Every day of summer, so far, had been launched on a wave of Mrs. Tracy's good will and optimism. Madeline settled back in bed and closed her eyes. Seven more days to Labor Day, she thought, and only then did she remember that it was her birthday. Three years ago, she had been fourteen. In another three, she would be twenty. She was unmarried and not in love and without a trace of talent in any direction. It seemed to her the worst of all possible days.

Turning to the window, she looked with distaste at the top of a pear tree. Someone, Paul or Allie, was scratching at her door.

"Paul, if that's you, then come in. Please don't lurk in the hall."

He slid around the door, spectacles gleaming, with an armful of books. Too wary to speak until he had judged her temper, he sat down on one of the blue-and-white striped chairs, balancing his books.

"Have you come to wish me happy birthday?" Madeline asked. She sat up in bed, tugging halfheartedly at a strap of her nightgown that had broken in the night. With everybody but Paul, she was almost nunlike in her decorum, but she had decided early in the summer that he would put up with anything, and immodesty was only one of the ways she showed her contempt for his unmanliness.

He smiled, or gave way to a nervous tic—Madeline could never be sure which it was. "No," he said, fidgeting. "I did not come for your birthday but to ask you to read this paper and correct the English." He seemed to Madeline doomed for life to ask for help and speak with a slight accent.

"Say 'this,'" she said. "Not 'ziss.'"

"Ziss," he repeated after her.

Mrs. Tracy had hoped that Paul and Madeline would become friends, but, as it happened, they were without interest in each other. Their only common ground was the help Madeline could give him with his studies, and this she did with an ill grace.

"They're nearly of an age—only three years or so apart," Mrs. Tracy had told her husband in the spring, before she opened the house in the country. "They're both adrift, in a way—Paul on account of the war, and Madeline from her family. A summer there might do wonders."

Edward Tracy had said nothing. Technically, the Connecticut house belonged to his wife, who had inherited it. Loving it and remembering her own childhood there, she looked upon her summers as a kind of therapy to be shared with the world. Edward, therefore, merely added this summer of Paul and Madeline to his list of impossible summers. These included the summer of the Polish war orphans, the summer of the tennis court, the summer of Mrs. Tracy's cousins, the summer of the unmarried mother, the summer of the Friends of France, and the summer of Bundles for Britain.

Paul and Madeline were less destructive than the Poles and less expensive than the tennis court. Unlike the unmarried mother, they did not leave suicide notes in the car. They were, on the face of it, quiet and undemanding. But there was an unhappiness about them, a lack of ease, that trailed through the house, affecting the general atmosphere. Sometimes Edward felt that having them there was bad for Allie, but he wasn't certain why or how. He said nothing about it, since, as he told himself, he saw them only weekends and couldn't judge.

The morning of Madeline's birthday, searching for an excuse to leave the city a day early and so have a long weekend, Edward remembered that he and Madeline had had a quarrel of a sort, and he thought, aggrieved, She is keeping me out of my own house. Edward had been drinking the evening before and felt, if not ill, at least indecisive. He sat at the dining-room table unable to drink his coffee or leave it alone, uncomfortable in the empty apartment but reluctant to go out into the heat of the street. Feeling sorry for himself, half wishing himself out of town, he thought of his last conversation with Madeline.

He had found her before one of his wife's white-painted bookcases. Madeline had been sunbathing and smelled of scented oil. Her hair, too long and thick for the season, had been pinned up and was beginning to straggle. Through the window, Edward could see the lawn sloping away to one of Anna's gardens. Anna, with Allie at her heels, moved along the flower border, doing something. They were fair-haired and unhurried. Edward looked at them and approved. He turned to Madeline and frowned. She, ignoring him, knelt on the floor to examine the bottom shelf.

"Looking for something special?" he asked.

Without turning, she said, "I found one book I liked and I thought you might have another."

"What was that?"

"You probably haven't read it," Madeline said, intending the insult. "It was about a girl who worked in a travel agency and fell in love with a lawyer. It was more than that, really, but that was the main thing."

"It sounds like a woman's book," Edward said. "What happened to the girl and the lawyer?" It seemed to him impossible to stop talking.

"He deceived the girl, so she ran a car into something and killed them both."

"Are you sure it belongs to us?" Edward asked.

"Yes. And it was good. I think someone gave it to you." She looked at him for the first time. "I can always tell your books by the funny little plate at the front."

Edward looked back at her with loathing and said, "It doesn't sound like terribly healthy reading for a young girl. I think you should spend more time at other things."

"Do you?" Madeline said. "Excuse me, I have to get by you to get out."

She left the room and ran upstairs, her heart pounding with fright and anger.

"Do you know what I hate more than anything?" Madeline said to Paul on the morning of her birthday. "I hate older men who look at girls and insult them." It was an unusually chatty remark for Madeline, but Paul was not listening.

"That little pear tree is dying," he said.

"Let it." Madeline was a city child. The country, with its hills and stretches and unexplained silences, bored and depressed her. Paul considered her.

"Where would you rather be?"

"I don't know," Madeline said indifferently. "Camp was worse."

"But Mrs. Tracy found you alone in an apartment," he said, as if he were telling her about someone else.

Madeline made a face. She was accustomed to being discussed, and she could imagine Mrs. Tracy's version of the story. It was true; she had been found alone in her mother's apartment. Madeline was to have slept there overnight in the interval between the end of school and the start of her holidays, but her mother had forgotten to write and tell her that she was spending the summer with the Tracys, or had neglected to post the letter, and Madeline had remained in the apartment three weeks.

Her mother had been away since Christmas. The apartment was shrouded in white dust covers, the telephone disconnected. No one knew that Madeline was there except the janitor, who had given her the key. Her allowance for the summer, a lump sum from her father, had arrived before the closing of school. She lived on chocolates and liverwurst sandwiches, went to the movies every day, and was ideally happy. All around her in the building was a pleasant bustle of latchkeys, footsteps, voices in the kitchen air shaft, sometimes a radio. Then Anna Tracy had arrived and carried her off like a scoop of ice cream.

"I think I like cities," Madeline said. She lay back with her head on the pillow and closed her eyes. "Are you never going?" she said, not intending it as a question. "If you want to use the bathroom, please go now. I'm going to wash my hair."

The birthday must have put her in an excellent temper, Paul thought. Otherwise, she would never have suggested that he use the bathroom first, for it was a constant grievance between them. It adjoined both their rooms, but Madeline treated it entirely as her own. She left powder on the bathmat, towels on the floor. Every morning, Paul found his towels pushed aside and Madeline's underthings hanging to dry. Ashamed for her, Paul would mop the tub and cap the toothpaste. Madeline would admit no part of Paul into her life. They did not even have a cake of soap in common. *He* might be one of Anna Tracy's casualties; she was not. Without finding words for it, Paul knew that her untidiness had something to do with her attitude toward him and the entire household. He wished she would employ a less troublesome method of showing it.

He stood up and, taking advantage of her humor, paused at the door, and said, "If I go now, will you read my term paper while I'm gone? I must give it to the mailman this morning."

He stepped aside as he said it, and for an astonished moment Madeline thought he expected her to throw something at him. But it was only because of Allie, who had been struggling with the door handle and now burst into the room, hairbrush in hand.

"I was told to tell you a happy birthday," she said to Madeline. "Will you do my hair?"

Madeline sat up. "Am I the only person in this house who can do things?" she asked. "No, I am not going to do your hair and I'm not going to read Paul's paper, because it's my birthday."

Allie sat down on the bed, leaning comfortably across Madeline's feet. She offered the hairbrush as if she hadn't heard. "What an adorable nightgown that is," she said. "Doris is making you a cake."

Madeline kicked at her from under the covers. "Get off and get out," she said. "You're more annoying than Paul." She looked at Paul and he smiled foolishly, backing into the hall with his books.

"I'll be back later," he promised.

"Now, as for you—" Madeline said to Allie. She took the hairbrush and began brushing Allie's hair so hard that it hurt.

Allie, accustomed to this daily punishment, said only, "Braid it good and tight, otherwise it comes undone in the water."

"Since it's my birthday," said Madeline, "could you do me a favor and leave me alone all day? Without even speaking to me?"

"No," Allie said, and added warningly, "Don't yell at me— Mummy's coming."

"Happy birthday!" Mrs. Tracy said as she opened the door. She was wearing blue and looked younger than Madeline. "Allie, let Madeline get dressed. Go on downstairs and put her present in front of her place." She moved quietly about the room picking up and straightening Madeline's belongings. It had been her own room before she married, and it was perfect for a *jeune fille*, but Madeline, she felt, would have been just as happy in a tent on the lawn.

"You're a very sloppy girl," she observed, "even for your age. But I daresay it's a reaction to boarding school. That's one good thing about this house. People can relax in it and be what they are. I mean I couldn't survive the winter without a summer here."

"Couldn't you?" said Madeline. "I could, with pleasure."

No one—not even Madeline—was ever rude to Mrs. Tracy, and she stood still, rooted with shock, Madeline's bathing suit in her hand. Then she saw that Madeline was crying. "Oh!" Mrs. Tracy exclaimed. "Not on your birthday! Allie, honey, will you do what Mummy tells you and go downstairs?"

She sat down on the bed where Allie had been. "I can't think what can be wrong," she said. She did not touch Madeline but folded her hands on her lap and looked at them, frowning. "On your birthday," she repeated wonderingly. "I know it sounds trite, but this is the best time of your life, this and the next four or five years. Why, when I think of your mother at your age! All the gardenias and the orchids! These are the years that should be absolute heaven for you."

From behind her hands, Madeline said, "I wish you had left me in town. I was perfectly all right."

"I can't listen to such nonsense," Mrs. Tracy said. She stood up, smoothing the covers at Madeline's feet. "Allie, will you please, for the love of God, do what Mummy tells you for once and go downstairs?"

"I don't like Mr. Tracy," Madeline said, "and he doesn't like me."

"You're being dramatic," Mrs. Tracy said, "but it's normal at your age." More gently, she added, "But you mustn't cry over nothing. In a few years, you can do anything you please, as I do, or your mother does. Now get dressed and come to breakfast, like a good girl. This is a terrible start for a birthday."

Still hiding her face, Madeline nodded, and Mrs. Tracy fled down the staircase, relieved to be away from so much emotion. Perhaps Madeline had been miserable all summer.

In the kitchen, she found Allie sitting on a high stool, holding a large mixing bowl between her knees. She was scraping the sides of the bowl with a rubber spatula and licking off bits of cake batter. Her pale hair, brushed but unbraided, was smeared with batter and stuck to her cheeks.

"Allie! Not before breakfast," Mrs. Tracy said, from habit. Allie, aware of the absentminded voice, went on without answering. Mrs. Tracy sat down at the table and leaned her head on her hand. Finally, she said, "When you were upstairs, before I came in, how did Madeline act?"

"Like always."

"What does that tell me? Put that thing—that bowl—down. What is 'always'?"

"With Madeline, it means to be rude."

"Yes. But was she crying? Did she say anything about me?"

"No," Allie said, embarrassed.

"This is dreadful," said Mrs. Tracy. "I can't live for the rest of the summer, even seven days of it, with someone in the house who is thinking only of the train to New York."

This was beyond Allie. She murmured, "If she is going, will we have a birthday party just the same?"

"There! The party!" Mrs. Tracy cried. "And your father won't be here. This is his fault. If he had been here, if he had spent more time with us, none of this would have happened."

"We could call him," Allie said. "I can get long distance."

"Maybe he doesn't like this house, either," Mrs. Tracy said. "I can't understand any of this. Everyone I know has always been happy. My summers have always been so perfect, ever since I was a child." And, bursting into tears, she ran out to the garden, past the astonished postman, who had walked up from the road with a package too large for the mailbox. It contained a present for Madeline, an unsuitable evening dress chosen by her stepmother, whom she had never met.

From the window of his room, Paul saw Mrs. Tracy run across the lawn. She stopped and bent down to pull three or four bits of wild grass from a flower bed. Then she wiped her eyes with her hands and walked calmly back to the house.

He turned to his books and wondered how soon it would be safe to approach Madeline again. A moment later, he heard the postman drive away and knew that he had missed the deadline for his term paper.

Mrs. Tracy put in a call to Mr. Tracy, and Paul began composing a letter to the head of the extension course, asking if he might submit his paper a few days late. He would show the letter to Madeline, he thought.

In the next room, Madeline had stopped crying and fallen asleep. She dreamed that someone had given her a dollhouse. When a bell rang downstairs, it merged into her dream as something to do with school. Actually, the ringing was caused by the long-distance operator, who had at first reported that the circuits to New York were busy and was now ready to complete the call. Mrs. Tracy entered the house in time to take the receiver from Allie's hand and assure her husband that nothing was the matter, that she had called only to say good morning.

"It's a lovely morning here," she said. "Couldn't you come up in time for dinner tonight? It's for Madeline's sake—you know what a birthday means to a young girl."

"I don't know," Edward said. "I suppose I could." His office would be unbearably hot, and he was beginning to feel foolish about his quarrel with Madeline. "She's only a kid," he said aloud.

"That's just the point. We mustn't take her too seriously. And it's her birthday," Mrs. Tracy said, as if this fact were a talisman, something that would cause the day to fall into place.

When she had hung up, Allie, who had been listening, looked at her accusingly. "I heard Madeline say she didn't like him," she said.

"People often say things," Mrs. Tracy said. "You must never pay attention to what people say if you know the opposite to be true."

"Like what?" said Allie.

"Well, for instance," Mrs. Tracy said seriously, "I could believe I was the only person who had enjoyed being here this summer. But I know it isn't reasonable."

She had, in fact, put the idea out of her head while pulling grass from the garden.

"Now," she said, "will you please, for the last time, call Paul and Madeline, so that we can get breakfast over with and get this day under way?"

*1951*

# ONE MORNING IN MAY

BY HALF past ten, a vaporish heat had gathered on the road above the Mediterranean, and the two picnickers, Barbara Ainslie and Mike Cahill, walked as slowly as they could. Scuffing their shoes, they held themselves deliberately apart. It was the first time they had been alone. Barbara's aunt, with whom she was staying in Menton, had begun speaking to Mike on the beach—she thought him a nice young boy—and it was she who had planned the picnic, packing them off for what she termed a good romp, quite unaware that her words had paralyzed at once the tremulous movement of friendship between them.

So far, they had scarcely spoken at all, passing in silence—in the autobus—between the shining arc of the beach and the vacant hotels that faced it. The hotels, white and pillared like Grecian ruins, were named for Albert and Victoria and the Empire. Shelled from the sea during the war, they exposed, to the rain and the road, cube-shaped rooms and depressing papered walls that had held the sleep of a thousand English spinsters when the pound was still a thing of moment. At sixteen, Barbara was neutral to decay but far too shy in the presence of Mike to stare at anything that so much as suggested a bedroom. She had looked instead at the lunch basket on her lap, at her bitten nails, at the shadow of her canvas hat, as if they held the seed of conversation. When they were delivered from the bus at last and had watched it reeling, in its own white dust, on to Monte Carlo, they turned together and climbed the scrambling path to Cap Martin.

"What will we talk about?" Barbara had asked her aunt, earlier that morning. "What will I say?"

Barbara's aunt could see no problem here, and she was as startled as if a puppy tumbling in a cushioned box had posed the same question.

"Why, what do young people have to say anywhere?" she had asked. "Tell him about your school, if you like, or your winter in Paris." Having provided that winter, she did not see why its value should be diminished in May, or, indeed, why it should not remain a conversational jewel for the rest of Barbara's life.

"I suppose so," Barbara had said, determined not to mention it at all. She was in France not as a coming-out present or because she had not smoked until she was eighteen but ignominiously, because she had failed her end-of-term examinations for the second year running. She had been enrolled in one of the best day schools in New York, a fact that she was frequently reminded of and that somehow doubled her imperfection. Her mother had consulted a number of people—an analyst she met at a party, two intimate women friends, the doctor who had delivered Barbara but had noticed nothing unusual about her at the time—and finally, when the subject was beginning to bore her, she had dispatched Barbara to Paris, to the distressed but dutiful sister of Barbara's late father. Barbara was conscious, every moment of the day, that she was to get something from her year in France, and return to America brilliant, poised, and educated. Accordingly, she visited all the museums and copied on slips of paper the legends of monuments. Her diary held glimpses of flint tools, angular modern tapestries, cave drawings, the *Gioconda* ("quite small"), and the *Venus de Milo* ("quite big"); of a monument "that came by ship from Africa and was erected to the cheers of a throng"; and of a hotel where Napoleon had stayed as a young man, "but which we did not really see because it had been pulled down." These mementos of Paris she buttressed with snapshots in which ghostly buildings floated on the surface of the Seine, and the steps of the Sacré-Coeur, transparent, encumbered the grass at Versailles. The snapshots she mounted and shielded with tissue in an album called "Souvenirs de France."

She was proud of the year, and of the fact that she had shivered in unheated picture galleries and not spent her time drinking milk shakes in the American Embassy restaurant; still, she felt her year no match for Mike's. When her aunt, testing, asked him where he lived in Paris, he had replied, "Oh, St. Germain," and Barbara had been ill with envy, unaware that he stayed at a recommended *pension*, the owner of which sent fortnightly reports to his mother.

Glancing now at Mike shyly, as they walked along the upper road, Barbara caught from the corner of her eye the movement of her own earrings, Moroccan hoops she had bought, in the merciful absence of her aunt, from an Arab on the beach. With his sweaty fez and his impertinent speech, the Arab had seemed to Barbara the breathing incarnation of oil, greed, and problems. She had read a great deal in the winter, and she could have told anyone that Africa seethed, Asia teemed, and that something must be done at once about the Germans, the Russians, the Chinese, and the Spanish or Heaven only knew what would happen. She had also been cautioned that these difficulties were the heritage of youth, and this she acknowledged, picturing the youth as athletic, open-shirted, vaguely foreign in appearance, and marching in columns of eight.

"Straight over there is the Middle East," she said to Mike, placing him without question in those purposeful ranks. She pointed in the direction of Corsica, and went on, "All the Arabs! What are we going to do about the Arabs?"

Mike shrugged.

"And the Indians," Barbara said. "There are too many of them for the food in the world. And the Russians. What are we going to do about the Russians?"

"I don't know," Mike said. "Actually, I never think about it."

"I suppose you don't," she said. "You have your work to do."

He glanced at her sharply, but there was no need to look twice. He had already observed her to be without guile, a fact that confused and upset him. Her good manners, as well, made him self-conscious. Once, when she mentioned her school, he had not mentioned his own New York high school and then, annoyed with himself, had introduced it with belligerence. He might have saved himself the trouble; she had never heard of it and did not know that it was a public school. He blamed his uneasiness, unfairly, on the fact that she had money and he had not. It had not occurred to him, inexperienced as he was, placing her with the thinnest of clues, that she might not be rich.

Mike was older than Barbara, although not by a great deal. He had come to France because the words "art" and "Paris" were unbreakably joined in his family's imagination, the legend of Trilby's Bohemia persisting long after the truth of it had died. When his high school art teacher, a young woman whose mobiles had been praised, pronounced that his was a talent not to be buried under the study of medicine or law, his family had decided that a year in Paris would show whether or not his natural bent was toward painting. It was rather like exposing someone to a case of measles and watching for spots to break out.

In Paris, Mike had spent the first three weeks standing in the wrong queue at the Beaux-Arts, and when no one seemed able to direct him to the right one, he had given up the Beaux-Arts entirely and joined a class instructed by an English painter called Chitterley, whose poster advertisement he had seen in a café. It was Mr. Chitterley's custom to turn his young charges loose on the city and then, once a week or so, comment on their work in a borrowed studio on the quai d'Anjou. Mike painted with sober patience the bridges of the Seine, the rain-soaked lawns of the Tuileries, and a head-on view of Notre Dame. His paintings were large (Mr. Chitterley was nearsighted), askew (as he had been taught in the public schools of New York), and empty of people (he had never been taught to draw, and it was not his nature to take chances).

"Very *interesting*," said Mr. Chitterley of Mike's work. Squinting a little, he would add, "Ah! I *see* what you were trying to do here!"

"You do?" Mike wished he would be more specific, for he sometimes recognized that his pictures were flat, empty, and the color of cement. At first, he had blamed the season, for the Paris winter had been sunless; later on, he saw that its gray contained every shade in a beam of light, but this effect he was unable to reproduce. Unnerved by the pressure of time, he watched his work all winter, searching for the clue that would set him on a course. Prodded in the direction of art, he now believed in it, enjoying, above all, the solitude, the sense of separateness, the assembling of parts into something reasonable. He might have been equally happy at a quiet table, gathering into something ticking and ordered the scattered wheels of a watch, but this had not been suggested, and he had most certainly never given it a thought. At last, when the season had rained itself to an end (and his family innocently were prepared to have him exhibit his winter's harvest in some garret of the Left Bank and send home the critics' clippings), he approached Mr. Chitterley and asked what he ought to do next.

"Why, go to the country," said Mr. Chitterley, who was packing for a holiday with the owner of the quai d'Anjou studio. "Go south. Don't stop in a hotel but live on the land, in a tent, and paint, paint, paint, paint, paint!"

"I can't afford it," Mike said. "I mean I can't afford to buy the tent and stuff. But I can stay over here until August, if you think there's any point. I mean is it wasting time for me to paint, paint, paint?"

Mr. Chitterley shot him an offended look and then a scornful one, which said, How like an American! The only measuring rods, time and money. Aloud, he suggested Menton. He had stayed there as a child, and he remembered it as a paradise of lemon ice and sunshine. Mike, for want of a better thought, or even a contrastive one, took the train there a day later.

Menton was considerably less than paradise. Shelled, battered, and shabby, it was a town gone to seed, in which old English ladies, propelling themselves with difficulty along the Promenade George V, nodded warmly to each other (they had become com-

rades during the hard years of war, when they were interned together in the best hotels, farther up the coast) and ignored the
new influx of their countrymen—embarrassed members of the
lower middle classes, who refused to undress in the face of heat
and nakedness and who huddled miserably on the beach in hot
city clothing, knotted handkerchiefs on their heads to shield
them from the sun.

"*Not* the sort of English one likes," Barbara's aunt had said
sadly to Mike, who was painting beside her on the beach. "If you
had seen Menton before the war! I had a little villa, up behind
that hotel. It was shelled by the Americans. Not that it wasn't
necessary," she added, recalling her origins. "Still—And they
built a fortification not far away. I went up to look at it. It was full
of rusted wire, and nothing in it but a dead cat."

"The French built it," Barbara said. "The *pension* man told me."

"It doesn't matter, dear," her aunt said. "Before the war, and
even when it started, there was nothing there at all. It was so different." She dropped her knitting and looked about, as if just the
three of them were fit to remember what Menton had been. It was
the young people's first bond of sympathy, and Barbara tried not
to giggle; before the war was a time she didn't remember at all.
"In those days, you knew where you were *at*," her aunt said, summing up the thirties. She picked up her knitting, and Mike went
on with his painting of sea, sky, and tilted sailboat. Away from
Mr. Chitterley and the teacher who had excelled in mobiles, he
found that he worked with the speed and method of Barbara's
aunt producing a pair of Argyle socks. Menton, for all its draw-
backs, was considerably easier to paint than Paris, and he rendered with fidelity the blue of the sea, the pink and white of the
crumbling villas, and the red of the geraniums. One of his recent
pictures, flushed and accurate as a Technicolor still, he had given
to Barbara, who had written a touched and eager letter of thanks,
and then had torn the letter up.

Mike had brought his painting things along on the picnic, for,
as Barbara's aunt had observed with approbation, he didn't waste

an hour of his day. Barbara carried the picnic basket, which had been packed by the cook at Pension Bit o' Heather and contained twice as much bread as one would want. Around her shoulders was an unnecessary sweater that she had snatched up in a moment of compulsive modesty just before leaving her room. She carried her camera, slung on a strap, and she felt that she and Mike formed, together, a picture of art, pleasure, and industry which, unhappily, there was no one to remark but a fat man taking his dog for a run; the man gave them scarcely a glance.

Rounding a bend between dwarfed ornamental orange trees, they saw the big hotel Barbara's aunt had told them about. From its open windows came the hum of vacuum cleaners and the sound of a hiccuping tango streaked with static. The gardens spread out before them, with marked and orderly paths and beds of brilliant flowers. Barbara's aunt had assured them that this place was ideal for a picnic lunch, and that no one would disturb them. There was, on Cap Martin, a public picnic ground, which Barbara was not permitted to visit. "You wouldn't like it," her aunt had explained. "It is nothing but tents, and diapers, and hairy people in shorts. Whenever possible in France, one prefers private property." Still, the two were unconvinced, and after staring at the gardens and then at each other they turned and walked in the other direction, to a clearing around a small monument overlooking the bay.

They sat down on the grass in the shade and Mike unpacked his paints. Barbara watched him, working over in her mind phrases that, properly used, would give them a subject in common; none came, and she pulled grass and played with her wristwatch. "We're leaving tomorrow," she said at last.

"I know." After some peering and indecision he had decided to face the hotel gardens instead of the sea. "I may not stay much longer, either. I don't know."

Barbara, bound to her aunt's unyielding cycle of city, sea, and mountains, marveled at his freedom. She fancied him stepping out of his hotel one morning and suddenly asking himself, "Shall

I go back to Paris now, or another day?" and taking off at once for Paris, or Rome, or Lisbon, or, having decided he had had enough of this, his parents' house.

"My father thinks I should go to Venice and Florence, now that I'm south." He spoke with neither enthusiasm nor resentment; had his father ordered him home, he would have set off with the same equable temper.

"Then you might go to Italy soon," Barbara said. He nodded. "I'm going home in September," she said. "My mother's coming for the summer, and we're going back together. I guess I'll go back to school. I have to do something—learn something, I mean."

"What for?"

"Well, it's just that I have to do *something*. It's different for you," she said, helplessly. "You have something to do. You've got—" She blushed, and went on, with resolution, "You've got this art to do."

Startled by her reminder of his vocation, he dropped his arm. He knew he would have to decide very soon whether to go on with painting or begin something else. If someone who knows would come along and tell me what to do this minute, he thought, I would do whatever he said.

Barbara, believing him in contact with some life of the spirit from which she was excluded, looked at him with admiration; and when he did not move for a moment longer, she focused her camera and took his picture, so that her album called "Souvenirs de France" would include this image of Mike looking rapt and destined, his eyes secretively shadowed, high above the sea.

"It's different for me," Barbara said, forgetting once more to wind her film. "I can't do anything. There's nothing I'm good at. I'm really dumb in school." She laid her camera in the shade. "Really dumb," she repeated, shaking her head at the thought. Confronted with ruled examination paper, the electric clock purring on the wall, she was lost—sometimes she was sick and had to leave the room; sometimes she just wrote nonsense. At school, they had tested her for aptitudes and found only that she liked to cook and had played with dolls until it was a scandal; her mother had had to give the dolls away. Anybody could cook and grow up to be a parent, the brisk, sallow student psychologist from N.Y.U. who had tested her implied, and he had then written something terrible—Barbara could only imagine the summing up of her inadequacies—that had been shown to all her teachers and to her mother.

"You should worry," Mike said. "You'll probably get married sometime, anyway, so what does it matter what you learn?"

The effect of this was to strike her into silence.

She drew her knees up and examined her dusty sandals; she pulled at her skirt so that it covered her legs, and drew her sweater close. Does he mean to *him*, she wondered. It had occurred to her many times in this lonely winter that only marriage would save her from disgrace, from growing up with no skills and no profession. Her own mother did nothing all day, but she was excused by having once been married. It was the image of her aunt that Barbara found distressing—her aunt filling her day with scurrying errands, writing letters of complaint (Bus conductors were ruder than before the war. Why did young girls shrink from domestic service? The streets of Paris were increasingly dirtier) to the "Letters" column of the Continental *Daily Mail*. But who would marry me, Barbara had thought. From her reading she knew that she would never meet men or be of interest to them until she could, suddenly and brilliantly, perform on the violin, become a member of Macy's Junior Executive Squad, or, at the very least, take shorthand at a hundred and twenty words a minute.

She peered up at Mike now, but he was looking only at his canvas, daubing in another patch of perfectly red geraniums. "For a while, they thought I could act," she said, offering him this semiprecious treasure. "I had a radio audition last year, when I was still fifteen. Really," she said quickly, as if he were about to round on her with complete disbelief. "My speech-class teacher was nice. When my mother came to school to see why I wasn't doing so well, she met all my teachers. This teacher, Mr. Peppner, told her—something. He's the only man teacher in the whole school." She frowned, wondering once again what Mr. Peppner in his polished dark blue suit had found to say to Mrs. Ainslie; probably she, moist-eyed and smelling expensive, had been so warm, so interested, that Mr. Peppner had had no idea he was being treated like a meritorious cook and had said something extravagant. A few days later, Barbara's mother had asked to dinner a bald young man in spectacles, who had stared hard at Barbara and said, gracefully, that her coloring was much too delicate for television but that he would make an appointment for her with someone else.

"It's not that my mother wanted me to work, or anything," Barbara explained to Mike, "but a friend of hers said it would give me poise and confidence. So I went to be tested. I had to read lines in a play. There was someone else being tested, a man, and then there was a girl, a real actress. She was only helping. My name in the play was Gillian. It was called 'The Faltering Years.'"

Mike had never heard of it.

"Well, neither did I, but they all seemed to know it," Barbara said. "I don't think it was one of the great plays of our time, or anything like that. Of our time," she repeated thoughtfully, having frequently read this phrase on the jackets of books. "Anyway, I had to be this Mayfair debutante. I was the girlfriend of this man, but I was leaving him."

"For a rich lord?" Mike said, smiling.

"No," she said, seriously. "*He* was the lord, only poor. I was leaving him for a rich industrialist. I had to say, 'Peter, won't you try to understand?' Then he said something. I forget what. Then I had to say, 'It isn't you, Peter, and it isn't me. It's just.' The line ended that way, but like a question. That was my main part, or most of it. Then I went away, but I was sorry. They skipped all that. Then the man being tested had this big scene with the actress. She was the nurse to his sick mother, who wins his heart. I forget what *they* said."

"It sounds to me like she had the best part," said Mike.

"She was around thirty," Barbara said. "I think she was the director's girlfriend. He took her to lunch afterwards. I saw them going out. Anyway, at the end I had to say to her, 'You love Peter very much, don't you?' And she had to say, 'Terribly.' Just the way she said that, the director told me, showed she was an actress. I guess he meant I wasn't. Anyway, they said I'd hear from them, but I never did."

"It's the craziest audition I ever heard of," Mike said. He stopped working and turned to look at her. "You a Mayfair debutante, for God's sake. It wasn't a fair audition."

She looked up at him, troubled. "But they must know what they're doing, don't you think?" At this reminder of knowledge and authority, Mike agreed that they probably did. "Are you hungry?" she asked. She was tired of the conversation, of exposing her failures.

The sun was nearly overhead, and they moved under a parasol pine. "There's nothing to drink," Barbara said apologetically, "but she put in some oranges."

They ate their lunch in silence, like tired Alpinists resting on a ledge. Barbara screwed her eyes tight and tried to read the lettering on the monument; it was too hot to walk across the grass, out of their round island of shade. "It's to some queen," she said at last, and read out: "'Elizabeth, impératrice d'Autriche et reine de la Hongrie.' Well, I never heard of her, did you? Maybe she stayed at this hotel." Mike seemed to be falling asleep. "About Hungary, you know," she said, speaking rapidly. "One time, I went to a funny revue in Paris with my aunt. It was supposed to be in the war, and this lady was going to entertain the Russian ambassador. She wanted to dress up her little dog in the Russian costume, in his honor, but she had only a Hungarian one. So she called all the embassies and said, 'Which side of the war is Hungary on?' and nobody knew. So then she finally called the Russian ambassador and she said, 'I want to dress my little dog in your honor but I have only a Hungarian costume. Do you know which side the Hungarians are on?' And the ambassador said, 'Yes, I do know, but I can't tell you until I've talked to Moscow.'" Barbara looked anxiously at Mike. "Do you think that's funny?"

"Sure."

Neither of them had laughed.

"Do you remember the war?" he asked.

"A little." She got up as if she were suddenly uncomfortable, and walked to the edge of the grass, where the Cap fell away sharply to the sea.

"I remember quite a lot," said Mike. "My father was in Denver the whole time—I don't know why. We stayed home because they couldn't find us a place to live there. When he came home for leaves, we—my brother and I—wouldn't mind him, we were so used to our mother. When he'd tell us to do something, we'd ask her if it was all right." He smiled, remembering. "Was yours away?"

"Well, mine was killed," she said diffidently, as if by telling him this she made an unfair claim on his attention. "I was only five when he went away, so I don't remember much. He was killed later, when I was seven. It was right before my birthday, so I couldn't have a party." She presented, like griefs of equal value, these two facts. "People are always asking me—friends of my mother, I mean—do I remember him and what a wonderful sense of humor he had and all that. When I say no, I don't re- member, they look at me and say –" Her voice went up to an in- credulous screech: "'But it can't be that long ago!'"

"Well, it is," Mike said, as if he were settling a quarrel. He stood up and moved beside her. Together, they looked down to the curving beach, where the sea broke lightly against the warm rocks, and the edge of the crumbling continent they had never seen whole. From above, they could see that beside each of the tumbled hotels a locked garden, secure against God knew what marauders, had gone wild; they could distinguish the film of weeds that brushed the top of the wall, the climbing roses that choked the palms. Above, out of their vision, was the fortification that had offended Barbara's aunt, and down on the beach was the aunt herself, a dot with a sunshade, knitting forever

Say we might get married later, Barbara willed, closing her eyes against the quiet sea and the moldering life beside it. But

Mike said nothing, thinking only of how dull a town Menton was, and wondering if it had been worth two weeks. He had been taught that time must be reckoned in value—and fiscal value, at that. At home, he would be required to account both for his allowance and for his days and weeks. "Did you get anything out of Menton?" his father would ask. "Was it worth it?"

"Oh, yes," he might tell them. "I worked a lot, and I met a rich girl."

His parents would be pleased. Not that they were vulgar or mercenary, but they considered it expedient for young artists to meet the well-born; they would accept, Mike was certain, the fact of his friendship with Barbara as a useful acquirement, justifying a fortnight of lounging about in the sun. When he thought of Barbara as a patroness, commissioning him, perhaps, for a portrait, he wanted to laugh: yet the seed of the thought—that the rich were of utility—remained, and to rid himself of it he asked her sharply if she had brought her bathing suit.

Stricken, looking about as if it might be lying on the grass, she said, "I didn't think—But we can go home and get it."

They gathered up their scattered belongings and walked back the way they had come. Barbara, in her misery, further chastened herself by holding a geranium leaf on her nose—she had visions of peeling and blisters—and she trotted beside Mike in silence.

"Do you write letters?" he said at last, for he had remembered that they both lived in New York, and he felt that if he could maintain the tenuous human claim of correspondence, possibly his acquaintance with Barbara might turn out to be of value; he could not have said how or in terms of what. And although he laughed at his parents, he was reluctant to loosen his hold on something that might justify him in their sight until he had at least sorted out his thoughts.

She stood stock-still in the path, the foolish green leaf on her nose, and said solemnly, "I will write to you every day as long as I live."

He glanced at her with the beginning of alarm, but he was

spared from his thoughts by the sight of the autobus on the highway below. Clasping hands, they ran slipping and falling down the steep embankment, and arrived flushed, bewildered, exhausted, as if their romp had been youthful enough to satisfy even Barbara's aunt.

*1952*

# THE PICNIC

THE THREE Marshall children were dressed and ready for the picnic before their father was awake. Their mother had been up since dawn, for the coming day of pleasure weighed heavily on her mind. She had laid out the children's clothes, so that they could dress without asking questions—clean blue denims for John and dresses sprigged with flowers for the girls. Their shoes, chalky with whitening, stood in a row on the bathroom windowsill.

John, stubbornly, dressed himself, but the girls helped each other, standing and preening before the long looking glass. Margaret fastened the chain of Ellen's heart-shaped locket while Ellen held up her hair with both hands. Margaret never wore her own locket. Old Madame Pégurin, in whose house in France the Marshalls were living, had given her something she liked better—a brooch containing a miniature portrait of a poodle called Youckie, who had died of influenza shortly before the war. The brooch was edged with seed pearls, and Margaret had worn it all summer, pinned to her navy-blue shorts.

"How very pretty it is!" the children's mother had said when the brooch was shown to her. "How nice of Madame Pégurin to think of a little girl. It will look much nicer later on, when you're a little older." She had been trained in the school of indirect suggestion, and so skillful had she become that her children sometimes had no idea what she was driving at.

"I guess so," Margaret had replied on this occasion, firmly fastening the brooch to her shorts.

She now attached it to the front of the picnic frock, where, too

34

heavy for the thin material, it hung like a stone. "It looks lovely," Ellen said with serious admiration. She peered through their bedroom window across the garden, and over the tiled roofs of the small town of Virolun, to the blooming summer fields that rose and fell toward Grenoble and the Alps. Across the town, partly hidden by somebody's orchard, were the neat rows of gray-painted barracks that housed American troops. Into this tidy settlement their father disappeared each day, driven in a jeep. On a morning as clear as this, the girls could see the first shining peaks of the mountains and the thin blue smoke from the neighboring village, some miles away. They were too young to care about the view, but their mother appreciated it for them, often reminding them that nothing in her own childhood had been half as agreeable. "You youngsters are very lucky," she would say. "Your father might just as easily as not have been stationed in the middle of Arkansas." The children would listen without comment, although it depressed them inordinately to be told of their good fortune. If they liked this house better than any other they had lived in, it was because it contained Madame Pégurin, her cat, Olivette, and her cook, Louise.

Olivette now entered the girls' bedroom soundlessly, pushing the door with one paw. "Look at her. She's priceless," Margaret said, trying out the word.

Ellen nodded. "I wish one of us could go to the picnic with *her*," she said. Margaret knew that she meant not the cat but Madame Pégurin, who was driving to the picnic grounds with General Wirtworth, commander of the post.

"One of us might," Margaret said. "Sitting on the General's lap."

Ellen's shriek at the thought woke their father, Major Marshall, who, remembering that this was the day of the picnic, said, "Oh, God!"

The picnic, which had somehow become an Army responsibility, had been suggested by an American magazine of such grandeur that the Major was staggered to learn that Madame Pégurin had never heard of it. Two research workers, vestal maidens in dirndl skirts, had spent weeks combing France to find the most typically French town. They had found no more than half a dozen; and since it was essential to the story that the town be near an American Army post, they had finally, like a pair of exhausted doves, fluttered to rest in Virolun. The picnic, they had explained to General Wirtworth, would be a symbol of unity between two nations—between the troops at the post and the residents of the town. The General had repeated this to Colonel Baring, who had passed it on to Major Marshall, who had brought it to rest with his wife. "Oh, really?" Paula Marshall had said, and if there was any reserve—any bitterness—in her voice, the Major had failed to notice. The mammoth job of organizing the picnic had fallen just where he knew it would—on his own shoulders.

The Major was the post's recreation officer, and he was beset by many difficulties. His status was not clear; sometimes he had to act as public relations officer—there being none, through an extraordinary oversight on the part of the General. The Major's staff was inadequate. It was composed of but two men: a lieutenant, who had developed measles a week before the picnic, and a glowering young sergeant who, the Major feared, would someday write a novel depicting him in an unfavorable manner. The Major had sent Colonel Baring a long memo on the subject of his status, and the Colonel had replied in person, saying, with a comic, rueful smile, "Just see us through the picnic, old man!"

The Major had said he would try. But it was far from easy. The research workers from the American magazine had been joined by a photographer who wore openwork sandals and had so far not emerged from the Hotel Bristol. Messages in his languid handwriting had been carried to Major Marshall's office by the research workers, and answers returned by the Major's sergeant. The messages were grossly interfering and never helpful. Only yesterday, the day before the picnic, the sergeant had placed before the Major a note on Hotel Bristol stationery: "Suggest folk dances as further symbol of unity. French wives teaching American wives, and so on. Object: Color shot." Annoyed, the Major had sent a message pointing out that baseball had already been agreed on as an easily recognized symbol, and the afternoon brought a reply: "Feel that French should make contribution. Anything colorful or indigenous will do."

"Baseball is as far as I'll go," the Major had said in his reply to this.

On their straggling promenade to breakfast, the children halted outside Madame Pégurin's door. Sometimes from behind the white-and-gold painted panels came the sound of breakfast—china on china, glass against silver. Then Louise would emerge with the tray, and Madame Pégurin, seeing the children, would tell them to come in. She would be sitting up, propped with a pillow and bolster. Her hair, which changed color after every visit to Paris, would be wrapped in a scarf and Madame herself enveloped in a trailing dressing gown streaked with the ash of her cigarette. When the children came in, she would feed them sugared almonds and pistachio creams and sponge cakes soaked in rum, which she kept in a tin box by her bedside, and as they stood lined up rather comically, she would tell them about little dead Youckie, and about her own children, all of whom had married worthless, ordinary, social-climbing men and women. "In the end," she would say, sighing, "there is nothing to replace the love one can bear a cat or a poodle."

The children's mother did not approve of these morning visits, and the children were frequently told not to bother poor Madame Pégurin, who needed her rest. This morning, they could hear the rustle of paper as Madame Pégurin turned the pages of Le Figaro, which came to Virolun every day from Paris. Madame Pégurin looked at only one section of it, the Carnet du Jour—the daily account of marriages, births, and deaths—even though, as she told the children, one found in it nowadays names that no one had heard of, families who sounded foreign or commonplace. The children admired this single minded reading, and they thought it "commonplace" of their mother to read books.

"Should we knock?" Margaret said. They debated this until

their mother's low, reproachful "Children!" fetched them out of the upstairs hall and down a shallow staircase, the wall of which was papered with the repeated person of a shepherdess. Where a railing should have been were jars of trailing ivy they had been warned not to touch. The wall was stained at the level of their hands; once a week Louise went over the marks with a piece of white bread. But nothing could efface the fact that there were boarders, American Army tenants, in old Madame Pégurin's house.

During the winter, before the arrival of the Marshalls, the damage had been more pronounced; the tenants had been a Sergeant and Mrs. Gould, whose children, little Henry and Joey, had tracked mud up and down the stairs and shot at each other with water pistols all over the drawing room. The Goulds had departed on bad terms with Madame Pégurin, and it often worried Major Marshall that his wife permitted the Gould children to visit the Marshall children and play in the garden. Madame Pégurin never mentioned Henry's and Joey's presence; she simply closed her bedroom shutters at the sound of their voices, which, it seemed to the Major, was suggestion enough.

The Gould and Marshall children were to attend the picnic together; it was perhaps for this reason that Madame Pégurin rattled the pages of *Le Figaro* behind her closed door. She disliked foreigners; she had told the Marshall children so. But they, fortunately, did not consider themselves foreign, and had pictured instead dark men with curling beards. Madame Pégurin had tried, as well as she could, to ignore the presence of the Americans in Virolun, just as, long ago, when she traveled, she had overlooked the natives of whichever country she happened to be in. She had ignored the Italians in Italy and the Swiss in Switzerland, and she had explained this to Margaret and Ellen, who, agreeing it was the only way to live, feared that their mother would never achieve this restraint. For she *would* speak French, and she carried with her, even to market, a book of useful phrases.

Madame Pégurin had had many troubles with the Americans; she had even had troubles with the General. It had fallen to her, as the highest-ranking resident of Virolun, to entertain the high-est-ranking American officer. She had asked General Wirtworth to tea, and he had finished off a bottle of whiskey she had been saving for eleven years. He had then been moved to kiss her hand, but this could not make up for her sense of loss. There had been other difficulties—the tenancy of the Goulds, and a row with Colonel Baring, whose idea it had been to board the Goulds and their hoodlum children with Madame Pégurin. Madame Pégurin had, indeed, talked of legal action, but nothing had come of it. Because of all this, no one believed she would attend the picnic, and it was considered a triumph for Major Marshall that she had consented to go, and to drive with the General, and to be photo-graphed.

"I hope they take her picture eating a hot dog," Paula Marshall said when she heard of it.

"It was essential," the Major said reprovingly. "I made her see that. She's a symbol of something in this town. We couldn't do the thing properly without her."

"Maybe she just likes to have her picture taken, like anyone else," Paula said. This was, for her, an uncommonly catty remark.

The Major said nothing. He had convinced Madame Pégurin that she was a symbol only after a prolonged teatime wordplay that bordered on flirtation. This was second nature to Madame Pégurin, but the Major had bogged down quickly. He kept com-ing around to the point, and Madame Pégurin found the point uninteresting. She wanted to talk about little Youckie, and the difference between French and American officers, and how well Major Marshall looked in his uniform, and what a good idea it was for Mrs. Marshall not to bother about her appearance, run-ning as she did all day after the children. But the Major talked about the picnic and by the weight of blind obduracy won.

The little Marshalls, thinking of the sugared almonds and pista-chio creams in Madame Pégurin's room, slid into their places at the breakfast table and sulked over their prunes. Before each plate was a motto, in their mother's up-and-down hand: "I will be good at the picnic," said John's. This was read aloud to him, to circumvent the happy excuse that he could not yet read writing. "I will not simper. I will help Mother and be an example. I will not ask the photographer to take my picture," said Ellen's. Margaret's said, "I will mind my own business and not bother Madame Pégurin."

"What's simper?" Ellen asked.

"It's what you do all day," said her sister. To their mother she remarked, "Madame is reading the *Figaro* in her bed." There was, in her voice, a reproach that Paula Marshall did not spend her mornings in so elegant a manner, but Paula, her mind on the picnic, the eggs to be hard-boiled, scarcely took it in.

"You might, just this once, have come straight to breakfast," she said, "when you know I have this picnic to think of, and it means so much to your father to have it go well." She looked, as if for sympathy, at the portrait of Madame Pégurin's dead husband, who each day surveyed with a melancholy face these strangers around his table.

"It means a lot to Madame, too," Margaret said. "Riding there with the General! Perhaps one of us might go in the same car?"

There was no reply.

Undisturbed, Margaret said, "She told me what she is wearing. A lovely gray thing, and a big lovely hat, and diamonds." She looked thoughtfully at her mother, who, in her sensible cotton dress, seemed this morning more than ever composed of starch and soap and Apple Blossom cologne. She wore only the rings that marked her engagement and her wedding. At her throat, holding her collar, was the fraternity pin Major Marshall had given her fifteen years before. "Diamonds," Margaret repeated, as if their mother might take the hint.

"Ellen, *dear*," said Paula Marshall. "There is, really, a way to eat prunes. Do you children see *me* spitting?" The children loudly applauded this witticism, and Paula went on, "Do be careful of the table. Try to remember it isn't ours." But this the Army children had heard so often it scarcely had a meaning. "It isn't ours," they were told. "It doesn't belong to us." They had lived so much in hotels and sublet apartments and all-alike semi-detached houses that Madame Pégurin's table, at which minor nobility had once been entertained, meant no more to them than the cross-legged picnic tables at that moment being erected in the Virolun community soccer field.

"You're so fond of poor Madame," said Paula, "and all her little diamonds and trinkets. I should think you would have more respect for her furniture. Jewels are only a commodity, like tins of soup. Remember that. They're bought to be sold." She wondered why Madame Pégurin did not sell them—why she kept her little trinkets but had to rent three bedrooms and a drawing room to a strange American family.

"Baseball is as far as I'll go," said the Major to himself as he was dressing, and he noted with satisfaction that it was a fine day. Outside in the garden sat the children's friends Henry and Joey Gould. The sight of these fair-haired little boys, waiting patiently on a pair of swings, caused a cloud to drift across the Major's day, obscuring the garden, the picnic, the morning's fine beginning, for the Gould children, all unwittingly, were the cause of a prolonged disagreement between the Major and his wife.

"It's not that I'm a snob," the Major had explained. "God knows, no one could call me that!" But was it the fault of the Major that the Goulds had parted with Madame Pégurin on bad terms? Could the Major be blamed for the fact that the father of Henry and Joey was a sergeant? The Major personally thought that Sergeant Gould was a fine fellow, but the children of officers and the children of sergeants were not often invited to the same parties, and the children might, painfully, discover this for themselves. To the Major, it was clear and indisputable that the friendship should be stopped, or at least tapered. But Paula, unwisely, encouraged the children to play together. She had even asked Mrs. Gould to lunch on the lawn, which was considered by the other officers' wives in Virolun an act of great indelicacy.

Having the Gould children underfoot in the garden was particularly trying for Madame Pégurin, whose window overlooked their antics in her lily pond. She had borne with much; from her own lips the Major had heard about the final quarrel of the previous winter. It had been over a head of cauliflower—only slightly bad, said Madame Pégurin—that Mrs. Gould had dropped, unwrapped, into the garbage can. It had been retrieved by Louise, Madame Pégurin's cook, who had suggested to Mrs. Gould that it be used in soup. "I don't give my children rotten food," Mrs. Gould had replied, on which Louise, greatly distressed, had carried the slimy cauliflower in a clean towel up to Madame Pégurin's bedroom. Madame Pégurin, considering both sides, had then composed a message to be read aloud, in English, by Louise: "Is Mrs. Gould aware that many people in France have not enough to eat? Does she know that wasted food is saved for the poor by the garbage collector? Will she please in future wrap the things she wastes so that they will not spoil?" The message seemed to Madame Pégurin so fair, so unanswerable, that she could not understand why Mrs. Gould, after a moment of horrified silence, burst into tears and quite irrationally called Louise a Communist. This political quarrel had reached the ears of the General, who, insisting he could not have that sort of thing, asked Colonel Baring to straighten the difficulty out, since it was the Colonel's fault the Goulds had been sent there in the first place.

All this had given Virolun a winter of gossip, much of which was still repeated. One of the research workers had, quite recently, asked Major Marshall whether it was true that when young Mrs. Gould asked Madame Pégurin if she had a vacuum cleaner, she had been told, "No, I have a servant." Was this attitude widespread, the research worker had wanted to know. Or was the Army helping break down the feudal social barriers of the little town. Oh, yes, the Major had replied. Oh, yes, indeed.

Passing Louise on the staircase with Madame Pégurin's break-fast tray, the Major smiled, thinking of Madame Pégurin and of how fond she was of his children. Often, on his way to breakfast, he saw the children through the half-open door, watching her as she skimmed from her coffee a web of warm milk; Madame Pégurin's levees, his wife called them. Paula said that Madame Pégurin was so feminine it made her teeth ache, and that her influence on the children was deplorable. But the Major could not take this remark seriously. He admired Madame Pégurin, confusing her, because she was old and French and had once been rich, with courts and courtesans and the eighteenth century. In her presence, his mind took a literary turn, and he thought of vanished glories, something fine that would never return, gallant fluttering banners, and the rest of it.

He found his wife in the dining room, staring moodily at the disorder left by the children. "They've vanished," she said at once. "I sent them to wait in the garden with Joey and Henry, but they're not out there now. They must have crept in again by the front door. I think they were simply waiting for you to come down so that they could go up to *her* room." She was flushed with annoyance and the unexpected heat of the morning. "These red walls," she said, looking around the room. "They've made me so uncomfortable all summer I haven't enjoyed a single meal." She longed to furnish a house of her own once more, full of chintz and robin's-egg blue, and pictures of the children in frames.

In the red dining room, Madame Pégurin had hung yellow curtains. On a side table was a vase of yellow late summer flowers. The Major looked around the room, but with an almost guilty enjoyment, for, just as the Methodist child is seduced by the Roman service, the Major had succumbed in Madame Pégurin's house to something warm and rich, composed of red and yellow, and branching candelabra.

"If they would only stay in the garden," Paula said. "I hate it, always having to call them and fetch them. The girls, at least, could help with the sandwiches." She began to pile the plates one on another, drawing the crumbs on the tablecloth toward her with a knife. "And they're probably eating things. Glacéed pineapple. Cherries in something—something *alcoholic*. Really, it's too much. And you don't help."

She seemed close to tears, and the Major, looking down at his cornflakes, wondered exactly how to compose his face so that it would be most comforting. Paula was suspicious of extravagant tastes or pleasures. She enjoyed the nursery fare she gave the children, sharing without question their peas and lamb chops, their bland and innocent desserts. Once, long ago, she had broken off an engagement only because she had detected in the young man's eyes a look of sensuous bliss as he ate strawberries and cream. And now her own children came to the table full of rum-soaked sponge cake and looked with condescension at their lemon Jello.

"You exaggerate," the Major said, kindly. "Madame Pégurin takes a lot of trouble with the children. She's giving them a taste of life they might never have had."

"I know," Paula said. "And while she's at it, she's ruining all my good work." She often used this expression of the children, as if they were a length of Red Cross knitting. As the Major drank his coffee, he made marks in a notebook on the table. She sighed and, rising with the plates in her hands, said, "We'll leave it for now, because of the picnic. But tomorrow you and I must have a long talk. About everything."

"Of course," the Major said. "We'll talk about everything—the little Goulds, too. And you might try, just this once, to be nice to Mrs. Baring."

"I'll try," said Paula, "but I can't promise." There were tears in her eyes, of annoyance at having to be nice to Colonel Baring's wife.

Madame Pégurin, in the interim, descended from the shuttered gloom of her room and went out to the garden, trailing wings of gray chiffon, and followed by the children and Louise, who were bearing iced tea, a folding chair, a parasol, a hassock, and a blanket. Under the brim of her hat her hair was drawn into tangerine-colored scallops. She sat down on the chair and put her feet on the hassock. On the grass at her feet, Margaret and Ellen lay prone, propped on their elbows. John sat beside them, eating something. The little Goulds, identical in striped jerseys, stood apart, holding a ball and bat.

"And how is your mother?" Madame Pégurin asked Joey and Henry. "Does she still have so very much trouble with the vegetables?"

"I don't know," Henry said innocently. "Where we live now, the maid does everything."

"Ah, of course," Madame Pégurin said, settling back in her chair. Her voice was warm and reserved— royalty at a bazaar. Between her and the two girls passed a long look of feminine understanding.

In the kitchen, attacking the sandwiches, Paula Marshall wondered what, if anything, Mrs. Baring would say to Madame Pégurin, for the Barings had been snubbed by her so severely that, thinking of it, Paula was instantly cheered. The Barings had wanted to live with Madame Pégurin. They had been impressed by the tidy garden, the house crowded with the salvage of something better, the portrait of Monsieur Pégurin, who had been, they understood, if not an ambassador, something just as nice. But they had offended Madame Pégurin, first by giving her a Christmas present, a subscription to the *Reader's Digest* in French, and then by calling one afternoon without an invitation. Mrs. Baring had darted about the drawing room like a fish, remarking, in the sort of voice reserved for the whims of the elderly, "*My* mother collects milk glass." And the Colonel had confided to Madame Pégurin that his wife spoke excellent French and would, if pressed, say a few words in that language—a confidence that was for Madame Pégurin the depth of the afternoon. "I wouldn't think of taking into my house anyone but the General," she was reported to have said, "Or someone on his immediate staff." The Barings had exchanged paralyzed looks, and then the Colonel, rising to it, had said that he would see, and the following week he had sent Sergeant Gould, who was the General's driver, and his wife, and the terrible children. The Barings had never mentioned the incident, but they often, with little smiles and movements of their eyebrows, implied that by remaining in a cramped room at the Hotel Bristol and avoiding Madame Pégurin's big house they had narrowly escaped a season in Hell.

Now they were all going to the picnic, that symbol of unity, Sergeant Gould driving the General and Madame Pégurin, the Barings following with the mayor of Virolun, and the Marshalls and the little Goulds somewhere behind.

The Major came into the kitchen, carrying his notebook, and Paula said to him, "It will be queer, this thing today."

"Queer?" he said absently. "I don't see why. Look," he said. "I may have to make a speech. I put everyone on the agenda but myself, but I may be asked." He frowned at his notes. "I could start with 'We are gathered together.' Or is that stuffy?"

"I don't know," Paula said. With care, and also with a certain suggestion of martyrdom, she rolled bread around watercress. "Actually, I think it's a quote."

"It could be." The Major looked depressed. He ate an egg sandwich from Paula's hamper. The basket lunch had been his idea; every family was bringing one. The Major had declared the basket lunch to be typically American, although he had never in his life attended such a function. "You should see them all in the garden," he said, cheering up. "Madame Pégurin and the kids. What a picture! The photographer should have been there. He's never around when you want him."

Describing this scene, which he had watched from the dining-room windows, the Major was careful to leave out any phrases that might annoy his wife, omitting with regret the filtered sunlight, the golden summer garden, and the blue shade of the parasol. It had pleased him to observe, although he did not repeat this either, that even a stranger could have detected which children were the little Goulds and which the little Marshalls. "I closed the dining-room shutters," he added. "The sun seems to have moved around." He had become protective of Madame Pégurin's house, extending his care to the carpets.

"That's fine," Paula said. In a few minutes, the cars would arrive to carry them all away, and she had a sudden prophetic vision of the day ahead. She saw the tiny cavalcade of motorcars creeping, within the speed limit, through the main street and stopping at the 1914 war memorial so that General Wirtworth could place a wreath. She foresaw the failure of the Coca-Cola to arrive at the picnic grounds, and the breakdown of the movie projector. On the periphery, scowling and eating nothing, would be the members of the Virolun Football Club, which had been forced to postpone a match with the St. Etienne Devils because of the picnic. The Major would be everywhere at once, driving his sergeant before him like a hen. Then the baseball, with the mothers of Virolun taking good care to keep their pinafored children away from the wayward ball and the terrible waving bat. Her imagination sought the photographer, found him on a picnic table, one sandaled foot next to a plate of doughnuts, as he recorded Mrs. Baring fetching a cushion for General Wirtworth and Madame Pégurin receiving from the little Goulds a cucumber sandwich.

Paula closed the picnic hamper and looked at her husband with compassion. She suddenly felt terribly sorry for him, because of all that was in store for him this day, and because the picnic was not likely to clarify his status, as he so earnestly hoped. There would be fresh misunderstandings and further scandals. She laid her hand over his. "I'm sorry," she said. "I should have been listening more carefully. Read me your speech, and start with 'We are gathered together.' I think it's quite appropriate and very lovely."

"Do you?" said the Major. His eyes hung on her face, trusting. "But then suppose I have to give it in French? How the hell do you say 'gathered together' in French?"

"You won't have to give it in French," Paula said, in just such a voice as she used to her children when they had a fever or nightmares. "Because, you see, the mayor will speak in French, and that's quite enough."

"That's right," said the Major. "I can say, in French, 'Our good French friends will excuse this little talk in English.'"

"That's right," Paula said.

Reassured, the Major thrust his notes in his pocket and strode from the kitchen to the garden, where, squaring his shoulders, he rallied his forces for the coming battle.

*1952*

# A DAY LIKE ANY OTHER

JANE AND Ernestine were at breakfast in the hotel dining room
when the fog finally lifted. It had clung to the windows for weeks,
ever since the start of the autumn rains, reducing a promised view
of mountains to a watery blur. Now, unexpectedly, the fog rose; it
went up all in one piece, like a curtain, and when it had cleared
away, the children saw that the mountains outside were covered
with snow. Because of their father's health, they had always, until
this year, wintered in warm climates. They abandoned their slopped
glasses of milk and stared at slopes that were rough with trees,
black and white like the glossy postcards their mother bought to
send to aunts in America. Down below, on a flat green plain, were
villages no bigger than the children's cereal plates. Some of the
villages were in Germany and some were over in France—their
governess, Frau Stengel, had explained about the frontier, with
many a glum allusion—but from here the toy houses and steeples
looked all alike; there was no hedge, no fence, no mysterious cleft
in the earth to set them apart, although, staring hard, one *could* see
something, a winding line, as thin as a hair. That was the Rhine.

"Look," said Jane, to the back of her mother's newspaper. She
said it encouragingly, preparing Mrs. Kennedy for shock. It did
not enter her head that her mother knew what snow was like. To
the two little girls winter meant walks in parks where every pebble had a correct place underfoot and geraniums grew in rows,
like soldiers marching. The sea was always there, but too cold to
bathe in. Overhead, and outside their window at night, palms
rustled bleakly, like unswept leaves.

"Look," Jane repeated, but Mrs. Kennedy, who read the local paper every day in order to improve her German, didn't hear. "You can see everything," said Jane, giving her mother up. "Mountains."

"Hitler's mountains," said Ernestine, repeating a phrase that Frau Stengel had used. The girls had no idea who Hitler was, but they had seen his photograph—Frau Stengel kept it pressed between two film magazines on her bookshelf—and she frequently spoke of his death, which she appeared to have felt keenly. The children, because of this, assumed that Hitler and Frau Stengel must have been related. "Poor Hitler, Frau Stengel's dead cousin," Ernestine sang, inventing a tune, making whirlpools in her porridge with a spoon. Some of the people at nearby tables in the dining room turned to smile mistily at the children. What angels the Kennedy girls were, the hotel guests often remarked—so pretty and polite, and always saying the most intelligent things! "Frau Stengel says there wouldn't have been a war that time, only all these other people were so greedy," and "Only one little, little piece of Africa, Frau Stengel says. Frau Stengel says..." Someone had started the rumor that Jane and Ernestine were not Mrs. Kennedy's daughters at all but had been adopted here in Germany. How else was one to account for their blond hair? Mrs. Kennedy was quite dark, and old enough to be, if not their grandmother (although some of the women in the hotel were willing to push it that far), at least a sort of elderly adoptive aunt. Mrs. Kennedy, looking up in time to catch the looks of tender good will beamed toward her daughters, would think, How fond they are of children! But then Jane and Ernestine are particularly attractive. She had no notion of the hotel gossip concerning their origins and would have been deeply offended if she had been told about it, for Jane and Ernestine were not German and not adopted. They had come along quite naturally, if disconcertingly, less than a year apart, just at a time when Mrs. Kennedy had begun to regard all children as a remote, alarming race. The second surprise had come when they had turned out to be more than commonly pretty. "Like little dolls," Frau Stengel had said on first seeing them. "Just like dolls."

"I have been told that they resemble little Renoirs," Mrs. Kennedy had replied, with just a trace of correction.

Their charm, after all, was not entirely the work of nature; one's character was just as important as one's face, and the girls, thanks to their mother's vigilance on their behalf, were as unblemished, as removed from the world and its coarsening effects, as their guileless faces suggested. Unlike their little compatriots, whom they sometimes met on their travels, and from whom they were quickly led away, they had never, Mrs. Kennedy was able to assure herself, heard a thought expressed that was cheapening or less than kind. They wore, in all seasons, clothing that matched the atmosphere created for their own special world—ribboned straw hats, fluffy little sweaters, starched frocks trimmed with rows and rows of *broderie anglaise*, made to order wherever a favorable exchange prevailed—and the result was that, with their long, brushed tresses, they did indeed resemble dolls, or even, in a rosy light, little Renoirs.

What marriages they would make! Mrs. Kennedy, without complaining of her own, nevertheless hoped her girls would accomplish something with just a little more glitter—a double wedding in a cathedral, for instance. Chartres would be nice, though damp. Observing the children now, over the breakfast table, she saw the picture again—perfumed, cloudy, with a pair of faceless but utterly suitable bridegrooms hovering in the background. Mr. Kennedy, who did not believe in churches and thought they should all be turned into lending libraries, would simply have to put aside his scruples for the occasion. Mrs. Kennedy, mentally, had it out with him. "Very well," he replied, vanquished. "I certainly owe you this much consideration after the splendid way you've brought them up." He led them into the cathedral, one on each arm. After a tuneful but, to spare Mr. Kennedy, nondenom inational ceremony, the two couples emerged under the crossed swords of a guard of honor. "The girls are charming, and they owe it all to their mother," someone was heard to remark in the crowd. Returning to the breakfast table, Mrs. Kennedy heard Jane saying, "Just this one movie, and I'll never ask again."

"One *what*!"

"This movie," said Jane. "The one I was just telling about, *Das Herz Einer Mutti*. Frau Stengel could take us this afternoon, she says. She already went twice. She cried like anything."

"Frau Stengel should know better than to suggest such a thing," said Mrs. Kennedy, looking crossly at her brides. "There's milk all over your mouth, and Ernestine's hands are filthy. Do you want to make my life a trial?"

"No," said Jane. She opened a picture book she had brought to the table and began to read aloud in German, in a high, stumbling recitative. One silky tress of hair lay on the buttered side of a piece of bread. She wiped her mouth on the fluffy sleeve of her pale blue sweater.

"Well, really, sometimes I just—" Mrs. Kennedy began, but Jane was reading, and Ernestine singing, and she said, annoyed, "What is that book, if you please?"

"Nothing," said Jane. It was a book Frau Stengel had given them, the comic adventures of Hansi, a baboon. Hansi was always in mischief, bursting in where grown-up people were taking baths, and that kind of thing, but the most enchanting thing about him, from the children's point of view, was his heart-shaped scarlet behind, on which the artist had dwelt with loving exactitude.

Mrs. Kennedy drew the book toward her. She glanced quickly through the pages, then put it down by her coffee cup. She said nothing.

"Is it cruel?" said Jane nervously. She tried again: "Is it too cruel, or something?"

"It is worse than cruel," said Mrs. Kennedy, when at last she could speak. "It is vulgar. I forbid you to read it."

"We already have."

"Then don't read it again. If Frau Stengel gave it to you, give it back this morning."

"It has our names written in it," said Jane.

Momentarily halted, Mrs. Kennedy looked out at the view. Absorbed with her own problem—the children, the book, whether or not she had handled it well—she failed to notice that the fog had lifted, and felt just as hemmed in and baffled as usual. If only one could consult one's husband, she thought. But Mr. Kennedy, who lay at this very moment in a nursing home half a mile distant, waiting for his wife to come and read to him, could not be counted on for advice. He cherished an obscure stomach complaint and a touchy liver that had withstood, triumphantly, the best attention of twenty doctors. It was because of Mr. Kennedy's stomach that the family moved about so much, guided by a new treatment in London, an excellent liver man on the Riviera, or the bracing climate of the Italian lakes. A weaker man, Mrs. Kennedy sometimes thought, might have given up and pretended he was better, but her husband, besides having an uncommon lot of patience, had been ailing just long enough to be faddish; this year it was a nursing home on the rim of the Black Forest that had taken his fancy, and here they all were, shivering in the unaccustomed damp, dosed with a bracing vitamin tonic sent over from America and guaranteed to replace the southern sun.

Mr. Kennedy seldom saw his daughters. The rules of the private clinics he frequented were all in his favor. In any case, he seldom asked to see the girls, for he felt that they were not at an interesting age. Wistfully, his wife sometimes wondered when their interesting age would begin—when they were old enough to be sent away to school, perhaps, or, better still, safely disposed of in the handsome marriages that gave her so much concern.

Reminded now of Mr. Kennedy and the day ahead, she looked around the dining room, wondering if anyone would like to come along to the nursing home for a little visit. She stared coldly past the young American couple who sat before the next window; they were the only other foreigners in the hotel, and Mrs. Kennedy had swept them off to the hospital one morning before they knew what was happening. The visit had not been a success. Cheered by a new audience, Mr. Kennedy had talked about his views—views so bold that they still left his wife quite breathless after fourteen years of marriage. Were people fit to govern themselves, for instance? Mr. Kennedy could not be sure. Look at France. And what of the ants? Was not their civilization, with its emphasis on industry and thrift, superior to ours? Mr. Kennedy thought that it was. And then there was God—or was there? Mr. Kennedy had talked about God at some length that morning, and the young couple had listened, looking puzzled, until, at last, the young woman said, "Yes, well, I see. Agnostic. How sweet."

"Sweet!" said Mr. Kennedy, outraged.

Sweet? thought his wife. Why, they were treating Mr. Kennedy as if he were funny and old-fashioned, somebody to be humored. If they could have heard some of the things he had said to the bishop that time, they might have more respect! She had given the young man a terrible look, and he had begun to speak valiantly of books, but it was too late. Mr. Kennedy was offended, and he interrupted sulkily to snap, "Well, no one had to revive Kipling for *me*," and the visit broke up right after that.

Really, no one would do for Mr. Kennedy, thought his wife—but she thought it without a jot of censure, for she greatly admired her husband and was ready to show it in a number of practical ways; not only did she ungrudgingly provide the income that permitted his medical excursions but she sat by his bedside nearly every day of the year discussing his digestion and reading aloud the novels of Upton Sinclair, of which he was exceedingly fond.

Sighing, now, she brought her gaze back from the window and the unsuitable hotel guests. "You might as well go to lessons," she said to the girls. "But remember, no movies."

They got down from their chairs. Each of them implanted on Mrs. Kennedy's cheek a kiss that smelled damply of milk. How grubby they looked, their mother thought, even though the day had scarcely begun. Who would believe, seeing them now, that they had been dressed not an hour before in frocks still warm from the iron? Ernestine had caught her dress on something, so that the hem drooped to one side. Their hair... But Mrs. Kennedy, exhausted, decided not to think about their hair.

"You look so odd sometimes," she said. "You look all untidy and forlorn, like children without mothers to care for them, like little refugees. Although," she added, conscientious, "there is nothing the matter with being a refugee."

"Like Frau Stengel," said Jane, straining to be away.

"Frau Stengel? What on earth has she been telling you about refugees?"

"That you should never trust a Czech," said Jane.

Mrs. Kennedy could not follow this and did not try. "Haven't you a message for your father?" she said, holding Jane by the wrist. "It would be nice if you showed just a little concern." They stood, fidgeting. "Shall I tell him you hope he feels much better?"

"Yes."

"And that you hope to see him soon?"

"Yes. Yes."

"He will be pleased," their mother said, but, released, they were already across the room.

Frau Stengel was, on the whole, an unsatisfactory substitute for a mother's watchful care, and it was only because Mrs. Kennedy had been unable to make a better arrangement that Frau Stengel had become the governess of Jane and Ernestine. A mournful *Volksdeutsch* refugee from Prague, she looked well over her age, which was thirty-nine. She lived— with her husband—in the same hotel as the Kennedy family, and she had once been a schoolteacher, both distinct advantages. The girls were too young for boarding school, and the German day school nearby, while picturesque, had a crucifix over the door, which meant, Mrs. Kennedy was certain, that someone would try to convert her daughters. Of course, a good firm note to the principal might help: "The children's father would be most distressed..." But no, the risk was too great, and in any case it had been agreed that the children's religious instruction would be put off until Mr. Kennedy had made up his mind about God. Frau Stengel, if fat, and rather commonplace, and given to tearful lapses that showed a want of inner discipline, was not likely to interfere with Mr. Kennedy's convictions. She admired the children just as they were, applauding with each murmur of praise their mother's painstaking efforts to see that they kept their bloom. "So sweet," she would say. "So *herzig*, the little sweaters."

The children were much too pretty to be taxed with lessons; Frau Stengel gave them film magazines to look at and supervised them contentedly, rocking and filing her nails. She lived a cozy, molelike existence in her room on the attic floor of the hotel, surrounded by crocheted mats, stony satin cushions, and pictures of kittens cut from magazines. Her radio, which was never still, filled the room with soupy operetta melodies, many of which reminded Frau Stengel of happier days and made her cry.

Everyone had been so cruel, so unkind, she would tell the children, drying her eyes. Frau Stengel and her husband had lived in Prague, where Herr Stengel, who now worked at some inferior job in a nearby town, had been splendidly situated until the end of the war, and then the Czechs sent them packing. They had left everything behind—all the tablecloths, the little coffee spoons!

Although the children were bored by the rain and not being allowed to go out, they enjoyed their days with Frau Stengel. Every day was just like the one before, which was a comfort; the mist and the rain hung on the windows, Frau Stengel's favorite music curled around the room like a warm bit of the fog itself, they ate chocolate biscuits purchased from the glass case in the dining room, and Frau Stengel, always good-tempered, always the same, told them stories. She told about Hitler, and the war, and about little children she knew who had been killed in bombardments or separated forever from their parents. The two little girls would listen, stolidly going on with their coloring or cutting out. They liked her stories, mostly because, like the room and the atmosphere, the stories never varied; they could have repeated many of them by heart, and they knew exactly at what point in each Frau Stengel would begin to cry. The girls had never seen anyone weep so much and so often.

"We like you, Frau Stengel," Jane had said once, meaning that they would rather be shut up here in Frau Stengel's pleasantly overheated room than be downstairs alone in their bedroom or in the bleak, empty dining room. Frau Stengel had looked at them and after a warm, delicious moment had wiped her eyes. After that, Jane had tried it again, and with the same incredulity with which she and Ernestine had learned that if you pushed the button the elevator would arrive, every time, they had discovered that either one of them could bring on the great, sad tears that were, almost, the most entertaining part of their lessons. "We like you," and off Frau Stengel would go while the two children watched, enchanted. Later, they learned that any mention of their father had nearly the same effect. They had no clear idea of the nature of their father's illness, or why it was sad; once they had been told that, because of his liver, he sometimes turned yellow, but this interesting evolution they had never witnessed.

"He's yellow today," Jane would sometimes venture.

"Ah, so!" Frau Stengel would reply, her eyes getting bigger and bigger. Sometimes, after thinking it over, she wept, but not always.

For the past few days, however, Frau Stengel had been less diverting; she had melted less easily. Also, she had spoken of the joyous future when she and Herr Stengel would emigrate to Australia and open a little shop.

"To sell what?" said Ernestine, threatened with change.

"Tea and coffee," said their governess dreamily.

In Australia, Frau Stengel had been told, half the people were black and savage, but one was far from trouble. She could not see the vision of the shop clearly, and spoke of coffee jars painted with hearts, a tufted chair where tired clients could rest. It was important, these days, that she fix her mind on rosy vistas, for her doctor had declared, and her horoscope had confirmed, that she was pregnant; she hinted of something to the Kennedy children, some revolution in her life, some reason their mother would have to find another governess before spring. But winter, the children knew, went on forever.

This morning, when Jane and Ernestine knocked on her door, Frau Stengel was sitting by her window in a glow of sunshine reflected from the snow on the mountains. "Come in," she said, and smiled at them. What pathetic little orphans they were, so sad, and so fond of her. If it had not been for their affection for her, frequently and flatteringly expressed, Frau Stengel would have given them up days ago; they reminded her, vaguely, of unhappy things. She had told them so many stories about the past that just looking at the two little girls made her think of it all over again—dolorous thoughts, certain to affect the character and appearance of the unborn.

"Mother doesn't want us to go to the movies with you," began Jane. She looked, expectant, but Frau Stengel said placidly, "Well, never do anything your mother wouldn't like." This was to be another of her new cheerful days; disappointed, the children settled down to lessons. Ernestine colored the pictures in a movie magazine with crayons, and Jane made a bracelet of some coral rosebuds from an old necklace her mother had given her.

"It's nice here today," said Jane. "We like it here."

"The sun is shining. You should go out," said Frau Stengel, yawning, quite as if she had not heard. "Don't forget the little rubbers."

"Will you come?"

"Oh, no," Frau Stengel said in a tantalizing, mysterious way. "It is important for me to rest."

"For us, too," said Ernestine jealously. "We have to rest. Everybody rests. Our father rests all the time. He has to, too."

"Because he's so sick," said Jane.

"He's dead," said Ernestine. She gave Gregory Peck round blue eyes.

Frau Stengel looked up sharply. "Who is dead?" she said. "You must not use such a word in here, now."

The children stared, surprised. Death had been spoken of so frequently in this room, on the same level as chocolate biscuits and coral rosebud bracelets.

"*He's* dead," said Ernestine. "He died this morning."

Frau Stengel stopped rocking. "Your father is *dead*?"

"Yes, he is," said Ernestine. "He died, and we're supposed to stay here with you, and that's all."

Their governess looked, bewildered, from one to the other; they sat, the image of innocence, side by side at her table, their hair caught up with blue ribbons.

"Why don't we go out now?" said Jane. The room was warm. She put her head down on the table and chewed the ends of her hair. "Come on," she said, bored, and gave Ernestine a prod with her foot.

"In a minute," her sister said indistinctly. She bent over the portrait she was coloring, pressing on the end of the crayon until it was flat. Waxy colored streaks were glued to the palm of her hand. She wiped her hand on the skirt of her starched blue frock. "All right, now," she said, and got down from her chair.

"Where are you going, please?" said Frau Stengel, breathing at them through tense, widened nostrils. "Didn't your mother send a message for me? When did it happen?"

"What?" said Jane. "Can't we go out? You said we could, before."

"It isn't true, about your father," said Frau Stengel. "You made it up. Your father is not dead."

"Oh, no," said Jane, anxious to make the morning ordinary again. "She only said it, like, for a joke."

"A joke? You come here and frighten me in my condition for a *joke*?" Frau Stengel could not deliver sitting down the rest of the terrible things she had to say. She pulled herself out of the rocking chair and looked down at the perplexed little girls. She seemed to them enormously fat and tall, like the statues in Italian parks. Fascinated, they stared back. "What you have done is very wicked," said Frau Stengel. "Very wicked. I won't tell your mother, but I shall never forget it. In any case, God heard you, and God will punish you. If your father should die now, it would certainly be your fault."

This was not the first time the children had heard of God. Mrs. Kennedy might plan to defer her explanations to a later date, in line with Mr. Kennedy's eventual decision, but the simple women she employed to keep an eye on Jane and Ernestine (Frau Stengel was the sixth to be elevated to the title of governess) had no such moral obstacles. For them, God was the catch-all answer to most of life's perplexities. "Who makes this rain?" Jane had once asked Frau Stengel.

"God," she had replied cozily.

"So that we can't play outside?"

"He makes the sun," Frau Stengel said, anxious to give credit.

"Well, then—" Jane began, but Frau Stengel, sensing a paradox, went on to something else.

Until now, however, God had not been suggested as a threat. The children stayed where they were, at the table, and looked wide-eyed at their governess.

Frau Stengel began to feel foolish; it is one thing to begin a scene, she was discovering, and another to sustain it. "Go to your room downstairs," she said. "You had better stay there, and not come out. I can't teach girls who tell lies."

This, clearly, was a dismissal, not only from her room but from her company, possibly forever. Never before had they been abandoned in the middle of the day. Was this the end of winter?

"Is he dead?" cried Ernestine, in terror at what had become of the day.

"Goodbye, Frau Stengel," said Jane, with a ritual curtsy; this was how she had been trained to take her leave, and although she often forgot it, the formula now returned to sustain her. She gathered up the coral beads—after all, they belonged to her—but Ernestine rushed out, pushing in her hurry to be away. "Busy little feet," said an old gentleman a moment later, laboriously pulling himself up with the aid of the banisters, as first Ernestine and then Jane clattered by.

They burst into their room, and Jane closed the door. "Anyway, it was you that said it," she said at once.

Ernestine did not reply. She climbed up on her high bed and sat with her fat legs dangling over the edge. She stared at the opposite wall, her mouth slightly open. She could think of no way to avert the punishment about to descend on their heads, nor could she grasp the idea of a punishment more serious than being deprived of dessert.

"It was you, anyway," Jane repeated. "If anything happens, I'll tell. I think I could tell anyway."

"I'll tell, too," said Ernestine.

"You haven't anything to tell."

"I'll tell everything," said Ernestine in a sudden fury. "I'll tell you chewed gum. I'll tell you wet the bed and we had to put the sheets out the window. I'll tell everything."

The room was silent. Jane leaned over to the window between their beds, where the unaccustomed sun had roused a fat, slumbering fly. It shook its wings and buzzed loudly. Jane put her finger on its back; it vibrated and felt funny. "Look, Ern," she said.

Ernestine squirmed over on the bed; their heads touched, their breath misted the window. The fly moved and left staggering tracks.

"We could go out," said Jane. "Frau Stengel even said it." They went, forgetting their rubbers.

Mrs. Kennedy came home at half past six, no less and no more exhausted than usual. It had not been a lively day or a memorably pleasant one but a day like any other, in the pattern she was now accustomed to and might even have missed. She had read aloud until lunch, which the clinic kitchen sent up on a tray—veal, potatoes, shredded lettuce, and sago pudding with jelly—and she had noted with dismay that Mr. Kennedy's meal included a bottle of hock, fetched in under the apron of a guilty-looking nurse. How silly to tempt him in this way when he wanted so much to get well, she thought. After lunch, the reading went on, Mrs. Kennedy stopping now and then to sustain her voice with a sip of

Vichy water. They were rereading an old Lanny Budd novel, but Mrs. Kennedy could not have said what it was about. She had acquired the knack of thinking of other things while she read aloud. She read in a high, uninflected voice, planning the debut of Jane and Ernestine with a famous ballet company. Mr. Kennedy listened, contentedly polishing off his bottle of wine. Sometimes he interrupted. "Juan-les-Pins," he remarked as the name came up in the text.

"We were there." This was the chief charm of the novels, that they kept mentioning places Mr. Kennedy had visited. "Aix-les-Bains," he remarked a little later. Possibly he was not paying close attention, for Lanny Budd was now having it out with Göring in Berlin. Mr. Kennedy's tone of voice suggested that something quite singular had taken place in Aix-les-Bains, when as a matter of fact Mrs. Kennedy had spent a quiet summer with the two little girls in a second-class pension while Mr. Kennedy took the mud-bath cure.

Mr. Kennedy rang for his nurse and, when she came, told her to send in the doctor. The reading continued; Jane and Ernestine found ballet careers too strenuous, and in any case the publicity was cheapening. For the fortieth time, they married. Jane married a very dashing young officer, and Ernestine the president of a university. A few minutes later, the doctor came in; another new doctor, Mrs. Kennedy noted. But it was only by constantly changing his doctor and reviewing his entire medical history from the beginning that Mr. Kennedy obtained the attention his condition required. This doctor was cheerful and brisk. "We'll have him out of here in no time," he assured Mrs. Kennedy, smiling.

"Oh, *grand*," she said faintly.

"Are you sure?" her husband asked the doctor. "There are two or three things that haven't been checked and attended to."

"Oh?" said the doctor. At that moment, he saw the empty wine bottle and picked it up. Mrs. Kennedy, who dreaded scenes, closed her eyes. "You waste my time," she heard the doctor say. The door closed behind him. She opened her eyes. These awful rows, she thought. They were all alike—all the nurses, all the clinics, all the doctors. Mr. Kennedy, fortunately, did not seem unduly disturbed.

"You might see if you can order me one of those books of crossword puzzles," he remarked as his wife gathered up her things to leave.

"Shall I give your love to Jane and Ernestine?" she said. But Mr. Kennedy, worn out with his day, seemed to be falling asleep.

Back at the hotel, Jane and Ernestine were waiting in the upper hall. They clung to Mrs. Kennedy, as if her presence had reminded them of something. Touched, Mrs. Kennedy said nothing about the mud on their shoes but instead praised their rosy faces. They hung about, close to her, while she rested on the chaise longue in her room before dinner. "How I should love to trade my days for yours," she said suddenly, thinking not only of their magic future but of these days that were, for them, a joyous and repeated holiday.

"Didn't you have fun today?" said Jane, leaning on her mother's feet.

"Fun! Well, not what you chicks would call fun."

They descended to dinner together; the children held on to her hands, one on each side. They showed, for once, a nice sensibility, she thought. Perhaps they were arriving at that special age a mother dreams of, the age of gratitude and awareness. In the dining room, propped against the mustard jar, was an envelope with scrolls and curlicues under the name "Kennedy." Inside was a note from Frau Stengel explaining that, because she was expecting a child and needed all her strength for the occasion, she could no longer give Jane and Ernestine their lessons. So delicately and circuitously did she explain her situation that Mrs. Kennedy was left with the impression that Frau Stengel was expecting the visit of a former pupil. She thought it a strange way of letting her know. I wonder what she means by "harmony of spirit," she thought. The child must be a terror. She was not at all anxious to persuade Frau Stengel to change her mind; the incident of the book at breakfast, the mention of movies, the mud on the children's shoes all suggested it was time for someone new.

"Is it bad news?" said Jane.

Mrs. Kennedy was touched. "You mustn't feel things so," she said kindly. "No, it is only that Frau Stengel won't be your governess anymore. She is expecting"—she glanced at the letter again and, suddenly getting the drift of it, folded it quickly and went on—"a little boy or girl for a visit."

"Our age?"

"I don't know," said Mrs. Kennedy vaguely. Would this be a good occasion, she wondered, to begin telling them about... about... But no, not in a hotel dining room, not over a plate of alphabet soup. "I suppose I could stay home for a few days, until we find someone, and we could do lessons together. Would you like that?" They looked at her without replying. "We could do educational things, like nature walks," she said. "Why, what ever is the matter? Are you so unhappy about Frau Stengel?"

"Is he dead?" said Jane.

"Who?"

"Our father," said Jane in a quavering voice that carried to every table and on to the kitchen.

"Good heavens!" Mrs. Kennedy glanced quickly around the dining room; everyone had heard. Damp clouds of sympathy were forming around the table. "As a matter of fact, he is much better," she said loudly and briskly. "Perhaps, to be reassured, you ought to see him. Would you like that?"

"Oh, yes."

She was perplexed but gratified. "Father didn't want you to see him when he was so ill," she explained. "He wanted you to remember him as he was."

"In case he died?"

"I think we'll go upstairs," said Mrs. Kennedy, pushing back her chair. They followed her across the room and up the staircase without protest. She had never seen them looking so odd. "You seem all pinched," she said, examining them by the light between their beds. "And a few minutes ago you seemed so rosy! Where are my little Renoir faces? I'm getting you liver tablets tomorrow. You'd better go to bed."

It was early, but they made no objection. "Are you really going to be home tomorrow?" said Jane.

"Well, yes. I can't think of anything else to do, for the moment."

"He's dead," said Jane positively.

"Really," said their mother, exasperated. "If you don't stop this at once, I don't know what I'll do. It's morbid."

"Will you read to us?" said Ernestine, shoeless and in her petticoat.

"Read?" Mrs. Kennedy said. "No, I couldn't." With quick, tugging motions, she began to braid their hair for the night. "I don't even want to speak. I want to rest my voice."

"Then could you just sit here?" said Jane. "Could we have the light?"

"Why?" said Mrs. Kennedy, snapping elastic on the end of a braid. "Have you been having bad dreams?"

"I don't know," said Jane, standing uncertainly by her bed.

"Healthy children don't dream," her mother said, confident that this was so. "You have no reason whatever to dream." She rose and put the hairbrush away. "Into bed, now, both of you."

They crept wretchedly into their separate beds. Mrs. Kennedy kissed each of them and opened the window. She was at the door, her hand on the light switch, when Jane said, "Can God punish you for something?"

Mrs. Kennedy dropped her hand. She had been, she found with annoyance, about to say vaguely, "Well, that all depends." She said instead, "I don't know."

It was worse than anything the children had bargained for. "If *she* doesn't know—" said Ernestine. It was not clear whom she was addressing. "—then who does?"

"Nobody, really," said Mrs. Kennedy. They had certainly chosen a singular approach to the subject, and an odd time to speak of it, she thought, but curiosity of this sort should always be dealt with as it came up. "Many people think they know, one way or the other, but it is impossible for a thinking person—Father will tell you about it," she finished. "We'll arrange a visit very soon."

"If you don't *know*," said Jane from her pillow, "then we don't know what can happen." She lay back and pulled the bedsheet up to her eyes. Mrs. Kennedy put out the light, promising again an interesting talk with their father, who would explain all over again how he didn't know, either, and why.

Just before going to bed, shortly after ten o'clock, Mrs. Kennedy softly re-entered the children's room. She carried a large dish of applesauce, two spoons, and two buttered rolls for the girls to discover in the morning. The room was totally dark, and stuffy; someone—one of the children—had closed the window and drawn the heavy double curtains straight across. Groping in the dark to their bedside table, she put down her burden of food, and then, as quietly as she could, pulled the draperies to one side. Moonlight filled the squares of the window. The breeze that came in when she unlatched the window smelled of snow. In the bright, cold, clear night, the lights from the villages down below blinked and wavered like stars. It was not often that Mrs. Kennedy had time to enjoy or contemplate something not directly dependent on herself or fated by one of her or her husband's decisions. For nearly a full minute, she stood perfectly still and admired the night. Then she remembered one of the reasons she had come into the room, and bent over to draw the covers up over her daughters.

Ernestine had got into bed with Jane, which was odd; they lay facing the same direction, like two question marks. With one hand Ernestine limply clutched at her sister's braids. Both children had wormed down into the middle of the bed, well below the pillow, under a tent of blankets; it was a wonder they hadn't smothered.

Mrs. Kennedy drew back the blankets and gently pulled Ernestine away. Without waking, but muttering something, Ernestine got up and walked to her own bed. The hair at her temples was wet, and she generated the nearly feverish warmth of sleeping children. Sleeping, she put her thumb in her mouth. Mrs. Kennedy turned to Jane and pulled her carefully up to the pillow. "I left my book outside," said Jane urgently and distinctly. Straightening up, Mrs. Kennedy gave the covers a final pat. She looked down at her little girls, frowning; they seemed at this moment not like little Renoirs, not like little dolls, but like rather ordinary children who for some reason of their own had shut and muffled the window and then crept into one bed, the better to hide. She was tempted to wake Jane, or Ernestine, and ask what it was all about, this solicitude for Mr. Kennedy, this irrelevant talk of God. Perhaps Frau Stengel, in some blundering way, had mentioned her pregnancy. Despairing, Mrs. Kennedy wished she could gather her children up, one under each arm, and carry them off to a higher mountain, an emptier hotel, where nothing and no one could interfere, or fill their minds with the kind of thought she feared and detested. Their *minds*. Was she really, all alone, without Mr. Kennedy to help her, expected to cope with their minds as well as everything else?

But I am exaggerating, she thought, looking out at the peaceful night. They haven't so much as begun to think, about anything. Without innocence, after all, there was no beauty, and no one could deny the beauty of Jane and Ernestine. She did not look at them again as they lay, damp and vulnerable, in their beds, but, instantly solaced with the future and what it contained for them, she saw them once again drifting away on a sea of admiration, the surface unmarred, the interior uncorrupted by thought or any one of the hundred indecisions that were the lot of less favored human beings. Meanwhile, of course, they had still to grow up—but after all what was there between this night and the magic time to come but a link of days, the limpid days of children? For, she thought, smiling in the dark, pleased at the image, were not their days like the lights one saw in the valley at night, starry, indistinguishable one from the other? She must tell that to Mr. Kennedy, she thought, drawing away from the window. He would be sure to agree.

*1953*

# GOING ASHORE

AT TANGIER it was surprisingly cold, even for December. The sea was lead, the sky cloudy and low. Most of the passengers going ashore for the day came to breakfast wrapped in scarves and sweaters. They were, most of them, thin-skinned, elderly people, less concerned with the prospect of travel than with getting through another winter in relative comfort; on bad days, during the long crossing from the West Indies, they had lain in deck chairs, muffled as mummies, looking stricken and deceived. When Emma Ellenger came into the breakfast lounge barelegged, in sandals, wearing a light summer frock, there was a low flurry of protest. Really, Emma's mother should take more care! The child would catch her death.

Feeling the disapproval almost as an emanation, like the salt one breathed in the air, Emma looked around for someone who liked her—Mr. Cowan, or the Munns. There were the Munns, sitting in a corner, frowning over their toast, coffee, and guidebooks. She waved, although they had not yet seen her, threaded her way between the closely spaced tables, and, without waiting to be asked, sat down.

Miss and Mrs. Munn looked up with a single movement. They were daughter and mother, but so identically frizzy, tweedy, and elderly that they might have been twins. Mrs. Munn, the kindly twin, gazed at Emma with benevolent, rather popping brown eyes, and said, "Child, you'll freeze in that little dress. Do tell your mother—now, don't forget to tell her—that the North African winter can be treacherous, very treacherous indeed." She tapped one of the brown paper-covered guidebooks that lay beside her coffee tray. The Munns always went ashore provided with books, maps, and folders telling them what to expect at every port of call. They differed in every imaginable manner from Emma and her mother, who seldom fully understood where they were and who were often daunted and upset (particularly Mrs. Ellenger) if the people they encountered ashore were the wrong color or spoke an unfamiliar language.

"You should wear a thick scarf," Mrs. Munn went on, "and warm stockings." Thinking of the Ellengers' usual wardrobe, she paused, discouraged. "The most important parts of the—" But she stopped again, unable to say "body" before a girl of twelve. "One should keep the throat and the ankles warm," she said, lowering her gaze to her book.

"We can't," Emma said respectfully. "We didn't bring anything for the cruise except summer dresses. My mother thought it would be warm all the time."

"She should have inquired," Miss Munn said. Miss Munn was crisper, taut; often the roles seemed reversed, and it appeared that she, of the two, should have been the mother.

"I guess she didn't think," Emma said, cast down by all the things her mother failed to do. Emma loved the Munns. It was distressing when, as now, they failed to approve of her. They were totally unlike the people she was accustomed to, with their tweeds, their pearls, their strings of fur that bore the claws and muzzles of some small, flattened beast. She had fallen in love with them the first night aboard, during the first dinner out. The Munns and the Ellengers had been seated together, the dining-room steward having thought it a good plan to group, at a table for four, two solitary women and their solitary daughters.

The Munns had been so kind, so interested, asking any number of friendly questions. They wondered how old Emma was, and where Mr. Ellenger might be ("In Heaven," said Emma, casual), and where the Ellengers lived in New York.

"We live all over the place." Emma spoke up proudly. It was

evident to her that her mother wasn't planning to say a word. *Somebody* had to be polite. "Most of the time we live in hotels. But last summer we didn't. We lived in an apartment. A big apartment. It wasn't our place. It belongs to this friend of my mother's, Mr. Jimmy Salter, but he was going to be away, and the rent was paid anyway, and we were living there already, so he said—he said—" She saw her mother's face and stopped, bewildered.

"That was nice," said Mrs. Munn, coloring. Her daughter looked down, smiling mysteriously.

Emma's mother said nothing. She lit a cigarette and blew the smoke over the table. She wore a ring, a wedding band, a Mexican necklace, and a number of clashing bracelets. Her hair, which was long and lighter even than Emma's, had been carefully arranged, drawn into a tight chignon and circled with flowers. Clearly it was not for Miss or Mrs. Munn that she had taken such pains; she had expected a different table arrangement, one that included a man. Infinitely obliging, Mrs. Munn wished that one of them were a man. She bit her lip, trying to find a way out of this unexpected social thicket. Turning to Emma, she said, a little wildly, "Do you like school? I mean I see you are not in school. Have you been ill?"

Emma ill? The idea was so outrageous, so clearly a criticism of Mrs. Ellenger's care, that she was forced, at last, to take notice of this pair of frumps. "There's nothing the matter with my daughter's health," she said a little too loudly. "Emma's never been sick a day. From the time she was born, she's had the best of everything—the best food, the best clothes, the best that money can buy. Emma, isn't that right?"

Emma said yes, hanging her head and wishing her mother would stop.

"Emma was born during the war," Mrs. Ellenger said, dropping her voice. The Munns looked instantly sympathetic. They waited to hear the rest of the story, some romantic misadventure doomed by death or the fevered nature of the epoch itself. Mrs.

Munn puckered her forehead, as if already she were prepared to cry. But evidently that part of the story had ceased to be of interest to Emma's mother. "I had a nervous breakdown when she was born," Mrs. Ellenger said. "I had plenty of troubles. My God, *troubles*!" Brooding, she suddenly dropped her cigarette into the dregs of her coffee cup. At the sound it made, the two ladies winced. Their glances crossed. Noticing, Emma wondered what her mother had done now. "I never took my troubles out on Emma," Mrs. Ellenger said. "No, Emma had the best, always the best. I brought her up like a little lady. I kept her all in white—white shoes, white blankets, white bunny coats, white hand-knitted angora bonnets. When she started to walk, she had little white rubbers for the rain. I got her a white buggy with white rubber tires. During the *war*, this was. Emma, isn't it true? Didn't you see your pictures, all in white?"

Emma moved her lips.

"It was the very best butter," Miss Munn murmured.

"She shows your care," Mrs. Munn said gently. "She's a lovely girl."

Emma wanted to die. She looked imploringly at her mother, but Mrs. Ellenger rushed on. It was important, deeply important, that everyone understand what a good mother she had been. "Nobody has to worry about Emma's school, either," she said. "I teach her, so nobody has to worry at all. Emma loves to study. She reads all the time. Just before dinner tonight, she was reading. She was reading Shakespeare. Emma, weren't you reading Shakespeare?"

"I had this book," Emma said, so low that her answer was lost. The Munns began to speak about something else, and Emma's mother relaxed, triumphant.

In truth, Emma had been reading Shakespeare. While they were still unpacking and settling in, she had discovered among their things a battered high school edition of *The Merchant of Venice*. Neither she nor her mother had ever seen it before. It was in the suitcase that contained Mrs. Ellenger's silver evening slippers and Emma's emergency supply of comic books. Emma opened the book and read, "You may do so; but let it be so hasted that supper be ready at the farthest by five of the clock." She closed the book and dropped it. "It must have come from Uncle Jimmy Salter's place," she said. "The maid must have put it in when she helped us pack." "I didn't know he could read," Mrs. Ellenger said. She and Mr. Salter had stopped being friends. "We'll mail it back sometime. It'll be a nice surprise."

Of course, they had never mailed the book. Now, at Tangier, it was still with them, wedged between the comic books and the silver slippers. It had never occurred to Emma's mother to give the book to a steward, or the purser, still less take it ashore during an excursion; the mechanics of wrapping and posting a parcel from a strange port were quite beyond her. The cruise, as far as she was concerned, had become a series of hazards; attempting to dispatch a volume of Shakespeare would have been the last straw. She was happy, or at least not always unhappy, in a limited area of the ship—the bar, the beauty salon, and her own cabin. As long as she kept to this familiar, hotel-like circuit, there was almost no reason to panic. She had never before been at sea, and although she was not sickened by the motion of the ship, the idea of space, of endless leagues of water, perplexed, then frightened, then, finally, made her ill. It had come to her, during the first, dismal dinner out, that her life as a pretty young woman was finished. There were no men on board—none, at least, that would do—and even if there had been, it was not at all certain that any of them would have desired her. She saw herself flung into an existence that included the Munns, censorious, respectable, prying into one's affairs. At that moment, she had realized what the cruise would mean: She was at sea. She was adrift on an ocean whose immenseness she could not begin to grasp. She was alone, she had no real idea of their route, and it was too late to turn back. Embarking on the cruise had been a gesture, directed against the person Emma called Uncle Jimmy Salter. Like any such gesture, it had to be carried through, particularly since it had been received with total indifference, even relief.

Often, even now, with twenty-four days of the cruise behind and only twenty more to be lived through, the fears she had experienced the first evening would recur: She was at sea, alone. There was no one around to tip stewards, order drinks, plan the nights, make love to her, pay the bills, tell her where she was and what it was all about. How had this happened? However had she mismanaged her life to such a degree? She was still young. She looked at herself in the glass and, covering the dry, darkening skin below her eyes, decided she was still pretty. Perplexed, she went to the beauty salon and had her hair washed by a sympathetic girl, a good listener. Then, drugged with heat, sated with shared confidences, she wandered out to the first-class bar and sat at her own special stool. Here the sympathetic girl was replaced by Eddy, the Eurasian bartender from Hong Kong. Picking up the thread of her life, Mrs. Ellenger talked to Eddy, describing her childhood and her stepmother. She told him about Emma's father, and about the time she and Emma went to California. Talking, she tried to pretend she was in New York and that the environment of the ship was perfectly normal and real. She played with her drink, smiling anxiously at herself in the mirror behind the bar.

Eddy wasn't much of an audience, because he had other things to do, but after a time Mrs. Ellenger became so engrossed in her own recital, repeating and recounting the errors that had brought her to this impasse, that she scarcely noticed at all.

"I was a mere child, Eddy," she said. "A child. What did I know about life?"

"You can learn a lot about life in a job like mine," Eddy said. Because he was half Chinese, Eddy's customers expected him to deliver remarks tinged with Oriental wisdom. As a result, he had got into the habit of saying anything at all as if it were important.

"Well, I got Emma out of it all." Mrs. Ellenger never seemed to hear Eddy's remarks. "I've got my Emma. That's something. She's a big girl, isn't she, Eddy? Would you take her for only twelve? Some people take her for fourteen. They take us for sisters."

"The Dolly Sisters," Eddy said, ensconced on a reputation that had him not only a sage but a scream.

"Well, I never try to pass Emma off as my sister," Mrs. Ellenger went on. "Oh, it's not that I couldn't. I mean enough people have told me. And I was a mere child myself when she was born. But I don't care if they know she's my daughter. I'm *proud* of my Emma. She was born during the war. I kept her all in white..."

Her glass slid away, reminding her that she was not in New York but at sea. It was no use. She thought of the sea, of travel, of being alone; the idea grew so enormous and frightening that, at last, there was nothing to do but go straight to her cabin and get into bed, even if it was the middle of the day. Her head ached and so did her wrists. She took off her heavy jewelry and unpinned her hair. The cabin was gray, chintzed, consolingly neutral; it resembled all or any of the hotel rooms she and Emma had shared in the past. She was surrounded by her own disorder, her own scent. There were yesterday's clothes on a chair, trailing, smelling faintly of cigarette smoke. There, on the dressing table, was an abandoned glass of brandy, an unstoppered bottle of cologne.

She rang the service bell and sent someone to look for Emma.

"Oh, Emma, darling," she said when Emma, troubled and apprehensive, came in. "Emma, why did we come on this crazy cruise? I'm so unhappy, Emma."

"I don't know," Emma said. "I don't know why we came at all." Sitting on her own bed, she picked up her doll and played with its hair or its little black shoes. She had outgrown dolls as toys years before, but this doll, which had no name, had moved about with her as long as she could remember. She knew that her mother expected something from this winter voyage, some miracle, but the nature of the miracle was beyond her. They had shopped for the cruise all summer—Emma remembered that—but when she thought of those summer weeks, with Uncle Jimmy Salter away, and her mother sulking and upset, she had an impression of heat and vacancy, as if no one had been contained in the summer season but Mrs. Ellenger and herself. Left to themselves, she and her mother had shopped; they had bought dresses and scarves and blouses and bathing suits and shoes of every possible color. They bought hats to match the dresses and bags to match the shoes. The boxes the new clothes had come in piled up in the living room, spilling tissue.

"Is he coming back?" Emma had asked once.

"I'm not waiting for *him* to make up *his* mind," her mother had said, which was, to Emma, scarcely an answer at all. "I've got my life, too. I mean," she amended, "we have, Emma. We've got a life, too. We'll go away. We'll go on a cruise or something."

"Maybe he'd like that," Emma had said, with such innocent accuracy that her mother, presented with the thought, stared at her, alarmed. "Then he could have the place all to himself."

In November, they joined the cruise. They had come aboard wearing summer dresses, confident in the climate promised by travel posters—the beaches, the blue-painted seas, the painted-yellow suns. Their cabin was full of luggage and flowers. Everything was new—their white bags, the clothes inside them, neatly folded, smelling of shops.

"It's a new life, Emma," said Mrs. Ellenger.

Emma had caught some of the feeling, for at last they were doing something together, alone, with no man, no Uncle Anyone, to interfere. She felt intensely allied to her mother, then and for several days after. But then, when it became certain that the miracle, the new life, had still to emerge, the feeling disappeared. Sometimes she felt it again just before they reached land—some strange and unexplored bit of coast, where anything might happen. The new life was always there, just before them, like a note indefinitely suspended or a wave about to break. It was there, but nothing happened.

All this, Emma sensed without finding words, even in her mind, to give the idea form. When her mother, helpless and lost, asked why they had come, she could only sit on her bed, playing with her doll's shoe, and, embarrassed by the spectacle of such open unhappiness, murmur, "I don't know. I don't know why we came at all."

Answers and explanations belonged to another language, one she had still to acquire. Even now, in Tangier, longing to explain to the Munns about the summer dresses, she knew she had better not begin. She knew that there must be a simple way of putting these things in words, but when Mrs. Munn spoke of going ashore, of the importance of keeping the throat and ankles warm, it was not in Emma's grasp to explain how it had come about that although she and her mother had shopped all summer and had brought with them much more luggage than they needed, it now developed that they had nothing to wear.

"Perhaps we shall see you in Tangier, later today," said Mrs. Munn. "You must warn your mother about Tangier. Tell her to watch her purse."

Emma nodded vigorously. "I'll tell her."

"And tell her to be careful about the food if you lunch ashore," Mrs. Munn said, beginning to gather together her guidebooks. "No salads. No fruit. Only bottled water. Above all, no native restaurants."

"I'll tell her," Emma said again.

After the Munns had departed, she sat for a moment, puzzled. Certainly they would be lunching in Tangier. For the first time, now she remembered something. The day before (or had it been the day before that?) Emma had invited Eddy, the bartender, to meet them in Tangier for lunch. She had extended the invitation with no sense of what it involved, and no real concept of place and time. North Africa was an imaginary place, half desert, half jungle. Then, this morning, she had looked through the porthole above her bed. There was Tangier, humped and yellowish, speckled with houses, under a wintry sky. It was not a jungle but a city, real. Now the two images met and blended. Tangier was a real place, and somewhere in those piled-up city blocks was Eddy, waiting to meet them for lunch.

She got up at once and hurried back to the cabin. The lounge was clearing; the launch, carrying passengers ashore across the short distance that separated them from the harbor, had been shuttling back and forth since nine o'clock.

Emma's mother was up, and—miracle—nearly dressed. She sat at the dressing table, pinning an artificial camellia into her hair. She did not turn around when Emma came in but frowned at herself in the glass, concentrating. Her dress was open at the back. She had been waiting for Emma to come and do it up. Emma sat down on her own bed. In honor of the excursion ashore, she was wearing gloves, a hat, and carrying a purse. Waiting, she sorted over the contents of her purse (a five-dollar bill, a St. Christopher medal, a wad of Kleenex, a comb in a plastic case), pulled on her small round hat, smoothed her gloves, sighed.

Her mother looked small and helpless, struggling with the awkward camellia. Emma never pitied her when she suffered—it was too disgraceful, too alarming—but she sometimes felt sorry for some detail of her person; now she was touched by the thin veined hands fumbling with flower and pins, and the thin shoulder blades that moved like wings. Her pity took the form of exasperation; it made her want to get up and do something crazy and rude—slam a door, say all the forbidden words she could think of. At last, Mrs. Ellenger stood up, nearly ready. But, no, something had gone wrong.

"Emma, I can't go ashore like this," her mother said. She sat down again. "My dress is wrong. My shoes are wrong. Look at my eyes. I look old. Look at my figure. Before I had you, my figure was wonderful. Never have a baby, Emma. Promise me."

"O.K.," Emma said. She seized the moment of pensive distraction—her mother had a dreamy look, which meant she was thinking of her pretty, fêted youth—and fastened her mother's dress. "You look lovely," Emma said rapidly. "You look just beautiful. The Munns said to tell you to dress warm, but it isn't cold. Please, let's go. Please, let's hurry. All the other people have gone. Listen, we're in *Africa*."

"That's what so crazy," Mrs. Ellenger said, as if at last she had discovered the source of all her grievances. "What am I doing in Africa?"

"Bring a scarf for your head," said Emma. "Please, let's go."

They got the last two places in the launch. Mrs. Ellenger bent and shuddered and covered her eyes; the boat was a terrible ordeal, windy and smelling of oil. She felt chilled and vomitous. "Oh, Emma," she moaned.

Emma put an arm about her, reassuring. "It's only a minute," she said. "We're nearly there now. Please look up. Why don't you look? The sun's come out."

"I'm going to be sick," Mrs. Ellenger said.

"No, you're not."

At last they were helped ashore, and stood, brushing their wrinkled skirts, on the edge of Tangier. Emma decided she had better mention Eddy right away.

"Wouldn't it be nice if we sort of ran into Eddy?" she said. "He knows all about Tangier. He's been here before. He could take us around."

"Run into *who*?" Mrs. Ellenger took off the scarf she had worn in the launch, shook it, folded it, and put it in her purse. Just then, a light wind sprang up from the bay. With a little moan, Mrs. Ellenger opened her bag and took out the scarf. She seemed not to know what to do with it, and finally clutched it to her throat. "I'm so cold," she said. "Emma, I've never been so cold in my whole life. Can't we get away from here? Isn't there a taxi or something?"

Some of their fellow passengers were standing a short distance away in a sheeplike huddle, waiting for a guide from a travel bureau to come and fetch them. They were warmly dressed. They carried books, cameras, and maps. Emma suddenly thought of how funny she and her mother must look, alone and baffled, dressed for a summer excursion. Mrs. Ellenger tottered uncertainly on high white heels.

"I think if we just walk up to that big street," Emma said,

pointing. "I even see taxis. Don't worry. It'll be all right." Mrs. Ellenger looked back, almost wistfully, to the cruise ship; it was, at least, familiar. "Don't look *that* way," said Emma. "Look where we're going. Look at Africa."

Obediently, Mrs. Ellenger looked at Africa. She saw hotels, an avenue, a row of stubby palms. As Emma had said, there were taxis, one of which, at their signals, rolled out of a rank and drew up before them. Emma urged her mother into the cab and got in after her.

"We might run into Eddy," she said again.

Mrs. Ellenger saw no reason why, on this particular day, she should be forced to think about Eddy. She started to say so, but Emma was giving the driver directions, telling him to take them to the center of town. "But what if we *did* see Eddy?" Emma asked.

"Will you stop that?" Mrs. Ellenger cried. "Will you stop that about Eddy? If we see him, we see him. I guess he's got the same rights ashore as anyone else!"

Emma found this concession faintly reassuring. It did not presage an outright refusal to be with Eddy. She searched her mind for some sympathetic reference to him—the fact, for instance, that he had two children named Wilma and George— but, glancing sidelong at her mother, decided to say nothing more. Mrs. Ellenger had admitted Eddy's rights, a point that could be resurrected later, in case of trouble. They were driving uphill, between houses that looked, Emma thought, neither interesting nor African. It was certainly not the Africa she had imaged the day she invited Eddy—a vista of sand dunes surrounded by jungle, full of camels, lions, trailing vines. It was hard now to remember just why she had asked him, or if, indeed, she really had. It had been morning. The setting was easy to reconstruct. She had been the only person at the bar; she was drinking an elaborate mixture of syrup and fruit concocted by Eddy. Eddy was wiping glasses. He wore a white coat, from the pocket of which emerged the corner of a colored handkerchief.

The handkerchief was one of a dozen given him by a kind American lady met on a former cruise; it bore his name, embroidered in a dashing hand. Emma had been sitting, admiring the handkerchief, thinking about the hapless donor ("She found me attractive, et cetera, et cetera," Eddy had once told her, looking resigned) when suddenly Eddy said something about Tangier, the next port, and Emma had imagined the three of them together—herself, her mother, and Eddy.

"My mother wants you to go ashore with us in Africa," she had said, already convinced this was so.

"What do you mean, ashore?" Eddy said. "Take you around, meet you for lunch?" There was nothing unusual in the invitation, as such; Eddy was a great favorite with many of his clients. "It's funny she never mentioned it."

"She forgot," Emma said. "We don't know anyone in Africa, and my mother always likes company."

"I know *that*," Eddy said softly, smiling to himself. With a little shovel, he scooped almonds into glass dishes. "What I mean is your mother actually said"—and here he imitated Mrs. Ellenger, his voice going plaintive and high—"'I'd just adore having dear Eddy as our guest for lunch.' She actually said that?"

"Oh, Eddy!" Emma had to laugh so hard at the very idea that she doubled up over her drink. Eddy could be so witty when he wanted to be, sending clockwork spiders down the bar, serving drinks in trick glasses that unexpectedly dripped on people's clothes! Sometimes, watching him being funny with favorite customers, she would laugh until her stomach ached.

"I'll tell you what," Eddy said, having weighed the invitation. "I'll meet you *in* Tangier. I can't go ashore with you, I mean—not in the same launch; I have to go with the crew. But I'll meet you there."

"Where'll you meet us?" Emma said. "Should we pick a place?"

"Oh, I'll find you," Eddy said. He set his plates of almonds at spaced intervals along the bar. "Around the center of town. I know where you'll go." He smiled again his secret, superior smile.

They had left it at that. Had Eddy really said the center of town, Emma wondered now, or had she thought that up herself? Had the whole scene, for that matter, taken place, or had she thought that up, too? No, it was real, for, their taxi having deposited them at the Plaza de Francia, Eddy at once detached himself from the crowd on the street and came toward them.

Eddy was dapper. He wore a light suit and a square-shouldered topcoat. He closed their taxi door and smiled at Emma's mother, who was paying the driver.

"Look," Emma said. "Look who's here!"

Emma's mother moved over to a shop window and became absorbed in a display of nylon stockings; presented with a *fait accompli*, she withdrew from the scene—turned her back, put on a pair of sunglasses, narrowed her interest to a single stocking draped on a chrome rack. Eddy seemed unaware of tension. He carried several small parcels, his purchases. Jauntily he joined Mrs. Ellenger at the window.

"This is a good place to buy nylons," he said. "In fact, you should stock up on everything you need, because it's tax-free. Anything you buy here, you can sell in Spain."

"My daughter and I have everything we require," Mrs. Ellenger said. She walked off and then quickened her step, so that he wouldn't appear to be walking with them.

Emma smiled at Eddy and fell back very slightly, striking a balance between the two. "What did you buy?" she said softly. "Something for Wilma and George?"

"Lots of stuff," said Eddy. "Now, this café right here," he called after Mrs. Ellenger, "would be a good place to sit down. Right here, in the Plaza de Francia, you can see everyone important. They all come here, the high society of two continents."

"Of two continents," Emma said, wishing her mother would pay more attention. She stared at all the people behind the glass café fronts—the office workers drinking coffee before hurrying back to their desks, the tourists from cruise ships like their own.

Mrs. Ellenger stopped. She extended her hand to Emma and

said, "My daughter and I have a lot of sightseeing to do, Eddy. I'm sure there are things you want to do, too." She was smiling. The surface of her sunglasses, mirrored, gave back a small, distorted public square, a tiny Eddy, and Emma, anguished, in gloves and hat.

"Oh, Eddy!" Emma cried. She wanted to say something else, to explain that her mother didn't understand, but he vanished, just like that, and moments later she picked out his neat little figure bobbing along in the crowd going downhill, away from the Plaza. "Eddy sort of expected to stay with us," she said.

"So I noticed," said Mrs. Ellenger. They sat down in a café— not the one Eddy had suggested, but a similar café nearby. "One Coca-Cola," she told the waiter, "and one brandy-and-water." She sighed with relief, as if they had been walking for hours.

Their drinks came. Emma saw, by the clock in the middle of the square, that it was half-past eleven. It was warm in the sun, as warm as May. Perhaps, after all, they had been right about the summer dresses. Forgetting Eddy, she looked around. This was Tangier, and she, Emma Ellenger, was sitting with the high society of two continents. Outside was a public square, with low buildings, a café across the street, a clock, and, walking past in striped woollen cloaks, Arabs. The Arabs were real; if the glass of the window had not been there, she could have touched them.

"There's sawdust or something in my drink," Mrs. Ellenger said. "It must have come off the ice." Nevertheless, she drank it to the end and ordered another.

"We'll go out soon, won't we?" Emma said, faintly alarmed.

"In a minute."

The waiter brought them a pile of magazines, including a six-month-old *Vogue*. Mrs. Ellenger removed her glasses, looking pleased.

"We'll go soon?" Emma repeated.

There was no reply.

The square swelled with a midday crowd. Sun covered their table until Mrs. Ellenger's glasses became warm to the touch.

"Aren't we going out?" Emma said. "Aren't we going to have anything for lunch?" Her legs ached from sitting still.

"You could have something here," Mrs. Ellenger said, vague.

The waiter brought Emma a sandwich and a glass of milk. Mrs. Ellenger continued to look at *Vogue*. Sometimes passengers from their ship went by. They waved gaily, as if Tangier were the last place they had ever expected to see a familiar face. The Munns passed, walking in step. Emma thumped on the window, but neither of the ladies turned. Something about their solidarity, their sureness of purpose, made her feel lonely and left behind. Soon they would have seen Tangier, while she and her mother might very well sit here until it was time to go back to the ship. She remembered Eddy and wondered what he was doing.

Mrs. Ellenger had come to the end of her reading material. She seemed suddenly to find her drink distasteful. She leaned on her hand, fretful and depressed, as she often was at that hour of the day. She was sorry she had come on the cruise and said so again. The warm ports were cold. She wasn't getting the right things to eat. She was getting so old and ugly that the bartender, having nothing better in view, and thinking she would be glad of anything, had tried to pick her up. What was she doing here, anyway? Her life . . .

"I wish we could have gone with Eddy," Emma said, with a sigh.

"Why, Emma," Mrs. Ellenger said. Her emotions jolted from a familiar track, it took her a moment or so to decide how she felt about this interruption. She thought it over, and became annoyed. "You mean you'd have more fun with that Chink than with me? Is that what you're trying to tell me?"

"It isn't that exactly. I only meant, we *could* have gone with him. He's been here before. Or the Munns, or this other friend of mine, Mr. Cowan. Only, he didn't come ashore today, Mr. Cowan. You shouldn't say 'Chink.' You should say 'Chinese person,' Mr. Cowan told me. Otherwise it offends. You should never offend. You should never say 'Irishman.' You should say 'Irish person.' You should never say 'Jew.' You should say—"

"Some cruise!" said Mrs. Ellenger, who had been listening to this with an expression of astounded shock, as if Emma had been repeating blasphemy. "All I can say is some cruise. Some selected passengers! What else did he tell you? What does he want with a little girl like you, anyway? Did he ever ask you into his state-room—anything like that?"

"Oh, goodness, no!" Emma said impatiently; so many of her mother's remarks were beside the point. She knew all about not going anywhere with men, not accepting presents, all that kind of thing. "His stateroom's too small even for him. It isn't the one he paid for. He tells the purser all the time, but it doesn't make any difference. That's why he stays in the bar all day."

Indeed, for most of the cruise, Emma's friend had sat in the bar writing a long journal, which he sent home, in installments, for the edification of his analyst. His analyst, Mr. Cowan had told Emma, was to blame for the fact that he had taken the cruise. In revenge, he passed his days writing down all the things at fault with the passengers and the service, hoping to make the analyst sad and guilty. Emma began to explain her own version of this to Mrs. Ellenger, but her mother was no longer listening. She stared straight before her in the brooding, injured way Emma dreaded. Her gaze seemed turned inward, rather than to the street, as if she were concentrating on some terrible grievance and struggling to bring it to words.

"You think I'm not a good mother," she said, still not looking at Emma, or, really, at anything. "That's why you hang around these other people. It's not fair. I'm good to you. Well, am I?"

"Yes," said Emma. She glanced about nervously, wondering if anyone could hear.

"Do you ever need anything?" her mother persisted. "Do you know what happens to a lot of kids like you? They get left in schools, that's what happens. Did I ever do that to you?"

"No."

"I always kept you with me, no matter what anyone said. You mean more to me than anybody, any man. You know that. I'd give up anyone for you. I've even done it."

"I know," Emma said. There was a queer pain in her throat. She had to swallow to make it go away. She felt hot and uncomfortable and had to do something distracting; she took off her hat, rolled her gloves into a ball, and put them in her purse.

Mrs. Ellenger sighed. "Well," she said in a different voice, "if we're going to see anything of this town, we'd better move." She paid for their drinks, leaving a large tip on the messy table, littered with ashes and magazines. They left the café and, arm in arm, like Miss and Mrs. Munn, they circled the block, looking into the dreary windows of luggage and furniture stores. Some of the windows had been decorated for Christmas with strings of colored lights. Emma was startled; she had forgotten all about Christmas. It seemed unnatural that there should be signs of it in a place like Tangier. "Do Arabs have Christmas?" she said.

"Everyone does," Mrs. Ellenger said. "Except—" She could not remember the exceptions.

It was growing cool, and her shoes were not right for walking. She looked up and down the street, hoping a taxi would appear, and then, with one of her abrupt, emotional changes, she darted into a souvenir shop that had taken her eye. Emma followed, blinking in the dark. The shop was tiny. There were colored bracelets in a glass case, leather slippers, and piles of silky material. From separate corners of the shop, a man and a woman converged on them.

"I'd like a bracelet for my little girl," Mrs. Ellenger said.

"For Christmas?" said the woman.

"Sort of. Although she gets plenty of presents, all the time. It doesn't have to be anything special."

"What a fortunate girl," the woman said absently, unlocking the case.

Emma was not interested in the bracelet. She turned her back on the case and found herself facing a shelf on which were pottery figures of lions, camels, and tigers. They were fastened to bases marked "*Souvenir de Tanger*," or "*Recuerdo*."

"Those are nice," Emma said, to the man. He wore a fez, and leaned against the counter, staring idly at Mrs. Ellenger. Emma pointed to the tigers. "Do they cost a lot?"

He said something in a language she could not understand. Then, lapsing into a creamy sort of English, "They are special African tigers." He grinned, showing his gums, as if the expression "African tigers" were a joke they shared. "They come from a little village in the mountains. There are interesting old myths connected with them." Emma looked at him blankly. "They are magic," he said.

"There's no such thing," Emma said. Embarrassed for him, she looked away, coloring deeply.

"This one," the man said, picking up a tiger. It was glazed in stripes of orange and black. The seam of the factory mold ran in a faint ridge down its back; the glaze had already begun to crack. "This is a special African tiger," he said. "It is good for ten wishes. Any ten."

"There's no such thing," Emma said again, but she took the tiger from him and held it in her hand, where it seemed to grow warm of its own accord. "Does it cost a lot?"

The man looked over at the case of bracelets and exchanged a swift, silent signal with his partner. Mrs. Ellenger, still talking, was hesitating between two enameled bracelets.

"Genuine Sahara work," the woman said of the more expensive piece. When Mrs. Ellenger appeared certain to choose it, the woman nodded, and the man said to Emma, "The tiger is a gift. It costs you nothing."

"A present?" She glanced toward her mother, busy counting change. "I'm not allowed to take anything from strange men" rose to her lips. She checked it.

"For Christmas," the man said, still looking amused. "Think of me on Christmas Day, and make a wish."

"Oh, I will," Emma said, suddenly making up her mind. "Thanks. Thanks a lot." She put the tiger in her purse.

"Here, baby, try this on," Mrs. Ellenger said from across the shop. She clasped the bracelet around Emma's wrist. It was too small, and pinched, but everyone exclaimed at how pretty it looked.

"Thank you," Emma said. Clutching her purse, feeling the lump the tiger made, she said, looking toward the man, "Thanks, I love it."

"Be sure to tell your friends," he cried, as if the point of the gift would otherwise be lost.

"Are you happy?" Mrs. Ellenger asked, kissing Emma. "Do you really love it? Would you still rather be with Eddy and these other people?" Her arm around Emma, they left the shop. Outside, Mrs. Ellenger walked a few steps, looking piteously at the cars going by. "Oh, God, let there be a taxi," she said. They found one and hailed it, and she collapsed inside, closing her eyes. She had seen as much of Tangier as she wanted. They rushed downhill. Emma, her face pressed against the window, had a blurred impression of houses. Their day, all at once, spun out in reverse; there was the launch, waiting. They embarked and, in a moment, the city, the continent, receded.

Emma thought, confused, Is that all? Is that all of Africa?

But there was no time to protest. Mrs. Ellenger, who had lost her sunglasses, had to be consoled and helped with her scarf. "Oh, thank God!" she said fervently, as she was helped from the launch. "Oh, my God, what a day!" She tottered off to bed, to sleep until dinner.

The ship was nearly empty. Emma lingered on deck, looking back at Tangier. She made a detour, peering into the bar; it was empty and still. A wire screen had been propped against the shelves of bottles. Reluctantly, she made her way to the cabin. Her mother had already gone to sleep. Emma pulled the curtain over the porthole, dimming the light, and picked up her mother's scattered clothes. The new bracelet pinched terribly; when she unclasped it, it left an ugly greenish mark, like a bruise. She rubbed at the mark with soap and then cologne and finally most of it came away. Moving softly, so as not to waken her mother, she put the bracelet in the suitcase that contained her comic books and Uncle Jimmy Salter's *Merchant of Venice*. Remembering the tiger, she took it out of her purse and slipped it under her pillow.

The bar, suddenly, was full of noise. Most of it was coming from a newly installed loudspeaker. "Oh, little town of Bethlehem," Emma heard, even before she opened the heavy glass doors. Under the music, but equally amplified, were the voices of people arguing, the people who, somewhere on the ship, were trying out the carol recordings. Eddy hadn't yet returned. Crew members, in working clothes, were hanging Christmas decorations. There was a small silver tree over the bar and a larger one, real, being lashed to a pillar. At one of the low tables in front of the bar Mr. Cowan sat reading a travel folder.

"Have a good time?" he asked, looking up. He had to bellow because "Oh, Little Town of Bethlehem" was coming through so loudly. "I've just figured something out," he said, as Emma sat down. "If I take a plane from Madrid, I can be home in sixteen hours."

"Are you going to take it?"

"I don't know," he said, looking disconsolately at the folder. "Madrid isn't a port. I'd have to get off at Gibraltar or Malaga and take a train. And then, what about all my stuff? I'd have to get my trunk shipped. On the other hand," he said, looking earnestly at Emma, talking to her in the grown-up, if mystifying, way she liked, "why should I finish this ghastly cruise just for spite? They brought the mail on today. There was a letter from my wife. She says I'd better forget it and come home for Christmas."

Emma accepted without question the new fact that Mr. Cowan had a wife. Eddy had Wilma and George, the Munns had each other. Everyone she knew had a life, complete, that all but excluded Emma. "Will you go?" she repeated, unsettled by the idea that someone she liked was going away.

"Yes," he said. "I think so. We'll be in Gibraltar tomorrow. I'll get off there. How was Tangier? Anyone try to sell you a black-market Coke?"

"No," Emma said. "My mother bought a bracelet. A man gave me an African tiger."

"What kind of tiger?"

"A toy," said Emma. "A little one."

"Oh. Damn bar's been closed all day," he said, getting up. "Want to walk? Want to go down to the other bar?"

"No, thanks. I have to wait here for somebody," Emma said, and her eyes sought the service door behind the bar through which, at any moment, Eddy might appear. After Mr. Cowan had left, she sat, patient, looking at the folder he had forgotten.

Outside, the December evening drew in. The bar began to fill; passengers drifted in, compared souvenirs, talked in high, excited voices about the journey ashore. It didn't sound as if they'd been in Tangier at all, Emma thought. It sounded like some strange, imagined city, full of hazard and adventure.

"... so this little Arab boy comes up to me," a man was saying, "and with my wife standing right there, right there beside me, he says—"

"Hush," his wife said, indicating Emma. "Not so loud."

Eddy and Mrs. Ellenger arrived almost simultaneously, coming, of course, through separate doors. Eddy had his white coat on, a fresh colored handkerchief in the pocket. He turned on the lights, took down the wire screen. Mrs. Ellenger had changed her clothes and brushed her hair. She wore a flowered dress, and looked cheerful and composed. "All alone, baby?" she said. "You haven't even changed, or washed your face. Never mind, there's no time now."

Emma looked at the bar, trying in vain to catch Eddy's eye. "Aren't you going to have a drink before dinner?"

"No. I'm hungry. Emma, you look a mess." Still talking, Mrs.

Ellenger ushered Emma out to the dining room. Passing the bar, Emma called, "Hey, Eddy, hello," but, except to throw her a puzzling look, he did not respond.

They ate in near silence. Mrs. Ellenger felt rested and hungry, and, in any case, had at no time anything to communicate to the Munns. Miss Munn, between courses, read a book about Spain. She had read aloud the references to Gibraltar, and now turned to the section on Malaga, where they would be in two days. "From the summit of the Gibralfaro," she said, "one has an excellent view of the city and harbor. Two asterisks. At the state-controlled restaurant, refreshments…" She looked up and said, to Mrs. Munn, who was listening hard, eyes shut, "That's where we'll have lunch. We can hire a horse and *calesa*. It will kill the morning and part of the afternoon."

Already, they knew all about killing time in Malaga. They had never been there, but it would hold no surprise; they would make no mistakes. It was no use, Emma thought. She and her mother would never be like the Munns. Her mother, she could see, was becoming disturbed by this talk of Gibraltar and Malaga, by the threat of other ventures ashore. Had she not been so concerned with Eddy, she would have tried, helpfully, to lead the talk to something else. However, her apology to Eddy was infinitely more urgent. As soon as she could, she pushed back her chair and hurried out to the bar. Her mother dawdled behind her, fishing in her bag for a cigarette.

Emma sat up on one of the high stools and said, "Eddy, where did you go? What did you do? I'm sorry about the lunch."

At that, he gave her another look, but still said nothing. Mrs. Ellenger arrived and sat down next to Emma. She looked from Emma to Eddy, eyebrows raised.

Don't let her be rude, Emma silently implored an undefined source of assistance. Don't let her be rude to Eddy, and I'll never bother you again. Then, suddenly, she remembered the tiger under her pillow.

There was no reason to worry. Eddy and her mother seemed to

understand each other very well. "Get a good lunch, Eddy?" her mother asked.

"Yes. Thanks."

He moved away from them, down the bar, where he was busy entertaining new people, two men and a woman, who had come aboard that day from Tangier. The woman wore harlequin glasses studded with flashing stones. She laughed in a sort of bray at Eddy's antics and his funny remarks. "You can't get mad at him," Emma heard her say to one of the men. "He's like a monkey, if a monkey could talk."

"Eddy, our drinks," Mrs. Ellenger said.

Blank, polite, he poured brandy for Mrs. Ellenger and placed before Emma a bottle of Coca-Cola and a glass. Around the curve of the bar, Emma stared at the noisy woman, Eddy's new favorite, and the two fat old men with her. Mrs. Ellenger sipped her brandy, glancing obliquely in the same direction. She listened to their conversation. Two were husband and wife, the third a friend. They had picked up the cruise because they were fed up with North Africa. They had been traveling for several months. They were tired, and each of them had had a touch of colic.

Emma was sleepy. It was too much, trying to understand Eddy, and the day ashore. She drooped over her drink. Suddenly, beside her, Mrs. Ellenger spoke. "You really shouldn't encourage Eddy like that. He's an awful showoff. He'll dance around like that all night if you laugh enough." She said it with her nicest smile. The new people stared, taking her in. They looked at her dress, her hair, her rings. Something else was said. When Emma took notice once more, one of the two men had shifted stools, so he sat halfway between his friends and Emma's mother. Emma heard the introductions: Mr. and Mrs. Frank Timmins. Mr. Boyd Oliver. Mrs. Ellenger. Little Emma Ellenger, my daughter.

"Now, don't tell me that young lady's your daughter," Mr. Boyd Oliver said, turning his back on his friends. He smiled at Emma, and, just because of the smile, she suddenly remembered Uncle Harry Todd, who had given her the complete set of Sue

Barton books, and another uncle, whose name she had forgotten, who had taken her to the circus when she was six.

Mr. Oliver leaned toward Mrs. Ellenger. It was difficult to talk; the bar was filling up. She picked up her bag and gloves from the stool next to her own, and Mr. Oliver moved once again. Polite and formal, they agreed that that made talking much easier.

Mr. Oliver said that he was certainly glad to meet them. The Timminses were wonderful friends, but sometimes, traveling like this, he felt like the extra wheel. Did Mrs. Ellenger know what he meant to say?

They were all talking: Mr. Oliver, Eddy, Emma's mother, Mr. and Mrs. Timmins, the rest of the people who had drifted in. The mood, collectively, was a good one. It had been a wonderful day. They all agreed to that, even Mrs. Ellenger. The carols had started again, the same record. Someone sang with the music: "Yet in thy dark streets shineth the everlasting light..."

"I'd take you more for *sisters*," Mr. Oliver said.

"Really?" Mrs. Ellenger said. "Do you really think so? Well, I suppose we are, in a way. I was practically a child myself when she came into the world. But I wouldn't try to pass Emma off as my sister. I'm proud to say she's my daughter. She was born during the war. We only have each other."

"Well," Mr. Oliver said, after thinking this declaration over for a moment or so, "that's the way it should be. You're a brave little person."

Mrs. Ellenger accepted this. He signaled for Eddy, and she turned to Emma. "I think you could go to bed now. It's been a big day for you."

The noise and laughter stopped as Emma said her good nights. She remembered all the names. "Good night, Eddy," she said, at the end, but he was rinsing glasses and seemed not to hear.

Emma could still hear the carols faintly as she undressed. She knelt on her bed for a last look at Tangier; it seemed different again, exotic and remote, with the ring of lights around the shore, the city night sounds drifting over the harbor. She thought, Today I was in Africa...But Africa had become unreal. The café, the clock in the square, the shop where they had bought the bracelet, had nothing to do with the Tangier she had imagined or this present view from the ship. Still, the tiger was real: it was under her pillow, proof that she had been to Africa, that she had touched shore. She dropped the curtain, put out the light. To the sound of Christmas music, she went to sleep.

It was late when Mrs. Ellenger came into the cabin. Emma had been asleep for hours, her doll beside her, the tiger under her head. She came out of a confused and troubled dream about a house she had once lived in, somewhere. There were new tenants in the house; when she tried to get in, they sent her away. She smelled her mother's perfume and heard her mother's voice before opening her eyes. Mrs. Ellenger had turned on the light at the dressing table and dropped into the chair before it. She was talking to herself, and sounded fretful. "Where's my cold cream?" she said. "Where'd I put it? Who took it?" She put her hand on the service bell and Emma prayed: It's late. Don't let her ring...The entreaty was instantly answered, for Mrs. Ellenger changed her mind and pulled off her earrings. Her hair was all over the place, Emma noticed. She looked all askew, oddly put together. Emma closed her eyes. She could identify, without seeing them, by the sounds, the eau de cologne, the make-up remover, and the lemon cream her mother used at night. Mrs. Ellenger undressed and pulled on the nightgown that had been laid out for her. She went into the bathroom, put on the light, and cleaned her teeth. Then she came back into the cabin and got into bed with Emma. She was crying. She lay so close that Emma's face was wet with her mother's tears and sticky with lemon cream.

"Are you awake?" her mother whispered. "I'm sorry, Emma. I'm so sorry."

"What for?"

"Nothing," Mrs. Ellenger said. "Do you love your mother?"

"Yes." Emma stirred, turning her face away. She slipped a hand up and under the pillow. The tiger was still there.

"I can't help it, Emma," her mother whispered. "I can't live like we've been living on this cruise. I'm not made for it. I don't like being alone. I need friends." Emma said nothing. Her mother waited, then said, "He'll go ashore with us tomorrow. It'll be someone to take us around. Wouldn't you like that?"

"Who's going with us?" Emma said. "The fat old man?"

Her mother had stopped crying. Her voice changed. She said, loud and matter-of-fact, "He's got a wife someplace. He only told me now, a minute ago. Why? Why not right at the beginning, in the bar? I'm not like that. I want something different, a *friend*." The pillow between their faces was wet. Mrs. Ellenger rubbed her cheek on the cold damp patch. "Don't ever get married, Emma," she said. "Don't have anything to do with men. Your father was no good. Jimmy Salter was no good. This one's no better. He's got a wife and look at how—Promise me you'll never get married. We should always stick together, you and I. Promise me we'll always stay together."

"All right," Emma said.

"We'll have fun," Mrs. Ellenger said, pleading. "Didn't we have fun today, when we were ashore, when I got you the nice bracelet? Next year, we'll go someplace else. We'll go anywhere you want."

"I don't want to go anywhere," Emma said.

But her mother wasn't listening. Sobbing quietly, she went to sleep. Her arm across Emma grew heavy and slack. Emma lay still; then she saw that the bathroom light had been left on. Carefully, carrying the tiger, she crawled out over the foot of the bed. Before turning out the light, she looked at the tiger. Already, his coat had begun to flake away. The ears were chipped. Turning it over, inspecting the damage, she saw, stamped in blue: "Made in Japan." The man in the shop had been mistaken, then. It was not an African tiger, good for ten wishes, but something quite ordinary.

She put the light out and, in the dim stateroom turning gray with dawn, she got into her mother's empty bed. Still holding the tiger, she lay, hearing her mother's low breathing and the unhappy words she muttered out of her sleep.

Mr. Oliver, Emma thought, trying to sort things over, one at a time. Mr. Oliver would be with them for the rest of the cruise. Tomorrow, they would go ashore together. "I think you might call Mr. Oliver Uncle Boyd," her mother might say.

Emma's grasp on the tiger relaxed. There was no magic about it; it did not matter, really, where it had come from. There was nothing to be gained by keeping it hidden under a pillow. Still, she had loved it for an afternoon, she would not throw it away or inter it, like the bracelet, in a suitcase. She put it on the table by the bed and said softly, trying out the sound, "I'm too old to call you Uncle Boyd. I'm thirteen next year. I'll call you Boyd or Mr. Oliver, whatever you choose. I'd rather choose Mr. Oliver." What her mother might say then Emma could not imagine. At the moment, she seemed very helpless, very sad, and Emma turned over with her face to the wall. Imagining probable behavior was a terrible strain; this was as far as she could go.

Tomorrow, she thought, Europe began. When she got up, they would be docked in a new harbor, facing the outline of a new, mysterious place. "Gibraltar," she said aloud. Africa was over, this was something else. The cabin grew steadily lighter. Across the cabin, the hinge of the porthole creaked, the curtain blew in. Lying still, she heard another sound, the rusty cri-cri-cri of sea gulls. That meant they were getting close. She got up, crossed the cabin, and, carefully avoiding the hump of her mother's feet under the blanket, knelt on the end of her bed. She pushed the curtain away. Yes, they were nearly there. She could see the gulls swooping and soaring, and something on the horizon—a shape, a rock, a whole continent untouched and unexplored. A tide of newness came in with the salty air: she thought of new land, new dresses, clean, untouched, unworn. A new life. She knelt, patient, holding the curtain, waiting to see the approach to shore.

*1954*

# AUTUMN DAY

I WAS EIGHTEEN when I married Walt and nineteen when I followed him to Salzburg, where he was posted with the Army of Occupation. We'd been married eleven months, but separated for so much of it that my marriage really began that autumn day, when I got down from the train at Salzburg station. Walt was waiting, of course. I could see him in the crowd of soldiers, tall and anxious-looking, already a little bald even though he was only twenty-nine. The first thought that came into my head wasn't a very nice one: I thought what a pity it was he didn't look more like my brother in law. Walt and my brother-in-law were first cousins; that was how we happened to meet. I had always liked my brother-in-law and felt my sister was lucky to have him, and I suppose that was really why I wanted Walt. I thought it would be the same kind of marriage.

I waved at Walt, smiling, the way girls do in illustrations. I could almost see myself, fresh and pretty, waving to someone in uniform. This was eight years ago, soon after the war; the whole idea of arriving to meet a soldier somewhere seemed touching and brave and romantic. When Walt took me in his arms, right in front of everyone, I was so engulfed by the *idea* of the picture it made that I thought I would cry. But then I remembered my luggage and turned away so that I could keep an eye on it. I had matching blue plaid suitcases, given me by my married sister as a going-away present, and I didn't want to lose them right at the start of my married life.

"Oh, Walt," I said, nearly in tears, "I don't see the hatbox."

97

Those were the first words I'd spoken, except for hello or something like that.

Walt laughed and said something just as silly. He said, "You look around ten years old."

Immediately, I felt defensive. I looked down at my camel's-hair coat and my scuffed, familiar moccasins, and I thought, What's wrong with looking young? Walt didn't know, of course, that my married sister had already scolded me for dressing like a little girl instead of a grownup.

"You're not getting ready to go back to school, Cissy," she'd said. "You're married. You're going over there to be with your husband. You'll be mixing with grown-up married couples. And for goodness' sake stop sucking your pearls. Of all the baby habits!"

"Well," I told her, "you brought me up, practically. Whose fault is it if I'm a baby now?"

My pearls were always pink with lipstick, because I had a trick of putting them in my mouth when I was pretending to be stubborn or puzzled about something. Up till now, my sister had always thought it cute. I had always been the baby of the family, the motherless child; even my wedding had seemed a kind of game, like dressing up for a party. Now they were pushing me out, buying luggage, criticizing my clothes, sending me off to live thousands of miles away with a strange man. I couldn't understand the change. It turned all my poses into real feelings: I became truly stubborn, and honestly perplexed. I took the trousseau check my father had given me and bought exactly the sort of clothes I'd always worn, the skirts and sweaters, the blouses with Peter Pan collars. There wasn't one grown-up dress, not even a pair of high-heeled shoes. I wanted to make my sister sorry, to make her see that I was too young to be going away. Then, too, I couldn't imagine another way of dressing. I felt safer in my girlhood uniforms, the way you feel in a familiar house.

I remembered all that as I walked along the station platform with Walt, awkwardly holding hands, and I thought, I suppose now I'll have to change. But not too soon, not too fast.

That was how I began my married life.

In those days, Salzburg was still coming out of the war. All the people you saw on the streets looked angry and in a hurry. There were so many trucks and jeeps clogging the roads, so many soldiers, so much scaffolding over the narrow sidewalks that you could hardly get around. We couldn't find a place to live. The Army had taken over whole blocks of apartments, but even with the rebuilding and the requisitioning, Walt and I had to wait three months before there was anything ready for us. During those months—October, November, December—we lived in a farmhouse not far out of town. It was a real farm, not a hotel. The owner of the place, Herr Enrich, was a polite man and spoke English. When he first saw me, he said right away that he had taken in boarders before the war, but quite a different type—artists and opera singers, people who had come for the Salzburg Festival. "Now," he said politely, "one cannot choose." I wondered if that was meant for us. I looked at Walt, but he didn't seem to care. Later, Walt told me not to listen to Herr Enrich. He told me not to talk about the war, not to mix with the other people on the farm, to make friends with Army wives. Go for walks. I wrote it all down on a slip of paper like a little girl: Don't talk war. Avoid people on farm. Meet Army wives. Go for walks. Years later, I came across this list and I showed it to Walt, but he didn't remember what it was about. When I told him this was a line of conduct he had laid down for me, he didn't believe it. He hardly remembers our life on the farm. Yet those three months stand out in my memory like a special little lifetime, neither girlhood nor marriage. It was a time when I didn't like what I was, but didn't know what I wanted to be. In a way, I tried to do the right things. I followed Walt's instructions.

I didn't talk about the war; there was no one to talk to. I didn't mix with the people on the farm. They didn't want to mix with me. There were six boarders besides us: a Hungarian couple named de Kende—dark and fat with gold teeth; and a family from Vienna with two children. The family from Vienna looked like rabbits. They had moist noses and pink eyes. All four wore the Salzburg costume, and they looked like rabbits dressed up. Sometimes I smiled at the two children, but they never smiled back. I wondered if they had been told not to, and if they had a list of instructions like mine: Don't mix with Americans. Don't talk to Army wives...We ate at a long table in the dining room, all of us together. There was a tiled stove in a corner, and the room was often so hot that the windows steamed and ran as if it were raining inside. Most of the time Walt ate with the Army. He was always away for lunch, and then I would be alone with these people—the Enrichs, the de Kendes from Hungary, and the rabbity family from Vienna. Only Mr. de Kende and his wife ever tried to speak to me in English. Mr. de Kende had a terrible accent, but I once understood him to say that he had been a wealthy man in his own country and had owned four factories. Now he traveled around Austria in an old car selling dental supplies. "What do you think of that for Yalta justice?" he said, pointing his fork at me over the table. The others all suddenly stared at me, alert and silent, waiting for my reply. But I didn't understand. All I could think of then was that my brother-in-law was a dentist, and I remembered how he'd taken me into his home when my mother died, and how kind he had been, and I had to hold my breath to keep from crying in front of them all. At last, I said, "Well, goodness, it's quite a coincidence, because my sister happens to be married to a dental surgeon." Mr. de Kende just grunted, and they all went back to their food.

I told Walt about it, but all he said was, "Don't bother with them. Why don't you get to know some Army wives?"

He didn't understand how hard it was. We lived out of town, and I didn't know how to go about meeting anyone on my own. I thought it was up to Walt to take me around and introduce me to people, but he had only one friend in Salzburg and seemed to think that was enough. Walt's friend's name was Marvin McColl. He and Walt came from the same town and had gone to the same school. He seemed to have more in common with Marv than with me, but they were the same age, so it seemed only natural. Walt wanted me to be friends with Marv's wife, Laura.

He said we were going to be together a lot and it would help if we girls were friends. Laura was twenty-six. She had long hair and big eyes and always looked as if someone had just hurt her feelings. She had no girlfriends in Salzburg, other than me. She hated foreigners and couldn't stand Army wives. Three times a week, or more, Walt and I went out with the McColls. We went to the movies or drank beer in their apartment. Marv hardly spoke to me, except when he'd been drinking. Then he would get tears in his eyes and tell me I was the first and only girl Walt had ever taken seriously, and how they'd never thought Walt would ever marry. He said I was lucky to get Walt, and he hoped I'd make him happy.

"Dry your tears, Marv," Laura would say, rather sarcastically. She would leave Walt and Marv together and take me to another part of the room, so that we could talk. Our conversations were always the same. I would talk about home, and Laura would tell me how much she hated Salzburg and how Marv didn't understand her and her problems. Meanwhile, Marv and Walt drank beer and talked about people I didn't know and places I'd never been. On the way home, Walt would always ask me if I'd had a good time, and before I could answer he'd tell me again that Marv was his best friend and what a lot of fun the four of us were going to have together in Salzburg. I didn't mind the evenings so much, but I didn't care one bit for the afternoons I had to spend alone with Laura, because then she would curl up with a drink, girls together, and tell me the most awful things about her private life with Marv—the sort of thing my married sister would never have said. As for me, they could have cut my tongue out before I'd have talked about Walt. Naturally, I never repeated any of this to Walt. The truth was that he and I never talked much about anything. I didn't know him well enough, and I kept feeling that our real married life hadn't started, that there was nothing to say and wouldn't be for years.

I don't know if I was unhappy or happy in those days. It wasn't what I'd expected, none of it, being married, or being an Army wife, or living in Europe. Everything—even conversation—seemed so much in the future that I couldn't get my feet on the ground and start living. It seemed to me it had been that way all my life, and that being married hadn't settled anything at all. My mother died when I was little, and my father married again, and then I went to live with my married sister. Whenever I seemed low or moody, my sister would say, "Wait till you grow up. Wait till you have a home. Everything will seem different." Now I was married, and I still didn't have a home, and there was Walt saying, "We'll have our own place soon. You'll be all right then." I never told him I was unhappy—I wasn't sure myself if that was exactly the trouble—but often I could see that he was trying to think of the right thing to say to me, hesitating as if he was baffled or just didn't know me well enough to speak out. I was lonely in the daytimes, and terribly shy and unhappy at night. Walt was silent a lot, and often I simply burst into tears for no reason at all. Tears didn't seem to bother him. He expected girls to be nervous and difficult at times; he didn't like it, but he thought it was part of married life. I think he and Marv talked it over, and Marv told him how it was with Laura. Maybe Laura had been worse before they'd got the apartment. I know they had waited seven months, living in one room. Laura wouldn't be easy in one room. Anyway, I don't know where the notion came from, but Walt truly believed, if I was silent, or pale, or forlorn, that an apartment would make everything right.

I never thought about the apartment, except when Walt mentioned it. I wanted to be away from the farm, but I didn't know where I wanted to be. Our room at the farm was small, cold, and coldly clean. We slept in twin beds. At night, after Walt left me and went back to his own bed and went straight off to sleep, I lay close to the wall, trying to imagine it was a wall somewhere else—but where? At my married sister's, I had slept on a couch in the dining room. I didn't want to be there again. The daytime was worse, in a way, because I had to be up and around, and didn't know what to do with myself. I did a lot of laundering; I washed my sweaters until the wool matted. I'd always been clean, but now, being married, I felt I couldn't get things clean enough anymore. Walt had told me to go for walks. Once every day, at least, I set out for a walk, a scarf over my hair, my head bent into the wind. I never went far—I was afraid of getting lost—and I felt that I looked like a miserable cat as I skirted the muddy tracks on the road outside the farm. I had never lived in the country before, and it seemed crazy to just walk around with nothing special to look at. The sky was always gray and low, as if you could touch it. It seemed made of felt. The sky at home was never like that; at least, it didn't press down on you. Herr Enrich said this was the Salzburg autumn sky, and that the clouds were low because they were holding snow. It was frightening, in a way, to think that behind all that felt there were tireless whirlpools of snow, moving and silent.

One afternoon when I was tramping aimlessly around the yard, I heard somebody singing. I couldn't tell if the singer was a man or a woman, and I couldn't make out the words of the song. But the voice was the nicest I had ever heard. I stood still with my hands pulled up into my sleeves, because of the cold, and I looked up to the top of the house, where the voice was coming from. I wondered if it was the radio in someone's room, but then the singer stopped and sang the same phrase four or five times. The kitchenmaids were sitting on a bench in the yard, plucking chickens for supper in front of an open brazier. They stopped talking and listened, too, very still, and the yard was like one of those fairy tales where everyone is suddenly frozen for a thousand years. But then the voice stopped completely, and we became ourselves again, the girls working and giggling, and me trudging about on my eternal walks.

That night, Herr Enrich mentioned the singer. It was an American, a woman. Her name was Dorothy West. She had finished a concert tour in three countries and was here to rest. She was tired and didn't want to meet people and was having all her meals in her room.

"She used to come to us before the war," Herr Enrich said, looking conceited. "We are so pleased that she has remembered us and come back."

I said, timidly, "I'm American, too. Maybe she'd like to just meet me."

Herr Enrich said, "No, no one," like a dragon, so, of course, I didn't say more.

Every day, then, I heard Miss West. Her voice, deep and sure, filled the sky, and I heard her even in the woods far behind the house, where I dragged my feet on my dull walks. The people at the table told me she sang in French and Italian as well as English and German, but I didn't recognize a thing. Having her there had made them somewhat friendlier with me; also, I was beginning to understand a little German. It made a nicer atmosphere, but not one you would call home. Some days, Miss West's accompanist came out from Salzburg, where he stayed in a hotel. He was a small man in a shabby raincoat; it was a surprise to me that she should have anyone so poor. When he came, everyone was locked out of the dining room (the only really warm room of the house, because it contained the stove), and they worked together at a piano there. The accompanist had written a new song for her; that is, he had set a poem to music. The Enrichs stood out in the hall, where they could listen. Afterward, Herr Enrich told me it was a famous poem called "Herbsttag," which meant "Autumn Day," and he translated it for me. The translation was slow and clumsy, and didn't rhyme the way a real poem should. But when he came to the part about it being autumn and not having a house to live in, I suddenly felt that this poem had something to do with me. It was autumn here, and Walt and I hadn't a house, either. It was the first time I had ever had this feeling about a poem—that it had something to do with me. I got Herr Enrich to write it down in German, and I memorized the line, "*Wer jetzt kein Haus hat, baut sich keines mehr.*" The rest was all about writing letters and going for lonely walks—exactly the life I was leading. I wished more than ever that I might meet Miss West and tell her how much I liked her singing, and even how much this poet had understood me. I wanted to know someone outside my marriage. I felt that I would never get to know Walt, partly because he was ten years older, but more simply because he was a man. It seemed to me that a girlfriend was the only real friend you could have. I don't know why I attached so much to the idea of Miss West: I thought that because I had liked her voice this gave me some sort of claim on her. I realize now what a crazy idea this was, but I was only nineteen and in a foreign country.

Soon after this, the first snow fell. It snowed in the night. In the morning, the ground in the yard outside was covered with a lacy pattern, the imprints of the feet of birds. There were hundreds of tiny birds, yellow and brown, in the woods behind the farm. They came from Finland and were going to Italy and had got lost. Herr Enrich found one frozen and brought it in while we were at breakfast. It lay on the palm of his hand. Its feet stuck foolishly in the air, like matchsticks. Its eyes were glazed.

Herr Enrich stroked the yellow feathers in its brown wings. "This is the smallest bird in Europe," he said.

Walt never talked to anyone much, but this time he spoke up and said it was true: he had read it in the Salzburg paper. He got up and fished out the local paper from a pile on a bench by the stove and pointed to the headline. Herr Enrich read it aloud: "SMALLEST BIRD IN EUROPE VISITS SALZBURG." I just sat and stared at Walt. I didn't know until that minute that he read German or that he ever bothered to read the local paper. It wasn't important after all, you don't say to your wife, "Hey, I read German." But I felt more than ever that I needed a friend, someone simple enough for me to understand and simple enough to understand me. The rest of the people at the table went on talking about the bird, and when they had finished discussing it and had all touched its frozen wings, Herr Enrich opened the door of the tiled stove and threw the bird inside. I looked again at Walt, but he didn't seem to notice how horrible this was.

Mrs. de Kende, the Hungarian woman, smiled her toothy gold smile at me over the table, as if she sympathized. I had never liked her until then. We sat on after the others had left, and she leaned forward and whispered, "Come up to my room. We can talk." I was glad, although she was too old to be a friend for me, and I really disliked her looks. Her hair was black and dry, and rolled in an untidy bun. There were always ends trailing on her neck. Her room was next to ours, but I had never been in it before. It was stuffy and rather dark. She had an electric plate and a little coffeepot. "I creep up here to make coffee," she said, shutting the door. "I can't drink the stuff Frau Enrich makes. Don't ever tell her I've invited you here."

"Why not?"

"She might be jealous. She might take it as a slander against her coffee. She might think I was trying to get something from you; American coffee. She might make trouble. Much trouble." She spread out her fat fingers to show how big the trouble would be. "You don't know how people are," she said. "You don't know what the world is."

I sat straight in my chair, like a little girl on a visit. I drank the coffee she poured for me. It tasted like tap water.

"Good?" she asked me.

"Oh, yes."

I began to take in the room. It was littered with clothing. The bed wasn't made; just the covers pulled over the pillows. From the back of a chair, a dirty cotton brassiere hung by a strap. The word "marriage" came into my head. It reminded me of something—a glimpse of my married sister's bedroom on a Sunday morning, untidy and inexplicably frightening.

"What a funny little girl you are," Mrs. de Kende said. "You remind me of the little bird Herr Enrich brought in." She put down her cup and took my face in her hands. Her fingers were cold. I tried to smile. "One longs to speak to you," she said. "I long so for a friend." She let me go and looked around the room. "I have a terrible secret," she said. "The burden of a secret is too much for one person. Some things *must* be shared. Do you understand?"

"Yes," I said. "I do understand."

Mrs. de Kende looked at me for a long time in a rather dramatic way. I began to feel silly, and didn't know what to do with my empty cup. I hoped she wouldn't touch me again. Suddenly she said, "My husband is a Jew."

"Well," I said. I was still fretting about the cup, and finally put it on the floor.

"Never tell," Mrs. de Kende said. "Swear."

"I won't tell." There was no one I could tell. I still hadn't a friend. Walt wouldn't have found it interesting, and Laura Mc-Coll thought all foreigners were crazy.

Mrs. de Kende seemed disappointed, as if I should have had some reaction. But I didn't know what she wanted. She said, "Do you realize what would happen if it were known? We wouldn't be welcome in this house. It would be terrible," she said, clasping and unclasping her hands. "My husband would lose his clients. None of the dentists would buy from him. De Kende isn't our real name. How could it be? The Kendes were aristocrats. Oh, what a foolish woman I am," she said. "Look at my life, at the way I am forced to live. I am the daughter of an Army officer. God is punishing me for having married a Jew. Forgive me, Holy Mother of Jesus," she said, closing her eyes.

I sat with my hands in my lap and wished myself away. At last, because she didn't seem to notice me anymore, I got up quietly and went to my room. It was the first visit I'd had with anyone in Salzburg, except for the McColls.

That afternoon, I had to see Laura. Walt wanted us to be friends, so whenever she asked me over for tea, I took the bus in to Salzburg and listened to her complaints about Marv. Tea really meant having drinks. Laura would make sweet drinks for me, putting in lots of fruit and sugar so that I wouldn't taste the liquor, but I always had a headache coming home on the bus later on. Laura had a lot of time every day to think about her troubles. She had a maid, and a nurse for the baby, and the long autumn afternoons got on her nerves. She met me at the door, wearing velvet slacks and a pullover with a lot of jewelry. We settled down, and she started in right away about Marv. Although it was early, all the lights were on. They lived in a furnished apartment full of glass and china shelves, which seemed to take up all the air and light. It was the maid's day off, so the nurse brought in our drinks. She was young and thin and wore rouge. Laura watched her in silence as she carefully lowered a tray with bottles and glasses and a bowl of ice to a table near us. Suddenly Laura said, "Look at that bitch." I must have seemed stupid, because she said, "I mean *her*," and pointed with her foot to the nurse. "This bitch that Marv's brought in," she said. "Wouldn't you think he'd have more respect for his own baby? That's what it is now," she said. "He's not satisfied having them outside. Now he has to have them in the house." I looked at the nurse, but she didn't seem to understand. "Oh, Cissy," Laura cried, "he's got her in the house, to be around me, to look after my baby," and she sent the bowl of ice flying across the room. I heard glass shatter and closed my eyes, as if I were still with Mrs. de Kende, hearing that awful praying. When I opened them, Laura was crying softly, and the nurse was on her knees cleaning up the mess. There was more color than ever in her cheeks. She was young, but she looked hard. Laura was hard, too, but in a different way. I suddenly felt sorry for Marv, caught between these two women—although, of course, he didn't deserve pity.

Usually, I never talked to Walt about Marv and Laura. When he asked about my afternoons in town, I would say that Laura and I had drinks and told each other's fortune with Laura's Tarot cards. He seemed to think that was a good way of spending time. But that night, I thought I had better tell him something. It had been such a terrible day for me, with the scene in the morning, and Laura in the afternoon, it seemed to me that he might listen and be sympathetic. When we were alone, after dinner, I started to tell him about Laura and the nurse. He cut me off at once. He said that Marv was his best friend, and that Laura had a lot of imagination and not enough to do. All right, I thought, you big pig, see if I ever tell you anything again. I sulked a bit, but he didn't notice. So then I remembered my headache from the drinks, and complained about it, which made him nice. I decided to remember that: If I'm sick, he'll be nice.

After that, the days went on as before. I walked and washed and heard the singer and saw the trays going up to her room. I never saw her. I never seemed to be around at the right time. She went to Vienna for a week, and the house was so empty I could have cried. Then she came back, and there was a great hustle on the staircase, maids running up and down carrying things to be pressed. Herr Enrich said that she was going home to America soon.

"Couldn't I just meet her before she goes?" I asked him. "Would you even just take her a note from me? Just a note?"

He explained all over again, as if I were a dim-witted child, that Miss West came to the farm in order to rest, and had given strict orders about intruders. "If I begin carrying messages," he said, "she will never come again."

"Maybe I could just leave a note in her door," I said. "Then it wouldn't be your fault."

"I cannot prevent you," Herr Enrich said.

I went up to my room and began writing notes. The final note said:

Dear Miss West, I am an American girl, the wife of an Occupation Forces sergeant. We live one floor down from you. I would like to tell you how much I have loved your singing and how much I have specially enjoyed "Herbsttag," the most beautiful song I have ever heard in my life, with sincere best wishes, Cecilia Rowe, Mrs. Walter T. Rowe.

I copied it out on the monogrammed paper my married sister had given me, and I went quietly up the stairs and pushed the note under Miss West's door. I waited around all day, but nothing happened. Walt came home, and then we went out to the movies with Laura and Marv. Laura told me in detail how to make a custard with brown-sugar sauce, even though she knew I never did any cooking at the farm. Marv and Laura seemed normal together—at least, they weren't fighting—and later on, when we were back at the farm, Walt reminded me of the story I'd tried to tell him about the nurse. "Laura's talk doesn't mean a thing," he said. "Girls always talk about their husbands."

"I don't," I said.

"Not yet," said Walt. He meant it for a joke, but I was hurt. When he came over to my bed that night, I pretended to be asleep. I felt wicked and deceitful. At the same time, I couldn't help being surprised at how easily it worked, and I was annoyed that he didn't try harder to wake me up. I was so confused about how I felt that I didn't know how to behave anymore. In the morning, I sulked and didn't speak, but Walt didn't even notice. As soon as he had gone off to Salzburg, there was a telephone call from Laura. She asked me to come over right away. She said that she and Marv had had a terrible fight after the movies, and that she had tried to kill herself twice. I went in at once, and found her looking about the same as always. She had been drinking, and seemed restless and depressed. I stayed with her all day, and by midafternoon she had talked herself out and seemed calmer. She sat in a chair with her feet tucked up and sipped a glass of brandy. She had done talking about herself, and suddenly seemed ready to start in on me. She looked at me over the glass and said, "You don't look too well either, Cissy. Anything wrong?"

"No." I didn't want to tell her about Walt and the deceitful thing I had done. Besides, the whole story behind it—our marriage and Salzburg and my wanting a friend—was too complicated to explain.

But Laura kept on looking, and she laughed and said, "I'll bet you've started a baby."

I cried, "Oh, no, no, no! Don't say that."

Laura said, "Well, you will someday, you know. If you haven't already. You needn't be so upset."

"Oh," I cried, "I never will! Don't say that. I don't *want* to."

"Christ, you don't have to want it," Laura said. "Look at me. And look at the mess I'm in. If I hadn't had the baby, we wouldn't have needed a nurse. If we hadn't needed a nurse, Marv wouldn't have dared..."

She was off again, and, for once, I was glad, because it kept her from talking about me. A baby! My heart beat as if I had been running. How could I take care of a tiny baby when I wasn't ready to take care of myself, when I couldn't even wear high heels and dress like a grownup? All the way home, late that afternoon, I thought about it, and I realized what Walt's visits to my bed might mean. I don't know why I hadn't thought about it before. I'd taken it for granted that I was too young and unready, and that my real married life hadn't started, and that nothing would happen on that account. I knew better, of course. It was just that I hadn't given it much thought.

It was late November, and the days were short. When I arrived at the farm, it was already quite dark. I stood in the doorway, wiping my shoes on the mat, and looked through the hall into the dining room. There was Miss West's piano. There were the rabbity people and Mrs. de Kende, sitting by the stove. The lights were on. The clocks ticked. I could smell the *Sauerbraten* cooking for supper. It was the atmosphere of late evening, and I felt as if here, in this part of the world, one night ran into the next with no day in between. As I shut the door, Herr Enrich came toward me, smiling, holding out a pale blue envelope. I knew at once that it was from Miss West. I snatched it, and my hands shook so much that I tore into the note as well. It was a nice note, inviting me to have lunch with her the next day in her room. I folded the torn note carefully and put it back. I felt happy and curiously delivered. I thought. Here is someone whose room won't be dirty, who doesn't drink all day, who won't frighten me, *who hasn't got a husband*. The note had been friendly. I thought, I have a friend.

Herr Enrich stood there, waiting, curious. "I'm having lunch with Miss West," I told him. "Tomorrow, in her room." I wanted him to realize I had been right all along, that she had wanted to meet me.

"Tomorrow?" he said in his polite, smiling way. "That scarcely seems possible. Miss West has gone."

"Gone where?"

"To America," he said. "She took the afternoon train to Zurich. She flies from there."

"But she left me this note," I said. I can still see myself, somehow, as if I had been a spectator all along, standing in the hall with my camel's-hair coat and my cold bare legs and my childish bobby socks, looking at Herr Enrich, holding on to the pale blue note.

"The tomorrow was today," Herr Enrich said, as if the triumph were his after all. "She left the note for you yesterday. But you went out in the evening, and then again this morning." He spread his hands in mock despair, as if to say that I was always out.

I muttered stupidly, "But I never go out—" and then flew past him, up the stairs, up to her room. I flung open the door without knocking and turned on the light. A strong current from the window slammed the door behind me. The bed was stripped, the room was being aired. I opened the heavy wardrobe: a few hangers swayed on the crossbar. She had left nothing in the wardrobe, nothing in the chest of drawers. I went slowly down to my room and, in the darkened hall, saw Mrs. de Kende. She had come up from the dining room and was sitting quietly on a chair. Still sitting, she grabbed my arm and squeezed it.

"You told," she said.

"What?"

"About my husband. About his being—you know."

"I didn't," I said. "Leave me alone." I pulled away.

"He has just come in," she said in a low voice. "He has lost two clients in Salzburg, both the same day. There could only be one reason. They found out. You told."

"I didn't," I said again. "Leave me alone."

She didn't get hysterical but said quietly, "It is my fault. I wanted to trust someone. God is punishing me." She got up and went into her room.

I could feel my heart in my breast, as hard and cool as a pebble. I sat down where she had been, in the dark, until I heard Walt come in. He spoke to Herr Enrich and then came up the stairs. "Walt," I said. He stopped, looking around, and I flung myself at him and cried, "She's gone, the singer has gone home, it's all over and I'll never meet her, I'll never have a friend!"

Faces appeared on the stairs—white, astonished faces. I had always been so quiet. Walt said to them, "It's all right," and he led me into our room. "Who's gone?" he said, shutting the door.

"The singer," I said. I leaned against him and wept and wept. "I wanted to meet her. I wanted terribly much to meet her. I'm sick of this house. I'm sick of the woman next door. I'm sick of Laura. I don't want a baby."

"Are you having a baby?" said Walt.

"I don't know." I pulled away and went over to the chest of drawers to find a handkerchief. I dried my eyes and blew my nose. Walt stood by the door, watching me. His arms hung at his sides. He looked helpless.

"Are you having a baby?" he said again.

"I told you, I don't know. I don't think so. It was just something Laura said."

"It might be a good thing for you," said Walt.

"You mean a good thing like having an apartment?" I combed my hair, tugging at it. I think I hated him at that moment. Then I caught sight of him in the mirror; he looked helpless, and unhappy, and I remembered what Marv had said—that I was the first girl Walt had taken seriously, and how his friends had never thought he'd get married. I wondered if he was sorry he'd got married, and, for the first time, I wondered if being married was as hard for him as for me.

In the next room, Mrs. de Kende was muttering—praying, I supposed. I felt guilty about her, in a vague way, as if I had let her down; as if I were really the one who had told about her husband. But that was just a momentary feeling. Mrs. de Kende was old and crazy, not a young girl like me. I began to dress to go out. Walt and I were having supper with Marv and Laura, and then we were going to the movies. I didn't want to spend my evening that way, but I felt there was no stopping things now that I was married and had better take things as they came. The singer had gone. I'd have to manage without help, without a friend more important than Walt. I wondered if all of this—my crying, Walt being bewildered—was married life, not just the preliminary.

Walt moved away from the door and sat down on his bed. "What about this singer?" he said. "Was she going to give you lessons, or something?"

"It was just crazy," I said.

"You'll be all right, Cissy," he said. "Living out here has got you down."

"I know," I said. "When we get our own place." We looked briefly, almost timidly, at each other in the mirror, and I knew we were thinking the same thing: the apartment will make the difference; something's got to.

Your girlhood doesn't vanish overnight. I know, now, what a lot of wavering goes on, how you step forward and back again. The frontier is invisible; sometimes you're over without knowing it. I do know that some change began then, at that moment, and I felt an almost unbearable nostalgia for the figure I was leaving behind, the shell of the girl who had got down from the train in September, the pretty girl with all the blue plaid luggage. I could never be that girl again, not entirely. Too much had happened in between.

"We'll be all right," I echoed to Walt, and I repeated it to myself, over and over, "I'll be all right; we'll be all right."

But we're not safe yet, I thought, looking at my husband—this stranger, mute, helpless, fumbling, enclosed. Oh, we're not safe. Not by a long shot. But we'll be all right. Take my word for it. We'll be all right.

*1955*

# THIEVES AND RASCALS

When the telephone on the desk rang just before lunch, Charles Kimber picked up the receiver and laid it down softly. The voice of the long-distance operator came through, thin and fitful, in conversation with his secretary. He crossed the room and, opening the door of his office, told his secretary that she could put the phone down, that he would take the call himself. She obeyed, close to tears. She had been upset ever since the morning of the previous day, when she had brought him a letter with the envelope slit down the side.

"I'm awfully sorry," she had said. "It wasn't marked personal or anything, and when I saw it was from Saint Hilda's, I just thought it was the term bill for your little girl."

"Don't worry about it," Charles had replied, surprised at her distress. Then he had read the letter. It was from the headmistress of St. Hilda's School, writing, with evident unease, that Charles's sixteen-year-old daughter, Joyce, had violated the rules of the school and of normal propriety by vanishing for a weekend. Miss Mercer had cause to believe—all the more since Joyce herself had admitted this—that she had spent the weekend in Albany, in a hotel, with a young man. "A young man of good family, and from a good school," she noted, as if this altered or improved the misdemeanor.

He walked back to his desk and picked up the telephone. The voice of Miss Mercer followed that of the operator, a surprisingly young and healthy voice.

"Of course, the responsibility is ours," said Miss Mercer. "We often let some of the senior girls go to Albany on Saturdays, always in pairs. They usually shop or go to an approved movie or something like that, and they always come back together, in our own station wagons, in time for dinner. Nothing like this has ever happened, until now. And Joyce is so...well, reliable. She's the last girl one wouldn't expect to trust. She's so..."

She's so plain, Charles supplied mentally. He had a quick image of Joyce, too big for her age and, by his standards, much too fat. Her hair was straight and of an indeterminate brown. At sixteen she still stood in a babyish manner, the toe of one moccasin over the other. She called her parents "Daddy" and "Mummy," and she had never in her life expressed a willful or unsuitable thought.

"I'm putting her on the train tomorrow," said Miss Mercer. "One of the junior teachers will be with her, although she's not likely to run away or anything like that. She's sensible. It sounds strange to say that now, but she *is* sensible. That's why...it's so hard to understand..."

"I know," said Charles. "I suppose we'll all have to meet."

"Yes," said Miss Mercer. "I, of course, have to meet the board. Well, it's all rather unfortunate. In any case, Joyce gets in at four tomorrow."

"Grand Central?" said Charles, although he knew very well that it was.

"Yes," said Miss Mercer. Her voice for the first time became indistinct.

"I can't hear you," said Charles.

"I said," she repeated, as if she had taken a breath, "that you mustn't be alarmed when you see her. She's cut her hair off."

"Oh, yes?" said Charles.

"Yes, the night she came back," said Miss Mercer. "With her manicure scissors, in front of the mirror, in her room. She...well, it's the only really odd thing in her behavior since she came back to school. She seemed to expect that she could go to classes, as usual."

"Yes, as usual," Charles repeated, until Miss Mercer cut off the embarrassed exchange, saying she could arrange a meeting between Charles and his wife, and herself, and someone whose name sounded official.

He put back the telephone. I'll have to tell Marian, he thought. Charles had not yet mentioned the letter to his wife. Marian was a fashion model, and her strenuous hours and her need to diet kept her tense and edgy. The morning this letter arrived, Charles had left his office and gone for a walk, although he found that walking helped him think of nothing in particular. He did not feel a sense of outrage that his daughter had been dishonored. He had no desire to shoot the young man, nor even to meet him, except, perhaps, out of curiosity. His mind could not construct the image of stolid Joyce, in the moccasins, the tweed skirt, the innocent sweaters, registering (as she surely had) in a shabby hotel on a side street in Albany. He wondered not so much how it had happened, but that it had happened at all. Joyce, as far as he knew, didn't know any young men, except, perhaps, the brothers of her classmates. And why, he wondered, would any young man, even the most callow and inexperienced, pick Joyce? There are so many girls her age who are graceful, pretty, knowing, and who have weekends here and there written all over them. Yes, even girls—and here his mind mimicked Miss Mercer—of good family and from good schools. Charles was a lawyer and knew the difficulties young girls of good family could cause themselves and their parents.

Thinking this as he walked, turning it over and over, he had noticed a small crowd outside the Museum of Modern Art and, advancing, he saw that they were looking at his wife who stood, posed, against the glass doors. She was wearing a thin black dress and a small hat. She must be frozen, Charles thought, for it was a cold day and many of the women in the crowd held their collars close to their faces. But there was not a shiver, not a movement, as she stood, looking through her black-gloved fingers in the curious way the photographer had caused her to remain. The photographer said something, and she dropped one arm. She paid no attention to the crowd, and although she stared, one would have said, straight into her husband's face, she appeared not to see him. She looked, he thought, gaunt and tired. The shadow under her cheekbone, which photographed as a clean curve, seemed, under the hard winter sun, the concavity of illness. The eye framed by her fingers looked vampish and absurd, the over-darkened eye of silent films.

He thought all this without criticism, for he greatly admired his wife, and he was proud of her impersonal beauty when he saw it on the pages of *Vogue* and *Harper's Bazaar*. She was the most physically disciplined human being he had ever known. She rose each morning at half-past six and went off to work, her thin body supplied with nothing more than coffee. At noon she ate cottage cheese and a raw tomato. For dinner she allowed herself a steak and ate it scrupulously to the last bite, without any visible enjoyment. Her consumption of this slice of meat had something about it that was ritualistic and cannibalistic, and it had, for a while, interfered with Charles's enjoyment of his own food.

Her moral discipline was just as pronounced. There was not an appetite of mind or spirit she could not control as she controlled the limbs of her body before a camera. Once, when she had been interviewed for a magazine that described the home lives of fashion models, she had said, in Charles's hearing: "I'm always too cold in winter and too hot in summer. I always have a slight headache. I'm always just a little bit hungry." He had been surprised to hear her say this. She had never volunteered anything to him that would suggest she found her métier disagreeable. Her edginess, usually, was caused by other agents: the telephone, servants, people who drank too much, parties that went on too long, and noise of any kind. She groomed herself with the absorbed concentration of a cat; and she often sat before a mirror, chin on hand, contemplating, quite objectively, her own image. She was self-contained, and she had few friends and almost no enemies. She never gossiped, and it was doubtful if she had, even in fancy, been unfaithful to her husband. Charles, indeed, had long ceased even to wonder about this.

So, thought Charles, summing up this picture as he walked back to his office, it was not from her mother that Joyce had inherited this unexpected streak of waywardness. Of course, one could not compare the two: Joyce was still a child, in a sense. She was gauche and untidy. She talked, it seemed to Charles, about nothing; and she ate far too many sweets, although Marian was surprisingly indulgent about this.

"It's up to you. You're old enough to know what you want to look like," she would say, not unkindly, picking up from the floor the empty wrapper of a bar of chocolate. Joyce ate candy in her room at night, after the light was put out. She had done this from the time she was old enough to have her own allowance. It was difficult for Charles to picture her before her adolescence. When he thought of her as a small child, it was in terms of photographs. There was a photograph of her at four, in a sun suit, blinking into the sun from a sandbox. It was an enlarged snapshot which Marian had had framed and kept on her dressing table. There were baby pictures, of course, the face shadowed by the hood of a pram, or looking up blankly from a tasseled cushion. There was the far-fetched photograph from the mother-and-daughter series that had appeared in a fashion magazine, and which Charles kept on his desk, although the child in the picture was not remotely like his daughter.

He tried to remember Joyce as a baby, Marian pushing a pram. But either this had never happened, or his mind had refused to retain so unlikely an image. In Charles's memory, Joyce appeared quite suddenly at twelve, the age at which she had been permitted to dine with her parents. Her untidy table manners had greatly annoyed him, and he had often complained to Marian about the expensive Swiss governess who, all these years, should have been grooming a model little girl, clean and silent as a watch, ready to take her place at her parents' table.

Well, Marian would have to be told. It was, in any case, a

problem for a woman, he thought, although he could not blame Joyce's delinquency on his wife. She had always been conscientious about spending time with Joyce. She seemed always to be meeting her at trains, or putting her on them. He recalled his wife's voice, from her bedroom, in conversation with Joyce's governess, saying eagerly, pleadingly almost: "But she has something, don't you think? Something pretty? Something about the eyes?" The governess, Miss Roefrich, had murmured something that was somehow flattering to Miss *and* Mrs. Kimber, which Charles considered a master stroke of tact. He, himself, could not have placed his wife and his daughter in the same breath.

He would not be seeing Marian until late that evening. Charles was dining with a Miss Lawrence, who lived near Columbia University, and at whose small apartment he spent two evenings a week. Miss Lawrence usually assembled the meal, since Charles felt they should not be seen too often in restaurants. Miss Lawrence, whose name was Bernice, but who called herself Bambi, was the secretary of a radio producer, but she had no opinions about radio, present or future, nor, for that matter, about anything else, and Charles found her conversation restful. In four years, she had complained only once or twice about their secluded relationship. The most difficult argument had taken place after she bought and read *Vogue's Book of Etiquette*. She had shown Charles the section on Dining with Married Men. "It says it's all right, if you don't do it too often with the same married man," she had explained.

"How many married men do you know, for God's sake?" Charles had demanded, and the evening had ended in tears and terms of reproach.

This evening, dinner began with a mushroom soup and ended with chocolate éclairs. Charles told Bernice about a case, and she related a tale of outrageous gossip about a program director and film star.

"I'm going on a diet, starting Monday," said Bernice, as she rose from the table. "Don't laugh. This time I mean it."

He watched her, thoughtfully, as she cleared the table. "What were you like at sixteen?" he said. "I mean, what were you doing?"

"It's not that long ago," said Bernice, looking at him. "I was in high school; what do you think?"

"Were you interested in men?"

"I don't know what you're getting at, exactly. I went to a good high school, all girls. Lauren Bacall was in my class. They were all nice girls. We never talked about men. We were interested in clothes, and world events. We had a very superior World Events teacher." She turned on the radio, moving away from him.

"What I mean is," said Charles, "would it have occurred to you... no, I'll put it this way: what would your family have done if you'd gone away for the weekend with some man, say a young boy from... from another good high school?"

"Killed me," said Bernice, simply. "My mother would have cried, but my father would have killed me." She looked at him. "Why?" she said.

"I just wondered," said Charles. "I was wondering about that kind of situation,"

"Well, I don't like it," said Bernice. "You're positively morbid. I'd rather talk to the cat."

"Come on, kitty-kitty-puss," Charles heard her say in the kitchen. "Come to your own mother, who loves you."

At eleven o'clock Charles let himself into his own apartment. His wife was sitting up in bed, reading.

"Tough client?" she said. Her hair was wrapped in a scarf. The room smelled of perfume, of cream, of toning lotion.

"Kind of," said Charles.

"Anything I'd be interested in?" said Marian.

"I don't *think* so," said Charles. "Something about airlines. Look, I think I'll get myself a drink. I don't suppose you want one," he said.

"No," said Marian. She closed her book as he came back into the room, glass in hand. "You look tired," she said. She pushed her pillows on the floor and slid down in bed. "Good night," she said, closing her eyes.

"Did you take a pill?" said Charles.

"No. I don't need one. I'm quite tired."

"Could you stay awake a minute, then?" said Charles. "I want to talk to you about something."

"About airlines?" She opened one eye and he was reminded of how, the previous day, she had peered at him, without seeing anything, through her gloves.

"I saw you yesterday morning, in front of the museum," he said. "You were wearing some black thing. God, you must have been cold."

"Yes, I was. Is that what you want to talk about?"

"No." He sat down on the edge of his own bed and gave her Miss Mercer's letter. Marian propped herself up on one elbow while she read it. She folded it and ran her long thumbnail along the fold.

"When is she coming home?" she said.

"Tomorrow," said Charles, "in the afternoon. What should we do?"

"Meet her," said Marian. "What else can we do?" She lay back in bed again. "If there was ever anything else to be done, it looks as though we've missed it. Will you meet her, or shall I?"

"I thought you should, perhaps," said Charles carefully. "Sometimes a woman is better...and if she sees me, she may be frightened."

Marian turned her head to look at him. "Now, why in the world would she be frightened?" she said.

"I don't know," said Charles, confused. "I think that in these cases, the father...I mean, traditionally, the father...."

"Never mind," said his wife. "We could, of course, both go."

"Oh, no," said Charles quickly. "The sight of us *both*...I mean, even if she hadn't done anything, it might be overwhelming."

"All right," said Marian. She settled into her bed. "Well, good night again."

"Is that all?" said Charles. He was surprised, and rather scandalized, that his wife could take it so calmly. He had known her to be greatly upset over much lesser things: a broken string of pearls, the accidental death of a cocker spaniel.

"What else can I say?" said Marian. "We can't lie here and discuss her character and all her little ways. Evidently neither of us knows anything about them. We can talk about what lousy parents we are. That won't help either. We might as well sleep, if we can."

Marian was wonderful, he thought. He turned out the lights, leaving only the small spotlight over his bed and the light from the half-opened bathroom door. He undressed quietly. His father had liked Marian, he remembered. "If you marry your own kind of person, you know exactly where you're at, every minute," he had said, and he had been right. Charles and Marian had never had a full-dress quarrel. In this, Charles congratulated himself that he had made many allowances for her nerves and the strain of her profession. He looked around and, finding nothing he wanted to read, put out the light over his bed.

A moment later, in the dark, he heard his wife's voice, so softly that he was not certain she had spoken at all.

"I said," Marian repeated, "is he coming too?"

"Who?" said Charles, thinking, for a second, that she was talking in her sleep.

"The party of the second part," said his wife. "Young Lochinvar. The boy with the good family and the good school."

"No," said Charles. "Why should he?"

"I thought not," said Marian. "I suppose she went back to school all alone, too?"

"I suppose so," said Charles, perplexed. "She cut her hair off," he said, suddenly remembering this. "With a pair of nail scissors, I think."

"Oh?" said Marian. "Well, that isn't too serious. It'll grow. I'll show her how to fix it. That, at least, I can do for her." Her voice dropped and he wondered if she could possibly be crying. She was silent and a few moments later she said quietly: "God, I don't like them."

"Who?" said Charles.

"Men," his wife said. It was quite unlike Marian to be dramatic: he wondered if the shock of the news had unhinged her, and if she were planning to talk like this, off and on, all night.

"It's the first inkling I've had that you hated men," he said, smiling in the dark.

Marian stirred in her bed. "I don't hate them," she said. "If I hated men, I'd probably hate women, too. *I don't like them.* It's quite different."

"I don't see the difference," said Charles, "but it doesn't matter." He sat up and switched on the light over his bed. His wife was crying. She had pulled the sheet up over her face and was drying her eyes on it.

"You mean," said Charles, "that you hate men because of this boy, this..." He stopped, realizing he must not undersell his daughter.

"Weak, frightened, lying..." said Marian. "Thieves and rascals." She sat up and, groping in the pocket of her dressing gown, found a handkerchief. "Thieves," she said. She blew her nose. "And never any courage, not a scrap. They can't own up. They can't be trusted. They can't face things. Not at that age. Not at any age."

"I think it's going a little far to say you can't trust any man, at any age," said Charles.

"I don't know any," said his wife.

"Well," he said, "there's me, for instance." When she did not reply, he said: "Well, it's a fine time to find out you don't trust me."

"The question isn't whether I do or not," said Marian. "I have to trust you. I mean, I either live with you, and keep the thing on the tracks, or I don't. So then, of course, I have to trust you."

"It's not good enough," said Charles. "You should trust me out of conviction, not because you think you have to."

"All right," said Marian.

"No," he insisted. "It's not good enough. Say you trust me."

"All right," said Marian. "I trust you. Don't put the light out. I have to get some ice for my eyes. I'm working in the morning."

"I'll get it," Charles said quickly, glad to end the conversation. One couldn't blame her if she sounded a little unreasonable, he thought. It would be a shock for any mother. He put the ice cubes in a bowl and carried them back through the dark apartment to their bedroom.

Marian had stopped crying. "Put them in that gadget over there," she said. "There, next to the lamp. That's it." She lay back again and Charles placed the mask of ice cubes across her eyes.

"You see," he said, "men are some use. Shall I get you anything else?"

She shook her head, then she said: "You know who used to say that about men, 'thieves and rascals'? My sister. You wouldn't remember her. She didn't come to our wedding. She didn't want me to marry you. It broke her heart, I think. She went out to the West Coast, and she died before Joyce was born. I didn't even know she was sick."

"Don't start crying about your sister, for God's sake," said Charles. "It's awfully late, and if you have a job in the morning..." Vaguely, he did recall a sister: a scowling female form that had chaperoned his early meetings with Marian and then disappeared.

"She brought me up," said Marian. "She thought I was so pretty. She used to wake me up in the morning, and say, 'Little pretty one.' She said it every day. Mother died ... And Father was pretty useless. She went everywhere with me. I was seventeen when I started modeling. Father was dead against it. We lived in New Canaan then."

"Darling, I know all this," said Charles. "I just happened to have forgotten about Margaret."

"No, listen to this," said Marian. "You can't imagine what a beautiful kid I was. No, really you can't. People used to stare at me on the street. I remember the men, mostly. They still look at me like that, like someone rubbing their dirty hands all over you.

Only now it doesn't frighten me. I was so beautiful that people hated me. Men hate beautiful girls, if they can't have them."

"I don't know where you picked up that idea," said Charles. "Everyone likes you. Everyone."

"That's not what I mean," said Marian. "My sister was with me all the time. She used to sit and read a book all the while I was working. The men were so scared of her that no one looked at me twice. I never minded. They did the best they could, though: a shove here, a little pat there. Then, the same year, when I was seventeen, I fell in love with a photographer. He was a Dane, or rather, his parents were. I don't know what happened to him. Maybe he was killed in the war."

She was silent for several minutes, and Charles, reaching overhead, put out his light. Then she began again: "We started passing notes, right under Margaret's nose, like a couple of school kids. I started coming in town without her, afternoons, saying I was shopping or something. I could only manage it afternoons, of course. So we decided to go away together. Up to then, it had all been pretty innocent. We were going to see if we liked each other—he told me that was how it was done in Europe, though I don't think he'd ever been there—and then we'd get married. We didn't run very far. We went to Philadelphia."

"You're making this up," said Charles. "It doesn't sound like you."

"Why?" said Marian. "Because now I don't run off to Philadelphia with photographers? I'm trying to tell you, I was seventeen."

"Do you think that makes it better, or something?" said Charles. "A girl of seventeen . . . and I met you a year later."

"Well, it wasn't too pleasant, if you're looking for a moral," his wife said. "In fact, I was so upset and frightened and unhappy that on the train when we were coming back to New York I said, 'You needn't look at me that way. It's just as sinful for you as it is for me.' He looked surprised, but he kept looking at me that funny way. Then he told me what they used to call me behind my back: this Lily Girl from New Canaan."

"There's nothing wrong with that," said Charles.

"Margaret met me at the door, when I got out of the taxi," said Marian. "My father was upstairs, collapsing, or writing me out of his will. She took me in her arms. She kissed me. She said, 'Little pretty one.' She looked around and she said, 'No, I guess he didn't come with you.' She put me to bed. She brought me my dinner, on a tray. She brushed my hair, and she said, once, under her breath, 'Thieves.' She never mentioned it again. No, not once. Until I said I was going to marry you. Then she called you a thief and a rascal."

"She didn't even know me. Frankly, I think she sounds neurotic."

"She was wonderful. And I wasn't even there when she died."

"I don't see why you're crying about it *now*," said Charles. "If she died before Joyce was even born, that's seventeen years. I wish you hadn't told me all this. When I think that a while back you were saying men couldn't be trusted. I'd certainly tell you...I mean, if something had happened nearly twenty years ago, I'd certainly tell you about it. As if we weren't upset enough about Joyce; or do you think this helps?"

"I'm sorry," said Marian. "I keep thinking about Margaret, and saying 'Thieves,' and bringing my dinner, and dying all by herself. I get it all mixed up with Joyce, being all by herself right now. Joyce sort of looks like her, something about the way she stands, something sturdy. Put on your light, will you? I've lost my handkerchief."

Charles looked at her critically. "You'll never be able to work tomorrow," he said. "Your eyelids are a mess."

"I don't care," said Marian. "Only I don't want to look too funny for Joyce. Oh, I want her hair to grow! Don't you see her, being alone, and cutting it off? Her femininity, because she's been made ashamed of it, or afraid?"

"Don't start on that," said Charles. "Don't give her complexes she hasn't got. It won't mark her for life. It didn't mark you. You made a happy marriage. And a career. Everyone respects you."

"Oh, I'll tell her about it," said Marian. "I should have talked to her before, but she seemed such a kid. I'll talk to her. I'll tell her how to live in the world with them as decently as one can."

"With who?" said Charles.

"With all of you," said his wife.

Charles turned off his light. "I don't see where I come into this at all," he said. He turned over to lie on his side, his sense of injury wrapped around him like an eiderdown. "Try to sleep," he said. "From the sound of your voice, you've given yourself a cold."

His wife did not reply. She was overwrought, Charles decided. As for her story, he scarcely knew whether to believe it or not. It's so plainly out of character, he thought, recalling their blameless courtship. She was never that interested in men, and she thinks all photographers are morons. But then, he thought, she may have made it all up so that I wouldn't be too hard on Joyce. He wanted to suggest this to Marian, but he was afraid of provoking another scene. He said, kindly: "Good night," and his wife whispered something back.

At last he fell asleep, undisturbed, leaving his wife to think and to weep alone in the dark, under her mask of ice cubes.

*1956*

# BERNADETTE

ON THE HUNDRED and twenty-sixth day, Bernadette could no longer pretend not to be sure. She got the calendar out from her bureau drawer—a kitchen calendar, with the Sundays and saints' days in fat red figures, under a brilliant view of Alps. Across the Alps was the name of a hardware store and its address on the other side of Montreal. From the beginning of October the calendar was smudged and grubby, so often had Bernadette with moistened forefinger counted off the days: thirty-four, thirty-five, thirty-six . . . That had been October, the beginning of fear, with the trees in the garden and on the suburban street a blaze of red and yellow. Bernadette had scrubbed floors and washed walls in a frenzy of bending and stretching that alarmed her employers, the kindly, liberal Knights.

"She's used to hard work—you can see that, of course," Robbie Knight had remarked, one Sunday, almost apologizing for the fact that they employed anyone in the house at all. Bernadette had chosen to wash the stairs and woodwork that day, instead of resting. It disturbed the atmosphere of the house, but neither of the Knights knew how to deal with a servant who wanted to work too much. He sat by the window, enjoying the warm October sunlight, trying to get on with the Sunday papers but feeling guilty because his wife was worried about Bernadette.

"She *will* keep on working," Nora said. "I've told her to leave that hard work for the char, but she insists. I suppose it's her way of showing gratitude, because we've treated her like a human being instead of a slave. Don't you agree?"

"I suppose so."

"I'm so tired," Nora said. She lay back in her chair with her eyes closed, the picture of total exhaustion. She had broken one of her nails clean across, that morning, helping Bernadette with something Bernadette might easily have done alone. "You're right about her being used to hard work. She's probably been working all her life." Robbie tried not answering this one. "It's so much the sort of thing I've battled," Nora said.

He gave up. He let his paper slide to the floor. Compelled to think about his wife's battles, he found it impossible to concentrate on anything else. Nora's weapons were kept sharp for two dragons: crooked politics and the Roman Catholic Church. She had battled for birth control, clean milk, vaccination, homes for mothers, homes for old people, homes for cats and dogs. She fought against censorship, and for votes for cloistered nuns, and for the provincial income tax.

"Good old Nora," said Robbie absently. Nora accepted this tribute without opening her eyes. Robbie looked at her, at the thin, nervous hand with the broken nail.

"She's not exciting, exactly," he had once told one of his mistresses. "But she's an awfully good sort, if you know what I mean. I mean, she's really a good sort. I honestly couldn't imagine not living with Nora." The girl to whom this was addressed had instantly burst into tears, but Robbie was used to that. Unreasonable emotional behavior on the part of other women only reinforced his respect for his wife.

The Knights had been married nearly sixteen years. They considered themselves solidly united. Like many people no longer in love, they cemented their relationship with opinions, pet prejudices, secret meanings, a private vocabulary that enabled them to exchange amused glances over a dinner table and made them feel a shade superior to the world outside the house. Their home held them, and their two daughters, now in boarding school. Private schools were out of line with the Knights' social beliefs, but in the case of their own children they had judged a private school essential.

"Selfish, they were," Robbie liked to explain. "Selfish, like their father." Here he would laugh a little, and so would his listeners. He was fond of assuming a boyish air of self-deprecation—a manner which, like his boyish nickname, had clung to him since school. "Nora slapped them both in St. Margaret's, and it cleared up in a year."

On three occasions, Nora had discovered Robbie in an affair. Each time, she had faced him bravely and made him discuss it, a process she called "working things out." Their talks would be formal, at first—a frigid question-and-answer period, with Robbie frightened and almost sick and Nora depressingly unreproachful. For a few nights, she would sleep in another room. She said that this enabled her to think. Thinking all night, she was fresh and ready for talk the next day. She would analyze their marriage, their lives, their childhoods, and their uncommon characters. She would tell Robbie what a Don Juan complex was, and tell him what he was trying to prove. Finally, reconciled, they were able to talk all night, usually in the kitchen, the most neutral room of the house, slowly and congenially sharing a bottle of Scotch. Robbie would begin avoiding his mistress's telephone calls and at last would write her a letter saying that his marriage had been rocked from top to bottom and that but for the great tolerance shown by his wife they would all of them have been involved in something disagreeable. He and his wife had now arrived at a newer, fuller, truer, richer, deeper understanding. The long affection they held for each other would enable them to start life again on a different basis, the letter would conclude.

The basic notion of the letter was true. After such upheavals his marriage went swimmingly. He would feel flattened, but not unpleasantly, and it was Nora's practice to treat him with tolerance and good humor, like an ailing child.

He looked at the paper lying at his feet and tried to read the review of a film. It was hopeless. Nora's silence demanded his attention. He got up, kissed her lightly, and started out.

"Off to work?" said Nora, without opening her eyes.

"Well, yes," he said.

"I'll keep the house quiet. Would you like your lunch on a tray?"

"No, I'll come down."

"Just as you like, darling. It's no trouble."

He escaped.

Robbie was a partner in a firm of consulting engineers. He had, at one time, wanted to be a playwright. It was this interest that had, with other things, attracted Nora when they had been at university together. Robbie had been taking a course in writing for the stage—a sideline to his main degree. His family had insisted on engineering; he spoke of defying them, and going to London or New York. Nora had known, even then, that she was a born struggler and fighter. She often wished she had been a man. She believed that to balance this overassertive side of her nature she should marry someone essentially feminine, an artist of some description. At the same time, a burning fear of poverty pushed her in the direction of someone with stability, background, and a profession outside the arts. Both she and Robbie were campus liberals; they met at a gathering that had something to do with the Spanish war—the sort of party where, as Nora later described it, you all sat on the floor and drank beer out of old pickle jars. There had been a homogeneous quality about the group that was quite deceptive; political feeling was a great leveler. For Nora, who came from a poor and an ugly lower-middle-class home, political action was a leg up. It brought her in contact with people she would not otherwise have known. Her snobbishness moved to a different level; she spoke of herself as working-class, which was not strictly true. Robbie, in revolt against his family, who were well-to-do, conservative, and had no idea of the injurious things he said about them behind their backs, was, for want of a gentler expression, slumming around. He drifted into a beer-drinking Left Wing movement, where he was welcomed for his money, his good looks, and the respectable tone he lent the group. His favorite phrase at that time was "of the people." He mistook Nora for someone of the people, and married her almost before he had discovered his mistake. Nora then did an extraordinary about-face. She reconciled Robbie with his family. She encouraged him to go into his father's firm. She dampened, ever so gently, the idea of London and New York.

Still, she continued to encourage his interest in theatre. More, she managed to create such a positive atmosphere of playwriting in the house that many of their casual acquaintances thought he *was* a playwright, and were astonished to learn he was the Knight of Turnbull, Knight & Beardsley. Robbie had begun and abandoned many plays since college. He had not consciously studied since the creative-writing course, but he read, and criticized, and had reached the point where he condemned everything that had to do with the English-language stage.

Nora agreed with everything he believed. She doggedly shared his passion for the theatre—which had long since ceased to be real, except when she insisted—and she talked to him about his work, sharing his problems and trying to help. She knew that his trouble arose from the fact that he had to spend his daytime hours in the offices of the firm. She agreed that his real life was the theatre, with the firm a practical adjunct. She was sensible: she did not ask that he sell his partnership and hurl himself into uncertainty and insecurity—a prospect that would have frightened him very much indeed. She understood that it was the firm that kept them going, that paid for the girls at St. Margaret's and the trip to Europe every second summer. It was the firm that gave Nora leisure and scope for her tireless battles with the political and ecclesiastical authorities of Quebec. She encouraged Robbie to write in his spare time. Every day, or nearly, during his "good" periods, she mentioned his work. She rarely accepted an invitation without calling Robbie at his office and asking if he wanted to shut himself up and work that particular night. She could talk about his work, without boredom or exhaustion, just as she could discuss his love affairs. The only difference was that when they were mutually explaining Robbie's infidelity, they drank whiskey. When they talked about his play and his inability to get on with it, Nora would go to the refrigerator and bring out a bottle of milk. She was honest and painstaking; she had at the tip of her tongue the vocabulary needed to turn their relationship and marriage inside out. After listening to Nora for a whole evening, agreeing all the way, Robbie would go to bed subdued with truth and totally empty. He felt that they had drained everything they would ever have to say. After too much talk, he would think, a couple should part; just part, without another word, full of kind thoughts and mutual understanding. He was afraid of words. That was why, that Sunday morning toward the end of October, the simple act of leaving the living room took on the dramatic feeling of escape.

He started up the stairs, free. Bernadette was on her knees, washing the painted baseboard. Her hair, matted with a cheap permanent, had been flattened into curls that looked like snails, each snail held with two crossed bobby pins. She was young, with a touching attractiveness that owed everything to youth.

"*Bonjour, Bernadette.*"

"*'Jour.*"

Bending, she plunged her hands into the bucket of soapy water. A moment earlier, she had thought of throwing herself down the stairs and making it seem an accident. Robbie's sudden appearance had frightened her into stillness. She wiped her forehead, waiting until he had closed the door behind him. Then she flung herself at the baseboard, cloth in hand. Did she feel something—a tugging, a pain? "*Merci, mon Dieu,*" she whispered. But there was nothing to be thankful for, in spite of the walls and the buckets of water and the bending and the stretching.

Now it was late December, the hundred and twenty-sixth day, and Bernadette could no longer pretend not to be certain. The

Knights were giving a party. Bernadette put the calendar back in the drawer, under her folded slips. She had counted on it so much that she felt it bore witness to her fears; anyone seeing it would know at once.

For weeks she had lived in a black sea of nausea and fear. The Knights had offered to send her home to Abitibi for Christmas, had even wanted to pay her fare. But she knew that her father would know the instant he saw her, and would kill her. She preferred going on among familiar things, as if the normality, the repeated routine of getting up in the morning and putting on Mr. Knight's coffee and Mrs. Knight's tea would, by force of pattern, cause things to be the way they had been before October. So far, the Knights had noticed nothing, although the girls, home for Christmas, teased her about getting fat. Thanks to St. Joseph, the girls had now been sent north to ski with friends, and there was no longer any danger of their drawing attention to Bernadette's waist.

Because of the party, Bernadette was to wear a uniform, which she had not done for some time. She pressed it and put it back on its hanger without trying it on, numb with apprehension, frightened beyond all thought. She had spent the morning cleaning the living room. Now it was neat, unreal, like a room prepared for a color photo in a magazine. There were flowers and plenty of ashtrays. It was a room waiting for disorder to set in.

"Thank you, Bernadette," Nora had said, taking, as always, the attitude that Bernadette had done her an unexpected service. "It looks lovely."

Nora liked the room; it was comfortable and fitted in with her horror of ostentation. Early in her marriage she had decided that her taste was uncertain; confusing elegance with luxury, she had avoided both. Later, she had discovered French-Canadian furniture, which enabled her to refer to her rooms in terms of the simple, the charming, even the amusing. The bar, for example, was a *prie-dieu* Nora had discovered during one of her forays into rural Quebec just after the war, before American tourists with a nose for a bargain had (as she said) cleaned out the province of its greatest heritage. She had found the *prie-dieu* in a barn and had bought it for three dollars. Sandpapered, waxed, its interior recess deepened to hold bottles, it was considered one of Nora's best *trouvailles*. The party that evening was being given in honor of a priest—a liberal priest from Belgium, a champion of modern ecclesiastical art, and another of Nora's finds. (Who but Nora would have dreamed of throwing a party for a priest?)

Robbie wondered if the *prie-dieu* might not offend him. "Maybe you ought to keep the lid up, so he won't see the cross," he said.

But Nora felt that would be cheating. If the priest accepted her hospitality, he must also accept her views.

"He doesn't know your views," Robbie said. "If he did, he probably wouldn't come." He had a cold, and was spending the day at home, in order to be well for the party. The cold made him interfering and quarrelsome.

"Go to bed, Robbie," said Nora kindly. "Haven't you anything to read? What about all the books you got for Christmas?"

Considering him dismissed, she coached Bernadette for the evening. They rehearsed the handing around of the tray, the unobtrusive clearing of ashtrays. Nora noticed that Bernadette seemed less shy. She kept a blank, hypnotized stare, concentrating hard. After a whole year in the household, she was just beginning to grasp what was expected. She understood work, she had worked all her life, but she did not always understand what these terrifying, well-meaning people wanted. If, dusting a bookcase, she slowed her arm, lingering, thinking of nothing in particular, one of them would be there, like a phantom, frightening her out of her wits.

"Would you like to borrow one of these books, Bernadette?"

Gentle, tolerant, infinitely baffling, Mr. or Mrs. Knight would offer her a book in French.

"For me?"

"Yes. You can read in the afternoon, while you are resting."

Read while resting? How could you do both? During her afternoon rest periods, Bernadette would lie on the bed, looking out the window. When she had a whole day to herself, she went down-town in a bus and looked in the windows of stores. Often, by the end of the afternoon, she had met someone, a stranger, a man who would take her for a drive in a car or up to his room. She accepted these adventures as inevitable; she had been so over-warned before leaving home. Cunning prevented her giving her address or name, and if one of her partners wanted to see her again, and named a time and a street number, she was likely to forget or to meet someone else on the way. She was just as happy in the cinema, alone, or looking at displays of eau de cologne in shops.

Reduced to perplexity, she would glance again at the book. Read?

"I might get it dirty."

"But books are to be read, Bernadette."

She would hang her head, wondering what they wanted, wish-ing they would go away. At last she had given in. It was in the autumn, the start of her period of fear. She had been dusting in Robbie's room. Unexpectedly, in that ghostly way they had, he was beside her at the bookcase. Blindly shy, she remembered what Mrs. Knight, all tact and kindness and firm common sense, had said that morning: that Bernadette sometimes smelled of perspi-ration, and that this was unpleasant. Probably Mr. Knight was thinking this now. In a panicky motion her hand flew to *L'Amant de Lady Chatterley*, which Nora had brought from Paris so that she could test the blundering ways of censorship. (The English version had been held at customs, the French let through, which gave Nora ammunition for a whole winter.)

"You won't like that," Robbie had said. "Still..." He pulled it out of the bookcase. She took the book to her room, wrapped it carefully in newspaper, and placed it in a drawer. A few days later she knocked on the door of Robbie's room and returned *L'Amant de Lady Chatterley*.

"You enjoyed it?"

"*Oui. Merci.*"

He gave her *La Porte Etroite*. She wrapped it in newspaper and placed it in a drawer for five days. When she gave it back, he chose for her one of the Claudine series, and then, rather doubtfully, *Le Rouge et le Noir*.

"Did you like the book by Stendhal, Bernadette?"

"*Oui. Merci.*"

To dinner guests, Nora now said, "Oh, our Bernadette! Not a year out of Abitibi, and she was reading Gide and Colette. She knows more about French literature than we do. She goes through Stendhal like a breeze. She adores Giraudoux." When Bernadette, grim with the effort of remembering what to do next, entered the room, everyone would look at her and she would wonder what she had done wrong.

During the party rehearsal, Robbie, snubbed, went up to bed. He knew that Nora would never forgive him if he hadn't recovered by evening. She regarded a cold in the head as something that could be turned off with a little effort; indeed, she considered any symptom of illness in her husband an act of aggression directed against herself. He sat up in bed, bitterly cold in spite of three blankets and a bathrobe. It was the chill of grippe, in the center of his bones; no external warmth could reach it. He heard Nora go out for some last-minute shopping, and he heard Bernadette's radio in the kitchen.

"*Sans amour, on est rien du tout,*" Edith Piaf sang. The song ended and a commercial came on. He tried not to hear.

On the table by his bed were books Nora had given him for Christmas. He had decided, that winter, to reread some of the writers who had influenced him as a young man. He began this project with the rather large idea of summing himself up as a person, trying to find out what had determined the direction of his life. In college, he remembered, he had promised himself a life of action and freedom and political adventure. Perhaps everyone had then. But surely he, Robbie Knight, should have moved on to something other than a pseudo-Tudor house in a suburb of Montreal. He had been considered promising—an attractive young man with a middling-good brain, a useful background, unexpected opinions, and considerable charm. He did not consider himself unhappy, but he was beginning to wonder what he was doing, and why. He had decided to carry out his reassessment program in secret. Unfortunately, he could not help telling Nora, who promptly gave him the complete Orwell, bound in green.

He read with the conviction of habit. There was Orwell's Spain, the Spain of action and his university days. There was also the Spain he and Nora knew as tourists, a poor and dusty country where tourists became colicky because of the oil. For the moment, he forgot what he had seen, just as he could sometimes forget he had not become a playwright. He regretted the Spain he had missed, but the death of a cause no longer moved him. So far, the only result of his project was a feeling of loss. Leaving Spain, he turned to an essay on England. It was an essay he had not read until now. He skipped about, restless, and suddenly stopped at this: "I have often been struck by the peculiar easy completeness, the perfect symmetry as it were, of a working-class interior at its best. Especially on winter evenings after tea, when the fire glows in the open range and dances mirrored in the steel fender, when Father, in shirt-sleeves, sits in the rocking chair at one side of the fire reading the racing finals, and Mother sits on the other with her sewing, and the children are happy with a penn'orth of mint humbugs, and the dog lolls roasting himself on the rag mat..."

Because he had a cold and Nora had gone out and left him on a snowy miserable afternoon, he saw in this picture everything missing in his life. He felt frozen and left out. Robbie had never been inside the kitchen of a working-class home; it did not occur to him that the image he had just been given might be idyllic or sentimental. He felt only that he and Nora had missed something, and that he ought to tell her so; but he knew that it would lead to a long bout of analytical talk, and he didn't feel up to that. He blew his nose, pulled the collar of his dressing gown up around his ears, and settled back on the pillows.

Bernadette knocked at the door. Nora had told her to prepare a tray of tea, rum, and aspirin at four o'clock. It was now half past four, and Bernadette wondered if Mr. Knight would betray her to Mrs. Knight. Bernadette's sleeves were rolled up, and she brought with her an aura of warmth and good food. She had, in fact, been cooking a ham for the party. Her hair was up in the hideous snails again, but it gave her, Robbie thought, the look of a hard-working woman—a look his own wife achieved only by seeming totally exhausted.

"*Y a un* book, too," said Bernadette, in her coarse, flat little voice. She put the tray down with care. "*Je l'ai mis sur le* tray." She indicated the new Prix Goncourt, which Robbie had lent her the day it arrived. He saw at once that the pages were still uncut.

"You didn't like it?"

"Oh, *oui*," she said automatically. "*Merci*."

Never before had a lie seemed to him more pathetic, or more justified. Instead of taking the book, or his tea, he gripped Bernadette's plump, strong forearm. The room was full of warmth and comfort. Bernadette had brought this atmosphere with her; it was her native element. She was the world they had missed sixteen years before, and they, stupidly, had been trying to make her read books. He held her arm, gripping it. She stared back at him, and he saw that she was frightened. He let her go, furious with himself, and said, rather coldly, "Do you ever think about your home in Abitibi?"

"*Oui*," she said flatly.

"Some of the farms up there are very modern now, I believe," he said, sounding as if he were angry with her. "Was yours?"

She shrugged. "*On a pas la* television, *nous*," she said.

"I didn't think you had. What about your kitchen. What was your kitchen like at home, Bernadette?"

"*Sais pas*," said Bernadette, rubbing the released arm on the back of her dress. "It's big," she offered, after some thought.

"Thank you," said Robbie. He went back to his book, still furious, and upset. She stood still, uncertain, a fat dark little creature not much older than his own elder daughter. He turned a page, not reading, and at last she went away.

Deeply bewildered, Bernadette returned to the kitchen and contemplated the cooling ham. She seldom thought about home. Now her memory, set in motion, brought up the image of a large, crowded room. The prevailing smell was the odor of the men's boots as they came in from the outbuildings. The table, masked with oilcloth, was always set between meals, the thick plates turned upside down, the spoons in a glass jar. At the center of the table, never removed, were the essentials: butter, vinegar, canned jam with the lid of the can half opened and wrenched back, ketchup, a tin of molasses glued to its saucer. In winter, the washing hung over the stove. By the stove, every year but the last two or three, had stood a basket containing a baby—a wailing, swaddled baby, smelling sad and sour. Only a few of Bernadette's mother's children had straggled up past the infant stage. Death and small children were inextricably knotted in Bernadette's consciousness. As a child she had watched an infant brother turn blue and choke to death. She had watched two others die of diphtheria. The innocent dead became angels; there was no reason to grieve. Bernadette's mother did all she could; terrified of injections and vaccines, she barred the door to the district nurse. She bound her infants tightly to prevent excess motion, she kept them by the flaming heat of the stove, she fed them a bouillon of warm water and cornstarch to make them fat. When Bernadette thought of the kitchen at home, she thought of her mother's pregnant figure, and her swollen feet, in unlaced tennis shoes.

Now she herself was pregnant. Perhaps Mr. Knight knew, and that was why he had asked about her mother's kitchen. Sensing a connection between her mother and herself, she believed he had seen it as well. Nothing was too farfetched, no wisdom, no perception, for these people. Their mental leaps and guesses were as mysterious to her as those of saints, or of ghosts.

Nora returned and, soon afterward, Robbie wandered downstairs. His wife had told him to get up (obviously forgetting that it was she who had sent him to bed) so that she could tidy the room. She did not ask how he felt and seemed to take it for granted that he had recovered. He could not help comparing her indifference with the solicitude of Bernadette, who had brought him tea and rum. He began comparing Bernadette with other women he had known well. His mistresses, *faute de mieux*, had been girls with jobs and little apartments. They had in common with Nora a desire to discuss the situation; they were alarmingly likely to burst into tears after lovemaking because Robbie didn't love them enough or because he had to go home for dinner. He had never known a working-class girl, other than the women his wife employed. (Even privately, he no longer used the expression "of the people.") As far as he could determine now, girls of Bernadette's sort were highly moral, usually lived with their parents until marriage, and then disappeared from sight, like Moslem women. He might have achieved an interesting union, gratifying a laudable social curiosity, during his college days, but he had met Nora straightaway. He had been disappointed to learn that her father did not work in a factory. There was an unbridgeable gap, he had since discovered, between the girl whose father went off to work with a lunch pail and the daughter of a man who ate macaroni-and-cheese in the company cafeteria. In the midst of all her solicitude for the underprivileged, Nora never let him forget it. On the three occasions when she had caught him out in a love affair, among her first questions had been "Where does she come from? What does she do?"

Robbie decided to apologize to Bernadette. He had frightened her, which he had no right to do. He no longer liked the classic role he had set for himself, the kindly educator of young servant girls. It had taken only a glimpse of his thin, busy wife to put the picture into perspective. He allowed himself one last, uncharitable thought, savoring it: Compared with Bernadette, Nora looked exactly like a furled umbrella.

Bernadette was sitting at the kitchen table. The ham had been put away, the room aired. She was polishing silver for the party, using a smelly antiseptic pink paste. He no longer felt the atmo-sphere of warmth and food and comfort Bernadette had brought up to his room. She did not look up. She regarded her own up-side-down image in the bowl of a spoon. Her hands moved slowly, then stopped. What did he want now?

Before coming to Montreal, Bernadette had been warned about the licentious English—reserved on the surface, hypocriti-cal, infinitely wicked underneath—and she had, in a sense, ac-cepted it as inevitable that Mr. Knight would try to seduce her. When it was over, she would have another sin to account for. Mr. Knight, a Protestant, would not have sinned at all. Unique in her sin, she felt already lonely. His apology sent her off into the strange swamp world again, a world in which there was no foot-ing; she had the same feeling as when they tried to make her read books. What was he sorry about? She looked dumbly around the kitchen. She could hear Nora upstairs, talking on the telephone.

Robbie also heard her and thought: Bernadette is afraid of Nora. The idea that the girl might say something to his wife crossed his mind, and he was annoyed to realize that Nora's first concern would be for Bernadette's feelings. His motives and his behavior they would discuss later, over a drink. He no longer knew what he wanted to say to Bernadette. He made a great show of drinking a glass of water and went out.

By evening, Robbie's temperature was over ninety-nine. Nora did not consider it serious. She felt that he was deliberately trying to ruin the party, and said so. "Take one good stiff drink," she said. "That's all you need."

He saw the party through a feverish haze. Nora was on top of the world, controlling the room, clergy-baiting, but in the most charming manner. No priest could possibly have taken offense, particularly a nice young priest from Belgium, interested in mod-ern art and preceded by a liberal reputation. He could not reply; his English was limited. Besides, as Nora kept pointing out, he didn't know the situation in Quebec. He could only make little grimaces, acknowledging her thrusts, comically chewing the stem of a cold pipe.

"Until you know this part of the world, you don't know your own Church," Nora told him, smiling, not aggressive.

The English-Canadians in the room agreed, glancing nervously at the French. French Canada was represented by three journalists huddled on a couch. (Nora had promised the priest, as if offering hors d'oeuvres, representatives of what she called "our chief ethnic groups.") The three journalists supported Nora, once it was made plain that clergy-baiting and French-baiting were not going to be combined. Had their wives been there, they might not have concurred so brightly; but Nora could seldom persuade her French-Canadian finds to bring their wives along. The drinking of Anglo-Saxon women rather alarmed them, and they felt that their wives, genteel, fluffy-haired, in good little dresses and strings of pearls, would disappoint and be disappointed. Nora never insisted. She believed in emancipation, but no one was more vocal in deploring the French-Canadian who spoke hard, flat English and had become Anglicized out of all recognition. Robbie, feverish and disloyal, almost expected her to sweep the room with her hand and, pointing to the trio of journalists, announce, "I found them in an old barn and bought them for five dollars each. I've sandpapered and waxed them, and there they are."

From the Church she went on to Bernadette. She followed the familiar pattern, explaining how environment had in a few months overcome generations of intellectual poverty.

"Bernadette reads Gide and Lawrence," she said, choosing writers the young priest was bound to disapprove of. "She adores Colette."

"Excellent," he said, tepid.

Bernadette came in, walking with care, as if on a tightrope. She had had difficulty with her party uniform and she wondered if it showed.

"Bernadette," Nora said, "how many children did your mother have?"

"Thirteen, Madame," said the girl. Accustomed to this interrogation, she continued to move around the room, remembering Nora's instructions during the rehearsal.

"In how many years?" Nora said.

"Fifteen."

"And how many are living?"

"Six, Madame."

The young priest stopped chewing his pipe and said quietly, in French, "Are you sorry that your seven brothers and sisters died, Bernadette?"

Jolted out of her routine, Bernadette replied at once, as if she had often thought about it, "Oh, no. If they had lived, they would have had to grow up and work hard, and the boys would have to go to war, when there is war, to fight—" About to say, "fight for the English," she halted. "Now they are little angels, praying for their mother," she said.

"Where?" said the priest.

"In Heaven."

"What does an angel look like, Bernadette?" he said.

She gave him her hypnotized gaze and said, "They are very small. They have small golden heads and little wings. Some are tall and wear pink and blue dresses. You don't see them because of the clouds."

"I see. Thank you," said Nora, cutting in, and the student of Gide and Colette moved off to the kitchen with her tray.

It ruined the evening. The party got out of hand. People stopped talking about the things Nora wanted them to talk about, and the ethnic groups got drunk and began to shout. Nora heard someone talking about the fluctuating dollar, and someone else said to her, of television, "Well, Nora, still holding out?"—when only a few months ago anyone buying a set had been sheepish and embarrassed and had said it was really for the maid.

When it was all over and Nora was running the vacuum so that there would be less for Bernadette to do the next day, she frowned and looked tired and rather old. The party had gone wrong. The guest of honor had slipped away early. Robbie had gone to bed before midnight without a word to anybody. Nora had felt outside the party, bored and disappointed, wishing to God they would all clear out. She had stood alone by the fireplace, wondering at the access of generosity that had led her to invite these ill-matched and noisy people to her home. Her parties in the past had been so different: everyone had praised her hospitality, applauded her leadership, exclaimed at her good sense. Indignant with her over some new piece of political or religious chicanery, they had been grateful for her combativeness, and had said so—more and more as the evening wore on. Tonight, they seemed to have come just as they went everywhere else, for the liquor and good food. A rot, a feeling of complacency, had set in. She had looked around the room and thought, with an odd little shock: How old they all seem! Just then one of her ethnic treasures—a recently immigrated German doctor—had come up to her and said, "That little girl is pregnant."

"What?"

"The little servant girl. One has only to look."

Afterward, she wondered how she could have failed to notice. Everything gave Bernadette away: her eyes, her skin, the characteristic thickening of her waist. There were the intangible signs, too, the signs that were not quite physical. In spite of her own motherhood, Nora detested, with a sort of fastidious horror, any of the common references to pregnancy. But even to herself, now, she could think of Bernadette only in terms of the most vulgar expressions, the terminology her own family (long discarded, never invited here) had employed. Owing to a "mistake," Bernadette was probably "caught." She was beginning to "show." She was at least four months "gone." It seemed to Nora that she had better go straight to the point with Bernadette. The girl was under twenty-one. It was quite possible that the Knights would be considered responsible. If the doctor had been mistaken, then Bernadette could correct her. If Bernadette were to tell Nora to mind her own business, so much the better, because it would mean that Bernadette had more character than she seemed to have. Nora had no objection to apologizing in either instance.

Because of the party and the extra work involved, Bernadette had been given the next afternoon off. She spent the morning cleaning. Nora kept out of the way. Robbie stayed in bed, mulishly maintaining that he wasn't feeling well. It was after lunch, and Bernadette was dressed and ready to go downtown to a movie, when Nora decided not to wait any longer. She cornered Bernadette in the kitchen and, facing her, suddenly remembered how, as a child, she had cornered field mice with a flashlight and then drowned them. Bernadette seemed to know what was coming; she exuded fear. She faced her tormentor with a beating, animal heart.

Nora sat down at the kitchen table and began, as she frequently had done with Robbie, with the words "I think we ought to talk about a certain situation." Bernadette stared. "Is there anything you'd like to tell me?" Nora said.

"No," said Bernadette, shaking her head.

"But you're worried about something. Something is wrong. Isn't that true?"

"No."

"Bernadette, I want to help you. Sit down. Tell me, are you pregnant?"

"I don't understand."

"Yes, you do. *Un enfant. Un bébé.* Am I right?"

"*Sais pas,*" said Bernadette. She looked at the clock over Nora's head.

"*Bernadette.*"

It was getting late. Bernadette said, "Yes. I think so. Yes."

"You poor little mutt," said Nora. "Don't keep standing there like that. Sit down here, by the table. Take off your coat. We must talk about it. This is much more important than a movie." Bernadette remained standing, in hat and coat. "Who is it?" said Nora. "I didn't know you had . . . I mean, I didn't know you knew anyone here. Tell me. It's most important. I'm not angry." Bernadette continued to look up at the clock, as if there were no other point in the room on which she dared fix her eyes. "Bern*adette*!" Nora said. "I've just asked you a question. Who is the boy?"

"*Un monsieur*," said Bernadette.

Did she mean by that an older man, or was Bernadette, in using the word "*monsieur*," implying a social category? "*Quel monsieur?*" said Nora.

Bernadette shrugged. She stole a glance at Nora, and something about the oblique look suggested more than fear or evasiveness. A word came into Nora's mind: sly.

"Can you . . . I mean, is it someone you're going to marry?" But no. In that case, he would have been a nice young boy, someone of Bernadette's own background. Nora would have met him. He would have been caught in the kitchen drinking Robbie's beer. He would have come every Sunday and every Thursday afternoon to call for Bernadette. "Is it someone you *can* marry?" Nora said. Silence. "Don't be afraid," said Nora, deliberately making her voice kind. She longed to shake the girl, even slap her face. It was idiotic; here was Bernadette in a terrible predicament, and all she could do was stand, shuffling from one foot to the other, as if a movie were the most important thing in the world. "If he isn't already married," Nora said, "which I'm beginning to suspect is the case, he'll marry you. You needn't worry about that. I'll deal with it, or Mr. Knight will."

"*Pas possible*," said Bernadette, low.

"Then I was right. He *is* married." Bernadette looked up at the clock, desperate. She wanted the conversation to stop. "A married man," Nora repeated. "*Un monsieur.*" An unfounded and wholly outrageous idea rushed into her mind. Dismissing it, she said, "When did it happen?"

"*Sais pas.*"

"Don't be silly. That really is a very silly reply. Of course you know. You've only had certain hours out of this house."

The truth of it was that Bernadette did not know. She didn't know his name or whether he was married or even where she could find him again, even if she had desired such a thing. He seemed the least essential factor. Lacking words, she gave Nora the sidelong glance that made her seem coarse and deceitful. She is so uninnocent, Nora thought, surprised and a little repelled. It occurred to her that in spite of her long marriage and her two children, she knew less than Bernadette. While she was thinking about Bernadette and her lover, there came into her mind the language of the street. She remembered words that had shocked and fascinated her as a child. That was Bernadette's fault. It was Bernadette's atmosphere, Nora thought, excusing herself to an imaginary censor. She said, "We must know when your baby will be born. Don't you think so?" Silence. She tried again: "How long has it been since you . . . I mean, since you missed . . ."

"One hundred and twenty-seven days," said Bernadette. She was so relieved to have, at last, a question that she could answer that she brought it out in a kind of shout.

"My God. What are you going to do?"

"*Sais pas.*"

"Oh, Bernadette!" Nora cried. "But you must think." The naming of a number of days made the whole situation so much more immediate. Nora felt that they ought to be doing some-thing—telephoning, writing letters, putting some plan into mo-tion. "We shall have to think for you," she said. "I shall speak to Mr. Knight."

"No," said Bernadette, trembling, suddenly coming to life. "Not Mr. Knight."

Nora leaned forward on the table. She clasped her hands together, hard. She looked at Bernadette. "Is there a special reason why I shouldn't speak to Mr. Knight?" she said.

"*Oui.*" Bernadette had lived for so many days now in her sea of nausea and fear that it had become a familiar element. There were greater fears and humiliations, among them that Mr. Knight, who was even more baffling and dangerous than his wife, should try to discuss this thing with Bernadette. She remembered what he had said the day before, and how he had held her arm. "He must know," said Bernadette. "I think he must already know."

"You had better go on," said Nora, after a moment. "You'll miss your bus." She sat quite still and watched Bernadette's progress down the drive. She looked at the second-hand imitation-seal coat that had been Bernadette's first purchase (and Nora's despair) and the black velveteen snow boots trimmed with dyed fur and tied with tasselled cords. Bernadette's purse hung over her arm. She had the walk of a fat girl—the short steps, the ungainly little trot.

It was unreasonable, Nora knew it was unreasonable; but there was so much to reinforce the idea—"*Un monsieur,*" and the fact that he already knew ("He must know," Bernadette had said)— and then there was Bernadette's terror when she said she was going to discuss it with him. She thought of Robbie's interest in Bernadette's education. She thought of Robbie in the past, his unwillingness to remain faithful, his absence of courage and common sense. Recalling Bernadette's expression, prepared now to call it corrupt rather than sly, she felt that the girl had considered herself deeply involved with Nora; that she knew Nora much better than she should.

Robbie had decided to come downstairs, and was sitting by the living-room fire. He was reading a detective novel. Beside him was a drink.

"Get you a drink?" he said, without lifting his eyes, when Nora came in.

"Don't bother."

He went on reading. He looked so innocent, so unaware that his life was shattered. Nora remembered how he had been when she had first known him, so pleasant and dependent and good-looking and stupid. She remembered how he had been going to write a play, and how she had wanted to change the world, or at least Quebec. Tears of fatigue and strain came into her eyes. She felt that the failure of last night's party had been a symbol of the end. Robbie had done something cheap and dishonorable, but he reflected their world. The world was ugly, Montreal was ugly, the street outside the window contained houses of surpassing ugliness. There was nothing left to discuss but television and the fluctuating dollar; that was what the world had become. The children were in boarding school because Nora didn't trust herself to bring them up. The living room was full of amusing peasant furniture because she didn't trust her own taste. Robbie was afraid of her and liked humiliating her by demonstrating again and again that he preferred nearly any other woman in bed. That was the truth of things. Why had she never faced it until now?

She said, "Robbie, can I talk to you?" Reluctant, he looked away from his book. She said, "I just wanted to tell you about a dream. Last night I dreamed you died. I dreamed that there was nothing I could do to bring you back, and that I had to adjust all my thoughts to the idea of going on without you. It was a terrible, shattering feeling." She intended this to be devastating, a prelude to the end. Unfortunately, she had had this dream before, and Robbie was bored with it. They had already discussed what it might mean, and he had no desire to go into it now.

"I wish to God you wouldn't keep on dreaming I died," he said.

She waited. There was nothing more. She blinked back her tears and said, "Well, listen to this, then. I want to talk about Bernadette. What do you know, exactly, about Bernadette's difficulties?"

"Has Bernadette got difficulties?" The floor under his feet heaved and settled. He had never been so frightened in his life.

Part of his mind told him that nothing had happened. He had been ill, a young girl had brought warmth and comfort into his room, and he wanted to touch her. What was wrong with that? Why should it frighten him so much that Nora knew? He closed his eyes. It was hopeless; Nora was not going to let him get on with the book. Nora looked without any sentiment at all at the twin points where his hairline was moving back. "Does she seem sort of unsettled?" he asked.

"That's a way of putting it. Sometimes you have a genuine talent for irony."

"Oh, hell," said Robbie, suddenly fed up with Nora's cat-and-mouse. "I don't feel like talking about anything. Let's skip it for now. It's not important."

"Perhaps you'd better tell me what you consider important," Nora said. "Then we'll see what we can skip." She wondered how he could sit there, concerned with his mild grippe, or his hangover, when the whole structure of their marriage was falling apart. Already, she saw the bare bones of the room they sat in, the rugs rolled, the cracks that would show in the walls when they took the pictures down.

He sighed, giving in. He closed his book and put it beside his drink. "It was just that yesterday when I was feeling so lousy she brought me—she brought me a book. One of those books we keep lending her. She hadn't even cut the pages. The whole thing's a farce. She doesn't even look at them."

"Probably not," said Nora. "Or else she does and that's the whole trouble. To get straight to the point, which I can see you don't want to do, Bernadette has told me she's having a baby. She takes it for granted that you already know. She's about four months under way, which makes yesterday seem rather pointless."

Robbie said impatiently, "We're not talking about the same thing." He had not really absorbed what Nora was saying; she spoke so quickly, and got so many things in all at once. His first reaction was astonishment, and a curious feeling that Bernadette had deceived him. Then the whole import of Nora's speech entered his mind and became clear. He said, "Are you crazy? Are you out of your mind? Are you completely crazy?" Anger paralyzed him. He was unable to think of words or form them on his tongue. At last he said, "It's too bad that when I'm angry I can't do anything except feel sick. Or maybe it's just as well. You're crazy, Nora. You get these—I don't know—You get these ideas." He said, "If I'd hit you then, I might have killed you."

It had so seldom occurred in their life together that Robbie was in the right morally that Nora had no resources. She had always triumphed. Robbie's position had always been indefensible. His last remark was so completely out of character that she scarcely heard it. He had spoken in an ordinary tone of voice. She was frightened, but only because she had made an insane mistake and it was too late to take it back. Bravely, because there was nothing else to do, she went on about Bernadette. "She doesn't seem to know what to do. She's a minor, so I'm afraid it rather falls on us. There is a place in Vermont, a private place, where they take these girls and treat them well, rather like a boarding school. I can get her in, I think. Having her admitted to the States could be your end of it."

"I suppose you think that's going to be easy," Robbie said bitterly. "I suppose you think they admit pregnant unmarried minors every day of the year."

"None of it is easy!" Nora cried, losing control. "Whose fault is it?"

"It's got nothing to do with me!" said Robbie, shouting at her. "Christ Almighty, get that through your head!"

They let silence settle again. Robbie found that he was trembling. As he had said, it was physically difficult for him to be angry.

Nora said, "Yes, Vermont," as if she were making notes. She was determined to behave as if everything were normal. She knew that unless she established the tone quickly, nothing would ever be normal again.

"What will she do with it? Give it out for adoption?" said Robbie, in spite of himself diverted by details.

"She'll send it north, to her family," said Nora. "There's always room on a farm. It will make up for the babies that died. They look on those things, on birth and on death, as acts of nature, like the changing of the seasons. They don't think of them as catastrophes."

Robbie wanted to say, You're talking about something you've read, now. They'll be too ashamed to have Bernadette or the baby around; this is Quebec. But he was too tired to offer a new field of discussion. He was as tired as if they had been talking for hours. He said, "I suppose this Vermont place, this school or whatever it is, has got to be paid for."

"It certainly does." Nora looked tight and cold at this hint of stinginess. It was unnatural for her to be in the wrong, still less to remain on the defensive. She had taken the position now that even if Robbie were not responsible, he had somehow upset Bernadette. In some manner, he could be found guilty and made to admit it. She would find out about it later. Meanwhile, she felt morally bound to make him pay.

"Will it be expensive, do you think?"

She gave him a look, and he said nothing more.


Bernadette sat in the comforting dark of the cinema. It was her favorite kind of film, a musical comedy in full color. They had reached the final scene. The hero and heroine, separated because of a stupid quarrel for more than thirty years, suddenly found themselves in the same nightclub, singing the same song. They had gray hair but youthful faces. All the people around them were happy to see them together. They clapped and smiled. Bernadette smiled, too. She did not identify herself with the heroine, but with the people looking on. She would have liked to have gone to a nightclub in a low-cut dress and applauded such a scene. She believed in love and in uncomplicated stories of love, even though it was something she had never experienced or seen around her. She did not really expect it to happen to her, or to anyone she knew.

For the first time, her child moved. She was so astonished that she looked at the people sitting on either side of her, wondering if they had noticed. They were looking at the screen. For the first time, then, she thought of it as a child, here, alive—not a state of terror but something to be given a name, clothed, fed, and baptized. Where and how and when it would be born she did not question. Mrs. Knight would do something. Somebody would. It would be born, and it would die. That it would die she never doubted. She was uncertain of so much else; her own body was a mystery, nothing had ever been explained. At home, in spite of her mother's pregnancies, the birth of the infants was shrouded in secrecy and, like their conception, suspicion of sin. This baby was Bernadette's own; when it died, it would pray for her, and her alone, for all of eternity. No matter what she did with the rest of her life, she would have an angel of her own, praying for her. Oddly secure in the dark, the dark of the cinema, the dark of her personal fear, she felt protected. She thought: *Il prie pour moi.* She saw, as plainly as if it had been laid in her arms, her child, her personal angel, white and swaddled, baptized, innocent, ready for death.

*1957*

# TRAVELERS MUST BE CONTENT

DREAMS OF chaos were Wishart's meat; he was proud of their diversity, and of his trick of emerging from mortal danger unscathed. The slightest change in pace provoked a nightmare, so that it was no surprise to him when, falling asleep in his compartment a few seconds before the train arrived at Cannes, he had a dream that lasted hours about a sinking ferryboat outside the harbor. Millions of limp victims bowled elegantly out of the waves, water draining from their skin and hair. There were a few survivors, but neither they nor the officials who had arrived in great haste knew what to do next. They milled about on the rocky shore looking unsteady and pale. Even the victims seemed more drunk than dead. Out of this deplorable confusion Wishart strode, suitably dressed in a bathing costume. He shook his head gravely, but without pity, and moved out and away. As usual, he had foreseen the disaster but failed to give warning. Explanations unrolled in his sleeping mind: "I never interfere. It was up to them to ask me. They knew I was there." His triumph was only on a moral level. He had no physical vanity at all. He observed with detachment his drooping bathing trunks, his skinny legs, his white freckled hands, his brushed-out fringe of graying hair. None of it humbled him. His body had never given him much concern.

Wishart was pleased with the dream. No one was gifted with a subconscious quite like his, tirelessly creative, producing without effort any number of small visual poems in excellent taste. This one might have been a ballet, he decided, or, better still, because of the black-and-white groupings and the unmoving light, an experimental film, to be called simply and cryptically "Wishart's Dream." He could manipulate this name without conceit, for it was not his own. That is, it was not the name that had been gummed onto his personality some forty years before without thought or care; "Wishart" was selected, like all the pieces of his fabricated life. Even the way he looked was contrived, and if, on bad days, he resembled nothing so much as a failed actor afflicted with dreams, he accepted this resemblance, putting it down to artistic fatigue. He did not consider himself a failed anything. Success can only be measured in terms of distance traveled, and in Wishart's case it had been a long flight. No wonder I look worn, he would think, seeing his sagged face in the glass. He had lived one of society's most gruelling roles, the escape from an English slum. He had been the sturdy boy with visions in his eyes. "Scramble, scrape, and scholarship" should have been written on his brow, and, inside balloons emerging from his brain, "a talent for accents" and "a genius for kicking the past from his shoes." He had other attributes, of course, but it wasn't necessary to crowd the image. Although Wishart's journey was by no means unusual, he had managed it better than nearly anyone. Most scramblers and scrapers take the inherited structure with them, patching and camouflaging as they can, but Wishart had knocked his flat. He had given himself a name, parents, and a class of his choice. Now, at forty-two, he passed as an English gentleman in America, where he lived, and as an awfully decent American when he went to England. He had little sense of humor where his own affairs were concerned, no more than a designer of comic postcards can be funny about his art, but he did sometimes see it as a joke on life that the quirks and crotchets with which he was laced had grown out of an imaginary past. Having given himself a tall squire of a father who adored horses and dogs, Wishart first simulated, then genuinely felt a disgust and terror of the beasts. The phantom parent was a brandy-swiller; Wishart wouldn't drink. Indeed, as created by his equally phantom son, the squire was impeccably *bien élevé* but rather a brute; he had not been wholly kind to Wishart, the moody, spindly boy. The only person out of the real past he remembered without loathing was a sister, Glad, who had become a servant at eleven and had taught him how to eat with a knife and fork. At the beginning, in the old days, before he had been intelligent enough to settle for the squire but had hinted at something grand, he had often been the victim of sudden frights, when an element, hidden and threatening, had bubbled under his feet and he had felt the soles of his shoes growing warm, so thin, so friable was the crust of his poor world. Nowadays, he moved in a gassy atmosphere of good will and feigned successes. He seemed invulnerable. Strangers meeting him for the first time often thought he must be celebrated, and wondered why they had never heard of him before. There was no earthly reason for anyone's having done so; he was a teacher of dramatics in a preparatory school, and once this was revealed, and the shoddiness of the school established, it required Wishart's most hypnotic gifts, his most persuasive monologue, to maintain the effect of his person. As a teacher he was barely adequate, and if he had been an American his American school would never have kept him. His British personality—sardonic, dry—replaced ability, or even ambition. Privately, he believed he was wasted in a world of men and boys, and had never bothered giving them the full blaze of his Wishart creation; he saved it for a world of women. Like many spiteful, snobbish, fussy men, or a certain type of murderer, Wishart chose his friends among middle-aged solitary women. These women were widowed or divorced, and lived in places Wishart liked to visit. Every year, then, shedding his working life, a shining Wishart took off for Europe, where he spent the summer alighting here and there, depending on the topography of his invitations. He lived on his hostesses, without shame. He was needed and liked. His invitations began arriving at Christmas. He knew that women who will fret over wasting the last bit of soap, or a torn postage stamp, or an unused return ticket, will pay without a murmur for the company of a man.

Wishart was no hired companion—carrier of coats, fetcher of aspirin, walker of dachshunds. He considered it enough to be there, supplying gossip and a listening ear. Often Wishart's friends took it for granted he was homosexual, which was all to the good. He was the chosen minstrel, the symbolic male, who would never cause "trouble." He knew this and it was a galling thought. But he had never managed to correct it. He was much too busy keeping his personality in place so that it wouldn't slip or collapse even in his dreams. He had never found time for such an enervating activity as proving his virility, which might not only divert the movement of his ambitions but could, indeed, take up an entire life. He had what he wanted, and it was enough; he had never desired a fleet of oil tankers. It sufficed him to be accepted here and there. His life would probably have been easier if he had not felt obliged to be something special on two continents, but he was compelled to return to England now, every year, and make them accept him. They accepted him as an American, but that was part of the buried joke. Sometimes he ventured a few risks, such as, "We were most frightfully poor when I was a child," but he knew he still hadn't achieved the right tone. The most successful impostures are based on truth, but how poor is poor, and how closely should he approach this burning fact? Particularly in England, where the whole structure could collapse for the sake of a vowel.

He got down from the train, holding his artfully bashed-up suitcase, and saw, in the shadow of the station, Mrs. Bonnie McCarthy, his American friend. She was his relay in the South of France, a point of refreshment between the nasal sculptress in London, who had been his first hostess of the season, and a Mrs. Sebastian in Venice. It would have been sweet for Wishart at this moment if he could have summoned an observer from the past, a control to establish how far he had come. Supposing one of the populated waves of his dream had deposited sister Glad on shore? He saw her in cap and apron, a dour little girl, watching him being greeted by this woman who would not have as much as spat in their direction if she had known them in the old days. At this thought he felt a faint stir, like the rumor of an earthquake some distance away. But he knew he had nothing to fear and that the source of terror was in his own mistakes. It had been a mistake to remember Glad.

"Wishart," his friend said gravely, without breaking her pose. Leaning on a furled peach-colored parasol, she gave the appearance of living a minute of calm in the middle of a hounding social existence. She turned to him the soft, myopic eyes that had been admired when she was a girl. Her hair was cut in the year's fashion, like an inverted peony, and she seemed to Wishart beautifully dressed. She might have been waiting for something beyond Wishart and better than a friend—some elegant paradise he could not imagine, let alone attain. His admiration of her (her charm, wealth, and aspirations) flowed easily into admiration of himself; after all, he had achieved this friend. Almost tearful with self-felicitation, he forgot how often he and Bonnie had quarrelled in the past. Their kiss of friendship here outside the station was real.

"Did you get my telegram?" he said, beginning the nervous remarks that preceded and followed all his journeys. He had prepared his coming with a message: "Very depressed London like old blotting paper longing for sea sun you." This wire he had signed "Baronne Putbus." There was no address, so that Bonnie was unable to return a killing answer she would have signed "Lysistrata."

"I died," Bonnie said, looking with grave, liquid eyes. "I just simply perished." After the nasal sculptress and her educated vowels, Bonnie's slight drawl fell gently on his ear. She continued to look at him gaily, without making a move, and he began to feel some unease in the face of so much bright expectancy. He suddenly thought, "Good God, has she fallen in love?," adding in much smaller print, "With me?" Accidents of that sort had happened in the past. Now, Wishart's personality being an object he used with discretion, when he was doubtful, or simply at rest, he became a sort of mirror. Reflected in this mirror, Bonnie McCarthy saw that she was still pretty and smart. Dear darling Wishart! He also gave back her own air of waiting. Each thought that the other must have received a piece of wonderful news. Wishart was not envious; he knew that the backwash of someone else's good fortune can be very pleasant indeed, and he waited for Bonnie's tidings to be revealed. Perhaps she had rented a villa, so that he would not have to stay in a hotel. That would be nice.

"The hotel isn't far," Bonnie said, stirring them into motion at last. "Do you want to walk a little, Wishart? It's a lovely, lovely day."

No villa, then; and if the hotel was nearby, no sense paying a porter. Carrying his suitcase, he followed her through the station and into the sudden heat of the Mediterranean day. Later he would hate these streets, and the milling, sweating, sunburned crowd; he would hurry past the sour-milk-smelling cafés with his hand over his nose. But now, at first sight, Cannes looked as it had sounded when he said the word in London—a composition in clear chalk colors: blue, yellow, white. Everything was intensely shaded or intensely bright, hard and yellow on the streets, dark as velvet inside the bars.

"I hope you aren't cross because Florence isn't here," Bonnie said. "She was perishing to meet your train, but the poor baby had something in her eye. A grain of sand. She had to go to an oculist to have it taken out. You'll love seeing her now, Wishart. She's getting a style, you know? Everyone notices her. Somebody said to me on the beach—a total stranger—somebody said, 'Your daughter is like a Tanagra.'"

"Of which there are so many fakes," Wishart remarked.

He did not have a great opinion of his friend's intelligence, and may have thought that a slight obtuseness also affected her hearing. It was insensitive of her to mention Flor now, just when Wishart was feeling so well. From the beginning, their friendship had been marred by the existence of Bonnie's daughter, a spoiled, sulky girl he had vainly tried to admire.

"There are literally millions of men chasing her," Bonnie said. "I've never seen anything like it. Every time we go to the beach or the casino—"

"I'm surprised she hasn't offered you a son-in-law," he said. "But I suppose she is still too young."

"Oh, she isn't!" Bonnie cried, standing still. "Wishart, that girl is twenty-four. I don't know what men want from women now. I don't even know what Flor wants. We've been here since the eighth of June, and do you know what she's picked up? A teeny little fellow from Turkey. I swear, he's not five three. When we go out, the three of us, I could die, I don't understand it—why she only likes the wrong kind. 'Only likes,' did I say? I should have said 'only *attracts*.' They're awful. They don't even propose. She hasn't even got the satisfaction of turning them down. I don't understand it, and that's all I can say. Why, I had literally hundreds of proposals, and not from little Turkeys. I stuck to my own kind."

He wanted to say, "Yes, but you were among your own kind. The girl is a floater, like me." He sensed that Bonnie's disappointment in what she called her own kind had affected her desires for Flor. Her own kind had betrayed her; she had told him so. That was why she lived in Europe. Outside her own kind was a vast population of men in suspenders standing up to carve the Sunday roast. That took care of Americans.

They walked on, slowly. A store window they passed reflected the drawn, dried expression that added years to Wishart's age but removed him from competition and torment. He found time to admire the image, and was further comforted by Bonnie's next, astonishing words: "Someone like you, Wishart, would be good for Flor. I mean someone older, a person I can trust. You know what I mean—an Englishman who's been in America, who's had the best of both."

He knew that she could not be proposing him as a husband for Florence, but he could have loved her forever for the confirmation of the gentleman he had glimpsed in the window, the sardonic Englishman in America, the awfully decent American in England. He slipped his hand under her elbow; it was almost a caress.

They reached the Boulevard de la Croisette, crossed over to the sea side, and Bonnie put up her parasol. Wishart's good humor hung suspended as he looked down at the beaches, the larva-like bodies, the rows of chairs. Every beach carried its own social stamp, as distinct as the strings of greasy flags, the raked pullulating sand, and the squalid little bar that marked the so-called "students' beach," and the mauve and yellow awnings, the plastic mattresses of the beach that were a point of reunion for Parisian homosexuals. Wishart's gaze, uninterested, was about to slide over this beach when Bonnie arrested him by saying, "This is where we bathe, Wishart, dear." He turned his head so suddenly that her parasol hit him in the eye, which made him think of her falsehood (for it was a falsehood, unquestionably) about Flor and the grain of sand. He looked with real suspicion now at the sand, probably treacherous with broken bottles, and at the sea, which, though blue and sparkling, was probably full of germs. Even the sky was violated; across the face of it an airplane was writing the name of a drink.

"Oh, my sweet heaven!" Bonnie said. She stood still, clutching Wishart by the arm, and said it again. "Sweet heaven! Well, there she is. There's Flor. But that's not the Turk from Turkey. No, Wishart, her mother is to have a treat. She's got a new one. Oh, my sweet heaven, Wishart, where does she find them?"

"I expect she meets them in trains."

From that distance he could admire Bonnie's girl, thin and motionless, with brown skin and red hair. She leaned on the low wall, looking down at the sea, braced on her arms, as tense as if the decision between this beach and some other one was to decide the course of her life. "She does have extraordinary coloring," he said, as generously as he could.

"She gets it from me," said Bonnie, shortly, as if she had never noticed her own hair was brown.

The man with Florence was stocky and dark. He wore sneakers, tartan swimming trunks of ample cut, a gold waterproof watch, a gold medal on a chain, and a Swedish-university cap some sizes too small. He carried a net bag full of diving equipment. His chest was bare.

"Well, I don't know," Bonnie said. "I just don't know."

By a common silent decision, the two rejected the beach and turned and came toward Bonnie. They made an impression as harsh and unpoetical as the day. The sun had burned all expression from their faces—smooth brown masks, in which their eyes, his brown and hers green, shone like colored glass. Even though Wishart had never dared allow himself close relations, he was aware of their existence to a high degree. He could detect an intimate situation from a glance, or a quality of silence. It was one more of his gifts, but he would have been happier without it. Pushed by forces he had not summoned or invented, he had at these moments a victim's face—puzzled, wounded, bloodless, coarse. The gap between the two couples closed. Bonnie had taken on a dreamy, vacant air; she was not planning to help.

"This is Bob Harris," Florence said. "He's from New York."

"I guessed that," Bonnie said.

It was plain to Wishart that the new man, now sincerely shaking hands all around, had no idea that Mrs. McCarthy might want to demolish him.

Every day after that, the four met on Bonnie's beach and lunched in a restaurant Bonnie liked. If Wishart had disapproved of the beach, it was nothing compared to the restaurant, which was full of Bonnie's new friends. Wine—Algerian pink—came out of a barrel, there were paper flags stuck in the butter, the waiters were insolent and barefoot, the menu was written on a slate and full of obscene puns. Everyone knew everyone, and Wishart could have murdered Bonnie. He was appalled at her thinking he could possibly like the place, but remembered that her attitude was the result of years of neuter camaraderie. It didn't matter. On the tenth of July he was expected in Venice. It was not a pattern of life.

It seemed to Wishart that Bonnie was becoming silly with age. She had developed a piercing laugh, and the affected drawl was becoming real. Her baiting of Bob Harris was too direct to be funny, and her antagonism was forming a bond between them— the last thing on earth she wanted. Bob had the habit of many Americans of constantly repeating the name of the person he was talking to. Bonnie retaliated by calling him Bob Harris, in full, every time she spoke to him, and this, combined with her slightly artificial voice, made him ask, "Is that a Southern accent you've got, Mrs. McCarthy?"

"Well, it just might be, Bob Harris!" Bonnie cried, putting one on. But it was a movie accent; she did it badly, and it got on Wishart's nerves. "Well, that's a nice breeze that's just come up," she would say, trailing the vowels. "We're certainly a nice little party, aren't we? It's nice being four." Nice being four? Nice for Wishart—the adored, the sought-after, Europe's troubadour? He closed his eyes and thought of Mrs. Sebastian, Venice, shuttered rooms, green canals.

Then Florence burst out with something. Wishart guessed that these cheeky outbursts, fit for a child of twelve, were innocent attempts to converse. Because of the way her mother had dragged her around, because she had never been part of a fixed society, she didn't know how people talked; she had none of the coins of light exchange. She said in an excited voice, "The Fox, the Ape, the Bumblebee were all at odds, being three, and then the Goose came out the door, and stayed the odds by making four. We're like that. Mama's a lovely bumblebee and I'm fox-colored." This left Wishart the vexing choice between being a goose and an ape, and he was the more distressed to hear Bob say placidly that it wasn't the first time he had been called a big ape. All at once it seemed to him preferable to be an ape than a goose.

"Have you got many friends in Paris, Bob Harris?" said Bonnie, who had seen Wishart's face pucker and shrink.

"Last year I had to send out one hundred and sixty-nine Christmas cards," said Bob simply. "I don't mean cards for the firm."

"The Bambino of the Eiffel Tower? Something real Parisian?"

Bob looked down, with a smile. He seemed to feel sorry for Mrs. McCarthy, who didn't know about the cards people sent now—nondenominational, either funny or artistic, depending on your friends.

He stayed in one of the spun-sugar palaces on the Croisette, and Wishart's anguished guess had been correct: Flor went to his room afternoons, while Bonnie was having her rest. The room was too noisy, too bright, and it was Flor who seemed most at ease, adjusting the blind so that slats of shade covered the walls, placing her clothes neatly on a chair. She seemed to Bob exclusive, a prize, even though the evidence was that they were both summer rats. He had met her in a café one afternoon. He saw his own shadow on her table, and himself, furtive, ratlike, looking for trouble.

Wishart had decided that Bob was no problem where he was concerned. His shrewdness was not the variety likely to threaten Wishart, and he took up Flor's time, leaving Bonnie free to listen to Wishart's chat. He did not desire Bonnie to himself as a lover might, but he did want to get on with his anecdotes without continual interruptions.

Alone with him, Bonnie was the person Wishart liked. When they laughed together on the beach, it was like the old days, when she had seemed so superior, enchanting, and bright. They lived out the fantasy essential to Wishart; he might have been back in London saying and thinking "Cannes." They had worked out their code of intimate jokes for the season; they called Bonnie's young friends "*les fleurs et couronnes*," and they made fun of French jargon, with its nervous emphasis on "*moderne*" and "*dynamique*." When Bonnie called Wishart "*un homme du vingtième siècle, moderne et dynamique*," they were convulsed. Flor and Bob, a little apart, regarded them soberly, as if they were a pair of chattering squirrels.

"Wishart is one of Mama's best friends," said Flor, apologizing for this elderly foolishness. "I've never liked him. I think he thinks they're like Oberon and Titania, you know—all malice and showing off. Wishart would love to have wings and power and have people do as he says. He's always seemed wormy to me. Have you noticed that my mother pays for everything?"

In point of fact, Bob paid for everything now. He expected to; it was as essential to his nature as it was to Wishart's to giggle and sneer. "Wishart doesn't like the way I look. The hell with him," he said placidly.

Lying on her back on the sand, Flor shaded her eyes to see him properly. He was turned away. He seemed casual, indifferent, but she knew that he stayed on in Cannes because of her. His holiday was over, and his father, business- and family-minded, was waiting for him in Paris. The discovery of Flor had disturbed Bob. Until now he had liked much younger girls, with straight hair and mild, anxious eyes; girls who were photographed in the living room wearing printed silk and their mother's pearls. His ideal was the image of some minor Germanic princess, whose nickname might be Mousie, and who, at sixteen, at twenty-nine, at fifty-three, seems to wear the same costume, the same hair, and the same air of patient supplication until a husband can be found. This picture, into which he had tried to fit so many women, now proved accommodating; the hair became red, the features hardened, the hands were thin and brown. She stared at him with less hopeless distress. At last the bland young woman became Flor, and he did not remember having held in his mind's eye any face but hers, just as he would never expect to look in the mirror one morning and see any face except his own.

"Bob is just a deep, creative boy looking for a girl with a tragic sense of life," Wishart said to Bonnie, who laughed herself to tears, for, having tried to trap Bob into saying "Stateside" and "drapes" and having failed, she needed new confirmation of his

absurdity. The conversation of the pair, devoid of humor, was repeated by Wishart or Bonnie—whichever was close enough to
hear. "Do you know what they're talking about *now*?" was a new
opening for discussion, amazement, and, finally, helpless laughter.

"They're on birds today," Wishart would say, with a deliberately solemn face.

"Birds?"

"Birds."

They collapsed, heaving with laughter, as if in a fit. The *fleurs
et couronnes*, out of sympathy, joined in.

"Do you know what bothered me most when I first came over
here?" Wishart had heard Flor say. "We were in England then,
and I didn't recognize a single tree or a single bird. They looked
different, and the birds had different songs. A robin wasn't a robin
anymore. It was terrible. It frightened me more than anything.
And they were so drab. Everything was brown and gray. There
aren't any red-winged blackbirds, you know—nothing with a
bright flash."

"Aren't there?" The urban boy tried to sound surprised. Wishart sympathized. The only quality he shared with Bob was igno-
rance of nature.

"Didn't you know? That's what's missing here, in everything.
There's color enough, but you don't know how I miss it—the
bright flash."

Bob saw the sun flash off a speedboat, and everywhere he
looked he saw color and light. The cars moving along the Croisette were color enough.

"Will you always live here now?" said Flor. "Will you never live
at home again?"

"It depends on my father. I came over to learn, and I'm practically running the whole Paris end. It's something."

"Do you like business?"

"Do you mean do I wish I was an actor or something?" He
gave her a resentful look, and the shadow of their first possible
difference fell over the exchange.

"My father never did anything much," she said. Her eyes were closed, and she talked into the sun. The sun bleached her words. Any revelation was just chat. "Now they say he drinks quite a lot. But that's none of my business. He married a really dull thing, they say. He and Mama are Catholics, so they don't believe in their own divorce. At least, Mama doesn't."

He noticed that Flor kissed her mother anxiously when they met, as if they had been parted for days, or as if he had taken Flor to another country. The affection between the two women pleased him. His own mother, having died, had elevated the notion of motherhood. He liked people who got on with their parents and suspected those who did not.

"I suppose he thinks he shouldn't be living with his second wife," Flor said. "If he still believes."

"How about you?"

"I'd believe anything I thought would do me or Mama any good."

This seemed to him insufficient. He expected women to be religious. He gave any amount of money to nuns.

These dialogues, which Wishart heard from a distance while seeming to concentrate on his tan, and which he found so dull and discouraging that the pair seemed mentally deficient, were attempts to furnish the past. Flor was perplexed by their separate pasts. She saw Bob rather as Bonnie did, but with a natural loyalty to him that was almost as strong as a family tie. She believed she was objective, detached; then she discovered he had come down to Cannes from Paris with a Swedish girl, the student from whom he had inherited the cap. Knowing that "student" in Europe is a generous term, covering a boundless field of age as well as activity, she experienced the hopeless jealousy a woman feels for someone she believes inferior to herself. It was impossible for Bonnie's daughter to achieve this inferiority; she saw the man already lost. The girl and Bob had lived together, in his room. Flor's imagina-

tion constructed a spiteful picture of a girl being cute and Swedish and larking about in his pajamas. Secretly flattered, he said
no, she was rather sickly and quiet. Her name was Eve. She was
off somewhere traveling on a bus. Cards arrived bearing the sticky
imprint of her lips—a disgusting practice. Trembling with feigned
indifference, Flor grabbed the cap and threw it out the window.
It landed on the balcony of the room below.

Bob rescued the cap, and kept it, but he gave up his hotel and
moved into Flor's. The new room was better. It was quiet, dark,
and contained no memories. It was in the basement, with a window high in one wall. The walls were white. There was sand everywhere, in the cracked red tiles of the floor, in the chinks of the
decaying armchair, caked to the rope soles of their shoes. It
seemed to Flor that here the grit of sand and salt came into their
lives and their existence as a couple began. When the shutters
were opened, late in the afternoon, they let in the peppery scent
of geraniums and the view of a raked gravel path. There must
have been a four-season mimosa nearby; the wind sent minute
yellow pompons against the sill, and often a gust of sweetish perfume came in with the dying afternoon.

Flor had not mentioned the change to Bonnie, but, inevitably,
Bonnie met her enemy at the desk, amiable and arrogant, collecting his key. "Has that boy been here all along?" she cried, in despair. She insisted on seeing his room. She didn't know what she
expected to find, but, as she told Wishart, she had a right to know.
Bob invited her formally. She came with Flor one afternoon, both
dressed in white, with skirts like lampshades, Bonnie on waves of
Femme. He saw for the first time that the two were alike, and
perhaps inseparable; they had a private casual way of speaking,
and laughed at the same things. It was like seeing a college friend
in his own background, set against his parents, his sisters, his
mother's taste in books. He offered Bonnie peanuts out of a tin,
brandy in a toothbrush glass. He saw everything about her except
that she was attractive, and here their difference of age was in the
way. Bob and Florence avoided sitting on the lumpy bed, strewn

with newspapers and photographs. That was Bonnie's answer. They knew she knew; Bonnie left in triumph, with an air she soon had cause to change. Now that Bonnie knew, the lovers spent more time together. They no longer slipped away during Bonnie's rest; they met when they chose and stayed away as long as they liked. If they kept a pretense of secrecy, it was because to Bob a façade of decency was needed. He had not completely lost sight of the beseeching princess into whose outline Flor had disappeared.

When he and Flor were apart, he found reason to doubt. She had told him the birds of Europe were not like the birds at home, but what about human beings? She never mentioned them. The breath of life for him was contained in relations, in his friendships, in which he did not distinguish between the random and the intense. All his relationships were of the same quality. She had told him that this room was like a place she had imagined. The only difference was that her imagined room was spangled, bright, perfectly silent, and full of mirrors. Years after this, he could say to himself "Cannes" and evoke a season of his life, with all the sounds, smells, light and dark that the season had contained; but he never remembered accurately how it had started or what it had been like. Their intimacy came first, then love, and some unclouded moments. Like most lovers, he believed that the beginning was made up of these moments only, and he would remember Flor's silent, mirrored room and believe it was their room at Cannes, and that he had lived in it, too.

One afternoon at the beginning of July, they fell asleep in this room, the real room, and when Flor woke it was dark. She knew it had begun to rain by the quickening in the air. She got up quietly and opened the shutters. A car came into the hotel drive; a bar of light swept across the ceiling and walls. She thought that what she felt now came because of the passage of light. It was a concrete sensation of happiness, as if happiness could be felt, lifted, carried around. She had not experienced anything of the kind before. She was in a watery world of perceptions, where impulses, doubts, intentions, detached from their roots, rise to the surface and expand. The difference between Bob and herself was that he had no attachments to the past. This was what caused him to seem inferior in her mother's view of life. He had told them freely that his father was self-educated and that his mother's parents were illiterate. There were no family records more than a generation old. Florence had been taught to draw her support from continuity and the past. Now she saw that the chain of fathers and daughters and mothers and sons had been powerless as a charm. In trouble, mistrusting her own capacity to think or move or enjoy living, she was alone. She saw that being positive of even a few things—that she was American, and pretty, and Christian, and Bonnie's girl—had not helped. Bob Harris didn't know his mother's maiden name, and his father's father had come out of a Polish ghetto, but Bob was not specifically less American than Florence, nor less proud. He was, if anything, more assertive and sure.

She closed the shutters and came toward him quietly, so that he would not wake and misinterpret her drawing near. Lacking an emotional country, it might be possible to consider another person one's home. She pressed her face against his unmoving arm, accepting everything imperfect, as one accepts a faulty but beloved country, or the language in which one's thoughts are formed. It was the most dangerous of ideas, this "Only you can save me," but her need to think it was so overwhelming that she wondered if this was what men, in the past, had been trying to say when they had talked to her about love.


The rainstorm that afternoon was not enough. Everyone agreed more rain was needed. Rain was wanted to wash the sand, clean the sea, cool their tempers, rinse the hot roofs of the bathing cabins along the beach. When Wishart thought "Cannes" now, it was not light, dark, and blueness but sand, and cigarette butts, and smears of oil. At night the heat and the noise of traffic kept him awake. He lay patient and motionless, with opened owl eyes. He and Bonnie compared headaches at breakfast; Bonnie's was like something swelling inside the brain, a cluster of balloons, while Wishart's was external, a leather band.

He could not understand what Bonnie was doing in this place; she had been so fastidious, rejecting a resort when it became too popular, seeming to him to have secret mysterious friends and places to go to. He still believed she would not be here, fighting through mobs of sweating strangers every time she wanted a slopped cup of coffee or a few inches of sand, if there had not been a reason—if she had not been expecting something real.

After a time, he realized that Bonnie was not waiting for anything to happen, and that her air of expectancy the day he arrived had been false. If she had expected anything then, she must have believed it would come through him. She talked now of the futility of travel. She said that Flor was cold and shallow and had broken her heart. There was no explanation for this, except that Flor was not fulfilling Bonnie's hopes and plans. Self-pity followed; she said that she, Bonnie, would spend the rest of her life like a bit of old paper on the beach, cast up, beaten by waves, and so forth. She didn't care what rubbish she said to him, and she no longer tried to be gay. Once she said, "It's no good, Wishart; she's never been a woman. How can she feel what I feel? She's never even had her periods. We've done everything—hormones, God knows what all. I took her to Zurich. She was so passive, she didn't seem to know it was important. Sometimes I think she's dumb. She has these men—I don't know how far she goes. I think she's innocent. Yes, I really do. I don't want to think too much. It's nauseating when you start to think of your own daughter that way. But she's cold. I know she's cold. That's why we have no contact now. That's why we have no contact anymore. I've never stopped being a woman. Thank God for it. If I haven't married again, it hasn't been because I haven't men after me. Wishart! It's tragic for me to see that girl. I'm fifty and I'm still a woman, and she's twenty-four and a piece of ice."

He was lying beside her on the sand. He pulled his straw hat over his face, perfectly appalled. It was a pure reaction, un-planned. If he let his thoughts move without restraint into the world of women, he discovered an area dimly lighted and faintly disgusting, like a kitchen in a slum. It was a world of migraines, miscarriages, disorder, and tears.

Another day, complaining of how miserable her life had been in Europe, she said, "I stopped noticing when the seasons changed. Someone would say that the trees were in bud. I hadn't even noticed that the leaves were gone. I stopped noticing every-thing around me, I was so concentrated on Flor."

She talked to him about money, which was new. When he discovered she was poor, she dwindled, for then she had nothing to make her different or better than anyone else. She had always been careful over pennies, but he had believed it was the passion-ate stinginess of the rich. But she was no better than Wishart; she was dependent on bounty, too. "I get no income at all, except from my brothers. And Stanley isn't required to support me, al-though he should, as I've had the burden of the child. And Flor's money is tied up in some crazy way until she's thirty. My father tied it up that way because of my divorce; he never trusted me again. Believe me, he paid for it. I never sent him as much as a postcard from that day until the day he died. Family, Wishart! God! Lovely people, but when it comes to m-o-n-e-y," she said, spelling it out. "Flor's allowance from Stanley was only until her majority, and now he hardly sends her anything at all. He forgets. He isn't made to do anything. She'll have to wait now until he dies. They say the way he's living now there won't be anything left. Wishart, my brain clangs like a cash register when I think about it. I never used to worry at all, but now I can't stop."

"You thought she would be married by the time her allowance from Stanley stopped," Wishart said. No tone could make this less odious. He thought he had gone too far, and was blaming her for having started it, when she relieved him by being simply angry.

"Do you think it's easy? Marriage proposals don't grow on trees. I can't understand it. I had so many."

Their conversation showed how worn their friendship had become. It was used down to the threads; they had no tolerance for each other anymore, and nothing new to give. They were more intimate than they needed to be. He blamed her. *He* had tried to keep it bright. Once, Bob had asked Bonnie why she lived in Europe, and Wishart had replied, "Bonnie had Flor and then, worn out with childbearing, retired to a permanently sunny beach." This was a flattering version of Bonnie's divorce and flight from home. "Don't you listen," Bonnie had said, immensely pleased. (She was pleased on another count: they were sitting on the outer edge of a café, and Bob was repeatedly jostled by the passing crowd. He had once said he liked people and didn't mind noise, and Bonnie saw to it that he had a basinful of both when it could be managed.) Wishart wanted their holiday to go on being as it had sounded when he said, in London, "I am going to Cannes to stay with a delightful American friend." The American friend now questioned Wishart about his plans. He perceived with horror that she was waiting for a suggestion from him. He might have been flattered by Bonnie's clinging to him, but in friendship he was like a lover who can only adore in pursuit. In a few days, he would be in Venice with Mrs. Sebastian—blessed Mrs. Sebastian, authentically rich. Snubbing Bonnie, he talked Venice to the *fleurs et couronnes*. Rejected by Wishart, abandoned by Flor, Bonnie took on a new expression; even more than Wishart, she looked like the failed comedian afflicted with dreams. He knew it, and was pleased, as if in handing over a disease he had reduced its malignant powers. Then, in time to bump him off his high horse, Wishart received a letter from Mrs. Sebastian putting him off until August. There were no apologies and no explanations; she simply told him not to come. He remembered then that she was cold and vulgar, and that she drank too much, and that, although she was a hefty piece, her nickname was Peewee and she insisted on being called by it. She was avaricious and had made Wishart pay her for a bottle of ddt and a spray one summer when the mosquitoes were killing him. He remembered that in American terms Bonnie was someone and Mrs. Sebastian nothing at all. Bonnie became generous, decent, elegant, and essential to Wishart's life. He turned to her as if he had been away; but as far as she was concerned he had been away, and he had lost ground. The dark glasses that seemed to condense the long curve of the beach into a miniature image were turned elsewhere. Even a diminished, penitent Wishart could not see his own reflection.

For her part, Bonnie was finding her withering Marchbanks tedious. His pursy prejudices no longer seemed delicious humor. He made the mistake of telling her a long, name-studded story of school politics and someone trying to get his job. It established him in reality—a master afraid for his grubby post—and reality was not what Bonnie demanded. She had enough reality on her hands: in the autumn that girl would be twenty-five.

Wishart tried to get back on their old plane. "Distract her," he said lazily. "Move on. Divert her with culture. Inspect the cathedrals and museums. Take her to the Musée de l'Homme."

"You don't meet any men in museums," said Bonnie, as if this were a sore point. "Anyway, what's the good? She only comes to life for slobs." After a moment she said quietly, "Don't you see, that's not what I want for Flor. I don't want her to marry just anybody. It may sound funny to you, but I don't even want an American. They've always let me down. My own brothers—But I don't want to go into it again. I want a European, but not a Latin, and one who has lived in the States and has had the best of both. I want someone much older than Flor, because she needs that, and someone I can trust. That's what I want for my girl, and that's what I meant when I said proposals don't grow on trees. Neither do men." But what did Wishart know about men? He was a woman-haunter, woman's best friend. She put on her sunglasses in order to hide her exasperation with him, because he was a man but not the right person.

Her expression was perfectly blank. There was no doubt now,

no other way of interpreting it. In spite of his recent indifference to her, she had not changed her mind. Wishart was being offered Flor.

He had never been foolish enough to dream of a useful marriage. He knew that his choice one season might damn him the next. He had thought occasionally of a charming but ignorant peasant child, whom he could train; he had the town boy's blurry vision of country people. Unfortunately, he had never met anyone of the kind. Certainly his peasant bride, who was expected to combine with her exceptional beauty a willingness to clean his shoes, was not Flor.

This was not the moment for false steps. He saw himself back in America with a lame-brained but perfect wife. Preposterous ideas made him say in imagined conversations, "The mother was a charmer; I married the daughter."

He forgot the dangers, and what it would be like to have Bonnie as a mother-in-law. A secret hope unfurled and spread. He got up, and in a blind, determined way began to walk across the beach. Not far away the lovers lay on the sand, facing each other, half asleep. Flor's arm was under her head, straight up. He saw Bob's back, burned nearly black, and Flor's face. They were so close that their breath must have mingled. Their intimacy seemed to Wishart established; it contained an implicit allegiance, like a family tie, with all the antagonism that might suggest as well. While he was watching, they came together. Wishart saw that Flor remained outside the kiss. Two laurels with one root. Where had he heard that? Each was a missing part of the other's character, and the whole, in the kiss, should have been unflawed.

Flor wondered what it was like for a man to kiss her, and remembered words from men she had not loved. It was a narcissism so shameful that she opened her eyes, and saw Wishart. He was the insect enemy met in an underground tunnel, the small, scratching watcher, the boneless witness of an insect universe—a tiny, scuttling universe that contained her mother, the pop-eyed Corsican proprietor of this beach, the *fleurs et couronnes*, her mother's procession of very best most intimate friends. (Before

Wishart a bestial countess, to whom Flor, as a girl, had been instructed to be nice.) In a spasm of terror, which Bob mistook for abandonment, she clung to him. He was outside this universe and from a better place.

Wishart returned to Bonnie and sank down beside her on the sand, adjusting his bony legs as if they were collapsible umbrellas. If he continued in error, it was Bonnie's fault, for she went on again about men, the right man, and Flor. The wind dropped. Cannes settled into the stagnant afternoon. The *fleurs et couronnes* were down from their naps and chattering like budgerigars. Bonnie had been polishing her sunglasses on the edge of a towel. She stopped, holding them, staring. "Last night I dreamed my daughter was a mermaid," she said. "What does it mean? Wishart, you know all about those things. What does it mean?"

"*Ravissant*," said one of her court. "I see the blue sea and the grottoes, everything coral and blue. Coral green and coral blue."

"There is no such thing as coral blue," said Wishart mechanically.

"And Florence, la belle Florence, floating and drifting, the bright hair spread like—"

"She sang and she floated, she floated and sang," took up a minor figure who resembled a guppy. At a look from Bonnie he gave a great gasp and shut up.

"It was nothing like that at all," said Bonnie snappily. "It was an ugly fishtail, like a carp's. It was just like a carp's, and the whole thing was a great handicap. The girl simply couldn't walk. She lay there on the ground and couldn't do a thing. Everybody stared at us. It was a perfectly hopeless dream, and I woke up in a state of *great distress*."

Wishart had been so disturbed by the kiss that moved into blankness. He could not form a coherent thought. What interested him, finally, was the confirmation of his suspicion that Flor was a *poseuse*. How conceited she had been, lying there exploring her own sensations as idly as a tourist pouring sand from one hand into the other. He recalled the expression in her eyes—shrewd, ratty eyes, he thought, not the eyes of a goddess—and he knew that she feared and loathed him and might catch him out. "It won't do," he said to Bonnie. "It wouldn't do, a marriage with Flor." He heard the words, "She has a crack across the brain," but was never certain afterward if he had said them aloud.

Bonnie turned her pink, shadowed face to him in purest amazement. She noticed that Wishart's eyes were so perturbed and desperate that they were almost beyond emotion—without feeling, like those of a bird. Then she looked up to the sky, where the plane was endlessly and silently writing the name of a drink. She said, "I wish he would write something for us, something useful."

His mistake in thinking that Bonnie considered him an equal and would want him for her daughter had been greater than the *gaffe* about Flor. Everything trembled and changed; even the color of the sky seemed extraordinary. Wishart was fixed and paralyzed in this new landscape, wondering if he was doing or saying anything strange, unable to see or stop himself. It was years since he had been the victim of such a fright. He had believed that Bonnie accepted him at his value. He had believed that the exact miniature he saw in her sunglasses was the Wishart she accepted, the gentleman he had glimpsed in the store window that first day. He had thought that the inflection of a voice, the use of some words, established them as a kind. But Bonnie had never believed in the image. She had never considered him anything but jumped-up. He remembered now that she had never let him know her family back home, had never suggested he meet her brothers.

When Bonnie dared look again, Wishart was picking his way into the sea. He was wearing his hat. He did not mind seeming foolish, and believed eccentricity added to his stature. After standing for a time, knee-deep, looking, with the expression of a brooding camel, first at the horizon and then back to shore, he began to pick his way out again. The water was too dirty for swimming, even if the other bathers had left him room. "Large colored balls were being flung over my head, and sometimes against it," he composed, describing for future audiences the summer at Cannes. "The shrieking children of butchers were being taught to swim."

Farther along the beach, Bob Harris carried two bottles of beer, crowned with inverted paper cups, down to Flor. Bonnie watched without emotion. Their figures were motionless, printed against her memory, arrested in heat and the insupportable noise.

Everyone around Bonnie was asleep. The sirocco, unsteady, pulled her parasol about on the sand. Sitting, knees bent, she clasped her white feet. There was not a blemish on them. The toes were straight, the heels rosy. She had tended her feet like twin infants, setting an example for Flor. Once, exasperated by Flor's neglect, she had gone down on her knees and taken Flor's feet on her lap and shown her how it ought to be done. She had creamed and manicured and pumiced, while Flor, listless, surreptitiously trying to get on with a book, said, "Oh, Mama, I can do it." "But you won't, honey. You simply don't take care of yourself unless I'm there." She had polished and tended her little idol, and for whom? For a Turk not sixty-three inches high. For Bob Harris in tartan trunks. It was no use; the minutes and hours had passed too quickly. She was perplexed by the truth that had bothered her all her life—that there was no distance between time and events. Everything raced to a point beyond her reach and sight. Everyone slid out of her grasp: her husband, her daughter, her friends. She let herself fall back. Her field of vision closed in, and from the left came the first, swimming molecules of pain.

Wishart, returning from the sea, making a detour to avoid being caught up and battered in a volleyball game, came up to Bonnie unobserved. Patting his yellowed skin with a towel, he watched the evolution of his friend's attack. Her face was half in sun. She twisted to find the shadow of the rolling parasol. Bitter, withdrawn, he was already pulling about himself the rags of imaginary Wishart: the squire father; Mrs. Sebastian, rolling in money above the Grand Canal. Bonnie believed she was really dying this time, and wondered if Flor could see.

Flor said, "I think Mama has one of her headaches."

"You two watch each other, don't you?" Bob Harris said.

A haze had gone over the sky. She finished her beer, spread her striped beach towel a little away from him, and lay still. He had told her that his father had telephoned from Paris, and that this time it was an order. He was leaving soon, perhaps the next day. This was July. The summer, a fruit already emptied by wasps, still hung on its tree. He was leaving. When he had gone, she would hear the question, the ghost voice that speaks to every traveler: "Why did you come to this place?" Until now, she had known; she was somewhere or other with her mother because her mother could not settle down, because every rented flat and villa was a horrible parody of home, or the home she ought to have given Flor. When he had gone, she would know without illusion that she was in Cannes in a rotting season, that the rot was reality, and that there was no hope in the mirrored room.

"Are you coming to Paris later on?" he asked. His father was waiting; he spoke with a sense of urgency, like someone trying to ring off, holding the receiver, eyes wandering around the room.

"I don't know. I don't know where we'll go from here, or how long Mama will stay. She and Wishart always finish with a fight, and Mama loses her head and we go rushing off. All our relations at home think we have such a glamorous life. Did you ever go out in the morning and find a spider's web spangled with dew?" she said suddenly. "You'll never find that here. It's either too hot and dry or it rains so much the spider drowns. At my grandmother's place, you know, summers, I used to ride, oh, early, early in the morning, with my cousins. All my cousins were boys." Her voice was lost as she turned her head away.

"Flor, why don't you go home?"

"I can't leave my mother, and she won't go. Maybe I don't dare. She used to need me. Maybe now I need her. What would I do at home? My grandmother is dead. I haven't got a home. I know I sound as if I feel sorry for myself, but I haven't got anything."

"You've got your mother," he said. "There's me."

Now it was here—the circumstance that Bonnie had loathed and desired. He moved closer and spoke with his lips to Flor's ear, playing with her hair, as if they were alone on the beach or in his room. He remembered the basement room as if they would never be in it again. He remembered her long hair, the wrinkled sheets, the blanket thrown back because of the heat. It was the prophetic instant; in it was the compression of feeling that occurs in childhood and in dreams. Wishart passed them; his shadow fell over their feet. They were obliged to look up and see his onion skin and pickled eyes. They were polite. No one could have said that they had agreed in that moment to change the movement of four lives, and had diverted the hopes, desires, and ambitions of Bonnie and of Bob's father, guides whose direction had suddenly failed.

Wishart went back to his hotel. It was the hour when people who lived in pensions began to straggle up from the sea. Whole families got in Wishart's way. They were badly sunburned, smelled of Ambre Solaire and Skol, and looked as if they couldn't stand each other's company another day. Wishart bathed and changed. He walked to the post office and then to the station to see about a bus. He was dryly forgiving when people stepped on his feet, but looked like someone who will never accept an apology again. He sent a telegram to an American couple he knew who had a house near Grasse. He had planned to skip them this year; the husband disliked him. (The only kind of husband Wishart felt easy with was the mere morsel, the half-digested scrap.) But he could not stay with Bonnie now, and Mrs. Sebastian had put him off. He summed up his full horror of Cannes in a heart-rending message that began, "Very depressed," but he did not sign a funny name, for fear of making the husband cross. He signed his own name and pocketed the change and went off to the station. This time he and Bonnie were parting without a quarrel.

That night there was a full moon. Bonnie woke up suddenly,

as if she had become conscious of a thief in the room; but it was only Flor, wearing the torn bathrobe she had owned since she was fourteen and that Bonnie never managed to throw away. She was holding a glass of water in her hand, and looking down at her sleeping mother.

"Flor, is anything wrong?"

"I was thirsty." She put the glass on the night table and sank down on the floor, beside her mother.

"That Wishart," said Bonnie, now fully awake and beginning to stroke Flor's hair. "He really takes himself for something."

"What is he taking himself for?"

Bonnie stroked her daughter's hair, thinking, My mermaid, my prize. The carp had vanished from the dream, leaving an iridescent Flor. No one was good enough for Florence. That was the meaning of the dream. "Your hair is so stiff, honey. It's full of salt. I wish you'd wear a bathing cap. Flor, have you got a fever or something?" She wants to tell me something, Bonnie thought. Let it be anything except about that boy. Let it be anything but that.

At dawn, Wishart, who had been awake most of the night, buckled his suitcase. No porter was around at that hour. He walked to the station in streets where there was still no suggestion of the terrible day. The southern scent, the thin distillation of lemons and geraniums, descended from the hills. Then heat began to tremble; Vespas raced along the port; the white-legged grub tourists came down from the early train. Wishart thought of his new hostess—academic, a husk. She chose the country behind Grasse because of the shades of Gide and Saint-Ex—ghosts who would keep away from her if they knew what was good for them. He climbed into the bus and sat down among workingmen who had jobs in Grasse, and the sea dropped behind him as he was borne away.

In the rocking bus, his head dropped. He knew that he was in a bus and traveling to Grasse, but he saw Glad, aged twelve, going off at dawn with her lunch wrapped in an apron. What about the dirty, snotty baby boy who hung on her dress, whose fingers she had to pry loose one at a time, only to have the hand clamp shut again, tighter than before? Could this be Wishart, clinging, whining, crying "Stay with me"? But Wishart was awake and not to be trapped. He took good care not to dream, and when the bus drew in at Grasse, under the trees, and he saw his new, straw-thin hostess (chignon, espadrilles, peasant garden hat), he did not look like a failed actor assailed with nightmares but a smooth and pleasant schoolmaster whose sleep is so deep that he never dreams at all.

*1959*

# ACCEPTANCE OF THEIR WAYS

PRODDED by a remark from Mrs. Freeport, Lily Littel got up and fetched the plate of cheese. It was in her to say, "Go get it yourself," but a reputation for coolness held her still. Only the paucity of her income, at which the *Sunday Express* horoscope jeered with its smart talk of pleasure and gain, kept her at Mrs. Freeport's, on the Italian side of the frontier. The coarse and grubby gaiety of the French Riviera would have suited her better, and was not far away; unfortunately it came high. At Mrs. Freeport's, which was cheaper, there was a whiff of infirm nicety to be breathed, a suggestion of regularly aired decay; weakly, because it was respectable, Lily craved that, too. "We seem to have finished with the pudding," said Mrs. Freeport once again, as though she hadn't noticed that Lily was on her feet.

Lily was not Mrs. Freeport's servant, she was her paying guest, but it was a distinction her hostess rarely observed. In imagination, Lily became a punishing statue and raised a heavy marble arm; but then she remembered that this was the New Year. The next day, or the day after that, her dividends would arrive. That meant she could disappear, emerging as a gay holiday Lily up in Nice. Then, Lily thought, turning away from the table, then watch the old tiger! For Mrs. Freeport couldn't live without Lily, not more than a day. She could not stand Italy without the sound of an English voice in the house. In the hush of the dead season, Mrs. Freeport preferred Lily's ironed-out Bayswater to no English at all.

In the time it took her to pick up the cheese and face the table again, Lily had added to her expression a permanent-looking smile. Her eyes, which were a washy blue, were tolerably kind when she was plotting mischief. The week in Nice, desired, became a necessity; Mrs. Freeport needed a scare. She would fear, and then believe, that her most docile boarder, her most pliant errand girl, had gone forever. Stealing into Lily's darkened room, she would count the dresses with trembling hands. She would touch Lily's red with the white dots, her white with the poppies, her green wool with the scarf of mink tails. Mrs. Freeport would also discover—if she carried her snooping that far—the tooled-leather box with Lily's daisy-shaped earrings, and the brooch in which a mother-of-pearl pigeon sat on a nest made of Lily's own hair. But Mrs. Freeport would not find the diary, in which Lily had recorded her opinion of so many interesting things, nor would she come upon a single empty bottle. Lily kept her drinking to Nice, where, anonymous in a large hotel, friendly and lavish in a bar, she let herself drown. "Your visits to your sister seem to do you so much good," was Mrs. Freeport's unvarying comment when Lily returned from these excursions, which always followed the arrival of her income. "But you spend far too much money on your sister. You are much too kind." But Lily had no regrets. Illiberal by circumstance, grudging only because she imitated the behavior of other women, she became, drunk, an old forgotten Lily-girl, tender and warm, able to shed a happy tear and open a closed fist. She had been cold sober since September.

"Well, there you are," she said, and slapped down the plate of cheese. There was another person at the table, a Mrs. Garnett, who was returning to England the next day. Lily's manner toward the two women combined bullying with servility. Mrs. Freeport, large, in brown chiffon, wearing a hat with a water lily upon it to cover her thinning hair, liked to *feel* served. Lily had been a paid companion once; she had never seen a paradox in the joining of those two words. She simply looked on Mrs. Freeport and Mrs. Garnett as more of that race of ailing, peevish elderly children whose fancies and delusions must be humored by the sane.

Mrs. Freeport pursed her lips in acknowledgment of the cheese. Mrs. Garnett, who was reading a book, did nothing at all. Mrs. Garnett had been with them four months. Her blued curls, her laugh, her moist baby's mouth, had the effect on Lily of a stone in the shoe. Mrs. Garnett's husband, dead but often mentioned, had evidently liked them saucy and dim in the brain. Now that William Henry was no longer there to protect his wife, she was the victim of the effect of her worrying beauty—a torment to shoe clerks and bus conductors. Italians were dreadful; Mrs. Garnett hardly dared put her wee nose outside the house. "You are a little monkey, Edith!" Mrs. Freeport would sometimes say, bringing her head upward with a jerk, waking out of a sweet dream in time to applaud. Mrs. Garnett would go on telling how she had been jostled on the pavement or offended on a bus. And Lily Littel, who knew—but truly knew—about being followed and hounded and pleaded with, brought down her thick eyelids and smiled. Talk leads to overconfidence and errors. Lily had guided her life to this quiet shore by knowing when to open her mouth and when to keep it closed.

Mrs. Freeport was not deluded but simply poor. Thirteen years of pension-keeping on a tawdry stretch of Mediterranean coast had done nothing to improve her fortunes and had probably diminished them. Sentiment kept her near Bordighera, where someone precious to her had been buried in the Protestant part of the cemetery. In Lily's opinion, Mrs. Freeport ought to have cleared out long ago, cutting her losses, leaving the servants out of pocket and the grocer unpaid. Lily looked soft; she was round and pink and yellow-haired. The imitation pearls screwed on to her doughy little ears seemed to devour the flesh. But Lily could have bitten a real pearl in two and enjoyed the pieces. Her nature was generous, but an admiration for superior women had led her to cherish herself. An excellent cook, she had dreamed of being a poisoner, but decided to leave that for the loonies; it was no real way to get on. She had a moral program of a sort—thought it wicked to set a poor table, until she learned that the sort of woman she yearned to become was often picky. After that she tried to put it out of her mind. At Mrs. Freeport's she was enrolled in a useful school, for the creed of the house was this: It is pointless to think about anything so temporary as food; coffee grounds can be used many times, and moldy bread, revived in the oven, mashed with raisins and milk, makes a delicious pudding. If Lily had settled for this bleached existence, it was explained by a sentence scrawled over a page of her locked diary: "I live with gentlewomen now." And there was a finality about the statement that implied acceptance of their ways.

Lily removed the fly netting from the cheese. There was her bit left over from luncheon. It was the end of a portion of Dutch so dry it had split. Mrs. Freeport would have the cream cheese, possibly still highly pleasing under its coat of pale fur, while Mrs. Garnett, who was a yogurt fancier, would require none at all.

"Cheese, Edith," said Mrs. Freeport loudly, and little Mrs. Garnett blinked her doll eyes and smiled: No, thank you. Let others thicken their figures and damage their souls.

The cheese was pushed along to Mrs. Freeport, then back to Lily, passing twice under Mrs. Garnett's nose. She did not look up again. She was moving her lips over a particularly absorbing passage in her book. For the last four months, she had been reading the same volume, which was called *Optimism Unlimited*. So as not to stain the pretty dust jacket, she had covered it with brown paper, but now even that was becoming soiled. When Mrs. Freeport asked what the book was about, Mrs. Garnett smiled a timid apology and said, "I'm *afraid* it is philosophy." It was, indeed, a new philosophy, counseling restraint in all things, but recommending smiles. Four months of smiles and restraint had left Mrs. Garnett hungry, and, to mark her last evening at Mrs. Freeport's, she had asked for an Italian meal. Mrs. Freeport thought it extravagant—after all, they were still digesting an English Christmas. But little Edith was so sweet when she begged, putting her head to one side, wrinkling her face, that Mrs. Freeport, muttering about monkeys, had given in. The dinner was prepared and served, and Mrs. Garnett, suddenly remembering about restraint, brought her book to the table and decided not to eat a thing.

It seemed that the late William Henry had found this capriciousness adorable, but Mrs. Freeport's eyes were stones. Lily supposed this was how murders came about—not the hasty, soon regretted sort but the plan that is sown from an insult, a slight, and comes to flower at temperate speed. Mrs. Garnett deserved a reprimand. Lily saw her, without any emotion, doubled in two and shoved in a sack. But did Mrs. Freeport like her friend enough to bother teaching her lessons? Castigation, to Lily, suggested love. Mrs. Garnett and Mrs. Freeport were old friends, and vaguely related. Mrs. Garnett had been coming to Mrs. Freeport's every winter for years, but she left unfinished letters lying about, from which Lily— a great reader—could learn that dear Vanessa was becoming meaner and queerer by the minute. Thinking of Mrs. Freeport as "dear Vanessa" took flexibility, but Lily had that. She was not "Miss" and not "Littel"; she was, or, rather, had been, a Mrs. Cliff Little, who had taken advantage of the disorders of war to get rid of Cliff. He vanished, and his memory grew smaller and faded from the sky. In the bright new day strolled Miss Lily Littel, ready for anything. Then a lonely, fretful widow had taken a fancy to her and, as soon as travel was possible, had taken Lily abroad. There followed eight glorious years of trains and bars and discreet afternoon gambling, of eating éclairs in English-style tearooms, and discovering cafés where bacon and eggs were fried. Oh, the discovery of that sign in Monte Carlo: "Every Friday Sausages and Mashed"! That was the joy of being in foreign lands. One hot afternoon, Lily's employer, hooked by Lily into her stays not an hour before, dropped dead in a cinema lobby in Rome. Her will revealed she had provided for "Miss Littel," for a fox terrier, and for an invalid niece. The provision for the niece prevented the family from coming down on Lily's head; all the same, Lily kept out of England. She had not inspired the death of her employer, but she had nightmares for some time after, as though she had taken the wish for the deed. Her letters were so ambiguous that there was talk in England of an inquest. Lily accompanied the coffin as far as the frontier, for a letter of instructions specified cremation, which Lily understood could take place only in France. The coffin was held up rather a long time at customs, documents went back and forth, and in the end the relatives were glad to hear the last of it. Shortly after that, the fox terrier died, and Lily appropriated his share, feeling that she deserved it. Her employer had been living on overdrafts; there was next to nothing for dog, companion, or niece. Lily stopped having nightmares. She continued to live abroad.

With delicate nibbles, eyes down, Lily ate her cheese. Glancing sidewise, she noticed that Mrs. Garnett had closed the book. She wanted to annoy; she had planned the whole business of the Italian meal, had thought it out beforehand. Their manners were still strange to Lily, although she was a quick pupil. Why not clear the air, have it out? Once again she wondered what the two friends meant to each other. "Like" and "hate" were possibilities she had nearly forgotten when she stopped being Mrs. Cliff and became this curious, two-faced Lily Littel.

Mrs. Freeport's pebbly stare was focussed on her friend's jar of yogurt. "Sugar?" she cried, giving the cracked basin a shove along the table. Mrs. Garnett pulled it toward her, defiantly. She spoke in a soft, martyred voice, as though Lily weren't there. She said that it was her last evening and it no longer mattered. Mrs. Freeport had made a charge for extra sugar—yes, she had seen it on her bill. Mrs. Garnett asked only to pay and go. She was never coming again.

"I look upon you as essentially greedy." Mrs. Freeport leaned forward, enunciating with care. "You pretend to eat nothing, but I cannot look at a dish after you have served yourself. The *wreck* of the lettuce. The *destruction* of the pudding."

A bottle of wine, adrift and forgotten, stood by Lily's plate. She had not seen it until now. Mrs. Garnett, who was fearless, covered her yogurt thickly with sugar.

"Like most people who pretend to eat like birds, you manage

to keep your strength up," Mrs. Freeport said. "That sugar is the equivalent of a banquet, and you also eat between meals. Your drawers are stuffed with biscuits, and cheese, and chocolate, and heaven knows what."

"Dear Vanessa," Mrs. Garnett said.

"People who make a pretense of eating nothing always stuff furtively," said Mrs. Freeport smoothly. "Secret eating is exactly the same thing as secret drinking."

Lily's years abroad had immunized her to the conversation of gentlewomen, their absorption with money, their deliberate over- or underfeeding, their sudden animal quarrels. She wondered if there remained a great deal more to learn before she could wear their castoff manners as her own. At the reference to secret drinking she looked calm and melancholy. Mrs. Garnett said, "That is most unkind." The yogurt remained uneaten. Lily sighed, and wondered what would happen if she picked her teeth.

"My change man stopped by today," said Mrs. Garnett, all at once smiling and widening her eyes. How Lily admired that shift of territory—that carrying of banners to another field. She had not learned everything yet. "I *wish* you could have seen his face when he heard I was leaving! There really was no need for his coming, because I'd been in to his office only the week before, and changed all the money I need, and we'd had a lovely chat."

"The odious little money merchant in the bright-yellow automobile?" said Mrs. Freeport.

Mrs. Garnett, who often took up farfetched and untenable arguments, said, "William Henry wanted me to be happy."

"Edith!"

Lily hooked her middle finger around the bottle of wine and pulled it gently toward her. The day after tomorrow was years away. But she did not take her eyes from Mrs. Freeport, whose blazing eyes perfectly matched the small sapphires hanging from her ears. Lily could have matched the expression if she had cared to, but she hadn't arrived at the sapphires yet. Addressing herself, Lily said, "Thanks," softly, and upended the bottle.

"I meant it in a general way," said Mrs. Garnett. "William Henry wanted me to be happy. It was nearly the last thing he said."

"At the time of William Henry's death, he was unable to say anything," said Mrs. Freeport. "William Henry was my first cousin. Don't use him as a platform for your escapades."

Lily took a sip from her glass. Shock! It hadn't been watered—probably in honor of Mrs. Garnett's last meal. But it was sour, thick, and full of silt. "I have always thought a little sugar would improve it," said Lily chattily, but nobody heard.

Mrs. Freeport suddenly conceded that William Henry might have wanted his future widow to be happy. "It was because he spoiled you," she said. "You were vain and silly when he married you, and he made you conceited and foolish. I don't wonder poor William Henry went off his head."

"Off his head?" Mrs. Garnett looked at Lily; calm, courteous Miss Littel was giving herself wine. "We might have general conversation," said Mrs. Garnett, with a significant twitch of face. "Miss Littel has hardly said a word."

"Why?" shouted Mrs. Freeport, throwing her table napkin down. "The meal is over. You refused it. There is no need for conversation of any kind."

She was marvelous, blazing, with that water lily on her head.

Ah, Lily thought, but you should have seen me, in the old days. How I could let fly... poor old Cliff.

They moved in single file down the passage and into the sitting room, where, for reasons of economy, the hanging lustre contained one bulb. Lily and Mrs. Freeport settled down directly under it, on a sofa; each had her own newspaper to read, tucked down the side of the cushions. Mrs. Garnett walked about the room. "To think that I shall never see this room again," she said.

"I should hope not," said Mrs. Freeport. She held the paper before her face, but as far as Lily could tell she was not reading it.

"The trouble is"—for Mrs. Garnett could never help giving herself away—"I don't know where to *go* in the autumn."

"Ask your change man."

"Egypt," said Mrs. Garnett, still walking about. "I had friends who went to Egypt every winter for years and years, and now they have nowhere to go, either."

"Let them stay home," said Mrs. Freeport. "I am trying to read."

"If Egypt continues to carry on, I'm sure I don't know where we shall all be," said Lily. Neither lady took the slightest notice.

"They were perfectly charming people," said Mrs. Garnett, in a complaining way.

"Why don't you do the *Times* crossword, Edith?" said Mrs. Freeport.

From behind them, Mrs. Garnett said, "You know that I can't, and you said that only to make me feel small. But William Henry did it until the very end, which proves, I think, that he was not o.h.h. By o.h.h. I mean *off his head.*"

The break in her voice was scarcely more than a quaver, but to the two women on the sofa it was a signal, and they got to their feet. By the time they reached her, Mrs. Garnett was sitting on the floor in hysterics. They helped her up, as they had often done before. She tried to scratch their faces and said they would be sorry when she had died.

Between them, they got her to bed. "Where is her hot-water bottle?" said Mrs. Freeport. "No, not that one. She must have her own—the bottle with the bunny head."

"My yogurt," said Mrs. Garnett, sobbing. Without her make-up she looked shrunken, as though padding had been removed from her skin.

"Fetch the yogurt," Mrs. Freeport commanded. She stood over the old friend while she ate the yogurt, one tiny spoonful at a time. "Now go to sleep," she said.

In the morning, Mrs. Garnett was taken by taxi to the early train. She seemed entirely composed and carried her book. Mrs. Freeport hoped that her journey would be comfortable. She and Lily watched the taxi until it was out of sight on the road, and then, in the bare wintry garden, Mrs. Freeport wept into her hands.

"I've said goodbye to her," she said at last, blowing her nose. "It is the last goodbye. I shall never see her again. I was so horrid to her. And she is so tiny and frail. She might die. I'm convinced of it. She won't survive the summer."

"She has survived every other," said Lily reasonably.

"Next year, she must have the large room with the balcony. I don't know what I was thinking, not to have given it to her. We must begin planning now for next year. She will want a good reading light. Her eyes are so bad. And, you know, we should have chopped her vegetables. She doesn't chew. I'm sure that's at the bottom of the yogurt affair."

"I'm off to Nice tomorrow," said Lily, the stray. "My sister is expecting me."

"You are so devoted," said Mrs. Freeport, looking wildly for her handkerchief, which had fallen on the gravel path. Her hat was askew. The house was empty. "So devoted...I suppose that one day you will want to live in Nice, to be near her. I suppose that day will come."

Instead of answering, Lily set Mrs. Freeport's water lily straight, which was familiar of her; but they were both in such a state, for different reasons, that neither of them thought it strange.

*1960*

# ROSE

CHILDHOOD recollected is often hallucination; who is to blame?

One of my father's brothers, Hans-Thomas, was a bigamist. He had a wife and sons in Europe, and a wife and a little girl in the United States. The mother of the little girl was a Catholic and would not have married him if she had known he had been married once before. She was doubly injured; his divorce from the European wife, too late to be of any good to anyone, was not recognized in Boston, where she had made her home, and in the eyes of her church, she had never married at all.

My uncle was supremely careless, but heaven knows that he hadn't been brought up that way. My grandparents were German. My grandfather died young, and the children were brought up by their mother. My uncle had been knocked about, physically and spiritually, as much as any disciplinarian could ask for. The education of my grandmother's five children was based on humiliation; when they grew up, they stitched together their torn personalities as best they could. Hans-Thomas had spent whole days in a room, deprived of food and light and air and voices. Regularly, his head was shaved. Since this was not a common punishment in America, it was much remarked and ought to have taught him grace and obedience once and for all. But he grew up to be just as willful and heedless as he had been as a boy, hurt his wives, neglected his children, and escaped to Mexico, where he failed in one thing after the other. His mother sent him money until she died.

I met Hans-Thomas once, in our house in Montreal. He gave

me two America five-dollar bills, which seemed to me more valuable than Canadian money—not that I had been given ten dollars to spend before. Lest the money go to my head, my mother made me buy presents for Germaine, the half-witted *bonne d'enfants*, and for her sisters and brothers and cousins. I had never been told about my uncle's scandal, or why he lived in Mexico. I had never been told that the Boston cousin existed; but I knew. I knew about it, although no one had told me a thing. Perhaps that intuitive knowledge, the piecing together of facts overhead, overcharges the mind. In any case, the prelude to the hallucination is this: Simple Germaine takes me by train to my grandmother's house, in northern Vermont, for the holidays. The towns, the snow, the shabby farms are all familiar; we cross the border, where there is a different way of speaking, different money, a different flag. We have made this trip a dozen times.

Christmas is a special season for us. My parents are atheists. My grandmother is a European of her time and her class—Socialist, bluestocking, agnostic, and a snob. Like my parents, she objects to Christmas, but on different grounds. My parents complain about the sentimentality, and the commercialization of a myth. My grandmother patiently explains her aversion to the pagan tree, and why she will not have one in her house. We seem to me entirely apart. In my Catholic *pensionnat* in Montreal, where I am a day student, instructed by my family to learn French and keep out of the chapel, Christmas is marked by four weeks of fever. On the last day, I receive a present—a pen-wiper—from a skimpy tree. There is a crèche; Bethlehem seems to be a town in Quebec. The holy family and the attending animals, angels, and kings are knee-deep in cotton snow. In my classroom, the board is decorated by the most artistic of the nuns. We watch her drawing with colored chalk: green holly, red berries, angels with yellow hair. The blackboard, no longer available for sums, holds all the excitement of a pagan season my parents despise.

We do, however, exchange presents. I am bearing gifts to Grandmother—three drawings on parchment, and a heavy book.

We arrive at Grandmother's without adventure. And here the hallucination begins.

Her name is Rose. She is about thirteen, with long hair that lies in ribbons on a velvet coat. The coat has braid trimming and gilt buttons. She wears a fur beret. She carries a muff. Her fur-and-velvet overshoes are in the hall closet, where my navy reefer has been hung. The overshoes are the first excitement; who is here? My cousins are boys. No girl comes to Grandmother's but me. Now someone has come—Rose.

I wear a Ferris waist, two pairs of bloomers because of the cold, a middy blouse with a whistle on a cord, a blue skirt, white stockings, black patent-leather shoes. I have left my coat and my gloves in the hall, but kept my hat: *H.M.S. Halifax*. From either side of the hat sprout braids and powder-blue grosgrain bows. I am much younger than Rose, and considerably smaller. She bends down to me; she smells of cold and of snow. The room is oddly dark. She cries, "Oh, this is Irmgard. Oh, isn't she cute!"

I wait for Grandmother to gather her thunderbolts, balance them, and let fly. I might conceivably be allowed to swear, but I would be husbanded from human society if I said "cute." "Cute" is an abomination, like Wagner, canaries, the radio, motorcycles, small dogs, chintz. There are no thunderbolts. My grandmother —our grandmother—smiles at Rose out of her cold hazel eyes. She smirks at her, *doting*. Rose responds with a positive simper. They would eat each other, like spun sugar, if they could.

Obviously, Germaine and I have come too early. We have broken into their tea. I have known of only one cake at Grandmother's—a lemon-scented yellow loaf my mother derisively calls "Lutheran folly." But Rose has a layer cake decorated with cherries. She has large, thick cookies, saucer-sized, iced with pink and white, sprinkled with colored sugar. She has ginger biscuits, crescents, stars, delicately iced. She has snowmen with cherry noses and currant eyes. They disappear, wrapped in spangled paper, into Rose's muff.

In the dark, warm, scented parlor Germaine winds the

gramophone, and we hear bells from a foreign cathedral and shrill little voices crying *"Süsser die Glocken nie klingen...."* Doors fly open, Rose has a tree. Beyond the doors is a sweet-smelling pagan cave; the sitting room is a blaze of candles, stars, moons, planets; a tree. Rose sits on Grandmother's lap; Grandmother smooths her hair. Rose is crying. Then, laden with presents, weeping, Rose departs.

It has the true quality of a hallucination, because I take no part. I can see them, but they cannot see me. And then (this is the very thing my grandmother had taught us—her own children, then me—to suspect and scorn) singing infants, little biscuits, shed tears, slops. For she worked on my education—hard; not as she had with her own children, for she knew it had failed, but with endless instructions, and kneadings and pummelings of the mind. Her Germany was hard and thin, shadeless and plain, thin and cold, a landscape illuminated with a cold lemon sun, without warmth or regular clouds. She read to me in German. I was expected to understand. I was expected to sit and listen and form my understanding of people and the way they behaved, on the things she read. But there was a heavy brown veil between us— the German tongue. I knew two words for everything, one in English and one in French. I could not admit three. My grandmother read; I sat on a chair, so high and steep that my legs stuck out before me and went to sleep. She read and read, and one day the veil melted. I began to see a woman in long skirts, walking to and fro, talking, explaining. Suddenly she stops and throws a glance into a mirror. She peeps into a mirror, and what she sees— her own face—will always be as important to her as anything she has to say. I knew instantly what grown women were like and how I would be one day. *Voilà les grandes.* The veil must have reappeared; I remember nothing else.

Now, was this grandmother mine, or Rose's? Was her Germany the dark, spruce-scented cave, of which I was given a glimpse, or the shadeless landscape, the clear lemon sun? Did Rose carry hers all her life as I did mine—hers mournful, mine sad; hers tearful, mine grim; her rich, mine thin? But here is the problem, and why it can never be answered: I never saw Rose at all. But if I never saw Rose, then everything fades with her: the tree, the bells, the dark parlor, the candles, the hanging suns.


The next day, the sitting room doors were closed, the rooms had been aired. My present—a book, of course—was by my plate at breakfast. My grandmother and I exchanged a diffident kiss. I saw that she had written on the flyleaf "*für Irmgard.*"

On the journey home, Germain and I do not discuss Rose. I suspect Germaine of being an accomplice. She wound the gramophone. But I tell my parents, I say that we saw Rose, that there were biscuits and a tree.

"Oh, she *wouldn't.*"

But they exchange a look, which I catch. They say I am making it up. "We shall ask Grandmother," they warn.

Instinct now says that Grandmother is old and tired, and will lie. She has failed, and will now say anything for the sake of peace and to bind the family to her.

They turn to Germaine. "What was she like, Germaine? What was she wearing?"

Germaine racks her brain, which means she is set down in an unknown country and stumbles over tree roots and rocks. "She had on a navy-blue coat, a sailor hat, a sailor blouse, a…"

But no! *I* am the one with the middy, the whistle, the stockings, the *H.M.S Halifax* hat. I see that they know perfectly well Rose exists and are curious, for they would love to know more. They would love to know how she looked and how she was dressed, but they have no more belief in my velvet coat and fur beret than in Germaine's navy-blue reefer and sailor hat. My mother is excited. She lights a cigarette, puts it out, lights another. She admires her brother-in-law for having "brought it off." He brought it off—kept out of prison, where he belongs, and there he is, in Mexico, in the sun. Her brother-in-law's wickedness, his escape, excites something ruthless in her own nature. He is in Mexico; she is in Canada, which she hates. My mother would like to hear about Rose. Rose's circumstances are more interesting than mine. Her legitimacy is in doubt, she is a Catholic, her father has "brought it off" and lives in a warm climate.

My circumstances are boring. My mother knows all about my clothes. I wake, I dress, I am taken to school by Germaine, I play with dolls. They would have preferred a boy. Well, it is too late now. I am here. They should have thought of it sooner. They should have stopped bickering for a moment and come to a decision. Now I am here, and we shall just have to put up with one another. Rose needn't put up with anyone; her father is in Mexico, shedding five-dollar bills like leaves.

Since Rose is favored from the start, why is she given things I am told are abomination? It is for Rose that Grandmother's sitting room is a dark, enchanted cave. And so the questions begin again. Did it amuse our grandmother to give us different glimpses of her world? Mine was surely the noblest and best, but there was a coarse, sentimental *Lumpendeutsch* part of her nature reserved for Rose?

Did she see her often? Did she like her best?

There is a core of the whole business; and even now the child's puppy ego wakes and shows its teeth: prefer me, if you don't mind.

Catching Germaine off guard, I ask cunningly, *"Rose est jolie?"*

*"Jolie!"* cries Germaine. "She has pretty hair, but an ugly face. She smiles like a monkey."

She smiles like a monkey. We did see her then. At any rate, we saw someone.


But let us begin with common sense. The scene, as I saw it, was impossible. My grandmother would not have had that tree and those candles. As for the record of "Süsser die Glocken," sung by

mosquito voices, why, she could never have heard it for one minute without intense intellectual suffering. As though an eraser
were coming down on the decorated blackboard, the memory
must be rubbed out, or life, and the possibilities of behavior, like
my grandmother's heart, will split in two. The holly, the berries,
the angels, the candles, the snow, white, red, green, blur together
and dissolve in an odor of dust and slate. Rose, reduced, is a plain
girl with a monkey's smile. The eraser crosses her face. Rose is not
my cousin. I never saw her. She had no legal reason to exist.

Chalk and dust hang suspended in the air; the air clears, and
we are in a world of black and white again, black and white of
nun's habits, of leafless trees and snow, of white chalk on the practical board. Germaine says she saw someone; she remembers it
well. But Germaine was simple-minded, and notorious for making legends last.

*1960*

# THE COST OF LIVING

LOUISE, my sister, talked to Sylvie Laval for the first time on the stairs of our hotel on a winter afternoon. At five o'clock the skylight over the stairway and the blank, black windows on each of the landings were pitch dark—dark with the season, dark with the cold, dark with the dark air of cities. The only light on the street was the blue neon sign of a snack bar. My sister had been in Paris six months, but she still could say, "What a funny French word that is, Puss—'*snack*.'" Louise's progress down the steps was halting and slow. At the best of times she never hurried, and now she was guiding her bicycle and carrying a trench coat, a plaid scarf, Herriot's *Life of Beethoven*, Cassell's English-French, a bottle of cough medicine she intended to exchange for another brand, and a notebook, in which she had listed facts about nineteenth-century music under so many headings, in so many divisions of divisions, that she had lost sight of the whole.

The dictionary, the Herriot, the cough medicine, and the scarf were mine. I was the music mistress, out in all weathers, subject to chills, with plenty of woolen garments to lend. I had not come to Paris in order to teach *solfège* to stiff-fingered children. It happened that at the late age of twenty-seven I had run away from home. High time, you might say; but rebels can't always be choosers. At first I gave lessons so as to get by, and then I did it for a living, which is not the same thing. My older sister followed me—wisely, calmly, with plenty of money for travel—six years later, when both our parents had died. She was accustomed to a busy life at home in Australia, with a large house to look after and our invalid mother to nurse. In Paris, she found time on her hands. Once she had visited all the museums, and cycled around the famous squares, and read what was written on the monuments, she felt she was wasting her opportunities. She decided that music might be useful, since she had once been taught to play the piano; also, it was bound to give us something in common. She was making a serious effort to know me. There was a difference of five years between us, and I had been away from home for six. She enrolled in a course of lectures, took notes, and went to concerts on a cut-rate student's card.

I'd better explain about that bicycle. It was heavy and old—a boy's bike, left by a cousin killed in the war. She had brought it with her from Australia, thinking that Paris would be an easy, dreamy city, full of trees and full of time. The promises that led her, that have been made to us all at least once in our lives, had sworn faithfully there would be angelic children sailing boats in the fountains, and calm summer streets. But the parks were full of brats and quarreling mothers, and the bicycle was a nuisance everywhere. Still, she rode it; she would have thought it wicked to spend money on bus fares when there was a perfectly good bike to use instead.

We lived on the south side of the Luxembourg Gardens, where streets must have been charming before the motorcars came. Louise was hounded by buses and small, pitiless automobiles. Often, as I watched her from a window of our hotel, I thought of how she must seem to Parisian drivers—the very replica of the governessy figure the French, with their passion for categories and their disregard of real evidence, instantly label "the English Miss." It was a verdict that would have astonished her, if she had known, for Louise believed that "Australian," like "Protestant," was written upon her, plain as could be. She had no idea of the effect she gave, with her slow gestures, her straight yellow hair, her long face, her hand-stitched mannish gloves and shoes. The inclination of her head and the quarter-profile of cheek, ear, and throat could seem, at times, immeasurably tender. Full-face, the head snapped to, and you saw the lines of duty from nose to mouth, and the too pale eyes. The Prussian ancestry on our mother's side had given us something bleached and cold. Our faces were variations on a theme of fair hair, light brows. The mixture was weak in me. I had inherited the vanity, the stubbornness, without the will; I was too proud to follow and too lame to command. But physically we were nearly alike. The characteristic fold of skin at the outer corner of the eye, slanting down—we both had that. And I could have used a word about us, once, if I dared: "dainty." A preposterous word; yet, looking at the sepia studio portrait of us, taken twenty-five years ago, when I was eight and Louise thirteen, you could imagine it. Here is Louise, calm and straight, with her hair brushed on her shoulders, and her pretty hands; there am I, with organdy frock, white shoes, ribbon, and fringe. Two little Anglo-German girls, accomplished at piano, Old Melbourne on the father's side, Church of England to the bone: Louise and Patricia—Lulu and Puss. We hated each other then.

Once, before Louise left Paris forever, I showed her a description of her that had been written by Sylvie Laval. It was part of a cast of characters around whom Sylvie evidently meant to construct a film. I may say that Sylvie never wrote a scenario, or anything like one; but she belonged to a Paris where one was "writer" or "artist" or "actor" without needing to prove the point. "The Australian," wrote Sylvie, in a hand that showed an emotional age of nine, "is not elegant. All her skirts are too long, and she should not knit her own sweaters and hats. She likes Berlioz and the Romantics, which means corrupt taste. She lives in a small hotel on the left bank because [erased] She has an income she tries to pass off as moderate, which she probably got from a poor old mother, who died at last. Her character is innocent and romantic, but she is a mythomaniac and certainly cold. This [here Sylvie tried to spell a word unknown to me] makes it hard to guess her age. Her innocence is phenomenal, but she knows more than she says. She resembles the Miss Bronty [crossed out] Bronthee [crossed out] Brounte, the English lady who wore her hair parted in front and lived to a great old age after writing many moral novels and also Wuthering Heights."

I found the notes for the film in a diary after Sylvie had left the hotel. Going by her old room, I stopped at the open door. I could see Monsieur Rablis, who owned the hotel and who had been Sylvie's lover, standing inside. He stood, the heart of a temper storm, the core of a tiny hurricane, and he flung her abandoned effects onto a pile of ragged books and empty bottles. I think he meant to keep everything, even the bottles, until Sylvie came back to settle her bill and return the money he said she had stolen from his desk. There were Javel bottles and whiskey bottles and yogurt bottles and milk bottles and bottles for olive oil and tonic water and medicine and wine. Onto the pile went her torn stockings, her worn-out shoes. I recognized the ribbons and the *broderie anglaise* of a petticoat my sister had once given her as a present. The petticoat suited Sylvie—the tight waist, and the wide skirt—and it suited her even more after the embroidery became unstitched and flounces began to hang. Think of draggled laces, sagging hems, ribbons undone; that was what Sylvie was like. Hair in the eyes, sluttish little Paris face—she was a curious friend for immaculate Louise. When Monsieur Rablis saw me at the door, he calmed down and said, "Ah, Mademoiselle. Come in and see if any of this belongs to you. She stole from everyone— miserable little thief." But "little thief" sounded harmless, in French, in the feminine. It was a woman's phrase, a joyous term, including us all in a capacity for frivolous mischief. I stepped inside the room and picked up the diary, and a Japanese cigarette box, and the petticoat, and one or two other things.

That winter's day when Sylvie talked to Louise for the first time, Louise was guiding her bicycle down the stairs. It would be presumptuous for me to say what she was thinking, but I can guess: she was more than likely converting the price of oranges, face powder, and Marie-biscuits from French francs to Australian shillings and pence. She was, and she is, exceptionally prudent. Questions of upbringing must be plain to the eye and ear—if not, better left unexplained. Let me say only that it was a long training in modesty that made her accept this wretched hotel, where, with frugal pleasure, she drank tea and ate Marie-biscuits, heating the water on an electric stove she had been farsighted enough to bring from home. Her room had dusty claret hangings. Silverfish slid from under the carpet to the cracked linoleum around the wash-stand. She could have lived in comfort, but I doubt if it occurred to her to try. With every mouthful of biscuit and every swallow of tea, she celebrated our mother's death and her own release. Louise had nursed Mother eleven years. She nursed her eleven years, buried her, and came to Paris with a bicycle and an income.

Now, Sylvie, who knew nothing about duty and less about remorse, would have traded her soul, without a second's bargaining, for Louise's room; for Sylvie lived in an ancient linen cupboard. The shelves had been taken out and a bed, a washstand, a small table, a straight chair pushed inside. In order to get to the window, one had to pull the table away and climb over the chair. This room, or cupboard, gave straight onto the stairs between two floors. The door was flush with the staircase wall; only a ravaged keyhole suggested that the panel might be any kind of door. As she usually forgot to shut it behind her, anyone who wanted could see her furrowed bed and the basin, in which underclothes floated among islands of scum. She would plunge down the stairs, leaving a blurred impression of mangled hair and shining eyes. Her eyes were a true black, with the pupil scarcely distinct from the iris. Later I knew that she came from the southwest of France; I think that some of her people were Basques. The same origins gave her a stocky peasant's build and thick, practical hands. Her hand, grasping the stair rail, and the firm tread of her feet specified a quality of strength that had nothing in common with the forced liveliness of Parisian girls, whose energy seemed to me as thin and strung up as their voices. Her scarf, her gloves flew from her like birds. Her shoes could never keep up with her

feet. One of my memories of Sylvie—long before I knew anything about her, before I knew even her name—is of her halting,
cursing loudly with a shamed smile, scrambling up or down a few
steps, and shoving a foot back into a lost ballerina shoe. She wore
those thin slippers out on the streets, under the winter rain. And
she wore a checked skirt, a blue sweater, and a scuffed plastic
jacket that might have belonged to a boy. Passing her, as she hung
over the banister calling to someone below, you saw the tensed
muscle of an arm or leg, the young neck, the impertinent head.
Someone ought to have drawn her—but somebody has: Sylvie
was the coarse and grubby Degas dancer, the girl with the shoulder thrown back and the insolent chin. For two pins, or fewer,
that girl staring out of flat canvas would stick out her tongue or
spit in your face. Sylvie had the voice you imagine belonging to
the picture, a voice that was common, low-pitched, but terribly
penetrating. When she talked on the telephone, you could hear
her from any point in the hotel. She owned the telephone, and she
read *Cinémonde*, a magazine about film stars, by the hour, in the
lavatory or (about once every six weeks) while soaking in the tub.
There was one telephone and one tub for the entire hotel, and one
lavatory for every floor. Sylvie was always where you wanted to be;
she had always got there first. Having got there, she remained,
turning pages, her voice cheerfully lifted in the newest and most
melancholy of popular songs.

"Have you noticed that noisy girl?" Louise said once, describing
her to me and to the young actor who had the room next to mine.

We were all three in Louise's room, which now had the look of
a travel bureau and a suburban kitchen combined; she had covered the walls with travel posters and bought a transparent plastic
tablecloth. Pottery dishes in yellow and blue stood upon the
shelves. Louise poured tea and gave us little cakes. I remember
that the young man and I, both well into the age of reason, sat up
very straight and passed spoons and paper napkins back and forth

with constant astonished cries of "Thank you" and "Please." It was something about Louise; she was so kind, so hospitable, she made one want to run away.

"I never notice young girls," said the young man, which seemed to me a fatuous compliment, but Louise turned pink. She appeared to be waiting for something more from him, and so he went on, "I know the girl you mean." It was not quite a lie. I had seen Sylvie and this boy together many times. I had heard them in his room, and I had passed them on the stairs. Well, it was none of my affair.

Until Louise's arrival, I had avoided meeting anyone in the hotel. Friendship in bohemia meant money borrowed, recriminations, complaints, tears, theft, and deceit. I kept to myself, and I dressed like Louise, which was as much a disguise as my bohemian way of dressing in Melbourne had been. This is to explain why I had never introduced Louise to anyone in the hotel. As for the rest of Paris, I didn't need to bother; Louise arrived with a suitcase of introductions and a list of names as long as the list for a wedding. She was not shy, she wanted to "get to know the people," and she called at least once on every single person she had an introduction to. That was how it happened that she and the actor met outside the hotel, in a different quarter of Paris. They had seen each other across the room, and each of them thought "I wonder who that is?" before discovering they lived in the same place. This sort of thing is supposed never to happen in cities, and it does happen.

She met him on the twenty-first of December in the drawing room of a house near the Parc Monceau. She had been invited there by the widow of a man in the consular service who had been to Australia and had stayed with an uncle of ours. It was one of the names on Louise's list. Before she had been many weeks in Paris, she knew far more than I did about the hard chairs, cheerless lights, and gray-pink antique furniture of French rooms. The hobby of the late consul had been collecting costumes. The drawing room was lined with glass cases in which stood headless dummies wearing the beads and embroidery of Turkey, Macedonia, and Greece. It was a room intended not for people but for things—this was a feeling Louise said she often had about rooms in France. Thirty or forty guests drifted about, daunted by the museum display. They were given whiskey to drink and sticky cakes. Louise wore the gray wool dress that was her "best" and the turquoise bracelets our Melbourne grandfather brought back from a voyage to China. They were the only ornaments I have ever seen her wearing. She talked to a poet who carried in his pocket an essay about him that had been printed years before— yellow, brittle bits of paper, like beech leaves. She consoled a wild-haired woman who complained that her daughter had begun to carry on. "How old is your daughter?" said Louise. The woman replied, "Thirty-five. And you know how men are now. They have no respect for girlhood anymore." "It is very difficult," Louise agreed. She was getting to know the people, and was pleased with her afternoon. The consul's widow looked toward the doors and muttered that Cocteau was coming, but he never came. All at once Louise heard her say, in answer to a low-toned question, "She's Australian," and then she heard, "She's like a coin, isn't she? Gold and cold. She's interested in music, and lives over on the Left Bank, just as you do—except that you don't give your address, little monkey, not even to your mother's friends. I had such a lot of trouble getting a message to you. Perhaps she's your sort, although she's much too old for you. She doesn't know how to talk to men." The consul's widow hadn't troubled to lower her voice—the well-bred Parisian voice that slices stone.

Louise accepted the summing up, which was inadequate, like any other. Possibly she did not know how to talk to men—at least the men she had met here. Because she thought people always said what they meant and no more than they intended, her replies were disconcerting; she never understood that the real, the un-mentioned, topic was implicit between men and women. I had often watched her and seen the pattern—obtuseness followed by visible surprise—which made her seem more than ever an English

Miss. She said to the young man who had asked the question about her, and who now was led across to be presented, "Yes, that's quite right. I don't talk to men much, although I do listen. I haven't any brothers and I went to Anglican convents."

That was abrupt and Australian and spinsterish, if you like, but she had been married. She had been married at eighteen to Collie Tate. After a few months his regiment was sent to Malaya, and before she'd had very many letters from him he was taken prisoner and died. He must have been twenty. Louise seemed to have forgotten Collie, obliterating, in her faithlessness, not only his death but the fact that he had ever lived. She wore the two rings he had given her. They had rubbed her fingers until calluses formed. She was at ease with the rings and with the protective thickening around them, but she had forgotten him.

The young actor gravely pointed out that the name he was introduced to her by—Patrick something—was a stage name, and after Louise had sat down on a gilt chair he sat down at her feet. She had never seen anyone sitting on the floor in France, and that made her look at him. She probably looked at his hands; most women think a man's character is shown in his hands. He was dressed like many of the students in the streets around our hotel, but her practical eye measured the cost and cut of the clothes, and she saw he was false-poor, pretending. There was something rootless and unclaimed in the way he dressed, the way he sprawled, and in his eagerness to explain himself; but for all that, he was French.

"You aren't what I think of as an Australian," he said, looking up at her. He must have learned to smile, and glance, and give his full attention, when he was still very young; perhaps he charmed his mother that way. "I didn't know there were any attractive women there."

"You might have met people from Sydney," Louise said. "I'm from Melbourne."

"Do the nice Australians come from Melbourne?"

"Yes, they do."

He looked at her briefly and suspiciously. Surely anyone so

guileless seeming must be full of guile? If he had asked, she would have told him that, tired of clichés, she met each question as it came up. She returned his look, as if glancing out of shadows. There must have been something between them then—a mouse squeak of knowledge. She was not a little girl freshly out of school, wishing she had a brother; she was thirty-eight, and had been widowed nineteen years.

They discovered they lived in the same hotel. He thought he must have seen her, he said, particularly when she spoke of the bicycle. He remembered seeing a bicycle, someone guiding it up and down. "Perhaps your sister," he said, for she had told him about me. "Perhaps," said serpent Louise. She thought that terribly funny of him, funny enough to repeat to me. Then she told him that she was certain she had heard his voice. Wasn't he the person who had the room next to her sister? There was an actor in that room who read aloud—oh, admirably, said Louise. (He did read, and I had told her so; he read in the groaning, suffering French classical manner that is so excruciating to foreign ears.) He was that person, he said, delighted. They had recognized each other then; they had known each other for days. He said again that "Patrick" was a stage name. He was sorry he had taken it—I have forgotten why. He told her he was waiting for a visa so that he could join a repertory company that had gone to America. He had been tubercular once; there were scars, or shadows, on his lungs. That was why the visa was taking so long. He tumbled objects out of his pockets, as if everything had to be explained to her. He showed a letter from the embassy, telling him to wait, and a picture of a house in the Dordogne that belonged to his family, where he would live when he grew old. She looked at the stone house and the garden and the cherry trees, and her manner when she returned it to him was stiff and shy. She said nothing. He was young, but old enough to know what that sudden silence meant; and he woke up. When the consul's widow came to see how they were getting on and if one of them wanted rescuing, they said together, "We live in the same hotel!" Had anything as marvelous ever happened in Paris, and could it ever happen again? The woman looked at Louise then and said, "I was wrong about you, was I? Discreet but sure—that's how Anglo-Saxons catch their fish."

It was enough to make Louise sit back in her chair. "What will people say?" has always been, to her, deeply real. In that light the gray wool dress she was wearing and the turquoise bracelets were cold as snow. She was a winter figure in the museum room. She was a thrifty widow; an abstemious traveler counting her comforts in shillings and pence. She was a blunt foreigner, not for an instant to be taken in. Her most profound belief about herself was that she was too honest to fall in love. She believed that men were basically faithless, and that women could not love more than once. She never forgave a friend who divorced. Having forgotten Collie, she thought she had never loved at all.

"Could you let me have some money?"

That was the first time Sylvie talked to Louise. Those were Sylvie's first words, on the winter afternoon, on the dark stairs. The girl was around the bend of a landing, looking down. Louise stopped, propping the bicycle on the wall, and stared up. Sylvie leaned into the stairwell so that the dead light from the skylight was behind her; then she drew back, and there was a touch of winter light upon her, on the warm skin and inquisitive eyes.

I may say that giving money away to strangers was not the habit of my sister, our family, or the people we grew up with. Louise stood, in her tweed skirt, her arm aching with the weight of so many useful objects. The mention of money automatically evoked two columns of figures. In all financial matters, Louise was bound to the rows of numbers in her account books. These account books were wrapped in patent leather, and came from a certain shop in Melbourne; our father's ledgers had never been bought in any other place. The columns were headed "Paid" and "Received," in the old-fashioned way, but at the top of each page our father, and then Louise, crossed out the printed words and wrote "Necessary" and "Unnecessary." When Louise was obliged to buy a Christmas or birthday present for anyone, she marked the amount she had spent under "Unnecessary." I had never attached any significance to her doing this; she was closer to our parents than I, and that was how they had always reckoned. She guarded her books as jealously as a diary. What can be more intimate than a record of money and the way one spends it? Think of what Pepys has revealed. Nearly everything we know about Leonardo is summed up in his accounts.

"Well, I do need money," said the girl, rather cheerfully. "Monsieur Rablis wants to put me out of my room again. Sometimes he makes me pay and sometimes he doesn't. Oh, imagine being on top of the world on top of a pile of money!" This was not said plaintively but with an intense vitality that was like a third presence on the stairs. Her warmth and her energy communicated so easily that there was almost too much, and some fell away and had its own existence.

That was all Louise could tell me later on. She had been asked to put her hand in her pocket for a stranger, for someone who had no claim on her at all, and she was as deeply shocked as if she had been invited to take part in an orgy—a comparison I do not intend as a joke.

"What if *I* asked you for money?" I suddenly said.

She looked at me with that pale-eyed appraisal and gently said, "Why, Puss, you've got what you want, haven't you? Haven't you got what you wanted out of life?" I had two woolen scarves, one plaid and one blue, which meant I had one to lend. Perhaps Louise meant that.

The absence of sun in Paris brought on a kind of irrationality at times, just as too much sun can drive one mad. If it had been anyone but my sister talking to me, I would have said that Sylvie was nothing but an apparition on the stairs. Who ever has heard of asking strangers for money? And one woman to another, at that. I know that I had never become accustomed to the northern solstice. The whitish sky and the evil Paris roofs and the cold red sun suggested a destiny so final that I wondered why everyone did not rebel or run away. Often after Christmas there was a fall of snow, and one could be amazed by the confident tracks of birds. But in a few weeks it was forgotten, and the tramps, the drunks, the unrepentant poor (locked up by the police so that they would not freeze on the streets) were released once more, and settled down in doorways and on the grilles over the Métro, where fetid air rose from the trains below, to await the coming of spring. I could see that Louise was perplexed by all this. She had been warned of the damp, but nothing had prepared her for those lumps of bodies, or for the empty sky. At four o'clock every day the sun appeared. It hung over the northwest horizon for a few minutes, like a malediction, and then it vanished and the city sank into night.

This is the moment to talk about Patrick. I think of him in that season—something to do with chill in the bones, and thermometers, and the sound of the rain. I had often heard his voice through the wall, and had guessed he was an actor. I knew him by sight. But I came home tired every night, disinclined to talk. I saw that everyone in this hotel was as dingy, as stationary, as I was myself, and I knew we were tainted with the same incompetence. Besides giving music lessons, I worked in a small art gallery on the Ile de la Cité. I received a commission of one half of one per cent on the paintings I sold. I was a foreigner without a working permit, and had no legal recourse. Every day, ten people came into that filthy gallery and asked for my job. Louise often said, "But this is a rich country, Puss. Why are there no jobs, and why are people paid nothing?" I can only describe what I know.

Patrick: my sister's lover. Well, perhaps, but not for long. An epidemic of grippe came into the city, as it did every year. Patrick was instantly felled. He went into illness as if it were a haven, establishing himself in bed with a record-player and a pile of books and a tape recorder. I came down with it, too. Every day, Louise knocked on his door, and then on mine. She came down the stairs—her room was one flight above ours—pushing her bicycle, the plaid scarf tied under her chin. She was all wool and tweed and leather again. The turquoise bracelets had been laid in a drawer, the good gray dress put away. She fetched soup, aspirin, oranges, the afternoon papers. She was conscientious, and always had the right change. Louise was a minor heiress now, but I had never been pardoned. I inherited my christening silver and an income of fifteen shillings a month. They might have made it a pound. It was only fair; she had stayed home and carried trays and fetched the afternoon papers—just as she was doing now— while I had run away. Nevertheless, although she was rich and I was poor, she treated me as an equal. I mean by that that she never bought me a cheese sandwich or a thermos flask of soup without first taking the money for it out of the purse on my desk and counting out the correct change. I don't know if she made an equal of Patrick. The beginning had already rushed into the past and frozen there, as if, from the first afternoon, each had been thinking, This is how it will be remembered. After a few days she declined, or rose, to governess, nanny, errand girl, and dear old friend. What hurts me in the memory is the thought of all that golden virtue, that limpid will, gone to waste. He was such an insignificant young man. Long eyelashes, grave smile—I could have snapped him out between thumb and finger like a bug. Poor Louise! She asked so many questions but never the right kind. God help you if you lose your footing in this country. There are no second tries. Was there any difference between a music teacher without a working permit, a tubercular actor trying to get to America, and a man bundled in newspapers sleeping on the street? Louise never saw that. She was as careful in her human judgments as she was in her accounts. Unable to squander, she wondered where to deposit her treasures of pity, affection, and love.

Patrick was reading to himself in English, with the idea that it would be useful in New York. Surely he might have thought of it before? Incompetence was written upon him as plainly as on me, and that was one of the reasons I averted my eyes. Louise was expected to correct his accent, and once he asked me to choose his texts. He read *End-game* and *Waiting for Godot*, which I heard through the wall. Can you imagine listening to Beckett when you are lying in bed with a fever? I struggled up one day, and into a dressing gown, and dumped on his bed an armload of poetry. "If you *must* have Irish misery," I said, and I gave him Yeats. English had one good effect; he stopped declaiming. The roughness of it took the varnish off his tongue. "Nor dread nor hope attend a dying animal," I heard through the wall one Thursday afternoon, and the tone was so casual that he might have been asking for a cigarette or the time of a train. "Nor dread nor hope..." I saw the window and heard the rain and realized it was my thirty-third birthday. Patrick had great patience, and listened to his own voice again and again.

Louise nursed us, Patrick and me, as if we were one: one failing appetite, one cracked voice. She was accustomed to bad-tempered invalids, and it must have taken two of us to make one of Mother. She fed us on soup and oranges and soda biscuits. The soda biscuits were hard to find in Paris, but she crossed to the Right Bank on her bicycle and brought them back from the exotic food shops by the Madeleine. They were expensive, and neither of us could taste them, but she thought that soda biscuits were what we ought to have. She planned her days around our meals. Every noon she went out with an empty thermos flask, which she had filled with soup at the snack bar across the street. The oranges came from the market, rue St.-Jacques. Our grippe smelled of oranges, and of leek-and-potato soup.

Louise had known Patrick seventeen days, and he had been ailing for twelve, when she talked to Sylvie again. The door to Sylvie's room was open. She sat up in her bed, with her back to a filthy pillow, eating *pain-au-chocolat*. There were crumbs on the blanket and around her chin. She saw Louise going by with a string bag and a thermos, and she called, "Madame!" Louise paused, and Sylvie said, "If you are coming straight back, would you mind bringing me a cheese sandwich? There's money for it in the chrysanthemum box." This was a Japanese cigarette box in which she kept her savings. "I am studying for the stage," she went on, without giving Louise a chance to reply. This was to explain a large mirror that had been propped against the foot of the bed so that she could look at herself. "It's important for me to know just what I'm like," she said seriously. "In the theatre, everything is enlarged a hundred times. If you bend your little finger"—she showed how—"from the top gallery it must seem like a great arc."

"Aren't you talking about films?" said Louise.

Sylvie screwed her eyes shut, thought, and said, "Well, if it isn't films it's Brecht. Anyway, it's something I've heard." She laughed, with her hands to her face, but she was watching between her fingers. Then she folded her hands and began telling poor Louise how to sit, stand, and walk on the stage—rattling off what she had learned in some second-rate theatrical course. Patrick had told us that every unemployed actor in Paris believed he could teach.

They still had not told each other their names; and if Louise walked into that cupboard room, and bothered to hear Sylvie out, and troubled to reply, it must have been only because she had decided one could move quite easily into another life in France. She worked hard at understanding, but she was often mistaken. I know she believed the French had no conventions.

"I stay in bed because my room is so cold," said Sylvie, rapidly now, as if Louise might change her mind and turn away. "This room is an icebox—there isn't even a radiator—so I stay in bed and study and I leave the door open so as to get some of the heat from the stairs." A tattered book of horoscopes lay facedown on the blanket. Tacked to the wall was a picture someone had taken of Sylvie asleep on a sofa, during or after a party, judging from the scene. The slit of window in the room gave on a court, but it was a bright court, with a brave tree whose roots had cracked the paving.

"My name is Sylvie Laval," she said, and, wiping her palm on the bedsheet, prepared to shake hands.

"Louise Tate." Louise set the thermos down on Sylvie's table, between a full ashtray and a cardboard container of coagulated milk. She saw the Japanese box with the chrysanthemum painted on the lid, and picked it up.

"What a new element you are going to be for me," said Sylvie, settling back and watching with some amazement. "I shall observe you and become like you. Yes, that's the money box, and you must take whatever you need for the sandwich."

"Why do you want to observe me?" said Louise, turning and laughing at her.

"You look like an angel," Sylvie said. "I'm sure angels look like you."

"I was once told I looked like an English poet in first youth," said Louise, trying to pretend that Sylvie's intention had been ironical.

Sylvie tilted her little chin as if to say she knew what that was all about. "Your friends are poets," she said. "They must be like you, too—wise and calm. I wish I knew your friends."

"They are very plain people," said Louise, still smiling. "They wouldn't be much fun for a bright little thing like you."

"Foreigners?"

"Some. French, too." Louise was proud of her introductions.

Sylvie looked with her bold black eyes and said, "French. I knew it."

"Knew what?"

"You and the type upstairs. The great actor—the comedian." She bit her fingers, hesitating. Her features were coarse and sly. "You're so comic, the two of you, creeping about with your secret. But love is love, and everyone knows."

I have wondered since about that bit of mischief. I suppose Patrick had given Sylvie a role to play, because it was the only way he could control her. She had found out, or he had told, and he had warned her not to hurt Louise. Louise was someone who must be spared. She must never guess that he and Sylvie had been lovers. They thought Louise could never stand up to the truth; they thought no one could bear to be told the truth about anything after a certain age.

Sylvie, launched in a piece of acting, could not help overloading. "Do you know any other French people?" she said. "Never mind. There's me." She flung out her arms suddenly—to the mirror, not to Louise—and cried, "I am your French friend."


"She's got a picture of herself sound asleep, curled up with no shoes on," said Louise, talking in a new, breathless voice. "It must be the first thing she looks at in the morning when she wakes up. And she seems terribly emotional and generous. I don't know why, but she gives you the feeling of generosity. I'm sure she does herself a lot of harm."

We were in Patrick's room. Louise poured the daily soup into pottery bowls. I have often tried to imagine how he must have seemed to Louise. I doubt if she could have told you. From the beginning they stood too close; his face was like a painting in which there are three eyes and a double profile. No matter how far she backed off, later on, she never made sense of him. Let me tell what *I* remember. I remember that it was easy for him to talk, easy for him to say anything, so that I can hear a voice, having ceased to think of a face. He seldom gestured. Only his voice, which was trained, and could never be disguised, told that he did not think he was an ordinary person; he did not believe he was like anyone else in the world, not for a minute. I asked myself a commonplace question: What does she see in him? I should have wondered if she saw him at all. As for me, I saw him twice. I saw him the first time when Louise described the meeting in the consul's widow's drawing room, and I understood that the dazzling boy was only that droning voice through the wall. From the time of our grippe, I can see a spiral of orange peel, a water glass with air bubbles on the side of the glass, but I cannot see him. There was the bluish smoke of his Caporal cigarettes, and the shape of Louise, like something seen against the light...None of it is sharp.

One day I saw Patrick and Sylvie together, and that was plain, and clear, and well remembered. I had gone out in the rain to give a music lesson to a spoiled child, the ward of a doting grand-mother. I came up the stairs, and because I heard someone laugh-ing, or because I was feverish and beyond despair, I went into Patrick's room instead of my own.

Sylvie was there. She knelt on the floor, wearing her nightdress (the time must have been close to noon), struggling with Patrick for a bottle of French vodka, which tastes of marsh water and smells like eau de cologne. "Louise says mustn't drink," said Syl-vie, in a babyish voice; "and besides it's mine." They stopped their puppy play when they saw me; there was a mock scurry, as if it were Puss who had the governess role instead of Louise. Then I noticed Louise. She sat before the window, reading a novel, tak-ing no notice of her brawling pair. Her face was calm and happy and the lines of moral obligation had disappeared. She said, "Well, Puss," with our mother's inflection, and she seemed so young—nineteen or so—that I remembered how Collie had been in love with her once, before going to Malaya to be killed. Sylvie must have been born that year, the year Louise was married. I hadn't thought of that until now.

"When Berlioz was living in Italy," I said, "he heard that Ma-rie Pleyel was going to be married, and so he disguised himself as a lady's maid and started off for Paris. He intended to assassinate Marie and her mother and perhaps the fiancé as well. But he changed his mind for some reason, and I think he went to Nice." This story rushed to my lips without reason. Berlioz and Marie Pleyel seemed to me living people, and the facts contemporary gossip. While I was telling it, I remembered they had all of them died. I forgot every word I had ever known of French, and told it in English, which Sylvie could not understand.

"You ought to be in bed, my pet," I heard Louise say.

Sylvie went on with something she had been telling before my arrival. She had an admirer who was a political cartoonist. His cartoons were ferocious, and one imagined him out on the boulevards of Paris doing battle with the police; but he was really a timid man, afraid of cats, and unable to cross most streets without trembling. "He spends thousands of francs," said Sylvie, sighing. She told how many francs she had seen him spending.

I said, "Money, money...it *does* bring happiness." I wondered if Louise recalled that Berlioz had written this, and that we had quarreled about it once.

Prone across the bed, leaning on his elbows, Patrick listened to Sylvie with grave attention, and I thought that here was a situation no amount of money could solve; for it must be evident to Louise, unless she were blind and had lost all feeling, that something existed between the two. The lark had stopped singing, but it had not died; it was alive and flying in the room. Sylvie, nibbling now on chocolates stuck to a paper bag, felt that I was staring at her, and turned her head.

"My room is so cold," she said humbly, "and I get so lonely, and finally I thought I'd come in to him."

"Quite right of you," I said, as if his time and his room were mine. But Sylvie seemed to think she had been dismissed. She licked the last of the chocolate from the paper, crumpled the bag, threw it at Patrick, and slammed the door. I sat down and leaned my head back and closed my eyes. I heard Patrick saying, "Read this," and when I looked again, Louise was on the edge of the bed with a letter in her hands. She bent over it. Her hair was like the sun—the real sun, not the sun we saw here.

"It says that your visa is refused," she said, in her flat, positive French. "It says that in six months you may apply again."

"That's what I understood. I thought you might understand more."

She smoothed the letter with both hands and made up her mind about saying something. She said, "Come to Australia."

"What?"

"Come to Australia. I'll see that they let you in; I can do that much for you. You can stay with me in Melbourne until you get settled. The house is enormous. It's too big for one person. The climate would be perfect for you."

Think of that courage: she'd have taken him home.

He looked as if she had said something completely empty of meaning, and then he appeared to understand; it was a splendid piece of mime. "What would I do in Australia? I can hardly talk the language."

"I've seen people arriving, without money, without English, without anything, and then they do as well as anyone."

"They were refugees," he said. "I've got my own country. I'm not a refugee."

"You were anxious enough to go to New York."

The apple never drops far from the tree; here was our mother all over again, saying something unpleasant but true. My dutiful sister, the good elder girl—I might have helped her then. I might have told her how men were, or what it was like in Paris. But I kept silent, and presently I heard him saying he was going home. He was going to the house in the Dordogne—the house he had shown her in the photograph. She may have been jealous of that house; in her place I should have been. He said that the winter in Paris had been bad for him; there hadn't been enough work. Next season he would try again.

"Your mother will be pleased to have you for a bit," said Louise, accepting it; but I doubt if any of us can accept humiliation so simply. She folded the letter and placed it quietly beside her on the blanket. She said, "I'd better put Puss to bed," and got to her feet. I don't believe they had much to say to each other after that. He went away for a week, came back to us for a fortnight, and then disappeared.

When I was recovering from that second attack of grippe, Louise made me go with her to the Faubourg St. Honoré to look at shops. Neither of us intended buying anything, but Louise thought the outing would do me good. Just as she was convinced invalids wanted soda biscuits, so she believed convalescents found a new purpose in living when they looked at pretty things. We looked at coats and ski boots and sweaters, and we stared at rare editions, and finally, fatigued and stupid, gazed endlessly at the brooches and strings of beads in an antique jewelry store.

"It can't be worth such an awful lot," said Louise, taking an interest in a necklace. The stones—agate, cornelian, red jasper— were rubbed and uneven, like glass that has been polished by waves. The charm of the necklace was in its rough, careless appearance and the warm color of the stones. I put one hand flat against the pane of the counter. When I took it away, I watched the imprint fade. I was accustomed to wanting what I could not have.

"Do you like it, Puss?" said Louise.

"Very much."

"So do I. It would be perfect for Sylvie."

That is all I can tell you: I am not Louise. She came out of the shop with a wrapped parcel in her hand, and said in a matter-of-fact tone that the stones were early-eighteenth-century seals, that the man had been most civil about taking her check, and that the necklace had cost a great deal of money. That was all until we reached the hotel, and then she said, "Puss, will you give it to her? She'll think it strange, coming from me."

"Why won't she think it just as odd if I give it?" I called, for Louise had simply moved on, leaving me outside Sylvie's door. I felt cross and foolish. Louise climbed slowly, one hand on the banister. I know now that she went straight upstairs to her room and marked the price of the necklace under "Necessary." It was not the real price but about a fifth of the truth. She absorbed the balance in the rest of her accounts by cheating heavily for a period of weeks. She charged herself an imaginary thousand francs for a sandwich and two thousand for a bunch of winter daisies, and inflated the cost of living until the cost of the necklace had disappeared.

I knocked on Sylvie's door, and heard her scuttling about behind it. "Come in!" she shouted. "Oh, it's you. I thought it was the horrible Rablis. I can't let him in when I'm not properly dressed, because...you know." She had pulled on a pair of slacks and a sweater I recognized as Patrick's.

"Louise wants you to have this," I said.

She took the box from me and sat down on the bed. She was terrified by this gift. Even the sight of the ribbons and tissue paper alarmed her. I saw that in terms of Sylvie's world Louise had made a mistake. The present was so extraordinary and it had been delivered in such a roundabout fashion that the girl thought she was being bought.

"My sister chose it for you on an impulse," I said. I felt huge and uniformed, like a policeman. "It seems to me a ridiculous present for a girl who hasn't proper shoes or a decent winter coat, but she thought you'd like it."

She lifted the necklace out of its box and held it over her head and let it fall. She was an actress, true enough—Sarah Bernhardt to the life. But then she turned away from me, leaning on her hands, straining forward toward the mirror, and she stopped pretending. I saw on her impudent profile surprise and greed, and we understood, together, at the same moment, what could be had from women like Louise. Sylvie said, "Your sister must be very rich."

That jolted me. "Consider the necklace a kind of insurance if you want to," I said. "You can sell it if you need money. You can give it back when you don't want it anymore." That stripped the giving of any intention; she was not obliged to admire Louise, or even be grateful.

She wore the necklace every day. It hung over her plastic coat, and on top of Patrick's old sweater. One night she fell up the stairs wearing it, and a piece of jasper broke away. The necklace had a grin to it then, with a cracked tooth. Louise scarcely noticed. Now that she had given the necklace away, she scarcely saw it at all. Giving had altered her perceptions. She walked in her sleep, and part of her character, smothered until now, began to live and breathe in a dream. "I've hardly worn it," I can hear her telling Sylvie. "I bought it for myself, but it doesn't suit me." She said it about the tweed skirts, the quilted dressing gown, the stockings, the gloves, all purchased with Sylvie in mind. (She never felt the need to give me anything. She never so much as returned my scarf until she went back to Australia, and then it was simply a case of forgetting it, leaving it behind. She also left her trumped-up accounts. Sylvie abandoned her empty bottles and a diary and a dirty petticoat; my sister left my scarf and her false accounts. The stuff of her life is in those figures: "Dentist for S." "Shoes for S." "Oil stove for S." I was touched to find under "Necessary" "Aspirin for Puss." She had listed against it the price of a five-course meal. The two went together, the giving and the lying.)

The days drew out a quarter-second at a time. Patrick, who had been away (though not to the house in the Dordogne; he did not tell us where he was), returned to a different climate. Louise and Sylvie had become friends. They were silly and giggly, and had a private language and special jokes. The most unexpected remarks sent them off into fits of laughter. At times they hardly dared meet each other's eyes. It was maddening for anyone outside the society. I saw that Patrick was intrigued and then annoyed. The day he left (I mean, the day he left forever) he returned the books I'd lent him—Yeats, and the other poets—and he asked me what was happening between those two. I had never known him to be blunt. I gave him an explanation, but it was beside the truth. I could have said, "You don't need her; you refused Australia; and now you're going home." Instead, I told him, "Louise likes looking after people. It doesn't matter which one of us she looks after, does it? Sylvie isn't worth less than you or me. She loves the stage as much as you do. She'd starve to pay for her lessons."

"But Louise mustn't take that seriously," he said. "There are thousands of girls like Sylvie in Paris. They all have natural charm, and they don't want to work. They imagine there's no work to acting. Nothing about her acting is real. Everything is copied. Look at the way she holds her arms, and that quick turn of the head. She never stops posing, trying things out; but acting is something else."

I took my books from him and put them on my table. I said, "This is between you and Sylvie. It's got nothing to do with me."

They were young and ambitious and frightened; and they were French, so that their learned behavior was all smoothness. There was no crevice where an emotion could hold. I was thinking about Louise. It is one thing to go away, but it is terrible to be left.

I wanted him to go away, or stop telling me about Sylvie and Louise, but he would continue and I had to hear him say, "The difference between Sylvie and me is that I work. I believe in work. Sylvie believes in one thing after the other. Now she believes in Louise, and one day she'll turn on her."

"Why should she turn on her?"

"Because Louise is good," he said. This was the only occasion I remember when he had trouble saying what he meant. We stood face to face in my room, with the table and books between us. We had never been as near. Twice in that conversation he slipped from "*vous*" to "*toi*," as if our tribal marks of incompetence gave us a right to intimacy. He stumbled over the words; stammered nearly. "She's so kind," he said. "She asks to be hurt."

"It's easy to be kind when you're an heiress."

"Aren't *you*?" I stared at him and he said, "Women like Louise make you think they can do anything, solve all your problems. Sylvie believes in magic. She believes in the good fairy, the endless wishes, the bottomless purse. I don't believe in magic." He had stopped groping. His actor's voice was as fluid and persistent as the winter rain. "But Sylvie believes, and one day she'll turn on Louise and hurt her."

"What do you expect me to do?" I said. "You keep talking about hurting and being hurt. What do you think my life is like? It's got nothing to do with me."

"Sylvie would leave Louise alone if you told her to," he said. "She isn't a clinger. She's a tough little thing. She's had to be." There was the faintest coloration of class difference in his voice. I remembered that Louise had met him in a drawing room, even though he lived here, in the hotel, with Sylvie and me.

I said, "It's not my affair."

"Sylvie is good," he said suddenly. That was all. He said "Sylvie," but he must have meant "Louise."

He left alone and went to the station alone. I was the only one to watch him go. Sylvie was out and Louise upstairs in her room. Unless I have dreamed it, it was then he told me he was ill. He was not going home after all but to a place in the mountains— near Grenoble, I think he said. That was why he had been away for a week; that was where he'd been. As he said those words, water rushed between us and we stood on opposite shores. He was sick, but I was well. We were both incompetent, but I was well. And I smiled and shook hands with him, and said goodbye.

In a book or a film one of us would have gone with him as far as the station. If he had disappeared in a country as big as Russia, one of us would have learned where he was. But he didn't disappear; he went to a town a few hundred miles distant and we never saw him again. I remember the rain on the skylight over the stairs. Louise may have looked out of her window; I would rather not guess. She may have wanted to come down at the last minute; but he had refused Australia, which meant he had refused her, and so she kept away.

Later on that day, she did something foolish: she stood in the passage and watched as his room was turned out by a maid. I managed to get her to sit on a chair. That was where Sylvie found her. Sylvie had come in from the street. Rain stood on her hair in perfect drops. She knelt beside Louise and began chafing her hands. "Tell me what it is," she said softly, looking up into her face. "How do you feel? What is it like? It must be something quite real."

"Of course it's real," I said heartily. "Come *on*, old girl."

Louise was clinging to Sylvie: she barely listened to me. "I feel as though I had no more blood," she said.

"That feeling won't last," said the girl. "He couldn't help leaving, could he? Think of how it would be if he had stayed beside you and been somewhere else—as good as miles and miles away." But I knew it was not Patrick but Collie who had gone. It was Collie who vanished before everything was said, turning his back, stopping his ears. I was thirteen and they were the love of my life. Sylvie said, "I wish I could be you and you could be me, for just this one crisis. I have too much blood and it never stops moving—never." She squeezed my sister's hand so hard that when she took her fingers away the mark of them remained in white bands. "Do you know what you must do now?" she said. "You must make yourself wait. Try to expect something. That will get the blood going again."

When I awoke the next day, I knew we were all three waiting. We waited for a letter, a telegram, a knock on the door. When Collie died, Louise went on writing letters. The letters began, "I can't believe that you are dead," which was chatty of her, not dramatic, and they went on giving innocent news. Mother and I found them and read them and tore them to shreds. We were afraid she would put them in the post and that they would be returned to her. Soon after Patrick had gone, Louise said to Sylvie, "I've forgotten what he was like."

"Like an actor," said Sylvie, with a funny little face. But I knew it was Collie Louise had meant.

Our relations became queer and strained. The final person, the judge, toward whom we were always turning for confirmation, was no longer there. Sylvie asked Louise outright for money now. If Patrick had been there to hear her, she might not have dared. Everything Louise replied touched off a storm. Louise seemed to be using a language every word of which offended Sylvie's ears. Sylvie had courted her, but now it was Louise who haunted Sylvie, sat in her cupboard room, badgered her with bursts of questions and pleas for secrecy. She asked Sylvie never to talk about her, never to disclose—she did not say what. When I saw them quarreling together, aimless and bickering, whispering and bored, I thought that a cloistered convent must be like that: a house without men.

"Did you have to stop combing your hair just because he left?" I heard Sylvie say. "You're untidy as Puss."

If you listen at doors, you hear what you deserve. She must have seemed thunderstruck, because Sylvie said, "Oh my God, don't look so helpless."

"I'm not helpless," said Louise.

"Why didn't you leave us alone?" Sylvie said. "Why didn't you just leave us with our weakness and our mistakes? You do so much, and you're so kind and good, and you get in the way, and no one dares hurt you."

That might have been the end of them, but the same afternoon Louise gave Sylvie a bottle of Miss Dior and the lace petticoat and a piece of real amber, and they went on being friends.

Soon after that scene, however, in March, Louise discovered two things. One was that Sylvie had an aunt and uncle living in Paris, so she was not as forsaken as she appeared to be. Sylvie told her this. The other had to do with Sylvie's social life, métier, and means. Monsieur Rablis made one of his periodic announcements to the effect that Sylvie would have to leave the hotel— clothes, mirror, horoscopes, money box, and all. Monsieur Rablis was, and is, a small truculent person. He keeps an underexercised dog chained to his desk. While the dog snarled and cringed, Louise said that she knew Sylvie had an aunt and uncle, and that she would make Sylvie go to them and ask them to pay their niece's back rent. Louise had an unshakable belief in the closeness of French families, having read about the welding influence of patriotism, the Church, and inherited property. She said that Sylvie would find some sort of employment. It was time to bring order into Sylvie's affairs, my sister said.

She was a type of client the hotel-keeper had often seen: the foreign, interfering, middle-aged female. He understood half she said, but was daunted by the voice, and the frozen eye, and the bird's-nest hair. The truth was that for long periods he forgot to claim Sylvie's rent. But he was not obsessed with her, and, in the long run, not French for nothing; he would as soon have had the money she owed. "She can stay," he said, perhaps afraid Louise might mention that he had been Sylvie's lover (although I doubt if she knew). "But I don't want her bringing her friends in at night. She never registers them, and whenever the police come around at night and find someone with Sylvie I have to pay a fine."

"Do you mean men?" said my wretched sister. "Do you mean the police come about men?"

Some of my sister's hardheaded common sense returned. She talked of making Sylvie a small regular allowance, which Sylvie was to supplement by finding a job. "Look at Puss," Louise said to her. "Look at how Puss works and supports herself." But Sylvie had already looked at me. Louise's last recorded present to Sylvie was a camera. Sylvie had told her some cocksure story about an advertising firm on the rue Balzac, where someone had said she had gifts as a photographer. Later she changed her mind and said she was gifted as a model, but by that time Louise had bought the camera. She moved the listing in her books from "Necessary" to "Unnecessary." Mice, insects, and some birds have secret lives. She harped on the aunt and uncle, until one day I thought, She will drive Sylvie insane.

"Couldn't you ask them to make you a proper allowance?" Louise asked her.

"Not unless I worked for them, either cleaning for my aunt or in my uncle's shop. Needles and thread and mending wool. Just the thought of touching those old maid's things—no, I couldn't. And then, what about my lessons?"

"You used to sew for me," said Louise. "You darned beautifully. I can understand their point of view. You could make some arrangement to work half days. Then you would still have time for your lessons. You can't expect charity."

"I don't mind charity," said Sylvie. "You should know."

I remember that we were in the central market, in Les Halles, dodging among the barrows, pulling each other by the sleeve whenever a cart laden with vegetables came trundling toward us. This outing was a waste of time where I was concerned; but Sylvie hated being alone with Louise now. Louise had become so nagging, so dull. Louise took pictures of Sylvie with the new camera. Sylvie wanted a portfolio; she would take the photographs to the agency on the rue Balzac, and then they would see how pretty she was and would give her a job. Louise had agreed, but she must have known it was foolish. Sylvie's bloom, divorced from her voice and her liveliness, simply disappeared. In any photograph I had ever seen of her she appeared unkempt and coarse and rather fat.

Her last words had been so bitter that I put my hand on the girl's shoulder, and at that her tension broke and she clutched Louise and cried, "I should be helped. Why shouldn't I be helped? I *should* be!"

When she saw how shocked Louise was, and how she looked to see if anyone had heard, Sylvie immediately laughed. "What will all those workmen say?" she said. It struck me how poor an actress she was; for the cry of "I should be helped" had been real, but nothing else had. All at once I had a strong instinct of revulsion. I felt that the new expenses in Louise's life were waste and pollution, and what had been set in motion by her giving was not goodness, innocence, courage, or generosity but something dark. I would have run away then, literally fled, but Sylvie had taken my sleeve and she began dragging me toward a fruit stall. "What if Louise took my picture here?" she said. "I saw something like that once. I make up my eyes in a new way, have you noticed? It draws attention away from my mouth. If I want to get on as a model, I ought to have my teeth capped."

I remember thinking, as Louise adjusted the camera, Teeth capped. I wonder if Louise will pay for that.

I think it was that night I dreamed about them. I had been dream-haunted for days. I watched Louise searching for Patrick in railway stations and I saw him departing on ships while she ran along the edge of the shore. I heard his voice. He said, "Haven't you seen her wings? She never uses them now." Then I saw wings, small, neatly folded back. That scene faded, and the dream continued, a dream of labyrinths, of search, of missed chances, of people standing on opposite shores. Awaking, I remembered a verse from a folkloric poem I had tried, when I was Patrick's age, to set to music:

> Es waren zwei Königskinder
> Die hatten einander so lief
> Sie konnten zusammen nicht kommen
> Das Wasser, es war zu tief.

I had not thought of this for years. I would rather not think about all the verses and all the songs. Who was the poem about? There were two royal children, standing on opposite shores. I was no royal child, and neither was Louise. We were too old and blunt and plain. We had no public and private manners; we were all one. We had secrets—nothing but that. Patrick was one child. Sylvie must be the other. I was still not quite awake, and the power of the dream was so strong that I said to myself, "Sylvie has wings. She could fly."

Sylvie. When she had anything particularly foolish to say, she put her head on one side. She sucked her fingers and grinned and narrowed her eyes. The grime behind her ears faded to gray on her neck and vanished inside her collar, the rim of which was black. She said, "I wonder if it's true, you know, the thing I'm not to mention. Do you think he loved her? What do you think? It's like some beautiful story, isn't it? . . . [hand on cheek, treacle voice]. It's pure Claudel. Broken lives. I *think*."

Cold and dry, I said, "Don't be stupid, Sylvie, and don't play detective." Louise and Collie, Patrick and Louise: I was as bad as Sylvie. My imagination crawled, rampant, unguided, flowering between stones. Supposing Louise had never loved Collie at all? Supposing Patrick had felt nothing but concern and some pity?

Sylvie knew. She knew everything by instinct. She munched sweets, listened to records, grimaced in her mirror, and knew everything about us all.

Patrick had been pushed to the very bottom of my thoughts. But I knew that Sylvie was talking. I could imagine her excited voice saying, "Patrick was an actor, although he hardly ever had a part, and she was good and clever, nothing of a man-eater..." I could imagine her saying it to the young men, the casual drifters, who stood on the pavement and gossiped and fingered coins, wondering if they dared go inside a café and sit down—wondering if they had enough money for a cup of coffee or a glass of beer. Sylvie knew everybody in Paris. She knew no one of any consequence, but she knew everyone, and her indiscretions spread like the track of a snail.

Patrick was behind a wall. I knew that something was living and stirring behind the wall, but it was impossible for me to dislodge the bricks. Louise never mentioned him. Once she spoke of her lost young husband, but Collie would never reveal his face again. He had been more thoroughly forgotten than anyone deserves to be. Patrick and Collie merged into one occasion, where someone had failed. The failure was Louise's; the infidelity of memory, the easy defeat were hers. It had nothing to do with me.

The tenants of the house in Melbourne wrote about rotten beams, and asked Louise to find a new gardener. She instantly wrote letters and a gardener was found. It was April, and the ripped fabric of her life mended. One could no longer see the way she had come. There had been one letter from Patrick, addressed to all three.

A letter to Patrick that Sylvie never finished was among the papers I found in Sylvie's room after she had left the hotel. "I have been painting pictures in a friend's studio," it said. "Perhaps art is what I shall take up after all. My paintings are very violent but also very tender. Some of them are large but others are small. Now I am playing Mozart on your old record-player. Now I am eating chocolate. Alas."

Patrick wrote to Sylvie. I found his letter on Monsieur Rablis' desk one day. I put my hand across the desk to reach for my key, which hung on a board on the wall behind the desk, and I saw the letter in a basket of mail. I saw the postmark and I recognized his hand. I put the letter in my purse and carried it upstairs. I sat down at the table in my room before opening it. I slit the envelope carefully and spread the letter flat. I began to read it. The first words were *"Mon amour."*

The new tenant of his room was a Brazilian student who played the guitar. The sun falling on the carpet brought the promise of summer and memories of home. Paris was like a dragonfly. The Seine, the houses, the trees, the wind, and the sky were like a dragonfly's wing. Patrick belonged to another season—to winter, and museums, and water running off the shoes, and steamy cafés. I held the letter under my palms. What if I went to find him now? I stepped into a toy plane that went any direction I chose. I arrived where he was, and walked toward him. I saw, on a winter's day (the only season in which we could meet), Patrick in sweaters. I saw his astonishment, and, in a likeness as vivid as a dream, I saw his dismay.

I sat until the room grew dark. Sylvie banged on the door and came in like a young tiger. She said gaily, "Where's Louise? I think I've got a job. It's a funny job—I want to tell her. Why are you sitting in the dark?" She switched on a light. The spring evening came in through the open window. The room trembled with the passage of cars down the street. She looked at the letter and the envelope with her name upon it but made no effort to touch them.

She said, "Everything is so easy for people like Louise and you. You go on the assumption that no one will ever dare hurt you, and so nobody ever dares. Nobody dares because you don't expect it. It isn't fair."

I realized I had opened a letter. I had done it simply and naturally, as a fact of the day. I wondered if one could steal or kill with the same indifference—if one might actually do harm.

"Tell Louise not to do anything more for me," she said. "Not even if I ask."

That night she vanished. She took a few belongings and left the rest of her things behind. She owed much rent. The hotel was full of strangers, for with the spring the tourists came. Monsieur Rablis had no difficulty in letting her room. Louise pushed her bicycle out to the street, and studied the history of music, and visited the people to whom she had introductions, and ate biscuits in her room. She stopped giving things away. Everything in her accounts was under "Necessary," and only necessary things were bought. One day, looking at the Seine from the Tuileries terrace, she said there was no place like home, was there? A week later, I put her on the boat train. After that, I had winter ghosts: Louise making tea, Sylvie singing, Patrick reading aloud.

Then, one summer morning, Sylvie passed me on the stairs. She climbed a few steps above me and stopped and turned. "Why, Puss!" she cried. "Are you still here?" She hung on the banister and smiled and said, "I've come back for my clothes. I've got the money to pay for them now. I've had a job." She was sunburned, and thinner than she had seemed in her clumsy winter garments. She wore a cotton dress, and sandals, and the necklace of seals. Her feet were filthy. While we were talking she casually picked up her skirt and scratched an insect bite inside her thigh. "I've been in a Christian cooperative community," she said. Her eyes shone. "It was wonderful! We are all young and we all believe in God. Have you read Maritain?" She fixed her black eyes on my face and I knew that my prestige hung on the reply.

"Not one word," I said.

"You could start with him," said Sylvie earnestly. "He is very materialistic, but so are you. I could guide you, but I haven't time. You must first dissolve your personality—are you listening to me?—and build it up again, only better. You must get rid of everything material. You must."

"Aren't you interested in the stage anymore?" I said.

"That was just theatre," said Sylvie, and I was too puzzled to say anything more. I was not sure whether she meant that her interest had been a pose or that it was a worldly ambition with no place in her new life.

"Oh," said Sylvie, as if suddenly remembering. "Did you ever hear from him?"

Everything was still, as still as snow, as still as a tracked mouse.

"Yes, of course," I said.

"I'm so glad," said Sylvie, with some of her old overplaying. She made motions as though perishing with relief, hand on her heart. "I was so silly, you know. I minded about the letter. Now I'm beyond all that. A person in love will do anything."

"I was never in love," I said.

She looked at me, searching for something, but gave me up. "I've left the community now," she said. "I've met a boy...oh, I wish you knew him! A saint. A modern saint. He belongs to a different group and I'm going off with them. They want to reclaim the lost villages in the South of France. You know? The villages that have been abandoned because there's no water or no electricity. Isn't that a good idea? We are all people for whom the theatre...[gesture]...and art...[gesture]...and music and all that have failed. We're trying something else. I don't know what the others will say when they see him arriving with me, because they don't want unattached women. They don't mind wives, but unattached women cause trouble, they say. *He* was against *all* women until he met *me*." Sylvie was beaming. "There won't be any trouble with me. All I want to do is work. I don't want anything..." She frowned. What was the word? "...anything material."

"In that case," I said, "you won't need the necklace."

She placed her hand flat against it, but there was nothing she could do. All the while she was lifting it off over her head and handing it down to me I saw she was regretting it, and for two pins would have taken back all she had said about God and materialism. I ought to have let her keep it, I suppose. But I thought of Louise, and everything spent with so little return. She had merged "Necessary" and "Unnecessary" into a single column, and when I added what she had paid out it came to a great deal. She must be living thinly now.

"I don't need it," said Sylvie, backing away. "I'd have been as well off without it. Everything I've done I've had to do. It never brought me *bonheur.*"

I am sorry to use a French word here, but "*bonheur*" is ambiguous. It means what you think it does, but sometimes it just stands for luck; the meaning depends on the sense of things. If the necklace had done nothing for Sylvie, what would it do for me? I went on down the stairs with the necklace in my pocket, and I thought, Selfish child. After everything that was given her, she might have been more grateful. She might have bitten back the last word.

*1962*

# NIGHT AND DAY

SITTING next to the driver, who was certainly his father, he saw the fine rain through the beam of the headlights, and the eyes of small animals at the edge of the road. They were driving from Shekomeko to Pulver's Corners, taking the route of the school bus. He felt a slight bump, nothing more, and sprawled on his face in an open field. Somebody, running, kicked him in the back. "Run," he heard a voice say. "Get up and run." They turned him over. "Be careful of my back," he said. "I've hurt my spine."

He knew without opening his eyes that he had been brought to a farmhouse. "I've been hurt," he tried to explain. They had placed him on a kitchen table, and now they stood round him and talked about him. They discussed his past, his character, and his destiny—and he powerless to reply! Then they all went out, and left him to die.

I must be careful, he said to himself. I don't know who these people are, or what they intend to do. He knew they were on the other side of the door, whispering, listening, waiting for him to die. He opened his eyes and saw the reflection of an oil lamp on the ceiling. The lamp had been placed out of his reach, on the kitchen floor.

Without moving his head, he sensed the weight, or the presence, of a large piece of furniture, such as a Welsh dresser, somewhere behind. A window had been left open; he could smell the snow, and he was rigid with cold.

"You poor devil," said the woman they had left in the room with him.

She got up from her chair and stood by the table. She bent over him; he could not see her face. "It's a drink you want," she said, "but I can't give you anything to drink. I can just give you something to wet your lips. Wait." She went outside to the yard and filled a cup with water at the pump. She poured the water from the cup onto his dry lips, but the water splashed to one side. None of it got to his tongue.

"I was in England twenty years," the woman said, close to his ear. "My husband was a schoolmaster. That is why my English is so fluent. They thought you would want to hear English when you came round."

They had placed his hands across his breast in preparation for his death, with the fingers of his right hand curled slackly on a worn piece of wood. In the dark—she had turned the lamp down, or else he had closed his eyes—he explored it, barely moving the muscles of his hand. His thumb came to the end of the piece of wood and pressed in.

"You don't need to ring for me," said the woman. "I am here. I shall be here until morning."

She was crouched on the floor, down beside the lamp. He knew she had his examination papers. He heard her rustling them, tearing them perhaps. He moved his jaw; his glued lips parted. His tongue was swollen and dry. He said, "What are you doing?," but all he heard of his words was "Aaah."

"You poor devil," she said. "It's a bad night for you. A week from now you won't remember it." She got to her feet, towered over him, and vanished. The room was rosy, then gray. The Welsh dresser dissolved. "Try to sleep," said the woman's voice, lingering after her person.

In his sleep they placed him upon a bed as hard to his back as the table had been. Someone at the foot of the bed asked him questions, tormenting him. He made no attempt to reply. He was troubled now only because he could not imagine his parents'

faces, or think of their name. The people at the foot of his bed
knew everything, but they did not know the name of his parents,
or how they could be reached. "Do you feel that?" they said to
him, grasping both his feet. They had tied electric wires between
his feet and his spine. He said, "Yes, I can feel it," and they all
went out once again and left him alone.

It occurred to him that he had been brought here for an important reason, dragged unwillingly, and had been injured when
he fought. He spread his hands on his chest, and touched the
turnback of the sheet, and then the blanket. He moved his hands
slowly, exploring.

The first thing he must remember was the name of the language these people spoke. He understood everything that was
said but had forgotten what the language was called. The room
was white and too bright, and the brightness was part of his pain.
He lay in pain, but presently he found small discomforts just as
serious. He was thirsty. The blanket covering him was heavy and
coarse. "Yes," he heard in answer to something he must have said
aloud, and a woman slipped her hand beneath his pillow and
gradually lifted the pillow and his head. She pushed a glass tube
between his lips and he drank orange juice and went to sleep.
Waking, he tested his fingers, then his wrists. He tried to change
the position of his legs but gave it up. He moved his hands cautiously and discovered the wooden bell. It had been pinned to
the garment he wore. There was a safety pin around the wire.
He ran his fingers along the pin and the wire, and then rang
the bell. He dreamed for a time of swimming. He felt the bedclothes drawn away and his hand gently lifted from the bell. He
had lost the sensation of swimming and all that accompanied
it—youth and pleasure—yet an indifference to his fate and future
made him joyous and pure, as a saint might feel. "I have no past
and no memories," he thought he said. "This is what it means to
be free." A light shone on his face; he addressed the darkness
around him.

"Drink some water now," she said. She laid the flashlight on the bed and brought the glass and tube toward him. He tried to lift his head.

One day a blond nurse of great beauty fed him little pieces of toast. The toast was slightly burned, and the texture of the butter disgusted him. He swallowed one bit, was revolted with the next, and spat it out. This girl, whose face floated above him, was of mythical beauty. Her hair was silk and her eyes sea blue. He wanted to see her clearly, but there was a veil. The aura of her own goodness blurred her features. He had never seen the physical evidence of goodness until now, but then he had never in his life been treated so kindly. Meanwhile, the goddess was putting yet a third piece of toast into his mouth. He swallowed it so as to make her pleased with him, and suddenly began to weep; and the goddess, on whom he now depended for everything, was obliged to wipe his tears.

They were speaking French. He understood everything they said, but had not been able to give the language a name. His language was English, which he had not forgotten—neither the name nor how to speak it. The people with secrets to keep, such as the little girls who swept the floor and were scolded by the nurses, talked in a dialect he could not follow, but he knew it was a dialect, and was not troubled as he would have been if it were something he ought to remember. It seemed to him that all anxieties and decisions concerning himself had passed into other hands. This lassitude, this trust, was a development of the vision he had been granted with the veiled goddess who fed him toast. He willed peace, harmony, and happiness to flow around his bed. He succeeded, and he understood how simple everything was going to be now. He smiled.

"That's a good sign," said the dark nurse. "Smiling is the best sign. We are bringing your telephone back today. We took it out so the ringing wouldn't disturb you. And look!" She whipped out her hand and held an envelope to his face. The handwriting said something to him, but his feeling was of apprehension, as if the letter had come too soon, and made too great a claim. He lifted his hand and took the letter. He had a wired arm attached to a wired spine. He was unable to read his own name. "There's too much light in this room," he said.

"It's the morphine," said the nurse. She had a sugary voice. "You can't focus. But you are getting smaller doses now."

That was all. From this momentary puzzle he moved on to his new state of bliss. He knew there would be nothing but brief periods of doubt followed by intervals of blessedness. Uncaring, impartial, he remembered the name for his condition: *la belle indifférence*.

"We have used the expression too often and I for one am sick to death of it," said the judge. Another voice remarked, "He is simulating indifference and knows very well what is in the balance." "I used the term in an ironical sense," said the consulting psychiatrist, rather crossly, "and did not intend the court to take it seriously."

He saw the prisoner, the judge. The prisoner was smiling, dreamy, unaware; they could do as they liked. Had he really seen this? No, he had read about it. It was an account of a trial he had read that summer, sitting on a beach. He had the airmail edition of the *Times*. The *Times* gave a long, thorough, and sober account of the case. He read it on the beach, with his children and wife nearby, and he wondered about *la belle indifférence*, which seemed a state of privileged happiness reserved for criminals and the totally insane. His younger son crawled away with his sunglasses, his cigarettes. It was because of his children, both babies, that his wife could not be with him now.

"When can I smoke?" he said, carefully putting the letter down.

"That is a very good sign, wanting to smoke," said the cooing nurse. "Your wife has called twice from Paris. We told her you were very quiet, no trouble at all. When you have the telephone you can talk to her. You must practice reaching, so that you can pick up the telephone. Pretend this is a telephone." It was his toothbrush.

In Europe, the doctors save you but the nurses kill you; before the operation someone had told him that. But he had a job in Paris and it was too expensive, out of the question, to go home. He had been told that in this place he would have care as good as any. What a mistake! The nursing was slipshod, slack. The girls were callous and unconcerned. They came and went, doing nothing really useful. They chattered together, and took little notice of him. And the doctor; what of the doctor? "Why hasn't the doctor been to see me?" he asked in a new, querulous voice—like an ailing countertenor's.

"Aren't three visits a day enough for you?" said the nurse, with all the honey gone from her voice. "You will be seeing less of him now. He has cases much more serious than yours. He is a celebrated surgeon, a busy man."


The goddess was a plain girl of about twenty-three. She was rough and impatient about his bath, and when she pulled the sheet taut underneath him it was an earthquake.

"You have to do too much for patients in Switzerland," she remarked. "I am French, and I am working here only to get an international certificate. All this washing and feeding..." She made a face and said, "In France, the patients look after themselves."

"I know it," he said. "That's why I came to Lausanne. I work in France." He had intended to tell her all about himself that morning—all about his children and wife. Now he would tell her nothing. In any case, he hardly needed her now. He could move his head when he wanted to, and reach for the telephone or his cigarettes. With only a little help he was able to turn on his side.

"You're getting better," the former goddess said placidly. "Bad temper is the best sign."

"You mean I'm a bad patient?" He resolved he would give as little trouble as possible, even if it meant hardship, hopeless neglect. Just the same, he thought, I think the doctor might come around more often than he does.

Now he knew everything, of course. What lingered of his amnesia was the sweetness of *la belle indifférence*. Sometimes he regretted it, and wished he had been in a state to observe it and put it away in his mind, but the return of memory, and reason, brought all the reasonable problems of the future as well—sensible problems of convalescence, work, money, home. Very soon he recalled everything he needed for everyday life, although there were crevices now and again: he forgot the names of close friends, and once the number of his own telephone. In conversation with the doctor, an amateur botanist, he forgot "trillium." And even much later, when nearly all of the first days had gone from his consciousness, he still could not believe he had ever come to this place voluntarily but secretly was certain he had somehow been tormented and then brought against his will.

*1962*

# ONE ASPECT OF A RAINY DAY

HE HAD SEEN his older brother, Günther, swear personal allegiance to Hitler when Günther was fifteen and he, Stefan, only six. Actually Günther promised nothing aloud, but stood with his lips tight. Later on, the boys' father said to Günther, "You haven't proven anything. No one knows what you were thinking. It was too late to drop out at the last minute. You have promised what the others promised, whether you wanted to or not."

What Stefan had never known and wondered now—it came back to him eighteen years later on a winter morning in France—was whether Günther was against the words because they were binding or against the idea they expressed. The formula of fidelity had been changed since the war (from 1939 until the capitulation, one swore to the person of Hitler instead of to the State), and perhaps Günther positively did not wish to make a gift of his life. Whatever his silence concealed, it stood for extreme feeling. Günther, now dead, had nothing more to say or conceal. And Stefan, walking among the French on a rainy morning, was wordless, as his brother had been eighteen years before.

In the laboratory outside Paris where Stefan's scholarship had taken him, the professors, the technicians, his friends and comrades, had put on their coats. Someone said, "Is Germany with us?" "Germany" meant Stefan. The rooms were dark and the heat in the building turned off; there was a general strike from eight until noon. Stefan went with the rest. It was too dark to work and he couldn't very well stay there alone.

There were nearly eighty of them straggling along the pave-

ment. They walked slowly, as if it were a mild spring day instead
of a winter morning of rain. They walked by the stone walls, the
brick houses, the drenched winter gardens of this town that had
been a quiet suburb and was now ringed with factories and
fragile-looking blocks of flats. Rain darkened Stefan's fair hair. If
the police came now and asked them what they were doing, he
intended to excuse himself. "Forgive me," he would say, "but it
was impossible to stay behind. I am in France with a scholarship.
I am a guest of the country. I regret any worry I might be causing
you by walking to the center of town instead of remaining at my
work."

He was more than a guest; they had sent for him. What is a
foreign scholarship if not a sort of bribe? Faint conceit made him
glance at a girl walking beside him—a girl who had flirted with
him in the halls. Now she walked with her hands in the pockets
of her raincoat. Her head, in a cotton scarf, was bent slightly forward. She was silent and thinking hard; he could see that because
of the way a tooth held her lower lip. It would have seemed to him
attractive, rather sensual, if she had not been so removed. Stefan
hoped for her sake that she was wearing a sweater under her thin
raincoat. Now and again she shivered. When they got back to the
laboratory, he would advise her to take aspirin, he thought.

The general strike made the country seem submerged; he felt
as if they were walking through waves. And now a smaller strike
of one hour had been called. Plenty of cars rushed by, splashing
the walkers on the pavement, but some taxis pulled up to the side
of the road, and some shops were locked, with the blinds drawn.
The main street, which they now descended, was the highway to
Paris. Here they seemed to Stefan conspicuous. How intent, how
uncasual they would seem if the police should appear now! He
hoped he would have time to say, "Excuse me, this is none of my
affair." In Germany the police broke up demonstrations with fire
hoses, and the most anyone got was a good wetting. He wondered
why the French police didn't copy this tactic instead of moving in
with clubs.

The leader of their group was a young man Stefan had seen in the laboratory but scarcely knew. Why should he be leader all at once? He had taken on authority without asking consent. This leader had a proclamation in his pocket, and they were on their way, all eighty of them, to the city hall of a Parisian suburb to read the proclamation to the mayor. The proclamation said they were against violence and murder, and that they stood for the Republic, whatever the Republic was. The owner of a fruit shop, who had joined in the one-hour strike, stood in his doorway, watching the fruit outside to make sure none of it was stolen. The pears under their protective netting looked delicious. If you bought one the merchant would say, "Is it for lunch, or dinner, or tomorrow?" If it was for lunch, it had to be eaten straightaway; tomorrow the interior would be spotted and brown.

At the city hall neither of the armed guards at the door moved an inch; not the guardian of the peace with his club and his gun, or the statue in dark blue with his machine gun. Being armed and in uniform, the two were not men. They were targets, objects, enemies—pictures of something. The group trailed past them and into the building and stood, scuffling their soaked shoes, in the dark lobby. A marble plaque, yellow now, gave the names of the dead in the 1914 war, and a much smaller, whiter piece of marble held the names of the few who had died twenty years ago. The building felt as if it had not been heated for days. The group waited, giving off an aura of coldness and dampness like a cloud. The leader had his proclamation to read, but the mayor was away—on a voyage, said the elderly clerk, who, if you forgot the armed guards outside, was the greeting committee. The mayor's assistant was away as well. There was no one to read the proclamation to, and so the young man read it aloud to Stefan, the shivering girl, and the rest of them. Stefan was aware of a feeling of dissatisfaction with the young leader—as if he had promised a victory and failed. Someone observed they could at least mark the occasion with one minute's silence, and that gave the leader another chance. He looked at his watch and said the minute had begun. In the long minute, Stefan heard people walking to and fro in the building and a telephone ringing. When the minute was up, the group pressed back out to the rain, which was warmer than indoors. The minute had tired them more than the walk. "Keep in line," the leader urged them. "Let us look as if..." He was losing his authority again; but surely it wasn't his fault if the mayor was away on a voyage? And the mayor's assistant, too?

Because of the strike, none of the traffic signals were working. Cars came from every direction. It was when they were trying to cross the main street of the town, the highway into Paris, that some of the group began to stamp in rhythm—three beats and three more—O. A. S. as-sas-sins. Everyone knew what three-three stood for, even without the syllables.

Now Stefan felt tricked and stubborn, as his brother might have done during the oath-of-allegiance ceremony eighteen years before. "Is Germany with us?" his comrades had asked. They knew he couldn't stay behind; but he hadn't come out on the streets to stamp and shout and risk his career for something that had nothing to do with him. Saying nothing, he thought he was saying everything. If the police came now, he would not even have time to explain, "I am a guest of France and deeply regret..." Then he noticed he was not the only one who was silent. Some were shouting and some were still, but no one knew what anyone thought, or what the silence contained. His own father had never known what Günther believed or why he behaved in a certain way.

When they turned up the hill to the laboratory, another group of marchers suddenly came around a corner and upon them. Both groups stopped and the slogans died in the rain. The men and women looked at each other. What had the others been shouting? Were they shouting and tramping the three beats and three, which made them friends, or had they been marching to the three-and-two that were Al-gé-rie Fran-çaise? Neither group had heard the other. Were they mortal enemies or close friends? At any rate, they weren't either of them the police. They stared as long as the silent minute in the city hall. Nothing happened; the groups passed without trouble. They mingled, parted, re-formed their lines, one going up the hill to the laboratory, the other along perhaps to the *lycée*; they had the look of teachers. No one stamped or called now. They were men and women in the rain. They might have been coming from anywhere—a cinema, or a funeral.

Foreign papers exaggerate; Stefan's mother sent him such anxious letters from Berlin! He would write tonight and tell her not to worry. Nothing was as serious as it seemed from the outside. Moreover, his superiors thought highly of him, and his work was going well.

*1962*

# SUNDAY AFTERNOON

ON A WET February afternoon in the eighth winter of the Algerian war, two young Algerians sat at the window table of a café behind Montparnasse station. Between them, facing the quiet street, was a European girl. The men were dressed alike in the dark suits and maroon ties they wore once a week, on Sunday. Their leather jackets lay on the fourth chair. The girl was also dressed for an important day. Her taffeta dress and crocheted collar were new; the coat with its matching taffeta lining looked home-sewn. She had thrown back the coat so that the lining could be seen, but held the skirt around her knees. She was an innocent from an inland place—Switzerland, Austria perhaps. The slight thickness of her throat above the crocheted collar might have been the start of a goiter. She turned a gentle, stupid face to each of the men in turn, trying to find a common language. Presently one of the men stood up and the girl, without his help, pulled on her coat. These two left the café together. The abandoned North African sat passively with three empty coffee cups and a heaped ashtray before him. He had either been told to wait or had nothing better to do. The street lamps went on. The rain turned to snow.

Watching the three people in the café across the street had kept Veronica Baines occupied much of the afternoon. Like the Algerian sitting alone, she had nothing more interesting to do. She left the window to start a phonograph record over again. She looked for matches, and lit a Gitane cigarette. It was late in the day, but she wore a dressing gown that was much too large and that did not belong to her, and last summer's sandals. Three plastic curlers along her brow held the locks that, released, would become a bouffant fringe. Her hair, which was light brown, straight, and recently washed, hung to her shoulders. She was nineteen, and a Londoner, and had lived in Paris about a year. She stood pushing back the curtain with one shoulder, a hand flat on the pane. She seldom read the boring part of newspapers, but she knew there was, or there had been, a curfew for North Africans. She left the window for a moment, and when she came back she was not surprised to find the second Algerian gone.

She wanted to say something about the scene to the two men in the room behind her. Surely it meant something—the Algerian boys and the ignorant girl? She held still. One of the men in the room was Tunisian and very touchy. He watched for signs of prejudice. When he thought he saw them, he was pleased and cold. He could be rude when he wanted to be; he had been educated in Paris and was schooled in the cold attack.

Jim Bertrand, whose flat this was, and Ahmed had not stopped talking about politics since lunch. Their talk was a wall. It shut out young girls and girlish questions. For instance, Veronica could have asked if there was a curfew, and if it applied to Ahmed as well as the nameless and faceless North Africans you saw selling flowers or digging up the streets; but Ahmed might consider it a racial question. She never knew just where he drew his own personal line.

"I am not interested in theories," she had taught herself to say, for fear of being invaded by something other than a dream. But she was not certain what she meant, and not sure that it was true.

Jim turned on a light. The brief afternoon became, abruptly, a winter night. The window was a black mirror. She saw how the room must appear to anyone watching from across the street. But no one peeped at them. Up and down the street, persiennes were latched, curtains tightly drawn. The shops were a line of iron shutters broken only by the Arab café, from which spilled a brownish and hideous light. The curb was lined with cars; Paris was like a garage. Shivering at the cold, and the dead cold of the lined-up automobiles, she turned to the room. She imagined a garden filled with gardenias and a striped umbrella. Veronica was a London girl. At first her dreams had been of Paris, but now they were about a south she had not yet seen.

She moved across the room, scuffling her old sandals, dressed in Jim's dressing gown. She dropped her cigarette on the marble hearth, stepped on it, and kicked it under the gas heater in the fireplace. Then she knelt and lifted the arm of the record-player on the floor, starting again the Bach concerto she had been playing most of the day. Now she read the name of it for the first time: "Concerto Italien en Fa Majeur bwv 971." She had played it until it was nothing more than a mosquito to the ear, and now that she was nearly through with it, about to discard it for something newer, she wanted to know what it had been called. Still kneeling, leaning on her fingertips, she reread the front page of a Sunday paper. Is Princess Paola sorry she has married a Belgian and has to live so far north? Deeply interested, Veronica examined the Princess's face, trying to read contentment or regret. Princess Paola, Farah of Iran, Grace of Monaco, and Princess Margaret were the objects of Veronica's solemn attention. Their beauty, their position, their attentive husbands should have been enough. According to *France Dimanche*, anonymous letters might still come in with the morning post. Their confidences went astray. None of them could say "Pass the salt" without wondering how far it would go.

When Jim and Ahmed talked on Sunday afternoon, Veronica was a shadow. If Princess Paola herself had lifted the coffeepot from the table between them, they would have taken no more notice than they now did of her. She picked up the empty pot and carried it to the kitchen. She saw herself in the looking glass over the sink: curlers, bathrobe—what a sight! Behind her was the music, the gas heater roaring away, and the drone of the men's talk.

Everything Jim had to say was eager and sounded as if it must be truthful. "Yes, I know," he would begin, "but look." He was too eager; he stammered. His Tunisian friend took over the idea, stated it, and demolished it. Ahmed was Paris-trained; he could be explicit about anything. He made sense.

"Sense out of hot air," said Veronica in the kitchen. "Perfect sense out of perfect hot air."

She took the coffeepot apart and knocked the wet grounds into the rest of the rubbish in the sink. She ran cold water over the pot and rinsed and filled it again; then she sat down on the low stepladder that was the only seat in the kitchen and ground new coffee, holding the grinder between her knees. At lunch the men had dragged chairs into the kitchen and stopped talking politics. But the instant the meal was finished they wanted her away; she sensed it. If only she could be dismissed, turned out to prowl like a kitten, even in the rain! But she lived here, with Jim; he had brought her here in November, four months ago, and she had no other home.

"I'm too young to remember," she heard Ahmed say, "and you weren't in Europe."

The coffeepot was Italian and composed of four aluminum parts that looked as if they never would fit one inside the other. Jim had written instructions for her, and tacked the instructions above the stove, but she was as frightened by the four strange shapes as she had been at the start. Somehow she got them together and set the pot on the gas flame. She put it on upside down, which was the right way. When the water began to boil, you turned the pot right way up, and the boiling water dripped through the coffee. You knew when the water was boiling because a thread of steam emerged from the upside-down spout. That was the most important moment.

Afraid of missing the moment, the girl leaned on the edge of the table, which was crowded with luncheon dishes; pushed together, behind her, were the remains of the rice-and-tomato, the bones and fat of the mutton chops. The Camembert dried in the kitchen air; the bread was already stale. She did not take her eyes from the spout of the coffeepot. She might have been dreaming of love.

"You still haven't answered me," said Jim in the next room. "Will Algeria go Communist? Yes or no."

"Tunisia didn't."

"You had different leaders."

"The Algerians are religious—the opposite of materialists."

"They could use a little materialism in Algeria," said Jim. "I've never been there, but you've only got to read. I've got a book here…"

Those two could talk poverty the whole day and never weary. They thought they knew what it was. Jim had never taken her to a decent restaurant—not even at the beginning, when he was courting her. He looked at the menu posted outside the door and if the prices seemed more than he thought simple working-class couples could pay he turned away. He wanted everyone in the world to have enough to eat, but he did not want them to enjoy what they were eating—that was how it seemed to Veronica. Ahmed lived in a cold room on the sixth floor of an old building, but he needn't have. His father was a fashionable doctor in Tunis. Ahmed said there was no difference between one North African and another, between Ahmed talking of sacrifice and the nameless flower seller whose existence was a sacrifice—that is to say, whose life appears to have no meaning; whose faith makes it possible; of whom one thinks he might as well be dead. All Veronica knew was that Ahmed's father was better off than her father had ever been. "I'm going to be an important personality," she had said to herself at the age of seventeen or so. Soon after, she ran away and came to Paris; someone got a job for her in a photographer's studio—a tidying-up sort of job, and not modeling, as she had hoped. In the office next to the studio, a drawer was open. She saw 100 Nouveaux Francs, a clean bill, on which the face of young Napoleon dared her, said, "Take it." She bought a pair of summer shoes for seventy francs and spent the rest on silly presents for friends. Walking in the shoes, she was new. She would never be the same unimportant Veronica again. The shoes were beige linen, and when she wore them in the rain they had to be thrown away. The friend who had got her the job made up the loss when it was discovered, but the story went round, and no photographer would have her again.

The coffeepot spitting water brought Jim to the kitchen. He got to the stove before Veronica knew what he was doing there. "I'm sorry," she said. "I was thinking about shoes."

"You need shoes?" He looked at her, as if trying to remember why he had loved her and what she had been like. His glasses were thumb-printed and steamed; all his talk was fog. He looked at her beautiful ankles and the scuffed sandals on her feet. He had come from America to Paris because he had a year to spend—just like that. Imagine spending a whole year of life, when every minute mattered! He had to be sure about everything before he was twenty-six; it was the limit he had set. But Veronica was going to be a great personality, and it might happen any day. She wanted to be a great something, and she wanted to begin, but not like Jim—reading and thinking—and not like that girl in taffeta, starting *her* experience with the two Algerians.

"I think I could be nearly anything, you know." That was what Veronica had said five months ago, when Jim asked what she was doing, sitting in a sour café with ashes and bent straws around her feet. She was prettier than any of the girls at the other tables. She had spoken first; he would never have dared. Her wrists were chapped where her navy-blue coat had rubbed the skin. That was the first thing he saw when he fell in love with her. That was what he had forgotten when he looked at her so vaguely in the kitchen, trying to remember what he had loved.

When he met her, she was homeless. It was a cause-and-effect she had not foreseen. She knew that when you run away from home you are brave—braver than anyone; but then you have nowhere to live. Until Jim found her, fell in love with her, brought her here, she spent hours on the telephone, ringing up any casual person who might give her a bed for the night. She borrowed money for bus tickets, and borrowed a raincoat because she lost hers—left it in a cinema—and she borrowed books and forgot who belonged to the name on the flyleaf. She sold the borrowed books and felt businesslike and proud.

She stole without noticing she was stealing, at first. Walking with Jim, she strolled out of a bookshop with something in her hand. "You're at the Camus age," he said, thinking it was a book she had paid for. She saw she was holding *La Chute*, which she had never read, and never would. They moved in the river of people down the Boulevard Saint-Michel, and he put his arm round her so she would not be carried away. The Boul'Mich was like a North African bazaar now; it was not the Latin Quarter of Baudelaire. Jim had been here three months and was homesick.

"It's wonderful to speak English," he said.

"You should practice your French." They agreed to talk French. "*Vous êtes bon*," she said, gravely.

"*Mais je ne suis pas beau*." It was true, and that was the end of the French.

They held hands on the Pont des Arts and looked down at the black water. He wanted to take her home, to an apartment he had rented in Montparnasse. It was a step for him; it was an event. He had to discuss it: love, honesty, the present, the past.

Yes, but be quick, I am dying of hunger and cold, she wanted to say.

She knew more about men than he did about women, and had more patience. She understood his need to talk about a situation without making any part of the situation clear.

"You ought to get a job," he said, when she had been living with him a month. He thought working would be good for her. He believed she should be working or studying—preparing for life. He thought life began only after it was prepared, but Veronica thought it had to start with a miracle. That was the difference between them, and why the lovely beginning couldn't last, and why he couldn't remember what he had loved. One day she said she had found work selling magazine subscriptions. He had never heard of that in France; he started to say so, but she interrupted him: "I used to sell the *Herald Tribune* on the street."

Soon after that, Jim met Ahmed, and every Sunday Ahmed came to talk. Jim wondered why he had been so hurt and confused by love. He discovered that it was easier to talk than read, and that men were better company than girls. After Jim met Ahmed, and after Veronica began selling magazine subscriptions, Jim and Veronica were happier. It was never as lovely as it had been at the beginning; that never came back. But Veronica had a handbag, strings of beads, a pink sweater, and a velvet ribbon for her hair. Perhaps that was all she wanted—a ribbon or so, the symbols of love that he should have provided. Now she gave them to herself. Sometimes she came home with a treasure; once it was a jar of caviar for him. It was a mistake—the kind of extravagance he abhorred.

"You shouldn't spend that way," he said. "Not on me."

"What does it matter? We're together, aren't we? As good as married?" she said sadly.

If they had been married, he would never have let her sell magazine subscriptions. They both knew it. She was not his wife but a girl in Paris. She was a girl, and although he would not have let her know it, almost his first. He was not attractive to women. His ugliness was unpleasant; it was the kind of ugliness that can make women sadistic. Veronica was the first girl pretty enough for Jim to want and desperate enough to have him. He had never met desperation at home, although he supposed it must exist. She was the homeless, desperate girl in Paris against whom he might secretly measure, one future day, a plain but confident wife.

"What's the good of saving money? If they come, they'll shoot me. If they don't shoot me, I shall wait for their old-age pensions. Apparently they have these gorgeous pensions." That was Veronica on the Russians. She said this now, putting the hot coffeepot down on a folded newspaper between the two men.

For Ahmed this was why women existed: to come occasionally with fresh coffee, to say pretty, harmless things. Bach sent spirals of music around the room, music that to the Tunisian still sounded like a coffee grinder. His idea of Paris was nearly just this—couples in winter rooms; coffee and coffee-grinder music on Sunday afternoon. Records half out of their colored jackets lay on the floor where Veronica had scattered them. She treated them as if they were toys, and he saw that she loved her toys best dented and scratched. "Come next Sunday," Jim said to Ahmed every week. Nearly every childless marriage has a bachelor friend. Veronica and Jim lived as though they were married, and Ahmed was the Sunday friend. Ahmed and Jim had met at the Bibliothèque Nationale. They talked every Sunday that winter. Ahmed lay back in the iron-and-canvas garden chair, and Jim was straight as a judge in a hard Empire armchair, the seat of which was covered with plastic cloth. The flat had always been let to foreigners, and traces of other couples and their passage remained—the canvas chair from Switzerland, the American pink bathmat in the ridiculous bathroom, the railway posters of skiing in the Alps.

Ahmed liked talking to Jim, but he was uneasy with liberals. He liked the way Jim carefully said "*Ak*med," having learned that was how it was pronounced; and he was almost touched by his questions. What did "Ben" mean? Was it the same as the Scottish "Mac"? However, Jim's liberalism brought Ahmed close to his mortal enemies; there were Jews, for instance, who wrote the kindest books possible about North Africa and the Algerian affair. Here was a novel by one of them. On the back of the jacket was the photograph of the author, a pipe-smoking earnest young intellectual—lighting his pipe, looking into the camera over the flame. "Well, yes, but still a Jew," said Ahmed frankly, and he saw the change in Jim—the face pink with embarrassment, the kind mouth opened to protest, to defend.

"I don't feel that way, I'm sorry." Jim brought out the useful answer. In his dismay he turned the book over and hid the author's face. He was sparing Ahmed now at the expense of the unknown writer; but the writer was only a photograph, and he looked an imbecile with that pipe.

Ahmed's attitudes were not acquired, like Jim's. They were as much part of him as his ears. He expected intellectual posturing from men but detested clever women. He judged women by merciless, frivolous, secret rules. First, a girl must never be plain.

Veronica was not an intellectual, nor was she plain. She moved like a young snake; like a swan. She put a new pot of coffee down upon the table. She started the same record again, the same coffee-grinder sound. She stretched her arms, sighing, in a bored, frantic gesture. He saw the rents in the dressing gown when she lifted her arms. He could have given her more than Jim; she was not even close to the things she wanted.

Jim knew Ahmed was looking at Veronica. He wondered if he would mind if Ahmed fell in love with her. She was not Jim's; she was free. He had told her so again and again, but it made her cry, and he stopped saying it. He had imagined her free and proud, but when he said "You're free" she just cried. Would the fact that Ahmed was his friend, and a North African, mean a betrayal? It was a useless exercise, as pointless as pacing a room, but it was the kind of problem he exercised his brain with. He thought back and forth for a minute: How would I feel? Hurt? Shocked?

In less than the minute it was played out. Ahmed looked at Veronica and thought she was not worth a quarrel with his friend. "*Pas pour une femme*," Sartre had said. Jim was too active in his private debate to notice Ahmed's interest withdrawn. Ahmed's look and its meaning were felt only by the girl. She turned to the window, with her back to the room. Suffering miserably, humiliated, she pressed her hands on the glass. The men had forgotten her. They laughed, as if Ahmed's near betrayal had made them closer friends. Jim poured his friend's coffee and pushed the sugar toward him. She saw the movement in the black glass.

She knew that Jim's being an American and Ahmed a North

African made their friendship unusual, but that was apart. She didn't care about politics and color. They had nothing to do with her life. No, the difficulty for Veronica was always the same: when a man was alone he wanted her, but when there were two men she was in the way. The admiration of men, when she was the center of attention, could not make up for their indifference when they had something to say to each other. She resented the indifference more than any amount of notice taken of another woman. She could have made pudding of a rival girl.

"The little things are so awful," said Jim. "Look, I was on the ninety-five bus. The bus stopped because they were changing drivers. There were two Algerians, and without even turning around to see why the bus stopped where it shouldn't, they pulled out their identity papers to show the police. It's automatic. Something unusual—the police."

"It is nearly finished," said Ahmed.

"Do you think so? That part?"

In one of the Sunday papers there was a new way of doing horoscopes. It was complicated and you needed a mathematician's brain, but anything was better than standing before the window with nothing to see. She found a pencil and sat down on the floor. I was born in '43 and Jim in '36. We're both the same month. That makes ten points in common. No, the ten points count against you.

"Ahmed, when were you born?"

"I am a Lion, a Leo, of the year 1939," Ahmed said.

"It'll take a minute to work out."

Presently she straightened up with the paper in her hand and said, "I can't work it out. Ahmed, you're going to travel. Princess Margaret's a Leo and she's going to travel. It must be the same thing."

That made them laugh, and they looked at her. When they looked, she felt brave again. She stood over them, as if she were one of them. "I can't tell if I'm going to have twins or have rheumatism," she said. "I'm given both. Actually, I think *I'll* travel. I've got to think of my future, as Jim says. I don't think Paris is the right place. Summer might be the time to move on. Some-where like the Riviera."

"What would you do there?" said Ahmed.

"Sell magazine subscriptions," she said, smiling. "Do you know I used to sell the *Herald Tribune*? I really and truly did. I wore one of those ghastly sweaters they make you wear. If I sold something like a hundred and ninety-nine, I could pay for my hotel room. That was before I met Jim. I had to keep walking with the papers because of the law. If you stand still on a street with a pile of newspapers in your arms, you're what's called a kiosk, and you need a special permit. Now I sell magazine subscriptions and I can walk or stand still, just as I choose."

"I've never seen you," said Ahmed.

"She makes a fortune," said Jim. "No one refuses. It's her face."

"I'm not around where you are," said Veronica to Ahmed. "I'm around the Madeleine, where the tourists go."

"I'll come and see you there," said Ahmed. "I'd like to see you selling magazine subscriptions to tourists around the Madeleine."

"I earn enough for my clothes," said Veronica. "Jim needn't dress me."

She could not keep off her private grievances. As soon as his friend was attacked, Ahmed turned away. He looked at the books on the shelf over the table where Jim did his thinking and read-ing. Jim was mute with unhappiness. He tried to remember the beginning. Had either of them said a word about clothes?

She could go on standing there, holding the newspaper and the futures she had been unable to work out. There must be some-thing she could do. In the kitchen, the washing up? The bed-room? She could dress. In the silence she had caused, she thought of questions she might ask. "Ahmed, are you the same as those Algerians in the café?" "Am I any better than that girl?"

They began to talk when Veronica was in the bedroom. Their voices were different. They were glad she was away. She knew it. Veronica thought she heard her name. They wanted her to be someone else. They didn't deserve her as she was. They wanted

Brigitte Bardot and Joan of Arc. They want everything, she said to herself. In the bedroom there was nothing but a double bed and pictures of ballet dancers someone had left tacked to the walls.

She returned to them, dressed in a gray skirt and sweater and high-heeled black shoes. She had put her hair up in a neat plait, and her fringe was brushed out so that it nearly touched her eyelashes.

Jim was in the kitchen. He had closed the door. She heard him pulling the ladder about. He kept books and papers on the top shelf of the kitchen cupboard. She sat down in his chair, primly, and folded her hands.

"You are well dressed these days," said Ahmed, as if their conversation had never stopped.

"I'm not what you think," she said. "You know that. I said 'around the Madeleine' for a joke. I sometimes take things. That's all."

"What things? Money?" He looked at her without moving. His long womanish hands were often idle.

"Where would I ever see money? Not *here*. *He* doesn't leave it around. Nobody does, for that matter. I take little things, in the shops. Clothes, and little things. Once a jar of caviar for Jim, but he didn't want it."

"You'll get into trouble," Ahmed said.

"It's all here, all safe," said Jim, coming back, smiling. "I'm like an old maid, you know, and I hate keeping money in the house, especially an amount like this."

He put the paper package on the table. It was the size of a pound of coffee. They looked at it and she understood. She was older than she had ever been, even picking Jim up in a café. There it is: money. It makes no difference to them. It is life and death for me. "What is it, Jim?" she said carefully, pressing her hands together. "What is it for? Is it for politics?" She remembered the two men in the café and the girl with the thick innocent throat. "Is it about politics? Is it for the Algerians? Was it in the kitchen a long time?" Slowly, carefully, she said, "What wouldn't you do for other people! Jim never spends anything. He needs a reason, and I'm not a reason. Ahmed, is it yours?"

"It isn't mine," said Ahmed.

"Why didn't you tell me it was here, Jim? Don't you trust me?"

"You can see we trust you," said Jim.

"We're telling you now."

"You didn't tell me you had it here because you thought I'd spend it," she said. She looked at the paper as if it were a stuffed object—a dead animal.

"I never thought of it as money," said Jim. "That's the truth."

"It's anything except the truth," she said, her hands tight. "But it doesn't matter. There's never a moment money isn't money. You'd like me to say 'It isn't money,' but I won't. If I'd known, I'd have spent it. Wouldn't I just! Oh, wouldn't I!"

"It wasn't money," said Jim, as if it had stopped existing. "It was something I was keeping for other people." Collected for a reason, a cause. And hidden.

None of them touched it. Ahmed looked sleepy. This was a married scene in a winter room; the bachelor friend is exposed to this from time to time. He must never take sides.

"You both think you're so clever," said the girl. "You haven't even enough sense to draw the curtains." While they were still listening, she said, "It's not my fault if you don't like me. Both of you. I can't help it if you wish I was something else. Why don't you take better care of me?"

*1962*

# WILLI

WHEN THEY need technical advice in films about the Occupation, they often send for Willi. There are other Germans in Paris with memories of the war, but they are uninterested or too busy. The students are too young. They don't know any of the marching songs. To tell the truth, these young people cannot be depended on to sing and march; they don't take to it seriously. Willi, whose job it is to drill them for the film, loses his patience. They like the acting, and seeing the movie stars, and clowning around in uniform, but they don't give their best.

"When I think I was ready to die for *you*!" Willi says.

Willi is short and thick and very fair. His eyes are cornflower blue. The lashes are stubby and nearly invisible. When he has been in the sun all day trying to work a squad of silly kids into some sort of organized endeavor, the whites of his eyes go red and his face looks as if he had dipped it in wine. Actually he never touches wine. Another thing he dislikes is cigarettes. He is unhappy when he sees a young girl smoking.

In the old days, he says—he must mean in his puberty—health was glory and he was taught something decent about girls.

Willi was a prisoner of war in France until the end of 1948. He dreamed of home, but when he got there one of his sisters had an American boyfriend and the whole family were happy as seals around a rich new brother-in-law, a builder in Stuttgart. Willi thought, The French had us four years but didn't learn a word of German, and if one of them could stick a knife in our back he did. He doesn't like the French better than he does the Germans; he

264

just despises them less. Back home was the ever-richer brother-in-law. Willi couldn't fit in, and presently he came to Paris. He must be in his middle thirties but looks twenty-five. He looks his age when he is puzzled, or doesn't understand what took place, or has lost control of a situation—has given someone else the upper hand.

The film business is occasional, but an economic pillar. He is paid fairly well for what he does. He sometimes meets a girl and hopes something will come of it—he is still looking for that—but he has never been sure he had the right girl.

When Willi was released from prison camp, and after he became disgusted with home, he thought he might join the Legion. He is glad he didn't now. Willi's friend Ernst did join; he was sick of being a prisoner and it was the only way out. They often talk about those days and what went on. Their decorations had been torn from them by enemy soldiers with private collections, but Ernst and Willi made each other decorations saying "Mother" and "Home Soon" and that kind of thing. Ernst was in the Legion in Indo-China and Algeria. He has had a troubling life; although he is a good soldier, he has all his life been part of a defeated army. The Legion was a total waste; they didn't teach him a trade. Also, they are slow about his pension. Ernst is in Paris waiting for the pension. It begins to look as if he might wait forever. Every time he goes to the pensions office, they tell him a document is missing from his file. When he comes back with the document, they say he has come on the wrong day. Ernst is going to be in trouble if the pension doesn't come through very soon; he has no residence permit in France. He hasn't been given one, because he has no income, no fixed domicile, and no trade. The wars are over; Ernst can go home. He doesn't want to go home. If he leaves France, he is sure he will never see the shadow of a pension. Everything depends on his turning up at the pensions office on the right day with every document assembled in the file.

The last time Willi worked on a film he got a small part for Ernst. It wasn't easy, because Ernst is brown-haired and slight. He is not a German military figure. Willi got the job for Ernst by saying he had been a German officer, which isn't true. He was too young—about sixteen when he was taken prisoner in 1944. In the film, Ernst plays an S.S. man who has to arrest a Jewish couple on the street outside their own house. This is what the scene is like: The husband, dressed like a modest middle-aged professor in a movie, and his wife, dressed as a humble professor's wife, are stopped by the two S.S. men (one of them Ernst) as they arrive at their door, arm in arm, one late-summer afternoon. The husband carries a folded newspaper and a loaf of bread.

Ernst has been told to push the professor, while the other S.S. man (a chemistry student) is to hold the woman by the elbow.

Ernst mutters to the actor, "I'm sorry," and gives him a push.

"Explain it to him in German," says the director to Willi.

"Don't apologize," says Willi quietly. "He doesn't mind being pushed. He expects it."

"If he expects it . . ." But Ernst says "I'm sorry" again.

If he fails a third time, they certainly won't use Ernst in the picture. It would be a pity, because Ernst is trying, and he does need the money. Willi understands: Ernst has too much respect for the professor. Ernst wouldn't hurt a fly. Somebody must have hurt a fly once, or they wouldn't keep on making these movies. But it wasn't Willi or Ernst.

"Give him a good push," says Willi, laughing suddenly, "and you'll get your pension tomorrow."

Ernst gives the professor such a push that the poor man falls against his wife. "The bread!" she cries, but it is too late: the bread has fallen on the dirty pavement. She and the professor bend down to pick it up. She keeps her arm around him. She puts the bread inside the folded newspaper and takes the parcel gently from the man. Ernst and the chemistry student have nothing more to do. The couple walk off between the two S.S. men as if they had always known this was how one afternoon would end.

"It's marvelous, that bit about the bread," says the director.

The star of the film, the French Resistance heroine, thinks it was overdone. They shoot two versions, one with the bread falling, and one with the professor losing his spectacles. Now Ernst has the hang of it and knocks the spectacles off without saying "I'm sorry."

The Resistance heroine is Italian. She glances at Willi, but she smokes and swears, and Willi can't bear that. Her skin is a mess. She looks as if she'd had smallpox. Someone tells Willi she was once a Roman prostitute.

He likes the young girl who has the part of the professor's daughter. She is a Parisian of sixteen who has spent her life, until now, in a convent school. She runs down the street screaming behind her parents. Willi thinks she does it well. She seems to him pure and good. He has already noticed that she is chaper-oned, and that she doesn't smoke. But if anyone gets to the girl it will be Ernst. Ernst has more luck with girls than Willi. He is in trouble, and girls will listen to that. Willi has nothing to com-plain about and lacks conversation. He knows that some weak-ness in his behavior makes him lose the upper hand, but he is not certain where it begins.

Two years ago, on another film, Willi met a girl who looked like this one. She had blond hair, short as a boy's, and wore a heart on a gold chain around her neck. She was calm and gentle—it is al-ways the same girl, the one they told him once he was going to have to defend. The blond girl invited Willi to her parents' flat one afternoon when no one was home. She lived in an old house with high ceilings. He remembers looking out the window into trees. She was proud to be entertaining a man, and she brought him ice and whiskey on a tray. When he refused, she sulked and sat as far away from him as she could. She crossed her legs, looked out the window, twisted and untwisted her gold chain.

He asked a stupid question. He said, "Don't you like me?" He always asks too soon, and the failure begins there.

"What does it matter?" said the young girl. The question an-noyed her. He had let her know she could be cruel.

Wondering what to say then, he touched a lapis-lazuli ashtray.

"My brother-in-law in Stuttgart has a bathroom tiled with this," he said.

"Don't be ridiculous," said the girl. "It's lapis lazuli."

"Whatever it is, my brother-in-law has a bathroom tiled with it."

"He can't have. Imagine what it would cost! Why, even an ashtray costs—I don't know what, exactly. You must mean blue tiles, or blue marble, or something like that."

Willi felt the weight of the ashtray and said, "I'm sure it's this."

"Then he must be so rich—a *gangster*. Besides, it would be vulgar."

She was impressed, though. He could see that. She stared at the ashtray. She had forgotten Willi's question. He had the upper hand, but only because of the brother-in-law. He suddenly thought she wasn't the girl he had expected. He stayed a few minutes longer, just to be polite, and then went away. He didn't see the girl again.

He has waited so long he must be certain; he has waited too long to afford a mistake.

*1963*

# MALCOLM AND BEA

WALKING diagonally over the sacred grass on his way up from the parking lot, Malcolm Armitage hears first the *gardien*'s whistle, then children shooting. To oblige the children, he doubles over his bent arm, wounded. Death, in children's wars, arrives by way of the stomach. Malcolm does not have to turn to know the children are Americans, just as the *gardien*, though he may not place Malcolm accurately, can tell he is not French. He can tell because Malcolm is walking on the grass between the apartment blocks, and because he is in his shirtsleeves, carrying his jacket. This is the only warm day in a cold spring. NATO is leaving, and by the time school has ended Malcolm and the embattled children will have disappeared. The children, talked of as rough, destructive, loud, laughed at for the boys' cropped heads and girls' strange clothes, are identifiable because they play. They play without admonitions and good advice. They tear over the grass shooting and killing. They shoot their mothers dead through picture windows, and each of them has died over and over, a hundred times. The *gardien* is not a real policeman, just a bad-tempered old man in a dirty collar, with a whistle and a caved-in cap. In the late warm afternoon the thinned army retreats in the direction of the wading pool, which is full of last year's leaves and fenced in, but this particular army knows how to get over a fence. The new children gradually replacing them do not mix and do not play. White net curtains cover their windows, and at night double curtains are drawn. The new children attend school on Saturdays, and when they come home they go indoors at once. They do their lessons;

then the blue light of television flashes in the chink of the curtains. When they walk, it is in a reasonable manner, keeping to the paths. They seem foreign, but of course they are not: they are French, and Résidence Diane, six miles west of Versailles, is part of France.

As he reaches the brick path edged with ornamental willows and one spared lime tree, Malcolm, unseen, comes upon his family. Bea has her back to him. Her bright-yellow dress is splashed with light. She carries the folding stool she takes to the playground and, tucked high under one arm, *Montcalm and Wolfe*, which she has been reading for weeks and weeks. When Malcolm asks how far along she is, she says, "Up to where it says Canada was the prey of jackals." Then she looks as if *he* were the jackal, because he was born in England. She looks as if she had access to historical information Malcolm will never understand. Only once he said, "Who do you hate most, Bea? The English, the French, or the Americans?" He has had to learn not to tease.

Behind her, for the moment abandoned, is the old blue stroller they bought after some other international baby had grown out of it. Ruth, Malcolm's child, is asleep in it, slumped to one side. Roy, astride his tricycle, faces Bea. Malcolm imagines himself as two miniatures—two perspiring stepfathers—on the child's eyes. Roy's eyes are mirrors. He never looks at you: there is no you. "Look at me," you say, and Roy looks over there.

The family scene set up and waiting for Malcolm consists of a fight for life. Roy, who is afraid of mosquitoes, has refused to ride his tricycle through a swarm of gnats. He is at a dead stop, with a foot on the path. His dark curls stick to his forehead. His resistance to Bea lies in his silence and stubbornness, or in sudden vandalism. Last weekend he snapped the head off every spaced, prized, counted, daffodil in reach of the playground. Malcolm heard Bea say, "I'll kill you!" He walked up to them—as he is doing now—trying to show the neighbors nothing was wrong. Bea is moved by an audience; Malcolm would like to be invisible. He drew Bea's arms back and Roy fell like a sack. She was crying. "Ah, he's not mine," she said. "He can't be. They made a mistake in the hospital." Only then did she notice Roy had been biting. She showed Malcolm her arm, mutely. He looked at the small oval, her stigmata. "He can't be mine," she said. "I had a lovely boy but some other mother got him. They gave me Roy by mistake."

"Listen," said Malcolm. "Never say that again."

Bea, suddenly cheerful, said, "But Roy's said worse than that to *me*!"

"Say right now, so he can hear you, that he's yours and there was no mistake."

Of course Roy was hers! She said so, laughing. He was hers like the crickets she kept in plastic cages and fed on scraps of lettuce the size of Ruth's fingernails; like the hedgehog she raised and trained to drink milk out of a wineglass; like the birds she buys on the quai de la Corse in Paris and turns out to freeze or starve or be pecked to death. It is always after she has said something harebrained, on the very limit of reason, that she seems most appealing. Her outrageousness is part of the coloration of their marriage, their substitute for a plot. "Poor kid," Malcolm will suddenly say, not about the wronged child but of Bea. It is easy for Bea to crave this pity of his, to feel unloved, bullied, to turn to him, though she thinks he is a bully too.

A rotary sprinkler now pivots on its stem. Roy is protected from Bea by rainbows. Bea, waiting for Roy to surrender, heaves her slight weight onto one foot. Her dress follows the line of her spine. "Honestly, Roy, you're just a coward, you know," she says. Accustomed to making animals trust her, she advances now almost without seeming to move. "Afraid of some old bugs! When I was your age I wasn't scared of anything." Bea has passed the lime tree. Her dress is in full sun. She will drop the stool and the book and shoot through rainbows. She will suddenly shove Roy off his tricycle and slap him twice, coming and going. She will drag the tricycle away and leave him there to mull over his defeat. No, none of it happens: Roy suddenly comes to life, pushes forward to meet her. When she turns back with him, she sees Malcolm. His whole family comes toward him now, and Bea is smiling.

A grievance overtakes her welcoming look. Something has come up. What now? On the way indoors she tells him: Leonard and Verna Baum, their closest friends, the only Canadians they know here, are not going to Belgium. Leonard is going to Germany, with the Army. Her interest in having Canadian friends, like her interest in history, is new. She does not always recognize a Canadian when she hears one.

"What's your father?" she said to a stray little boy who, like a puppy, followed Roy home one day. Just like that: not even "What's your name?"

"He's an Ayer Force Mayn," said the innocent, in syllables that should have rung like gongs to Bea.

"Well, Roy happens to be Canadian," said Bea haughtily, demonstrating how you put down any American aged about five.

By mistake, Bea has packed and shipped to Belgium pots and pans that belong to their landlord. She forgot to send their trunk of winter clothes. Ruth is back to baby food, and Roy (when he will eat) lives on marmalade sandwiches. Malcolm and Bea will have their dinner at the local bric-a-brac snack bar called Drug Diane. He knows, because she seems so comfortable in this ramshackle way of living, that she must have had something like it when she was a child. As if he had never seen her house, never known her father, she sometimes describes a house and a garden and a set of parents. "I liked it when we first came over to France and lived right in Versailles," she will say. "It was more like home."


The desire to be rid of Bea overtakes Malcolm at hopeless times, when he can do nothing about it. If she left him now, this second, it would settle every problem he ever has had in his life—even the problem of the winter clothes left behind. Bea, questioned about it, says she has never wanted to leave *him*. Sometimes she says, "All right, you take Roy, I'll keep Ruth." She forgets Roy isn't his. She thinks her difficulties would be resolved if she just knew something more about men. All she knows is Malcolm. The father of Roy hardly counted. She slept with him "only the once," as she puts it, and hated it. She warned Malcolm the other day: she would have an affair. If she waits too long, no one will want her. When Malcolm said, "With Leonard?" she burst out laughing. A few seconds later, evidently thinking of herself in bed with Leonard, she laughed again. "*Him*," she said. "It's too easy. Anybody can have him. They say any girl that ever worked in his office..." But her interest dies quickly. Malcolm has seldom heard her gossiping. Gossip implies at least a theory about behavior, and Bea has none. "Anyway, Leonard's losing his hair and all," she said, seriously.

So, she has an idea about a lover, Malcolm can see that, but it is still someone unreal.


Bea hasn't asked what Malcolm and Leonard were doing in Paris today, Saturday. She knows that Leonard rang just after lunch and said, "Can you come in and get me? I can't drive my car." He gave the address of a hospital.

"I think Leonard's had a heart attack," he said to Bea. "Don't say anything to Verna yet."

But when Malcolm found Leonard he discovered that Leonard's Danish girl, Karin, had cut her wrists with a fruit knife—one of those shallow cuts, with the knife held the wrong way. She isn't dead, but her stomach has been pumped out for good measure, and she is tied to her hospital bed. The police have Leonard's name.

Bea hasn't even said, "What was wrong with Leonard?" or "What did he want?"—which means she knows. If she knows, then Verna knows. Leonard is at this moment telling a carefully invented story to Verna, who may pretend to be taken in.

Bea sits very calmly on the balcony of the apartment, with Ruth in a pen at her feet, and waits for Malcolm to bring her a drink.

"Leonard's done a lot of lying to Verna," she says, out of the blue. "But I'm the sort of person no man would ever lie to."

She sits in a deck chair, serene, hair pulled into a dark ponytail so tense her black eyes look Asian. She means raw lying, such as a man's saying he is going out to buy cigarettes when he really wants to send a telegram. She would never think of a more subtle form, and might not consider it lying. She truly thinks that her face, her way of being invite the truth.

Malcolm is convinced he will never have an idea about Bea until he understands her idea of herself. Of course Bea has an idea; what woman hasn't? In her mind's eye she is always advancing, she is walking between lanes of trees on a June day. She is small and slight in her dreams, as she is in life. She advances toward herself, as if half of her were a mirror. In the vision she carries Ruth, her prettiest baby, newly born, or a glass goblet, or a bunch of roses. Whatever she holds must be untouched, fresh, scarcely breathed on.

What is her destination in this dream? Is it Malcolm?

She looks taken aback. It is herself. She *is* final. She can't go farther than herself, and Malcolm can't go any farther than Bea.

Malcolm, pouring straight gin, thinks "infantile" and then "conceited." Having her entire attention, he sits on the balcony railing and tries to tell her that no one is a destination, and no marriage simply endures: it is difficult to begin, and difficult to end. (Her dark eyes are full of love. She takes this for a declaration.) The only question, the correct question, about any marriage—the Baums', for instance—would be "What is it about?" Every marriage is about something. It must have a plot. Sometimes it has a puzzling or incoherent plot. If you saw it acted out, it would bore you. "Turn it off," you would say. "No one *I* know lives that way." It has a mood, a setting, a vocabulary, bone structure, a climate.

All Bea says to that is "Well, no man would ever lie to me."


It is not true that Bea put pressure on me to marry her, Malcolm decides. In her cloudiest rages she says, "You were maneuvered! I lied to you from the beginning! If that's what you think, why don't you come out with it?" But I have never thought it. There was no beginning. There were springs, and sources, but miles apart, uncharted. It would be like crossing a continent on foot to find them all. I would find some of them long before I knew she existed. The beginning, to her, would need a date to it—the day we met. I had been in Canada four months then, and was still without friends or money, waiting for a job I had been promised in London. Friends and money—I thought I was coming to a place where it would be easy to find both. One afternoon—a Saturday?—I was picked up in a movie by two giggling girls. Outside, I saw they were dumpy, narrow-eyed. They were twins, they told me, named Pattie and Claire. In that Western city every face bore a racial stamp, and because this was new to me I kept asking people what they were. The girls shrugged. They were called Griffith, whatever that was worth. Their father had come out here from Cape Breton Island after their mother died. I understood they might be blueberry blondes—Indians. I was still so ignorant then that I thought you could say this. The poisonous hate in their eyes lasted two or three seconds. My accent saved me. My English accent, so loathed, so resented out here, seemed hilarious to Pattie and Claire. I was hardly a generation away from signs reading, "Men Wanted. No British Need Apply," but the girls didn't know that. They must have been fifteen, sixteen. They wanted me to take them somewhere, but on a Saturday afternoon there was nowhere to go, nowhere I could take them, except my one-room flat ("suite," the girls called it). They drank rye and tap water, and told dirty stories, and laughed, and opened all the drawers and cupboards. They weren't tarts. They didn't want money. It was their idea of a normal afternoon. They wanted me to ring up some bachelor friend, but I didn't know anyone well enough. The upshot of the day was that they took me home with them. It was about eight o'clock; the sun was still high and hot.

"When you meet our Dad, just say you've always known us," said Pattie.

"No, say we went to see you for a summer job," said Claire. "Anyway, he won't ask."

They lived in a dark-green painted house behind a dried-up garden. Nearly blocking the entrance was a pram with a sleeping baby in it. His lips were slightly parted, his face flushed and mosquito-bitten. The baby's rasped thighs, his dark damp curls, the curdled-milk stain on the pillow had the print of that moment, as if I had already left Canada (I was, already, trying to do just that) and was getting ready to remember Bea, whom I hadn't met. I memorized the bright hot summer night, the stunning season that was new to me, a kind of endless afternoon, the street that seemed neither town nor country, the curtain at the window perfectly still behind a screen. The pram, the baby, and, once we were indoors, even the Seven Dwarfs on the fake chimneypiece, displayed like offerings in a museum, seemed reality, something important, from which my upbringing had protected me. I understood I had met the right people too late, for Canada had been a mistake, and it was already part of the past in my mind. The living room was spotless and cool; the linoleum on the floor gleamed pink and green. Upon it two dark-red carpets lay at pointless but evidently carefully chosen angles. Plants—dark furry begonias and a number of climbers—grew on the windowsill. A cat lay curled before the logs of the fire, exactly as if there were a real blaze. We did not stop here; the girls led me down a passage and into the kitchen. I remember a television set with the sound turned off. On the screen a man wearing a Stetson leaned against a fence, telling us to fly, fly, because the skies were falling—if the sound had been on, he would merely have been singing a song. On one wall was a row of cages with canaries, and there were still more green plants. We had walked into a quarrel. When two people are at right angles to each other they can only be quarrelling. I saw for the first time Bea's profile, and then heard her voice. The voices of most Canadian girls grated on me; they talked from a space between the teeth and the lips, as if breath had no part in speech. But the voices of all three Griffith girls were low-pitched and warm. The girls' father sat at the table drinking beer, leaning on a spread-out newspaper. Behind him was the photograph of a good-looking young man in Army uniform. At first I thought it must be his son.

"All Cath'lic girls are called Pat and Claire" was one of the first things Bea ever said to me. "I got my mother's name. *Beetriss.*" She mocked me, looking at me, gently exaggerating the way she and her sisters sounded, so as to make slight fun of me.

What did I fall in love with? A taciturn man who was anchored in the last war; two silly girls; quiet Bea. We ate quantities of toast and pickles and drank beer. "Come back any time," said Mr. Griffith, without smiling. Bea saw me out.

"I like it here," I said carefully, for I had learned something about the touchiness of Canadians, "but I may be going over to NATO. Somebody's pulling strings for me." I was diffident, in case she thought I thought I was being clever.

"That's like the Army, isn't it?"

"Not for me. I'm a civilian."

"I hope we'll see something of you before you go," she said. "But we're not very interesting for you."

"I love your family," I think I said. I said something else about "kitchen warmth."

"You like that, do you? I'd like to get out of it. But I'm stuck, and no one can help me. Well, I've got used to it. I mean, I guess I've got used to kitchens."

I wasn't the first person in her life. There was the father of Roy. What about him? "Oh, he was scared," she said. "Scared of what he'd done." She seemed curiously innocent—did not understand her sisters' jokes, or the words that sounded like other words and made them laugh. When I knew I was leaving, a few months after that, I felt I had no right to leave her behind. Even so, there was no beginning. Talking about her mother one day, we came close to talking about a common future.

"She died," Bea said, "but not at home. After the twins were born she thought everyone had it in for her, that Dad was getting secret messages over the radio, all that. She thought the cushions on the back of the sofa were watching her. She tried to drown the twins. Dad thinks we'll be like her. He thinks we already are."

"He's wrong," I said. "No one knows much about that kind of illness, but it isn't inherited." I went on—cautiously now, "Was your mother Indian? Indians are often paranoid, for some reason."

"No. Would you mind if she was?"

Nothing would have let her believe how interesting, how exotic I would have found it. "I'd mind other things more," I said. "Hemophilia, for instance."

It was exactly as if I were asking her to marry me. She looked at me, and decided not to trust me. "My mother was French-Canadian," she said. "Dad's Irish and Welsh."

I may have gone on talking then; I may have compressed my feelings about leaving her into a question. We were in a restaurant. She was a slow eater, never ate much, left half of everything on her plate. Now she stopped altogether and said quietly, "All right. I mean, yes, I want to. More than anything. But do something for me. Write it down."

"What do you want me to write? A proposal?"

"Yes. Say it in writing."

"Why?" I said. "Do you think I'm going to take it back?"

"No. I want it for Dad. Date it from three months back, so he won't be able to say I held a gun at your head."

"What is this?" I said. "What's it about?"

"Well, I'm pregnant," said Bea. "I was afraid if I told you you'd say it wasn't yours. Anyway there's nothing I could force you to do. There's no way of forcing a man to do anything. I could only wait for you to make up your mind about me. Dad thinks we're already engaged. I told him that to keep him quiet. I didn't want him to go down to your office and that."

The thought of what had been going on made my blood stop. I had never seen a change in him; there were always the same meals in the kitchen, the early supper, the noiseless television, the twins' laughter. Then Bea said, "I'll get rid of this one if you want, because of your new job and all. I suppose I can't keep my cat?"

I had expected "Can I keep Roy?"

"You can have another," I said. We seemed to be talking about the same thing.

Mr. Griffith asked me a few questions. One was "Been married before?" and another "What about the boy?"

"I'm adopting Roy," I said. This had not come up, except in my mind. Bea must have been waiting, once again, for me to decide. I remember that she looked completely astonished as I said it; not grateful, not even relieved. When she gave my written proposal to her father, her remark was "Don't say I never gave you anything for your old age."

It was nearly our farewell evening. We were around the kitchen table drinking wine I had brought. He read the proposal, made a ball of it, and threw it in the sink. Bea's face went dark, as if a curtain had been blown across the light. It was a dark look I saw later on Roy when he was learning to stand up to her. Mr. Griffith said, "Let's get back to something serious," and hoisted the bottle before him. His hand shook, and that made Bea smile. When she saw she had made him tremble, she smiled. That is all I know about her father and Bea.

Before we left she took her cat away to be destroyed. She had already stopped watering the plants, and the birdcages were empty. By the time we were married and she went away to start a new life with me, the household, the life in it, had been killed, or had committed suicide; anyway, it was dead.

Earlier today, in the tunnel of Saint-Cloud, between the western limit of Paris and the autoroute, stalled in Saturday traffic, Leonard Baum talked about his wife. The NATO removal coincides, for the Baums, with a fresh start. They have come to a "When all's said and done" stage of marriage. When all's said and done, it hasn't worked out too badly. When all's said and done, we did a good job with the children. We see absolutely eye to eye where the children are concerned. There's always that.

They are a raggle-taggle international family. They have been in Denmark, and in the Congo. Unless you know many varieties of North American accent (Bea knows none, as Malcolm can easily prove), they could be from anywhere. The girls, with their perpetual sniffles, their droopy skirts, their washed-out slacks, and their wide backsides, seem reasonably Canadian to Malcolm, though Bea says she has never seen anything like them in her life before.

"I feel like hell about Karin," Leonard said, "but that's what she wants me to feel. Suicide is always against somebody. She knew I wasn't responsible for her. I couldn't be. I am responsible for Martha and Susan and . . ." He forgot his wife's name. So did Malcolm. Both men searched for her name. Malcolm tried to pretend he was looking at her, straight across a room. She was tall and fair, her hair was pinned up, she looked like Malcolm's idea of a transfigured horse and like his idea of a missionary. "*Verna!*" said Leonard. "I'm responsible for Verna." Leonard now spoke so plainly that he must be suffering from shock. "When Verna turned Catholic, she said she didn't want any more sex. She didn't want any more children, and she had this new religion. Once there was no more of that to argue about, we got on better than before. I never missed a weekend at home and I never missed a meal. I didn't want my home to fall apart. I gave Karin as much time as I could. She poured all her life into the time I gave her. My life today makes no more sense than a sweeper's in India. I've been writing my own obituary: 'He left two young daughters and a hard-up wife.' 'His many friends were unanimous—the guy was a bastard.' 'All his life he thought he was going to Pichipoi.' You know what Pichipoi means?"

He's going to talk like this all the way home, Malcolm thought. He has talked about himself before now, but himself thirty years ago. We know about his mother and his father and his mother's cherry jam. He never talked about Verna, any more than I would talk about Bea. I know about Pichipoi. It was the name of an unknown place. The Jews in Paris invented it. It was their destination, but it was a place that might not be any worse than the present. Some of them thought it might even be better, because no one had come back yet to say it was worse. They couldn't imagine it. It was half magic. Sometimes in their transit camps they'd say, "Let's get to Pichipoi and get it over with." Leonard wasn't here. He must have been in Canada, in college. I was what—four, five? Roy's age? Leonard is still in control of his life. He was in control when he chose Verna over Karin. There is no more terror and mystery in Leonard's life than in mine. Now he thinks he has no control. His life is running away with him, because the girl tried to kill herself, the French have kicked us out and they hate us, the police have his name, he has to face Verna, and the future can't be worse than the way he feels now, stalled in the tunnel of Saint-Cloud. He shouldn't say "Pichipoi." It was a word that children invented. That makes it entirely magic. It is a sacred word. But it was such a long time ago, as long ago as the Children's Crusade. Leonard is generous; he knows he is presuming. He is on sacred ground, with his shoes on. *They* were on their way to dying. If every person thought his life was a deportation, that he had no say in where he was going, or what would happen once he got there, the air would be filled with invisible trains and we would collide in our dreams.

Leonard said, "I feel vindictive, now we're leaving. This is a private conversation, so I don't mind telling you. I get pleasure knowing a recession is on the way. When I see the sports cars with '*À Vendre*' in the windshield and I hear that cleaning women are coming round now and asking for work, I think of how we were gouged. Four hundred a month we paid for that dump. The phone never worked. We paid extra for hot water and heating and for using the elevator. Verna keeps asking, 'What's going to happen now?' Verna's very intelligent, but she asks me these questions, like 'Why are there wars?' She said, 'Leonard, explain to Martha and Susan about the new patterns of history. The girls are very interested in current affairs.' 'It's easy,' I said. 'Say Uganda has a project. They want to put a man on the moon. They'll apply to France.' 'Leonard, are you being serious?' Verna says."

Leonard knew he didn't have to say, "Don't repeat anything I've told you." He simply said, "Thanks a lot, I've talked your ear off." The shopping center of Résidence Diane looked like a giant motel. Where the lawns began, midges danced under the trees. Three American wives, in bare feet, holding mugs of coffee, stood on the holy grass. The *gardien* was furiously whistling, like a lifeguard who for some reason was unable to launch a boat. He stood at the edge of the grass and the three wives did not look at him; they stood laughing together with their mugs of coffee. Malcolm and Leonard saw something Malcolm, at least, had never seen before: a grown person dancing with rage. The *gardien* could not stop blowing his whistle; it seemed to be part of his breath. His arms were stiff with temper and he danced, there, on the path. Leonard raised his shoulders. He looked at Malcolm, and all at once seemed slightly foreign and droll.

In the midst of her packing and sorting and of Leonard's explanation, Verna Baum has remembered Malcolm and Bea. The ring at the door now is Verna, pushing a waterproof shopping cart. In it is an electric iron than cannot be plugged in anywhere except Hamilton, Ontario, two pairs of hand-painted porcelain doorknobs bought in the Paris Flea Market, a souvenir chessboard from Florence and about thirteen chessmen, a shoebox filled with old Christmas cards and Kodachrome holiday memories—these are for Roy. Roy will sit on the floor peering at them and sorting them over and over.

Bea, who has rubbish problems too, looks out of the corner of her eye and says, "Just leave it all in the hall."

Verna has also come because she wants to tell Bea exactly what her mistakes are as a mother. She may never see Bea and Malcolm again. They will exchange a letter or two, then Christmas greet-

ings, then nothing at all. She sits down in the kitchen. Her long
missionary horseface blocks Malcolm's view of Bea. Verna accepts sherry (half a tumbler), which she thinks has less alcohol in
it than beer. Does she know that Leonard's girl tried to kill herself, that Leonard was too scared afterward to drive his own car?
All she chooses to say is that she studied psychology in an American university and is in a position to analyze Roy, pass censure
on Bea, and caution Malcolm. He understands her to say "I was
a Syke-Major" and for a moment takes it to mean her maiden
name. Bea is making the children passive, Verna says. Roy will be
a homosexual and Ruth will be sucking her thumb at thirty-five
unless Malcolm at once confiscates the stroller and the tricycle.
Verna's words are "I want you to hear this, Mac. It's time somebody around here spoke up. Those two little kids should be walking on their own four feet. Roy doesn't trust you. He never asks a
question. When Martha was hardly older than Roy I told her
about you-know and she said, 'How long does it take?' She trusted
me then and she trusts me now."

"If Ruth ever asks me anything like that, I'll belt her one," says
Bea. "It's none of her damned business."

"It will have to be her business at some point," says Verna.

"Well, her business is none of mine. I don't want my own
daughter coming round telling me it's too much or not enough."

"Your reactions are so aggressive, Bea," says Verna. "I wish
you'd have someone take a look at Roy. I'm glad Mac's here, because I want him to hear this. Mac, Leonard is very worried about
Roy. He's a very sick child. He's an autistic child. You know that,
don't you?"

"Autistic my foot," says Bea. "He's bone lazy, that's all. He
talks when he wants to."

Malcolm, standing with his back to the sink, half sitting on
the edge of it, slides along to where he has a better view of Bea.
Verna has a red sherry flush right up to the edge of her eyes. "Mac
never looks at Ruthie," she says. "You wouldn't know she had a
father. If intelligent parents like you two can't do the right things,

what can you expect from people like the Congolese? I don't mean that racially. They make mistakes over weaning and that, but they have every excuse. Even our parents had an excuse. They didn't know anything."

"Mine did," says Bea. "My mother was a saint and my father worshipped her. We were very, very happy. Three girls. When I was thirteen my mother said to me, 'All men are filth.'" Bea laughs.

Verna swings round to Malcolm as if to say, "Now do you see what's wrong with Bea as a mother?"

Bea, glancing at Malcolm, says, "I can't talk openly if somebody thinks I'm telling lies."

"Oh, Bea, I don't!" This is Verna, but who cares what Verna says? The play is back to Malcolm and Bea.

Purified, exalted, because she has just realized what a good mother she is; sensing that Malcolm at this moment either wants to leave her or know something more about her, so that the marriage is at extremes of tension again, Bea calls happily, "Roy, there's a whole box of pictures for you in the hall."

She cuts the crusts off Roy's sandwiches and carries the plate to the living room. A puppet show is adjusted for him on the hired television and he is told to turn the sound off the instant it ends. Bea comes back and sits on a kitchen stool with her skirt at the top of her thighs. She grows excited, delaying Verna, keeping her because Malcolm wants her to go.

To say she had not wanted her children, as Verna sometimes hints, is a lie, Bea argues. She wanted a boy, then a girl—just what she was given. You have to take into account how Roy was conceived. She hardly knew the man. She never tried to hide Roy, or pretend he wasn't hers, though under the circumstances she might have been pardoned. She read Spock and gave Roy calcium and Vitamin D. "Mystery" had been her word for Roy unborn. But why hadn't anyone warned her the Mystery was so very ugly? Birth was ugly. Death was another ugly mystery. Her mother, dying...

"Now, Bea, that's just brooding over the past." Verna again.

But most of everything is just dirt and pain, says Bea. When she was pregnant with Ruth, she knew there was no mystery, she knew what to expect. She knew Malcolm wanted a child just to satisfy his ego, and because he felt guilty over something, and she woke him up in the night to say, "Look at how ugly you've made me."

Their lives are spread out for Verna like the wet tea leaves in the sink; like debris after a crash. No secret, dreaded destination could be worse than this. He leaves the room, walking between the two women, who seem too rapt to notice him. In the living room Roy is playing with Kodachromes, squinting, holding them up to the light. Malcolm bends down, as if helping the child. He sees the Baums' holiday in Spain, the Baums around a Christmas tree. Roy does not seem to notice Malcolm, but then he seldom does.

Neither Malcolm nor Roy heard the music rise and become poignant.

"Oh, *damn*!" Bea darts into the room. Roy kneels, staring at the screen. A woman lies on a large old-fashioned bed, surrounded by weeping children. Bea says, "The goddam mother's died. Roy shouldn't be looking at that."

Roy will speak now that Bea is here: "It's sad."

She raises her hand. "You know you're only supposed to watch the kids' programs." Her hand changes direction. She snaps off the sound.

Verna, looking as unhappy as Malcolm has ever seen any woman in his life, trails after Bea. In snatches, sometimes drowned in Ruth's bath water, he hears from sad Verna that it is depressing to live in rooms where half the furniture is gone. It reduces the feeling of stability. Tomorrow we'll be gone from here. No one will miss us. There will be homes for twelve hundred people now on a waiting list. As if a rich country could not house its people any other way. They will pay half the rents we are paying now. The landlords will paint and clean as they never had to for us. I'm not sad to be leaving.

A door is slammed. Behind the door, Verna whispers. Leonard's story is being retold.

Malcolm stood up as Bea came into the room. He said, "Don't come to Belgium." A blind movement of Roy at his feet drew his attention. "All right," he said. "I know you're there. Where do *you* want to go? Who do you want to go with, I mean?"

The child formed "Her" with his lips.

"You're sure? It beats me, but we won't discuss it now."

As if looking for help, Bea turned to the screen. Silently, washed by a driving rain (a defect of transmission), the President of the Republic's long bald head floated up the steps of a war memorial. The frames shot up wildly, spinning, like a window shade. Bea stood staring at the mute news, which seemed to be about stalled cars and middle-aged faces. Roy looked at his mother. His brow was furrowed, like an old man's.

I should have told Leonard, Malcolm thought: The real meaning of Pichipoi is being alone. It means each of us flung separately—Roy, Ruth, Bea—into a room without windows. It can't be done. It can't be permitted, I mean. No jumping off the train. I nearly made it, he said to himself. And then what?

"No," he said aloud.

A sigh escaped the child, as if he knew the denial was an affirmation, that it meant "Yes, I am still here, we are all of us together."

Breathing again, the child began his mindless sorting of old pictures and Christmas cards.

"Well, Roy," said Malcolm, as if answering some comment, "half the people in the world don't even get as far as I did just now."

That was the end of it—the end of the incident. It turned into a happy evening, one of their last in France.

*1968*

# THE REJECTION

HE SUPPOSED he had always been something of a sermonizer, but it was not really a failing; he had a mountain of information on many subjects, and silence worried him over and above the fear of being a bore. He had enjoyed, in particular, the education of his little girl. Even when she seemed blank and inattentive he went on with what he was saying. He thought it wrong of her to show so plainly she was sick to death of his voice; she ought to have learned a few of the social dishonesties by now.

They were in a warm climate, driving down to the sea. He must have been talking for hours. He said, "If indefinite time can be explained at all, it means there is another world somewhere, exactly like ours in every way."

"No, you're wrong," she said, finally answering him—high and irritable and clear. "To make it another world you'd have to change something. The ashtray in the dashboard could be red instead of silver. That would be enough to make *another* world. Otherwise it's just the same place."

This was her grandmother's training, he thought. She had been turned into a porcupine. Tears came to his eyes; none of it had been his fault.

"Who do you think tells the truth?" he said. "Your grandmother?"

"What do you mean?"

"Which of us do you like best? That must be what I meant."

"To tell you the God's truth," said the child, in a coarse voice he was not accustomed to hearing, "I'm not dying about either one of you."

In a rush of warm air the rest of her words were lost. She bent and picked up something that had been creeping on the floor—a reptile he could not identify. It was part lizard, or snake, or armadillo, the size of a kitten, and repulsive to see; but as the girl had made a pet of the thing—seemed attached to it, in fact—he said nothing.

He had lost her words, but he understood their meaning. "You don't want me to bring you up, is that it?"

"Yes. I said that."

"And your grandmother?"

"That's finished, too." Her voice was empty of anything except extreme conviction. She was a small girl, delicate of feature, but she wore, habitually, an expression so set and so humorless that her father felt weak and dispersed beside her—as if age and authority and second thoughts had, instead of welding his personality, pulled it to shreds.

I wonder, the man thought, if she *can* be mine? She had none of the qualities he recognized in himself, and for which he had been loved: warmth, tenacity, a sense of justice. Perhaps his desire to educate covered a profound unease, but he had never deserted the weak, never betrayed a friend. He was flooded with a great grievance all at once, as if he had been laughed at, his kindness solicited, his charity betrayed, for the sake of someone to whom he owed nothing. Perhaps, he thought—and this was even darker—perhaps she is not her mother's; for where were her qualities? Charm over shyness; gaiety over anxiousness; camouflage, dissimulation, myth-making to make life easier—myths explain the dark corners of life. Not even those! The child was the bottom of a pool from which both their characters had been drained away. She had nothing, except obstinacy, which he did not admire, and shallow judgment. Of course she was shallow; she had proved it: she did not love her father.

"If you do not love me," he wanted to say, "you will never care about anyone," but he felt so much pain at the possibility of not being loved that he added quickly, "I forgive you." Instantly the pain receded.

"Look here," he said. "How old are you, exactly?"

"Six and a half," said the child, without surprise.

"That would be it, that would be the right age," he said. She could be ours. With that, the pain returned.

He could not remember what they had been saying during much of the drive, but he must have been using the wrong language, or, worse, have allowed the insertion of silence. Everything had been a mistake. The child sat, perfectly self-contained, protected by an innocence that transformed her feelings and made them neutral. We must make a joke of this, her father thought, or the pain will make me so hideous, so disfigured, that she will be frightened of me. He opened his mouth, meaning to describe, objectively, what anguish was like, giving as examples the dupe on his way to be sacrificed, the runner overtaken by a tank, the loathed bearer of a disease, but he said instead, "I can't understand you," in a reasonable voice. "I was interested in you, I never neglected you. If you'd had more experience, you'd know when you were well off. You just don't know what other men can be like."

As if pleased with the effect she had produced, the child played with the monster's collar and bell. He heard the bell tinkle, and saw a flash of her small hands. She had not warned him, or prepared him, or even asked his advice. He could have stopped driving, flung himself down, appealed in the name of their past; but he had heard in his own last words a deliberate whine, which rendered any plea disgraceful.

He was dealing with a *child*, he suddenly recalled; it was not a father's business to plead for justice but to dispense it. Pride, yes, pride was important, but he was not to give up his role. He resumed reasonableness; he said, "I suppose you find me tiresome, sometimes."

"Yes, I did," said the child. "That was one of the things."

He was in the little girl's past, and she was so young that the past was removed from life. This is my fault, he said to himself. I've let her believe she was grown up; I have been too respectful. She thinks her life is her own; she doesn't know that she can't plan and think and provide for herself. He said, jokingly, as if they had been playing a game all along, "All right, who do you want to live with?," thinking she would laugh at the question, but instead she said at once, "With Mr. Mountford."

"Mountford? Are you sure that's the person you mean? You've hardly met him."

"I know," said the child, "but he's so much richer, and he has such lovely conversation."

It was further proof of shallowness, but also of her dismal innocence: If Mountford had been capable of saying one civil word to the child, it was only because he knew the little brat would not be in his house longer than an hour; she would eat her cake and drink her milk and be led away. He was the totality of everything the child's father despised; at the very sight of Mountford, his scorn for amateurs—amateur painters, actors, singers, poets, playwrights—rose and choked him. Any exchange was out of the question; they could not have discussed a crossword puzzle. Obviously, he could not translate such feelings into a child's language, while words such as "hypocrisy," "coldness," "greed" would convey nothing except a tone of adult spitefulness. She smiled to herself, perhaps remembering a "lovely conversation" in which she had mistaken a fatuous compliment for a promise. What did she mean by "richer," he wondered. It couldn't be money; not at that age. Meanwhile he saw Mountford clearly, with his slack mouth and light eyes. He did not seem like a man but like a discontented woman.

"All right," he said. "I'll take you to his house. We'll see if he can keep you. Remember," he added needlessly, "it was your decision."

Now he had relinquished her; they had put each other in the past. He wanted to say, "I didn't mean it," but she was beyond taking the slightest notice of anything he meant, or said, or did, or was. He went on, "You must do as you are told, for the last time. You are to stay in the car while I speak to Mr. Mountford." She seemed astonished, perhaps at her own power; and, after a brief gesture that might have been rebellious, sat quite still.

I was not the one who pushed things to the limit, he said to himself, as he walked up to Mountford's door. Did I abdicate? Let go too soon? It seemed settled in her mind; what else could I have done? Beside him trotted the monster with its collar and bell. She had thrust it out of the car, slyly, and sent it along to be her witness, to see if her father lied, later, about his conversation with Mountford. As though I would lie to the child, he said to himself, in despair at this new misunderstanding. But when the door was opened for him he stepped aside and let the creature scuttle through.

Mountford was dressed in his waffly felt gardening hat; a battered cream-colored corduroy jacket; dark-green hairy shirt with a hairy tie, woven for a Cottage Industry shop; trousers perpetually kneeling; shoes to which clay from a dreary promenade accrued.

How can I allow this child to live in a house where there are no flowers, no paintings, no books, and (this seemed the most miserly of all deprivations) no cigarettes? He knew there would be no musical instrument, and no records—it was a theory of Mountford's that right-thinking people went to concerts. If you lived in a provincial part of the world, in a resort, a watering place where you had to depend on military tunes played in the casino garden, then you did without. When you have heard an opera once in your life, it is up to you to remember it; it saves time, and any amount of money. The child's father supposed Mountford had said all of this to him once. He found he had a store of information concerning Mountford; how he felt about climates, sonnets, the sea, other people, the passage of time, the importance of pleasure; he possessed this knowledge, condensed, like a summary he had been given to read. He knew that Mountford went into the kitchen to see if his cook was using too much olive oil. Perhaps this was only gossip—but no, Mountford now held the bottle of oil up to the light of the kitchen window.

"You don't need all those ingredients for a simple *poulet chasseur*," Mountford said to the cook. "White wine, bouillon, brandy, butter, oil, flour, tomatoes, tarragon, chervil, shallots, salt and pepper... ridiculous. You can use a bouillon cube," he said, putting the bottle down. "Vinegar instead of wine. Cooking fat. No one will ever know. Go easy, now," he said, in his jovial way. "Go easy with the brandy and the flour. You know how things are... You can stay for lunch," he said, turning to the child's father, "but you understand I can't keep *her*. I scarcely know her. She's more of a stranger, if you know what I mean. We've had a few words together, nothing more. Tell her she has made a mistake, I don't know her and that's that."

That much is settled, the man thought. She will not live in a house where she can hear "No one will ever know." She will not he infected by meanness. As for himself, he had come out of it well. He had not bullied, or shown authority, or imposed a decision. He had not even suggested a course! She had been given free choice all the way.

"If I were you," said Mountford as they went into the front part of the house, "I would just give her to old Bertha in the kitchen."

"It isn't a matter of giving her away," he said. "I'm not *giving* her."

"Well, old Bertha would be one solution. We ought to repopulate those empty peasant areas—fill them with new stock, good blood."

"Not with *my* child," he said. He knew exactly how he ought to murder Mountford. He saw the place between his eyes, and his own hand flat, like a plate skimming. Mountford's eyes would start, fall out nearly, while the skin around them went black as ink. That was the way to show Mountford what he thought of him. He saw the kitchen again, the large stove, and the hag who must be old Bertha. Mountford, untouched, was still pink of face and smiling.

The child had disobeyed. She stood in the hall, fragile, composed, her hands bright in a shaft of light. This is her first shock, he remembered; I must tell her gently. She was so confident, so certain she would always be wanted. He thought, She *must* be mine—she is so independent. He spoke tenderly, but the small, resolute face did not alter. He felt the hopeless frustration of talking to someone whose mind is made up, and understood how difficult it must have been, sometimes, for someone to deal with him. He had a living memory of having once been secure in his ideas and utterly convinced. She has courage, too, he decided. But it was not courage—she was simply pretending not to mind. Perhaps she is stupid, he thought. All that acting, that pretending nothing matters. She must be her mother's, after all. "There," he wanted to say to the child's mother, "do you see how patient I had to be?"

As they walked away from the house, he heard the reptile. He recognized the frantic note of the creature abandoned; there was no mistaking the hysteria and terror, the fear that no one would ever come for it again.

"Go back and get him," he said.

"I don't want him."

"You can't leave him," said the man. "You've taken him out of his own life and made a pet of him. You can't abandon him now. You're responsible for him."

"I don't want him," the child said without emphasis.

Why, he thought, she is cruel. How horrible this has become—she can't belong to either of us, for surely we were never guilty of cruelty? The child sat in the car now, confident she would never be made to account for anything, that she had another choice, that her chances were eternal.

He stood with his hand on the door of the car and said once again, "Look here, how old are you exactly?"

"Six and a half."

"Then that's it," he said. "That would be the age. There's no getting away from it." He had to give in; he had to accept her.

Well, *she* will have to help me then, he decided, and an access of fierce and joyous hostility toward the child's mother made him think he was seeing clearly for the first time. I may have made some mistake, he said, but she got away with murder. Look at the pain and grief I thought were finished; *she* had nothing to remind her.

But then, he remembered, she does not know the child exists. I must have forgotten to tell her. How can I suddenly say, "Here is the result, the product, the thing we have left?" She could say, "Why didn't you mention it sooner?"

"I would like to take you to your mother," he said, "but it will take a little planning. She may not know anything about you. You are quite like her, I am afraid, though also like me. She may not want to admit who you are like. If she knew you had abandoned that creature, she might tell you there are two sorts of people, that the world is divided..." He thundered on, as if making himself heard, "People who give up...who destroy...though her own position is not all that good. Still, I'm certain she would say you are on the wrong side."

"Who do you think you're shouting at?" the calm child seemed to be saying. "And why are you bothering *me*?"

*1969*

# THE WEDDING RING

ON MY WINDOWSILL is a pack of cards, a bell, a dog's brush, a book about a girl named Jewel who is a Christian Scientist and won't let anyone take her temperature, and a white jug holding field flowers. The water in the jug has evaporated; the sand-and-amber flowers seem made of paper. The weather bulletin for the day can be one of several: No sun. A high arched yellow sky. Or, creamy clouds, stillness. Long motionless grass. The earth soaks up the sun. Or, the sky is higher than it ever will seem again, and the sun far away and small.

From the window, a field full of goldenrod, then woods; to the left as you stand at the front door of the cottage, the mountains of Vermont.

The screen door slams and shakes my bed. That was my cousin. The couch with the India print spread in the next room has been made up for him. He is the only boy cousin I have, and the only American relation my age. We expected him to be homesick for Boston. When he disappeared the first day, we thought we would find him crying with his head in the wild cucumber vine; but all he was doing was making the outhouse tidy, dragging out of it last year's magazines. He discovers a towel abandoned under his bed by another guest, and shows it to each of us. He has unpacked a trumpet, a hatchet, a pistol, and a water bottle. He is ready for anything except my mother, who scares him to death.

My mother is a vixen. Everyone who sees her that summer will remember, later, the gold of her eyes and the lovely movement of her head. Her hair is true russet. She has the bloom women have sometimes when they are pregnant or when they have fallen in love. She can be wild, bitter, complaining, and ugly as a witch, but that summer is her peak. She has fallen in love.

My father is—I suppose—in Montreal. The guest who seems to have replaced him except in authority over me (he is still careful, still courts my favor) drives us to a movie. It is a musical full of monstrously large people. My cousin sits intent, bites his nails, chews a slingshot during the love scenes. He suddenly dives down in the dark to look for lost, mysterious objects. He has seen so many movies that this one is nearly over before he can be certain he has seen it before. He always knows what is going to happen and what they are going to say next.

At night we hear the radio—disembodied voices in a competition, identifying tunes. My mother, in the living room, seen from my bed, plays solitaire and says from time to time, "That's an old song I like," and "When you play solitaire, do you turn out two cards or three?" My cousin is not asleep either; he stirs on his couch. He shares his room with the guest. Years later we will be astonished to realize how young the guest must have been—twenty-three, perhaps twenty-four. My cousin, in his memories, shared a room with a middle-aged man. My mother and I, for the first and last time, ever, sleep in the same bed. I see her turning out the cards, smoking, drinking cold coffee from a breakfast cup. The single light on the table throws the room against the black window. My cousin and I each have an extra blanket. We forget how the evening sun blinded us at suppertime—how we gasped for breath.

My mother remarks on my hair, my height, my teeth, my French, and what I like to eat, as if she had never seen me before. Together, we wash our hair in the stream. The stones at the bottom are the color of trout. There is a smell of fish and wildness as I kneel on a rock, as she does, and plunge my head in the water. Bubbles of soap dance in place, as if rooted, then the roots stretch and break. In a delirium of happiness I memorize ferns, moss, grass, seedpods. We sunbathe on camp cots dragged out in the long grass. The strands of wet hair on my neck are like melting icicles. Her "Never look straight at the sun" seems extravagantly concerned with my welfare. Through eyelashes I peep at the milky-blue sky. The sounds of this blissful moment are the radio from the house; my cousin opening a ginger-ale bottle; the stream, persistent as machinery. My mother, still taking extraordinary notice of me, says that while the sun bleaches her hair and makes it light and fine, dark hair (mine) turns ugly—"like a rusty old stove lid"—and should be covered up. I dart into the cottage and find a hat: a wide straw hat, belonging to an unknown summer. It is so large I have to hold it with a hand flat upon the crown. I may look funny with this hat on, but at least I shall never be like a rusty old stove lid. The cots are empty; my mother has gone. By mistake, she is walking away through the goldenrod with the guest, turned up from God knows where. They are walking as if they wish they were invisible, of course, but to me it is only a mistake, and I call and run and push my way between them. He would like to take my hand, or pretends he would like to, but I need my hand for the hat.

My mother is developing one of her favorite themes—her lack of roots. To give the story greater power, or because she really believes what she is saying at that moment, she gets rid of an extra parent: "I never felt I had any stake anywhere until my parents died and I had their graves. The graves were my only property. I felt I belonged somewhere."

*Graves?* What does she mean? My grandmother is still alive.

"That's so sad," he says.

"Don't you ever feel that way?"

He tries to match her tone. "Oh, I wouldn't care. I think everything was meant to be given away. Even a grave would be a tie. I'd pretend not to know where it was."

"My father and mother didn't get along, and that prevented me feeling close to any country," says my mother. This may be new to him, but, like my cousin at a musical comedy, I know it by heart, or something near it. "I was divorced from the landscape, as they were from each other. I was too taken up wondering what was going to happen next. The first country I loved was somewhere in the north of Germany. I went there with my mother. My father was dead and my mother was less tense and I was free of their troubles. That is the truth," she says, with some astonishment.

The sun drops, the surface of the leaves turns deep blue. My father lets a parcel fall on the kitchen table, for at the end of one of her long, shattering, analytical letters she has put "P.S. Please bring a four-pound roast and some sausages." Did the guest depart? He must have dissolved; he is no longer visible. To show that she is loyal, has no secrets, she will repeat every word that was said. But my father, now endlessly insomniac and vigilant, looks as if it were he who had secrets, who is keeping something back.

The children—hostages released—are no longer required. In any case, their beds are needed for Labor Day weekend. I am to spend six days with my cousin in Boston—a stay that will, in fact, be prolonged many months. My mother stands at the door of the cottage in nightgown and sweater, brown-faced, smiling. The tall field grass is gray with cold dew. The windows of the car are frosted with it. My father will put us on a train, in care of a conductor. Both my cousin and I are used to this.

"He and Jane are like sister and brother," she says—this of my cousin and me, who do not care for each other.

Uncut grass. I saw the ring fall into it, but I am told I did not —I was already in Boston. The weekend party, her chosen audience, watched her rise, without warning, from the wicker chair on the porch. An admirer of Russian novels, she would love to make an immediate, Russian gesture, but cannot. The porch is screened, so, to throw her wedding ring away, she must have walked a few steps to the door and *then* made her speech, and flung the ring into the twilight, in a great spinning arc. The others looked for it next day, discreetly, but it had disappeared. First it slipped under one of those sharp bluish stones, then a beetle moved it. It left its print on a cushion of moss after the first winter. No one else could have worn it. My mother's hands were small, like mine.

*1969*

# THE BURGUNDY WEEKEND

I

WHY DID the Girards let Lucie's cousin Gilles drive them to Burgundy? Lucie and Jérôme could so easily have rented a car or asked someone in their hotel about trains. The offer was not even a kindness: Gilles had to be in Dijon that weekend and he wanted company on the road.

In youth Gilles had looked like Julius Caesar, but now that he had grown thickly into his forties, he reminded people of Mussolini. Sometimes a relation from Quebec ran into Gilles—the cousin who had chosen the States, educated his daughters in Paris, had never come back to Canada except for funerals. "Gilles is like Mussolini now," Lucie had heard, but it was said with admiration.

As Mussolini might have been cavalier with lesser visitors, so Gilles kept Jérôme and Lucie waiting for seven hours, in Paris, on a Saturday in June. First he called at breakfast time (the Girards were already sitting in the hotel parlor with a packed suitcase between them), and then he called just before lunch, and again at three. It was Lucie who took the calls. She could not quite hear what Gilles' delays were about. The telephone at the hotel desk was greasy and certainly microbe-laden; she held it an inch away from her ear. The line was also being used by strangers frying bacon and popping corn. They lived under a tin roof on which hail was falling. A woman cried, "I told you he was a fool!" This thin, hysterical ghost voice was the tone for that weekend, a choir leader setting the pitch. Through the hail and the bacon frying came the Canadian voice of cousin Gilles making excuses.

After each of these calls, Lucie sent a telegram to a village in Burgundy, to a woman who was an old friend of Jérôme's, and who had been expecting the Girards in time for lunch. The telegrams were variations on a single mournful apology: "Desolated to inform you the unexpected retards our arrival." She signed Jérôme's name and trusted the choice of words to be suitable for Madame Henriette Arrieu, so important in...what? In recent French history? In the kind of history that was turned into films? Jérôme had never described her. Lucie, obliged to invent, composed someone slender and aged, not frighteningly clever, above all kind. She gave her creation a cloud of white hair, put five or six gold rings on her fingers, dressed her in pale chiffon. Henriette Arrieu, suddenly alive, approached Lucie across an acre of flawless grass, with her hands outstretched and her rings on fire and her weightless sleeves pushed back by the slightest, warmest movement of June—as if wind were the day.

I see pictures because I don't know as many words as Jérôme, said Lucie to herself, pleading inadequacy the way Gilles gave grounds for lateness.

Jérôme did not seem at all disturbed by the long wait. He stood looking over a window box of plastic geraniums at the traffic on quai Voltaire. Perhaps he was seeing only the pinpoint concentration of his thoughts, which Lucie imagined to be a minute ray of light in a dark curtain.

He is going to be all right this weekend, she said. The best signs were in place when he got up. Sun at the window. Breakfast. He seemed happy. The French coffee reminded him of something. Something pleasant, yes. His first cigarette. He showed me a map and explained about Burgundy. Only God could have known what he was thinking, but if you live with Jérôme you live without God, and so nobody knows anything.

Jérôme turned to speak to her (an excellent sign), but the traffic outside was like the purring of a monstrous cat. She had to close the parlor window—her gestures were gradual, calm—before she could hear. "About that advertisement in the Métro."

"Yes, which one?"

"The one I pointed out to you, to show what they are selling in Paris now. *'In Solitude, in Anguish, in Despair, call VAL* 70-50. *SOS Friendship.'* They used to sell soap, coffee, Dubonnet."

"Jérôme, you won't make sad remarks all weekend, will you?" said Lucie. "Or to Gilles while he's driving?"

Of course, it was the worst thing she could have said. He would not speak to her again for hours, might even refuse to acknowledge Gilles' greeting.

Every marriage is different, she said, and ours is like this. It can't be helped. I don't know of any that can be called better—only different.

Gilles had warned Lucie that he would not be allowed to park in front of their hotel. If he were to pause longer than it takes to shift gears the car would be hauled off to a motor graveyard, their passports would be impounded, and Lucie would be taken away by the police and shut up in a cage full of prostitutes. Gilles would slow down somewhere close to them, he had said, that was the best he could do, and the Girards would need to be poised, ready to leap like gazelles. And Lucie had promised that she and Jérôme would do that; they would leap like gazelles straight into Gilles' car. At three o'clock Gilles announced, "Twenty minutes from now. Remember what I told you." Jérôme and Lucie moved out to the edge of the pavement with their raincoats folded and their suitcase between them and stood without speaking until a quarter to four, at which time a blue BMW pulled out of the westbound flux on the quai and stopped dead. Gilles reached back and opened a door. "Hurry!" he said. He wore a tweed cap and 1910 goggles. Lucie started to get in until she saw a slavering black Labrador retriever sitting where she was meant to sit. She cried, "No, you go with him," to Jérôme and she ran round the front of the car to climb in next to Gilles. Jérôme put the coats and suitcase between himself and the animal and immediately closed his eyes. The car stank of cigars. The radio was turned on to a concert. "Hurry!" said Gilles again. They moved off at a crawl into the stream of traffic flowing west, then south.

Lucie leaned close to Gilles and said in a low voice, "He will probably sleep most of the way. He gets tired in cars, unless he happens to be driving. The time change was bad for his sleep. For his appetite, too. He'll say he's hungry and then he won't eat. I keep chocolate in my handbag. He is underweight for his height. He may seem indifferent sometimes. It is only tiredness. Pretend you don't notice."

Gilles said to himself, You would think he was her dog. You would think he was her infant. Christ, he must be what, now—thirty-nine? More?

Partly in French and sometimes in English, for he slid without hearing himself, Gilles began to speak as though Lucie had just recently interrupted him: "I don't want you to think I'm boasting. I don't need to boast. My first research grant was a personal one, one hundred thousand dollars."

"What kind of dollars?" said Lucie.

"I'm over in the States about ten months of the year," Gilles went on. "I was my own administrator when I got that first grant. No strings. I was about the age you are now. I'm a lot more sure of myself than when you remember me."

"I think I was twelve," said Lucie. "I didn't much notice how people were."

"I must be one of the top three or four in my field now," said Gilles. "Not in the States. In the world. I've published in the Soviet Union. I keep the apartment in Paris just for the girls' education. I want their French to be good. I don't want them to have what we had. Anyway, Laure won't live in the States. Our apartment is in Neuilly. André Maurois—you know?—used to have a place practically in the same building. Laure and the girls stay here most of the year. I've got this other beautiful place in New Haven built in 1728. Laure furnished it but she wouldn't stay. I don't insist. I believe in individual freedom. Laure feels she has more to contribute here. She wrote to the Prime Minister when they cut down the chestnut trees on place Saint-Sulpice. Got a nice answer, too. I don't work over there just for the money. If that's what you think, and if that's what they think at home, well, you don't know me. I'd take a lousy research-teaching job in a lousy French university any day if I thought it had real meaning. No, the reason why I'm there is because of my collections. Drawings, furniture. I've got these collections, they're so valuable I can't have them insured. Can't afford to. And I could never bring anything out of the country. The Americans would never allow it. They would say it was part of the national heritage."

"Do they say that about drawings?" said Lucie. "I thought heritage was just culture."

"Paris is the right place for my daughters," said Gilles. "They play with the Ruwenzori children, the little princesses. The Ruwenzoris send a car for them. Their mother was a Soplex, of the Soplex mineral water family. When the girls were in New Haven last year I had them tested. Sophie's I.Q. was one-eighty, Chantal's was one-seventy-five, and Diane's in between. We have to watch what they read, who their friends are. I'm not boasting. They get their brains from Laure."

All this was in English, of which Lucie understood a fair amount. She was a nurse; she had taken six months' special training in the psychiatric wing of an American hospital. She did not mind English, but Jérôme did. He lived in his own climate; he had made language one of the elements. Sometimes he seemed to be drenched by sleet no one else felt, or else he could not see out for a curtain of snow. Jérôme was more intelligent than anyone Lucie had ever heard of. He had taken university degrees in France. Lucie wanted her cousin to appreciate this; she wanted Gilles to respect Jérôme, who was careless with people but was not afraid of the night or of dying.

She turned her head slowly. His eyes were shut; his breath moved slowly and evenly. "Jérôme is asleep," she said to Gilles, who did not care one way or the other.

Jérôme was tuned to the radio, to a program of music by the composer End. The music was familiar, but who was End? It came to him as he saw a record sleeve with Jacqueline du Pré; he could see even her wedding ring. He opened his eyes and looked at Gilles' long graying-reddish hair fanned over a suede collar. Gilles was on his way to Dijon for an antiquarians' trade fair. He was to be the guest of famous professor somebody, a celebrated authority on medieval church carvings.

"Some medieval saints look like crocodiles," said Jérôme. "Some look like de Gaulle." No saint has ever looked like Gilles.

Gilles was a master of knowledge about saints, silver, tapestries, paintings, porcelain; he bought some things to keep and some to sell in America. He made a lot of money that way—so he was telling Lucie now.

The autoroute might have been taking them anywhere. The end of the road might even be Montreal.

"How is *he*?" said Gilles suddenly, with a slight jerk of the tweed cap. "I mean how is he really?"

"Who said anything was the matter with him?" said Lucie.

"Lucky thing you never had children," said Gilles. "He never had a job. I don't mean never held one, I mean never had one. Am I right?" He did not require an answer. "Did he ever write anything, finally?"

"I never heard him say he wanted to," said Lucie. "So I'm not sure what you mean by finally."

"Then why did he take degrees in literature?" said Gilles. "He could have taught. They were screaming for teachers then. Too late now. Degrees like his are a dime a dozen. Well, you aren't tied with children. That's one good thing."

"It isn't too late for children," said Lucie. "I'm twenty-eight."

"At least you'll never have problems like what to do about super-intelligent daughters," said Gilles. "Are you still a Catholic, Lucie? Practicing, I mean."

"Not now." That was something she could answer.

"Our upbringing was a disease," said Gilles.

"That's what Jérôme says. I don't know. God never hurt my feelings."

"It was easy for your generation," said Gilles. "You had a choice."

"No one mentioned it at the time," said Lucie. "Excuse me, Gilles, but your dog is slobbering on our raincoats."

"Saliva is only a saline solution," said Gilles. "It washes out."

". . . for cello and orchestra, by the composer Eye-hend," said the same announcer who had mentioned "End."

Gilles snapped the radio shut. "The French are twenty years behind the times," he said. "Still playing the wrong Haydn. Only *Michael* Haydn matters."

It occurred to Lucie that she had no clear early memory of what her cousin had been like before Mussolini and Julius Caesar; before Neuilly, New Haven, the goggles, the Labrador retriever, and the right Haydn.

With the stilling of music and of voices a freshness like the freshness of water filled the car. They had left the autoroute and crossed a river; no, the end of this journey would never be Montreal. Now Gilles drove them to the edge of a walled town whose ramparts rose above the road. Lucie observed Jérôme as he gave this wall his deepest attention. She looked too, and saw stone the color of leaves drying and a pair of towers like two of Jérôme's chessmen.

Between the towers there had once been houses, but they had been pulled apart, trodden to sand, probably when the Renaissance demanded horizons. Jérôme had explained that once. He had stood on the ramparts, looking down to the road where he and Gilles and Lucie and the slobbering dog were now stalled in Saturday traffic, and a girl standing beside him had asked, "Do they rent those towers? Couldn't we try to live in one?" The girl was one of the two or three he had been in love with before Lucie. Lucie had been a child then, not ready to be known. She had been so devout and solemn her sisters feared she might become a nun. But then she said no, that she would be a nurse and thereby marry a doctor. She turned herself into a nurse and had no home of her own, but slept in any of her married sisters' houses. The sisters were always making up spare beds for Lucie. Two of her brothers-in-law each tried to become Lucie's first lover because she looked like their wives but was a virgin still; but she was too devout, too tired, too afraid. At twenty-five she told her favorite sister, "I have waited too long now to marry just anybody. He will have to be special, rare. Intelligent, generous, faithful," making the choice so hard that she might never need to be chosen. She neglected to say, "Unbreakable, whole." Just when she was about to become indispensable as a babysitter, she married one of her patients, Jérôme.

Jérôme seemed to be counting something. As Lucie read his face, he might have been counting, "In Solitude, in Anguish, in Despair," wondering what could be added.

"A great thing about France is you can get Cuban cigars," said Gilles, throwing away the end of one. "By way of Geneva." He pulled in at an Elf service station and remarked, "Laure likes us to use Elf stations because they aren't backed by international capital. No other woman would think of that. I've got no change," he said, "Nothing small enough. They won't take a check here."

Now Lucie recalled her cousin. Yes, she remembered him before Mussolini, before Julius Caesar. There was a family joke, a joke still living, about rich cousin Gilles who never had the change for anything—not for a candy bar, not for a stamp.

"If you could let me have something like a hundred dollars—in francs, of course," said Gilles. "I won't be able to cash a check until Monday." He addressed himself to Lucie.

"Ask Jérôme," she said. She was remembering something she had been told: "Don't let Jérôme think he isn't competent. Don't take over his role. About money—he must learn to spend rationally." She saw Jérôme coming to life and giving Gilles three times one hundred francs—about sixty dollars, that would be. Was that rational? Was it too little? Was it miserly? Or else too much, the unnecessary gesture again? Gilles made no comment, but the matter of choosing bills and handing them over had started Jérôme off speaking, which was a good sign.

"I came to that town once with another student, one of three girls," he said. "I was trying to remember her name."

Gilles looked at Lucie. She knew the expression—a man confronted with another man's strangeness. Gilles had not seen the walls, high up over the road and to the right. He thought that Jérôme was raving. She said, "You know that Jérôme was a student here, in the nineteen-fifties." She weighted her voice with all that Gilles was supposed to keep in mind: Jérôme's precocious brilliance, Jérôme's degrees.

"The girls in the nineteen-fifties were the prettiest that ever lived," said Gilles, loudly and heartily. "Good old Jérôme! Of course he remembers them! Two or three of them, anyway." Lucie was used to that way of speaking too: a man's way of humoring a madman.

"Does anyone want chocolate?" she said. Gilles took a third of the bar; Jérôme closed his eyes, getting rid of Gilles, the Labrador, Lucie, chocolate, money, and Gilles' goggles and cap.

"Jérôme could have had a great career," said Lucie. "But he refused to work within the system. Of course he was right."

Like everyone else in Lucie's family, Gilles believed that Jérôme's relations had engineered the marriage because Jérôme had had a breakdown and Lucie was a nurse. As for Jérôme, said Gilles silently, he may have seemed like an intellectual pioneer all those years ago, but now there were crowds of younger men with degrees every bit as good as his, and all of them waiting for the handful of prestigious titles Free Quebec would throw out: Minister of Culture, Minister for the Restoration of Historical Monuments, Ambassador to the United Nations, to Unesco, to France, to London, to Rome, to the Vatican. Minister of Protocol. Minister of the Armed Forces. Minister in Charge of other Ministries. Minister in Discreet Control of the Self-Perpetuating Revolution. That was what Jérôme had been waiting for. It wasn't a breakdown he'd had. It was a sulking fit.

Well, just wait. Wait until it happens and there are one hundred and thirty candidates for the Ministry of Culture but not even one bright young man asking to be Minister of Potatoes. *I* never wanted that, Gilles thought, forcing his way back into southbound traffic. I was never sullen. I never had to be humored and led around like a blind man by my wife. I only wanted to be what I am now—one of the top three or four in my field. I support five people and a dog. I have beautiful homes in two countries. My education is a match for Jérôme's any day. I don't create social problems. I am on the side of life, not of failure. I am the equal of my wife, not her dependant. I shall never be poor.

"What do you live on, Lucie?" said Gilles. "How could you afford this trip?" He knew what Jérôme was said to have done with his money. Among other things, he had financed a string quartet and actually started it on tour before his trustees stepped in and left the musicians stranded in Rimouski. After five or six ventures of that kind Lucie had gone back to work as a private nurse.

"We have to be, well, careful," she said. Her attention was very much on the three hundred francs Gilles had pocketed. Sixty dollars mattered. In the Girards' life every dollar had a destination. "As for the trip here, he suddenly wanted it. He can't plan, you see. It's one of his . . . anyway, I was so glad when he said he wanted something."

"I never, never plan," said Gilles. "I never think farther ahead than five years. You don't believe me? Ask Laure." He forgot about Jérôme, which was easy, because Jérôme had never really been on his mind. Gilles suddenly said, "The girls in the nineteen-fifties—you know? No, you don't know. They were made out of butter. They had round faces and dimples and curly hair. Bright lipstick. They smiled. They wore these stiff petticoats. They could have fallen in the Seine and never drowned—they'd have floated downstream on their petticoats. They wore Italian shoes that were a disaster. All those girls have ruined feet now. They looked like children dressed up—too much skirt, mother's shoes. They smiled and smiled and wanted to get married. They were infantile, underdeveloped. Retarded. All except Laure. I married Laure."

"My sisters weren't retarded," said Lucie.

"There is a very important railway bridge named for Laure's family," said Gilles. "You and your sisters are peasants compared with Laure. She went to Vermont every summer. Her English was perfect. I took her to Venice for our honeymoon. In forty-eight hours she could order breakfast in Italian. I've got a picture of her in Venice feeding the pigeons. Skirt spread out. Big smile. We'd been married eleven days and she still didn't know what was what. Insisted on the dark. Married four weeks before she'd keep a light on. And then she kept her eyes shut."

"*I* knew what was what," said Lucie.

"You were a nurse," said Gilles. "Laure's upbringing—it was delicate, different. After we had Sophie and Chantal, she said to me, 'I don't want any more pregnancies, isn't there something I could be doing?' A doctor's wife! 'Isn't there something I could be doing?'" His voice rose to a squeak because he was trying to imitate a woman's. He was not mocking Laure; on the contrary, he seemed filled with awe in the face of her opaqueness, or obtuseness. It was proof of Laure's quality. "Training is everything," he said. "Training. The right word for every situation. She can tell where people come from before they open their mouths. The girls owe Laure every advantage they have. Looks. Brains. They play with the Ruwenzori children, the little princesses. Their mother—"

"You said that," Lucie reminded, wanting only to save her cousin the bother of repeating himself.

Jérôme, in the backseat, had suddenly become active. She had a special ear for him, as a person conscious of mice can detect the faintest rustling. He took a letter out, unfolded it, spread it on the suitcase, ran his thumbnail along the creases. With the letter was a hand-drawn map. He looked at Henriette Arrieu's instructions and then, without the slightest comprehension, out the window.

"We had better have that map up here," said Lucie, reaching for it.

"Laure says we have paid too much attention to beautiful objects that have no meaning," said Gilles. "She says the children will sell the silver for a pound of rice after our class has been reduced to begging."

"Is Laure a revolutionary?" said Lucie.

She had not seen Laure in Paris. One of Gilles' brilliant daughters had caught an ear infection in a selective swimming pool. Lucie had not understood why this should bar the apartment at Neuilly to herself and Jérôme. Perhaps Gilles and Laure had a rule about visiting Canadians. Perhaps Laure had been told cruel stories about Jérôme. It was possible that in a family with a bridge named after it no one worried about trouble with life from morning till night; perhaps it was not essential to understand other people or even be decent to them. And then Gilles could not leave the matter quiet, but had to keep adding new excuses. Laure was having the drawing room restyled; the place looked like Verdun after the battle. Also—he made it sound incidental—Laure suffered from a skin disease. It took the form of great patches of pigmentation, like freckles; the skin around the patches was drained of color, albino-pale. Gilles told Lucie the name of this ailment and said there was no cure for it. Laure had been told so too, but she would not listen; she had tried a new quack treatment in secret, a lotion you were supposed to dilute with mineral water one to twenty. Too highly bred for patience (think of racehorses, he said), she had used the stuff straight out of the bottle, dabbing poison around her mouth and eyes, burning the skin, raising blisters.

"She wouldn't consult me, of course," he said, still declaring his pride in her. "I'm only one of the world's top dermatologists—that's all I am. Is Laure a revolutionary? Is she a revolutionary? Let me consider that. She won't live in the States. Is that political? I'm not a dominating male. I don't ask questions."

Lucie considered what Gilles might be like as a husband. He was never moody or silent. He could jabber on for hours about anything. Whatever devils beset him he got rid of with words. Perhaps he did not object to living alone in the New Haven house and seeing his clever family only sometimes. Laure was certainly remarkable too, though she did have some lapses, such as using that powerful lotion just as it came from the bottle.

"We are not in Burgundy," Gilles presently said. "Though Jérôme can think so if he likes. What does your map say? Are you sure that is the house?" He was looking at a sandy ruin partly covered with tarpaulin. A sign near the road explained that restoration of this wreck was proceeding under the guidance of the Central Direction of Architecture and Historical Monuments of the Ministry for Cultural Affairs. "There, a job for Jérôme," said Gilles.

She was sure the remark was innocent. The question was, where were they?

"I know the site," said Gilles. "It was bought by a dentist in Paris. He will never live here, but it gives him prestige and something off his taxes."

"The house is across the road," said Jérôme, not only bringing them to their senses but showing that he could, sometimes, move the pinpoint of concentration away from himself and feel compassion for Lucie's anxious daisy-face, tenderness for the fair hair that stuck out in uncontrollable wisps like flower petals. She sensed that; smiled; and then all three saw with sudden shyness the unknown spiked fence with a low wall behind it, the shut gate, the dangling bell cord one of them would have to pull. Gilles was the first to move. He gave the bell a contemptuous look and pushed the gate open. They drove in over a curve of hissing gravel, under lime trees.

Lucie had never seen a house quite like this one. For one thing it had no door, but only four pairs of French windows. These stood open, allowing four pairs of streaked and faded red silk curtains to billow gently. The lawn was of scythed grass, like a pasture. Along a whitewashed wall trees had been trained flat to a lattice. Lucie knew an apple leaf when she saw one, but she had not seen trees crucified before. The emergence of two new persons, a girl of about eighteen and a slow old woman, out of separate windows at opposite ends of the house, turned her attention to herself. She saw everything she was wearing and had packed in the suitcase. This was a country weekend, but what is "country" when you are a total stranger? She could not grasp the meaning of this house, which was neither farm nor mansion; did not see why a scythed field required a fence and a wall around it; did not understand the running, breathless, scowling girl with her long cotton frock, bare arms, bare feet, flying hair; even less the plodding old woman who had a white mustache. The heels of Lucie's shoes sank into the loose gravel of the drive. Her ankles would not hold her. She felt herself clutching her white handbag. The dog had got out and was digging at the lawn: she saw that in white, as under lightning.

The running girl did not see anything, certainly not Lucie. She made for Jérôme; stopped; remembered her manners. It was Lucie who received her French coldness, her French handshake (a newborn white mouse was what it felt like). She said in delicate, musical English, "I am Nadine Besson, Madame Arrieu's granddaughter. My grandmother regrets endlessly, but she had to be in Paris for a memorial service today. A Resistance thing. They are old and keep on dying. Your telegrams kept arriving but no telephone number. We called the residence of your ambassador, but the ambassador..." (suspicious but sorry) "...had never heard of you. As for the embassy, no one could be obtained except a young girl who did not speak any known language at all, but who seemed to be in charge. She—when she could be understood—had never heard of you either. You neglected to tell my grandmother where you would be staying in Paris. She leaves you a thousand apologies and she will be here tomorrow."

Gilles at once detached himself from the Girards. They were peasants, he was only their cousin. "Someone slipped up on the arrangements," he said. He looked at Lucie with great good humor and all but slapped her on the back.

It was Jérôme who had been in constant touch with Madame Arrieu, who had received her instructions, her map. He had been incapable of booking seats on a flight to Paris, but he had known with exactitude where and when he was expected for lunch on a Saturday in June. The old woman meanwhile was circling the motor car, looking for luggage. Gilles made a tally of the entire situation. He added up the mown hay (these people must keep rabbits), the rows of salvia indifferently bedded out, the sun-bleached curtains, the barefoot girl. The house might have done, but it needed Laure, Laure's decorator, Laure's ideas on landscaping. Houses like this one were often on the market and sold like groceries.

"I remember everything here," said Jérôme.

"Are you sure you're all right?" said Gilles. "I can leave you?" He continued his sums: the servant in carpet slippers. The grand-daughter, a Latin Quarter leftover. Café student type. Probably sleeps with Arabs. My daughters play ping-pong with princesses. My wife knows the smartest people in Paris—dressmakers, the best hairdressers. Lucie looks like a farmer's wife got up for church. Well, she asked for it; she wanted Jérôme. "I'll pick you up on my way back to Paris on Monday," he said. "Ten, eleven. Try to be ready."

Both Girards looked at him. Lucie's round daisy face had gone narrow, as dark as Jérôme's. Gilles experienced a second of pro-phetic vision: under hostile pressure, felt equally, the Girards might grow to be alike. They could become savage, two wolves. One would need to speak softly to them, move cautiously, never make a move that might seem threatening. Having grasped this, having seen not only through layers of time but through walls of people, Gilles did not know if it was of any use to him. He did not know if understanding of people could be used, if the knowledge was good for anything, if it was even worth keeping in mind. "Does that plan suit you?" he said, which was not the kind of thing he usually said to anyone.

"Not the morning," said Nadine. "My grandmother will want her visitors to stay to lunch. Come for them in the afternoon—say, around three o'clock." Gilles was not included in that Mon-day lunch. Lucie noticed, Gilles noticed. As for Jérôme, he had taken the suitcase from the slippered old woman and was halfway to the house.


2


It would have been clear to the meanest intelligence that Nadine had no interest in the Girards. She had been ordered to entertain them. She was her grandmother's victim and by extension theirs. She was disappointed because they had spoken French to her: she had been hoping to show off her English.

Lucie could not sit still. She wanted a way through to Nadine's friendship, and the path she chose was to comment on everything she noticed in Henriette Arrieu's drawing room. After mentioning the loose white slipcovers, a fireplace with a jar of peonies standing in the grate, a series of six English hunting prints on one wall, she picked up a photograph in a silver frame and said to Nadine, "Is that your father?"

"My grandfather."

"He looks too young to be a grandfather."

"He wasn't a grandfather when the picture was taken. He wasn't even a grandfather when he died. Edouard Arrieu."

"Oh, yes. My husband always talked about him."

Jérôme, sitting one armchair away, reading a paperback novel found on a table, did not contradict. Nor did he help Lucie out. She wondered if he really *was* reading: he had opened the book at random.

"My husband didn't actually know your grandfather," Lucie went on. "He must have been already dead when they met. No, I don't mean that. I mean, when your grandmother met my husband. Only he wasn't my husband then. He was here in the nineteen-fifties. Let me see—your grandfather was killed during the war, so that means..."

"...that they never met," said Nadine. Her eyelids drooped. Annoyance? No, it was boredom. She was doing everything her grandmother had told her to do—she had offered the Girards drinks, shown Lucie to her room, she was making interesting conversation, or trying to, but all Lucie would discuss was the dead.

Lucie put the picture down. She was homesick. France was worse than any foreign country because the language was the same as her own. And yet it was not the same. It had a flat and glassy surface here. She felt better with her own people. That was where she came to life. Girls talked to each other at home—you didn't feel this coldness, this hostility. Walking about the room, she stopped at a card table. "Would you like me to play Scrabble with you?" she said to Nadine.

"After dinner, if you want to," said Nadine. She was remembering everything she had been told to do and say. "If you don't object, we shall have our dinner in here instead of the dining room. My grandmother might be on the eight o'clock news. Also, Marcelle, that was Marcelle you saw –"

"With the mustache," said Lucie. Jérôme stared, Nadine stared, and Lucie told herself, It was a mistake, but not a bad one.

Nadine's voice became firm, her diction precise: "Marcelle believes that serving dinner on the card table makes less work. Actually, it makes more. But she is quite old now. I am not suggesting looking at the news because I want to avoid conversation or anything like that. But I think you would like to see the memorial service."

Lucie said, "Is the memorial service for your father?"

"*Grand*father," said Nadine. "No, it isn't for him. It is an association—people who were deported. My grandfather's brother was deported to Buchenwald just because he was a relation. I never knew him either," she said quickly, seeing a question growing on Lucie's face. "My grandmother is invited to all those ceremonies."

And so the card table, cleared of ashtrays and Scrabble, was moved across the room. Marcelle, of the mustache and the felt slippers, brought plates in on a tray, fought off Lucie's attempts to help. Lucie felt herself to be a fluttering bird; even her words of help and protestation sounded like the piping of bird cries. Nadine looked at her; so did Jérôme. Lucie sat down and stared fixedly at the screen.

The most important piece of world news that night was a change in French methods of teaching grammar. A young man wearing a polka-dot tie was solemn about it, and at the same time rather excited: "Fourteen eminent persons will recycle..."

"What is recycle?" said Lucie.

"...the professors now teaching in lycées so that they can reorient their instruction on the basis of structural linguistics." It seemed to be true, for the young man now presented a living witness: "I am only about six weeks ahead of my students at the best of times," said the witness. Lucie would have taken him to be a professor except that he had a squint and a sagging eyelid. A man of his academic stature could have afforded surgery. "Much of this is heresy to me, as a grammarian," he said, "but I have also found it a bath in the fountain of youth."

Lucie tried to think of something courteous, something that would make Nadine proud of her country's school system. "It is interesting, but a pity about his eye," she said. "He must find it a handicap."

"Handicaps are an academic tradition," said Jérôme, and smiled. It was for that rare, unexpected, deeply personal smile that anyone, even musicians stranded at Rimouski, could forgive Jérôme.

Nadine looked as if she had seen nothing except Jérôme smiling from the very beginning.

I don't know what that remark means, thought Lucie. What if it doesn't mean anything? Very often when I haven't understood a remark, it had turned out not to mean anything.

She memorized the dinner they were eating for cousin Gilles, who was as interested in what other people fed on as he was in his own food. His first question when the Girards arrived in Paris had been, "What did they give you on the plane?" Some sort of soup, said Lucie to herself now. Green soup. Some sort of fish in a green sauce. Perhaps the whole meal will be green.

"There is my grandmother," said Nadine.

"Where?" cried Lucie, craning forward. "Where is she?" She could not see any women at all—nothing but old men.

To Jérôme they looked like elderly teachers at a seminary, controlled and withdrawn. Solemn music and torchlight. A priest with a country accent. They seem so quiet now. Old. Spent. They don't wear the striped pajama suits in public anymore.

He remembered a protest march in Paris. It must have been the first time Adenauer came to visit. Or when the French voted to rearm Western Germany after the war. Jérôme had been puzzled then by the men in pajama suits. They were one generation ahead of him: in a way, they had always been old. That day he had seen for the first time in his life how the police destroyed a crowd. They carved the whole into fragments and ground the fragments to crumbs. In those days the police carried capes with lumps of lead sewn in the hems. They rolled up the capes as if they were carpets and swung out. The men wearing the striped costumes tripped and fell and folded their arms for shelter. A head hitting a curb made one sound, a stick on a head made another. In those days you still remembered the brain beneath the bone: no one ever thought of that now. There were no crash helmets for protection, only hands and arms. Even Jérôme ran, though he still believed then that you could not have police running after you unless you deserved it.

In those days Jérôme was still a daily communicant and if he missed Mass he went to Vespers. He was scrupulous about giving Heaven as much as he wanted in return. He was thin at twenty, with a white frozen forehead and candid dark eyes. His eyes ran with the cold. Never in Canada had he been as miserable in winter as here in Paris. He pulled his neck down in the collar of his overcoat and walked with his hands in his pockets. He wore a gray scarf wound two or three times over his chin. His thoughts were like an invalid's, sparse and pale. Girls were drawn to him, but he failed them, they drifted off. Paris in those days was gritty and black. Even the streets looked diseased. The student restaurants smelled of steam and foul meat. He ate once a day, and he owed people money. People laughed at his accent. Then his grandfather died; he came into an inheritance; and he lost his pallor because he ate better food. He began to meet French persons of another sort.

Nadine's grandmother was one. She opened her house in Burgundy to a weekend seminar on Socialism and the French-Speaking Union. Even the name was bold, for everyone still thought "Empire" then. They talked about reforms in Morocco and about an army convoy of jeeps that had been shot at in Algeria. Morocco and Algeria were one in his mind, wave upon wave of vaguely biblical hills dotted with shepherds. Madame Arrieu predicted that one day France would lose her colonies. She made a gentle, visionary declaration. She was fair, blue-eyed, as quick as a bird. Jérôme got to his feet and suggested a strong French-speaking union in an old tradition, with an elected king at its head. Madame Arrieu countered with a proposal that seemed breathtakingly courageous: Why not a Negro king? The idea was so far-fetched, yet so forward-looking, that the seminar program was abandoned and the Negro king remained under consideration for much of the night. Jérôme and Madame Arrieu were still talking after everyone else had gone to bed. Their conversation slackened. They talked about regicide, fathers, men, men and women. She led him across a grassy courtyard to an open summer kitchen paved with black-and-white stones. Her thick yellow hair was pulled up on her head any way; her light shoes were wet with dew. He heard the first tentative sparrows. She made coffee, not very well—she explained that she had never done anything for herself. The canister of coffee beans slipped out of her grasp as she was saying it. It was all she could do not to sweep up the coffee, dust and all, and put everything back in the tin. She hated waste because of the war.

Jérôme had brought a girl with him from Paris for the weekend. She was the girl who had looked down over a stone wall to a motor road and said, "Do you think they rent those towers?" She had made a quick shift of roommates in order to have Jérôme, but she had given up waiting now and gone to sleep. She would remember that weekend and never forgive him. He would forget her for almost twenty years and then not remember her name. A girl from Paris was nothing now, because Henriette Arrieu was new. She had spent the war in England. She was a strict Anglophile.

"Your hereditary enemy," Jérôme reminded her. How can you define yourself without your enemies? he said. How can you know what you are? His face was radiant. She was the fine, pinpointed center of his attention. He had never looked at anyone but Henriette. That was how Jérôme seemed when he became passionate about an idea. She could have told him why women were attracted to him, and why they drifted off.

But all she said was that she had been in London with de Gaulle. (Poor de Gaulle—a forgotten figure now; a country gentleman writing his memoirs; but she had known him ten years ago, at his prime.)

Jérôme remembered de Gaulle. De Gaulle came to Quebec in nineteen forty-three. Jérôme's grandfather leaned one hand on the little boy's shoulder. He leaned with all his weight. "Vive Pétain!" the old man shouted when de Gaulle went by. Jérôme looked up, then back at the General. The General did not turn his head. Did not even blink. He was as straight as a capital I. That was de Gaulle, in Quebec, in nineteen forty-three. Lackey of the English. Puppet of the British Empire. Anti-Christ. Sold out to International Jewry and the Freemasons. Straw man. Terrorist. Playing Stalin's game. On Sundays Jérôme heard it in church. De Gaulle would never be honored in Quebec. He had come because he wanted cannon fodder for the English. Had been paid by Churchill, by the Rothschilds. The money was in Zurich. In the Argentine. Jérôme's grandfather wept tears of real happiness because he had said, "Vive Pétain!"

And as he was calling "Vive Pétain"—at that very moment, perhaps—Edouard Arrieu, sold out by his most trusted friend, went into the convulsion of cyanide poisoning. A week later Arrieu's brother was arrested and deported; he did not know why he had been arrested, or that Edouard was dead.

Jérôme listened to Henriette telling him about this and he tried to fuse "resistant" with "atheist terrorist," which was what he had been told, once, Resistant really meant. She let him finish drinking his bitter coffee out of a crockery bowl and then led him back to the drawing room. This time they went by way of the house, where one white room opened to another. She showed him the picture of a fair-haired man and told him the photograph was nearly all she remembered. She had two repeated nightmares. In one he came back from the dead, but so maimed and disfigured that his character had altered too. The change of person was the frightening part of the dream. In the second nightmare he was young, perfect, and said, "I see that you have started taking yourself seriously now." She did not know which fear was the more destructive, but she sometimes thought that one of the two was bound to kill her.

She parted new red curtains. A sunlit lawn had been unrolled for Jérôme. This day had a quicksilver surface. He thought for the first time in his life, "I could become another person," and knew that the transformation could come by way of a woman. But a few minutes later, in a room now bright and resistant to secrets, before a fireplace filled with field flowers, she put a generation between them.

It was not dignified—worse, it was not sensible—to confide in a young, foreign man. She said, "Is this your first visit to someone's house in France? I'm afraid we French are not hospitable." That was it, that was all, except that for almost twenty years she had answered his letters.

When he knew she was there with all the sad old men of the Resistance, the remnants, the survivors, he looked away in fear of losing her.

"Which one is she?" cried Lucie. "Where?"

"Well, there," said Nadine.

But all Lucie would have seen of the Resistance that night was its sad old men.

Nadine, eating a strawberry tart in her fingers, suddenly began speaking to Jérôme. Because he had smiled, she thought she knew him. He answered something—something concerning politics that Lucie did not try to follow. Well, then, said Nadine, Jérôme was not the Catholic reactionary her grandmother had prepared her for. She laughed as she said it, and Lucie saw that the pinpoint of attention he usually fixed on himself was directed towards Nadine. She watched and listened, cheek on hand. The fact was that Lucie was still hungry. She had just simply not been given enough to eat. Dessert had been cleared away. She dreamed of something more—say, a baked potato.

Jérôme and Nadine had dark eyes. It must be like looking at your own reflection on somebody's sunglasses, she thought. Nadine was a child, a pretty girl, but cold and awkward. Cold with women, at least. Lucie was glad that Jérôme could talk to Nadine, but she did wish he had made a similar effort during the trip from Paris, so that cousin Gilles might have been left with a better impression. Still, if Jérôme considered Nadine's giggles interesting, well, it was all to the good. Any contact he would accept was an opening to life. Lucie went to bed early in order to let them talk.

Hours after this she heard him tearing up every scrap of paper he could find, all but his passport. He always stopped short of real damage. Lucie lay in her bed, breathing as if she were far away, released. She supposed he had torn up Henriette Arrieu's letter and her map. Her breath caught and changed rhythm. She opened her eyes. He sat on the edge of a snowy bed, with his back to her, playing with a lighter, watching the flame. But he would not set this strange house on fire. He was never that careless; he was conscious of danger and knew what it meant.

Late in the night she woke. He was smoking, walking around the room. She thought of the white organdy curtains and of the lighter, but she was not awake enough to speak, only to hear her own mind saying, No, no, he never does the worst thing.

3

Morning. A wind like the sea. Low sky. From the bathroom window Jérôme saw a view that overlapped his memory of it. The house stood on a rise of land below which trees clustered like sponges. Lucie was still sleeping, just as the forgotten girl had slept twenty years before. He shut the bedroom door with care. Long corridor. Waxed stairs, white curve to the wall. Yesterday's ashtrays, yesterday's glasses, pineapple-shaped ice-bucket filled with water, records on the floor. Nadine's hair ribbon. He had played Scrabble with Nadine, using every language they knew, even Latin. Flies started up and circled the white morning air. He walked straight forward; one room led into another, and then he could not go any farther. The end was a small cold room containing a coal range covered over with last winter's newspapers. He smelled coffee and toasted bread, remembered that other kitchen, crossed the same grassy courtyard and found that the sleeping castle was alive. The servants were roused from the dead, the princess awake and eating honey. Two old women looked up at him. One was Marcelle, the other a crony who might have been her twin. They sat at opposite ends of a scrubbed table plucking ducks. The radio between them played an old nostalgic Beatles song, out of the years before Lucie.

On the edge of the table, perched, braced with the toes of one foot, soaking a long piece of buttered crust in a bowl of coffee, was dark-eyed Nadine. She brushed her hair away from her face with the back of her hand, leaving the toast crust sticking out of the bowl like the handle of a spoon. "These two know it all," she said. "They know what became of the Beatles. Has a survey been made about the effects of television on grandmothers?" He remained silent. He was like that sometimes. He might have been joyous beyond measuring, but who could have told? "Well, what are you looking at?" said Nadine, indulgently, like any woman.

He examined her bare feet, the white edge of her dressing gown, the black and white stones of the floor. "Good morning," said Jérôme, and smiled. She was not entirely new to him. He had known girls like Nadine before, had seen the same scowl, the same bold eyes. But those girls had been shabbier. They had worn navy blue raincoats and they had chapped grubby hands. They lived on hard-boiled eggs and weak coffee. In those days an advertisement in the Métro informed them that the purpose of soap was to improve their smell. When he went to the room of a Nadine-student of twenty years ago he saw a cold water tap on the landing.

Nadine walked barefoot over the morning grass, carrying Jérôme's breakfast tray to the dining room. He followed, just barely not treading on the ruffled edge of her gown. "I want to take a picture of you," she said, before he could begin. She pulled the curtains open (her gestures as brutal as Gilles') and showed him the other side of the house, yesterday's side, with the scythed grass and espaliered apple trees. He came out to the terrace just as the sun broke through. Nadine had vanished. Behind him she called, "Jérôme!," and when he swung round she caught the expression she wanted, which was private, meant for one person at a time.

Lucie wanted to believe that Jérôme had been quiet because she needed to rest, but he was far more likely to have forgotten all about her. Unlike Jérôme, she had understood the geography of the house from the beginning. She slipped off her shoes and walked over the grass until she came to the gravel terrace and the dining-room window. Inside the room Nadine, Jérôme, Marcelle, and some other old servant stood each facing a different corner, like a tableau of the four seasons. Marcelle held an upraised broom.

"A rat got in," said Nadine. She repeated yesterday's white-mouse handshake, then slapped hopelessly at the curtains.

"Do these rats run up curtains?" Lucie was merely after knowledge, but Nadine gave her a long cold glance instead of a reply. A few minutes later, as Lucie sat eating her breakfast, she saw the rat. He came along the terrace and thrust his elderly face under the curtain. Without saying anything, Lucie got up and closed the glass doors.

Nadine looked dirty to Lucie. She reminded Lucie of girls she had known in her hospital years, girls who would not wash their underclothes because their mothers had always done it for them. Nadine's sleeve grazed the honeypot. She smoked and sent ash flying. Women smokers are always making little private slums, said Lucie. She had to limit her disapproval to women, otherwise it implied a criticism of Jérôme.

"All our neutral descriptive words in French are masculine," said Nadine, putting Jérôme at the heart of the timeless conspiracy.

"A brute. A person. A victim. All feminine," said Jérôme.

"Brute, victim. Your choice is revealing," said Nadine. "All you people, you intellectuals, are still living in the nineteen sixties." Before then life had been nothing but legends: grandfather's death as a hero, great-uncle's deportation, grandmother in London being brave and bombed.

Lucie tried to break in to defend Jérôme: he most certainly was not a brute, if that was what Nadine had meant. This had the effect of halting, for the moment, the double monologue. Jérôme pulled a piece of cold toast toward him, smashed it carefully, began tormenting the crumbs.

"Only Michael Haydn matters," said Nadine suddenly. Jérôme began to laugh as if he would never stop. Her imitation of Gilles was nothing like him, but Jérôme must have repeated some of the conversation in the car. Harping on Gilles was at least a sign that he noticed other people. At the same time it worried Lucie to think that this spoiled, inexperienced child—Nadine—should mock a successful doctor. It was simply not anything Lucie was used to.

"Gilles is very intelligent," Lucie said. "His first research grant was five hundred thousand dollars—I think. He was younger than I am now."

If Nadine had been trained in any one thing, it was how to divert a conversation from shipwreck. "I have been meaning to ask you," she said to Jérôme. "What do you do?"

"Jérôme hasn't quite found what he wants to do yet," said Lucie, out of habit. She wasn't answering for him—it was just that sometimes he never answered at all. "He has degrees in literature and . . . all of that."

"What a waste," said Nadine. "I was hoping you had studied law, like Fidel Castro." This must have been tied to last night's conversation too, because it made Jérôme smile.

Lucie was not a jealous wife. At least, she did not wish to be one. As soon as she had finished her breakfast she left the two to their politics and private laughter and strolled over the courtyard to the summer kitchen. She would address herself to the servants, and learn something useful about French life.

"May I watch you preparing lunch?" she said.

Marcelle, the mustached senior servant, turned down the radio. She had been smoking a thin cigar while her assistant played Patience. The assistant gathered the cards together with two sweeping movements and put them in the pocket of her apron.

"I won't be cooking lunch for some time, little lady," said Marcelle. "Madame's train from Paris does not arrive until after one."

"I am longing to meet her," said Lucie. "There are no photographs of her in the house. Does she look like Nadine?"

Lucie was no threat to the servants: she was nothing to worry about. The assistant took out her cards again. Sitting down, drinking reheated coffee, homesick Lucie said, "Do you mean you have never been to Canada? You could easily go on a charter flight."

"That is true," said Marcelle.

"We speak the true French," said Lucie, pulling apart everything she had ever heard Jérôme say, as if unraveling a sweater. "The French of Louis XIII. Perhaps. Certainly Louis XV—no one can contradict that. Your kings talked just as I do. As for French cooking, the first settlers had to eat what they could find. They ate molasses." Marcelle said she had eaten molasses; the other woman had not. Allowing for the interruption, Lucie went on, "Also, buckwheat pancakes. The English were rich and ate meat. But our people lived on beans. Sometimes they owned just one plate for each person and they ate the beans on one side of the plate and then turned it over and ate the molasses out of the little hollow."

"What little hollow?" said Marcelle.

Lucie turned her saucer over; the bottom side was flat. "Those were different plates," she said.

"In the country, when I was a child, we ate that way," said Marcelle's crony suddenly. "Cleaned the plate with bread, turned it upside down, ate jam."

But Lucie did not need support. She had known she was right all along. "We suffer from the Oedipus feeling of having been abandoned," she said, unraveling more and more carelessly now. "Abandoned by the mother, by France—by *you*. Who knows what this new Oedipus won't do now that he has grown up? Nothing will ever be the same after the next elections."

Here came a pause, as all three thought of different elections. "It is true that nothing is the same," said the second old woman finally. "Now if it rains you have floods. In good weather the trees die. Only one person in this village was given a telephone, in spite of the last elections."

Marcelle agreed. Elections were meaningless. She told about how her nephew had come back blinded after a war, and how his wife had deserted him. Marcelle was still working at her age because she had spent all her postal savings to support the blind nephew's forsaken children. The other woman now began touching the playing cards, and from something hinted, Lucie understood she had overstayed. She also realized that the crony had not been playing Patience, but telling Marcelle's fortune—divining the risks, chances, and changes in love, health, and money that lay before her still.

Nadine had dressed meantime and she and Jérôme now walked through a gray and redbrick village. Every other façade looked lost and crumbling. He read, across the wall of one blind shuttered house, "The Rural Proletariat Needs Holidays Too."

"I painted that," said Nadine.

The house they stopped at was low and new; it stood in the

way of a much older house of brick and stone falling to ruin. They came straight into a kitchen full of women and small children dressed for church. Black currant liqueur was instantly served in heavy glasses. Jérôme, the only man in the room, sat on a narrow bench and heard a story about a last illness, a death, a will, lawyers' fees, and state taxation. The woman telling this had on a felt hat. An unborn child was considered a legal heir if it had attained five months of its pre-natal life; but if a foetus was unlucky enough to lose its father when it was only four and three-quarter months old, then it came into the world without any inheritance whatever. It could not inherit its father's land, his gold coins, his farm machinery, his livestock.

"What do you think of my washing machine?" said another woman, cutting off the story.

What made this room unlike a kitchen in a city? The smell, said Jérôme, though he could not have defined it. The crumbling house behind this must have been where the family had once lived—for hundreds of years, perhaps.

The owner of the new washing machine was named Pierrette. Her skin was pink, her eyes were blue, and although she spoke to Nadine, it was Jérôme's admiration she wanted. "We used to launder in the public wash-house, in spring water, and dry the sheets on the grass," she said. "God, that spring water was cold! We boiled the sheets with wood ash and rinsed them—it was like melted ice. Your grandmother gave all her linen to my mother to wash," she said to Nadine. "She used to send her sheets from Paris in winter."

"I think I remember," said Nadine. "The fresh scent of the sheets at my grandmother's house. Now everybody has a washing machine and the bedclothes smell of detergents." Nadine looked at the new machine as if expecting Pierrette to say she was sorry she owned it. "You probably laughed at your work," said Nadine severely. "A collective action is...well...collective. But the machine is lonely. Think of it, Jérôme," she said, suddenly turning to him. "Marcelle alone with her machine. Pierrette alone here."

"Our hands used to be chapped and covered with blood," said

the woman with the felt hat. "We had to leave off rinsing so as not to bloody the clothes. And I was allergic to wood ash, although we didn't know the word for allergy then."

"And the cold," said Pierrette. "My mother crossing her arms, trying to bring life back to her cold hands."

"It is true that we laughed," said another woman, so that the male guest would not feel uneasy among women's disagreements. "But we couldn't use the public wash-house now even if we still wanted to, because it is full of rubbish thrown there by Parisians after their picnics." As this was not a criticism, but something she would herself have done had she been a picnicking Parisian, she gave Jérôme a gap-toothed and reassuring smile.

"Why not laugh?" said Pierrette, whose new machine had come out of this conversation second-best. "Certain categories of people seem to be expected to laugh at their work."

"I know," said Nadine, but vaguely, for this conversation kept twisting and doubling back.

"Oh, you know, do you?" said Pierrette.

And now it was Nadine who was undervalued—not just the machine. Nadine had painted a slogan in favor of these people only a few houses away. She took out her change purse and paid for ducks, strawberries, and asparagus—standing very straight, granddaughter of Madame Arrieu and of a national hero for whom streets had been named.

On their way home, Nadine said to Jérôme, "Tell me—what do you think of me?" She wore a leather skirt, leather sandals, there were leather buttons on her blouse. The blouse was transparent. She had not dared to leave off her brassiere, in case Marcelle were to notice and inform her grandmother.

Jérôme said, "Whatever happened, I always liked women."

"All?"

"In a way, yes. Even that farmer's wife—what was her name? Pierrette? If she had said something to me..."

"Something friendly?" said Nadine, without sarcasm. She was considering this as a possibility, a way of looking at people.

"Well, friendly *too*. I could have found her charming. It could work. It could work with almost anyone."

"Then why do you stay with your wife?" said Nadine.

"Because she is my wife," said Jérôme.

There was a finality about this, a warning almost, that closed the subject. All the same, she was sure he had told her something Lucie would never know. She understood that he had no use for her, Nadine, because he had no use for any one person. She wanted to dash ahead and throw pebbles or kick at stone door-steps. But she walked along quietly thinking, I hope I won't grow old too suddenly. She stopped and said, laughing, "Well, kiss me," for that was all she knew about rites.

Lucie sat alone at the Scrabble board putting together high-scoring words in the best places. She jumped up when she heard the two, wishing this was her house and that she could welcome strangers to it. The minute Nadine saw Lucie, she seemed re-minded of an obligation, or a promise. She hung her head and muttered, "I have to fetch my grandmother at the station."

"I know," said Lucie. "They told me in the kitchen. Her train is after one."

"I am sorry to leave you here," said Nadine, as though Lucie had not been alone for much of the morning.

"Oh, but I'd love to come!" said Lucie. "Just to see—a French railway station."

"It is twenty-six kilometers from here, on a boring road. I have something to do in the town," said Nadine. Please don't come, but at the same time please don't think I don't want you, she was also saying.

Lucie wondered if Nadine and Jérôme had quarrelled, if their tense teasing at breakfast had gone straight through to hatred.

"Is it a town with a wall and two towers?" said Jérôme.

"You don't see the towers from the road," said Nadine. "Not the road I take. The old ramparts are there," drawing a half-moon from card table to window with her sandal, "but we drive this way, to the station, which is outside the walls, in the new town." That road ran along the edge of the carpet.

"I know the town," said Jérôme. "I might want to buy a house there. I'm thinking of coming back to France to live. Also," turning to Lucie, "I think we should get back to Paris. Go and pack. We can take a train from the station."

"Oh," said Nadine, flushed, staring from one to the other. She stated the most important objection first: "There is lunch, and the two ducks. And also... my grandmother... she will think I haven't been nice to you."

"We leave tomorrow afternoon, Jérôme, when Gilles stops by to fetch us," said Lucie. Sometimes everyone around her seemed half the size people ought to be. No one could handle Jérôme the way Lucie could—doctors had praised her for it. And it was all instinct on her part, or so she had been told. The more mysterious Jérôme seemed to those other half-sized people, the more Lucie seemed to grow tall.

He seemed under a strain just now; perhaps it had to do with Nadine's lowering of interest. He didn't take a sleeping pill last night, Lucie remembered. He walked round the room. She tidied the Scrabble letters; put the lid on the box; was supreme in her confidence.

Nadine now looked like a girl who might go in for spells of weeping. She muttered that she would get the car out. It was a car they used here in the country, just for running to the station. Not the best environment for Lucie's white dress. Also, the Girards would have to wait and be bored while Nadine did her errands.

"My husband is never bored," said Lucie, saying something she believed profoundly.


4


The car, of a make Lucie did not recognize, and whose shape she associated with the automobiles of her earliest childhood, was fit for a junk-heap. She appraised the worn seat covers, the torn rubber matting on the floor.

"Did anyone hear the thunder last night?" said Nadine.

There was no reply. Lucie, who had not had enough to eat for breakfast, was deep in a vision concerning the physical symptoms of hunger. She saw a stomach contracting and digestive juices pouring forth. Think about something else, she commanded, but all that she could see was home and her own table spread.

"The station," said Nadine, parking with her back to it. She did not trust these two to know a station when they saw one. "I shall meet you here, at the car, in one hour. Can you remember that?"

"We could help with your errands," Lucie said.

"They would bore you. My grandmother wants to have an extra key made for her gate. It is an old lock, over one hundred years old. No locksmith wants to be bothered. I know one who might."

"On a Sunday?" said Lucie—not prying, but simply interested.

"On a Sunday I am certain to find him at home. Don't lose your way if you walk about. Try to stay on the main street. The stores will stay open until one o'clock, if you want to look in windows. Please notice the number of the car—then you can recognize it." She was so anxious to get away that Lucie could feel the strain of it. Something tugged at Nadine, like the moon at the sea. Nadine didn't go to the church this morning, said Lucie suddenly. Neither did the two old servants. It isn't just Jérôme and myself.

She and Jérôme stood together, children abandoned, next to a row of parking meters in front of a provincial station, and watched Nadine trotting away. She had changed her blouse, Lucie noticed, and tied her hair back with a brown velvet ribbon. "Why is a key so important when she has guests to consider?" said Lucie. "What errand can she have that will take her an hour?" Nadine broke into a run. The ribbon came loose. "It's a lie about the key," Lucie said. "I don't believe it. She's going to meet someone. I'm sure it's a man. Probably married. Why else would she make such a mystery of it? Poor Nadine. She must be an orphan. She never mentions her parents—did you notice that, Jérôme? She forgot to put a coin in the meter. Do you think we should? Maybe you don't have to on Sundays. Who were her parents? Did you know them? I never heard you say that Madame Arrieu had any children."

"One stepdaughter," said Jérôme. "She had a husband, but he took cyanide. The two towers are on the far side of the town," he said. He raised a hand, wiping out of the present parking meters and cars. He began to walk, Lucie following. He seemed to have forgotten that she was with him. They turned into a street shaded by plane trees; the street presently became too narrow for trees, or even for people walking together. Lucie fell behind, pushed and jostled and sometimes separated from Jérôme by a Sunday provincial crowd. "I remember all of this," Jérôme said, but not really to her. He looked at his face on a plate glass window. "I remember," he said, walking again.

The antique china shop with plates against blue silk, said Jérôme. The tobacconist's with the yellow mailbox outside. The mailbox used to be another color—I think it was blue. (Lucie saw that he was once more beginning to count something on his fingers.) The fishmonger with the trays of cracked ice. The pastry shop. The café. The second café. The chapel.

"Jérôme, there is a sign saying Concert on the door," said Lucie, close behind him. She was bothered by the Sunday crowd, whose indifference to strangers seemed to her hostile. She wanted Jérôme to stop and rest and even a church would do, even though he said he had finished with religion. All the wrong omens for the day were in place, Jérôme's constellations of disaster: Jérôme not listening, looking at his face in a shopwindow as if he had forgotten what he was; Jérôme tearing paper, fiddling with breadcrumbs, saying he wanted to buy a house in France when they could barely even afford this trip.

Now he had come to a halt before another window and he stared in some puzzlement at stacks of men's shirts in magenta and blue. "Well, what do you think?" he asked, though not quite of Lucie. "I could easily live in this place. Look," he said, moving on. "Look at that." It was a glass bottle twisted in shape, as if it had been wrung out to dry. "In the old days they lowered iron shutters on Sunday. There must be less stealing now. Or else they never close."

"What was it for?" said Lucie. "That useless bottle?"

"To give to friends."

Well, at least it was an answer. But is that what people give each other here? she wondered. Is that what you are expected to bring when you are invited for a weekend? "We can't go on walking up and down the street," she said. "We could sit in that little church. Just for a minute."

It was small, a pink and white room with an almond pastry ceiling. "A private chapel," said Jérôme. "A patrician family with a resident priest. Corsicans. Transplanted Italians. The Stations of the Cross are even uglier than in Quebec." He perceived something Lucie had not noticed—the bare altar, the absence of a crucifix and of a sanctuary light.

He thinks I am praying, said Lucie. He won't interrupt me, because he never does the worst thing, but he is standing behind me despising me. She tried to clear her memory of shop windows; all her closed eyes could see were twisted bottles, magenta shirts. That is what you do on a holy day when there is no God, she said. You walk up and down and let strange people push you and you talk about what you might want to buy. I should have married a doctor after all, she said against her clasped hands. I would have been perfect for a doctor. I would have learned Spanish. Doctors like going to Mexico for their holidays. I could have answered the phone.

Jérôme knew that something had taken place in the chapel. The street had emptied and they could walk side by side now, but they had more trouble walking together than ever before. When they came to a corner, they collided, each attempting to cross in a different direction.

"Do you see that policeman?" said Jérôme, speaking to Lucie, only to her, now that she had stopped trying to listen. "I'm sure he was here twenty years ago. Look at his face. Red and stupid. Look at him with his red nose. Why won't you look? I remember this café," he went on. "We came here after a film." It was a café where they served nothing except pancakes. The waitresses wore Breton costumes, here, miles from the sea. It reminded him of the baroque ceiling in the chapel. The street was all a mistake, as if it had been knocked together by a child.

At home everything looks the same, said Lucie. We don't want these landslides, this strangeness. Who is "we"? What film? Was it Madame Arrieu? He doesn't want to see her again. He's afraid of seeing her. That is why he spent the night walking around the room instead of sleeping.

Nadine had left the car unlocked and the key stuck in the ignition; it showed how anxious she had been to get away from the Girards. Jérôme and Lucie sat in the back of the car holding hands. He told her about a girl he had brought to this town, a long time ago. Corinne was the girl's name. As soon as he had seen the Breton café the memory returned. Corinne worked in a bookshop in Montparnasse. She wanted Jérôme to think about nothing but her, and when she saw that he was interested in differences of opinion—oh, and in himself, and in girls in general, because they were unlike himself, they belonged to a different culture—Corinne could not understand it. Lucie was not like Corinne, he said. She had a natural goodness that welled up like a spring. Even if she wanted to be selfish and to put herself first, she would not know how to begin. He meant every word of this; she was not to forget what he was telling her now. "Even when you're asleep, you're better than other women," he said.

*This* was felicity. No one but Lucie knew what Jérôme could be like. He told her things he had never told anyone; even the doctors had said so. She gave him the simplest, most loving response she could think of, which was, "You didn't sleep well last night. You must be tired. Did you take anything this morning? Not even an Equanil?"

"For God's sake, stop asking me how I am," he shouted, and he flung out of the car and left her just as Nadine and her grandmother came walking across the square.

Through shock and horror that suddenly seemed like rain on a window, Lucie saw this new person—saw her sunglasses, her straw summer handbag, her linen suit; watched her greeting Jérôme, who now strolled back to the car as though he had left it for no purpose but this meeting. With the quick tally came a feeling of injustice, of unfairness, as though Lucie had been harshly treated. She could not attach the conviction to any one word or event. Jérôme was often impatient when she turned the conversation to his health, a turning she found too natural to avoid. Was it Lucie's fault if she had not looked her best yesterday? And what ought to be her best now, at the age of twenty-eight? Her sturdy blond beauty had suffocated under hospital training, and then this marriage. Was it Lucie's fault? Jérôme's?

"My grandmother," said Nadine.

"Did you have a good dinner last night?" said Madame Arrieu, shaking hands. "Are you pleased with your room? Did this child take good care of you?" Settled in, her profile to Lucie, she said, "Nadine, have you written your parents?"

"Oh, she has parents!" cried Lucie, from the back. "I am so glad."

Madame Arrieu quickly looked round. A miniature, eager Lucie was held on the surface of her glasses. Nadine frowned, half turned, elbow on the back of her seat, as she moved the car away from the curb. "Nadine! Answer Madame Girard."

"My parents are cruising around Greece," said Nadine.

"Nadine! Not Greece. The coast of Jugoslavia—please. Your parents would never spend a holiday in a fascist country."

"The postcards all look the same," said Nadine.

"In Nadine's ideal future there will be no need for holidays," said her grandmother.

"Or life will be one long holiday and the word will fall into disuse," said Jérôme. "If I could start my life over from the beginning, I would think along those lines." Lucie opened her mouth; stared; but before she could speak, he said under his breath, "Stop watching me!"

"And how are you, Jérôme?" said Henriette Arrieu. She seemed to mean something more than an ordinary greeting.

"He gets a little tired sometimes," said Lucie. It was not her fault—the words were out before she could stop and think about them. It was a bad habit, yes, but who had given her the habit? This time she met his eyes straight on. Why, I could hate him, she thought.

"I am all right," he said. "As much as anyone is."

"Oh, are you all right?" said Lucie. "What do you mean by all right? What about telling Nadine you wanted to buy a house here? What about last night, when you sat on your bed tearing paper? What about that other time, when the sun came out with Latin inscriptions in eighteenth-century lettering? One day you saw the sun with a perfect eye in its center—eyelashes, everything. When you saw the eyelashes again you called me and said, There, you can see them. You held your dark glasses at arm's length and looked out the window. But I had left the iron connected. There must have been a short circuit. The cord, the socket, everything began to smoke. I started to cry but you did the right thing, turned off the meter, disconnected the iron. How long are you going to keep insisting you're all right? Who else sees the sun with an eye and eyelashes? You can't even take an Equanil if I'm not there to remind you. Suppose I have to start taking your medicine too? Then where will we be?"

"Was there thunder in Paris?" said Nadine to her grandmother. "Did you hear thunder last night?"

Lucie understood that somehow, unheard, in a private family message code, Nadine was warning her grandmother: Be careful. The Girards do nothing but quarrel with each other and Lucie Girard may even be a little mad.

Ah, but why be angry? said Lucie. Why blame Jérôme? Anyone would think he owed me something. Perhaps there is a large unpaid debt and that is the paper he keeps tearing. Perhaps he had a bill he is too kind to present me with.

"Jérôme is fine," she said. "There are men worse than Jérôme. Oh, much worse. My brother-in-law held a knife to my sister's throat all one night. In the morning he went to the office as if nothing had happened. My sister thought it over and decided not to leave him. He had never done it before and might never again. Also, they hadn't finished paying for their house. Jérôme has only one thing the matter. He does not quite understand the effect he has on other people. Jérôme has had a superior education and he does not care what other people think."

"Did you pay Pierrette for the strawberries, Nadine?" said Madame Arrieu. "What about the key?"

Lucie turned and looked back at the town. Something was missing; once, during a long train journey in childhood, she had been disturbed to find the restaurant car had disappeared during the night. That is the way I feel now, she said. Forces are at work in the dark. We ought to reject sleep. Stay awake. Try to hear. Avoid being caught unawares. Jérôme is right when he walks up and down in the dark and refuses a sleeping pill. He would be right even to keep away from me; but he can't.

5.

"Do you want to take all those strawberries to Paris?" said Gilles. The seat next to Gilles was piled with fruit and flowers. The dog had been forced to lie on the floor. Jérôme and Lucie sat together; Lucie leaned forward so that she and Gilles could talk. "There was plenty to eat in Dijon, but nothing worth buying," said Gilles. "Imagine a world with nothing to eat and nothing to buy. That would be hell. It's probably the future, if anyone cares."

"Jérôme nearly bought a house," said Lucie.

Gilles repressed saying, With what money? He went on, "Saturday we had the damndest thing to eat—sauerkraut. In Dijon. It was supposed to be exotic. The Japanese buyers didn't only eat it, they asked for the recipe. I found out about your Madame Arrieu. Funny that I hadn't heard about her. Laure would know, of course. *He* was famous."

"He took cyanide," said Lucie. "He was very fair, he could have passed for a German. He did, in fact, and they caught him."

"They're friends of *Jérôme*? Are you sure?"

"We've been invited to go on a cruise next year with the whole family," said Lucie. "But not around any fascist state."

"Saturday they gave us the sauerkraut," said Gilles. "Sunday we had salmon. I could have sworn it was frozen. Then capon with a Beaujolais sauce. The sauce was gray. I think there was flour in it. Laure would have sent the whole thing back. Today we had shoulder of lamb. It was called *à la Washington* and basted in whiskey. That was to impress the American buyers, but there were complaints. Then we had *soufflé Hiroshima* for the sake of the Japanese. Do you know what *soufflé Hiroshima* is? Vanilla ice cream in an orange with a paper parasol. You don't eat the parasol. Why am I so interested in menus, I wonder? I should be writing cookbooks."

"Because you're a bachelor," said Jérôme. This was the first thing he had ever said to Gilles directly.

There, said Lucie to herself. He is making a contact. She hoped that Gilles understood and appreciated Jérôme's progress.

"Yes, a bachelor," Jérôme went on. "You are a bachelor with three children and whatever her name is. Laure. You'll end up shuffling around that New Haven house counting your medieval saints and testing the door locks. Wondering what you'll have to eat tomorrow and trying to recall yesterday's pudding. You will be wearing old tennis sneakers and the dog will trail along carrying a third shoe even more disgusting than those you will have on your feet. When you come to Paris on your annual bachelor visit, Laure will hear you in the hall and say, 'Is that you, darling?' because she will have forgotten your name and what part you play in the family, but she will have finally recognized the little bachelor shuffle."

"This weekend was good for Jérôme," said Lucie. "Though in my opinion he is still behind with his sleep."

Gilles reached over the pile of fruit and flowers to grope for the radio. "Shut up," he said to the silent dog. He was remembering his brief glimpse of the Girards with narrowed faces, as unpredictable as animals, and he said to himself, I've got two killers there in the back of the car.

"Be sure you turn on the right Haydn," Lucie said.

Between collar and cap, Gilles felt the coldest touch he had ever imagined. He gripped the wheel. It was a matter of keeping the car steady. But when he stole a look at them in the mirror he saw they had gone to sleep. He was alone in the world with something soothing—Vivaldi. No need to worry about the right one because there never had been another. He was not in any great danger, for the moment; the essential Gilles was not yet slumped, shot, hacked, with a dunce cap crowning the remains, though it seemed that nothing less than a murder could round off the Burgundy weekend. Why had he invited them into his car to begin with? If it was a matter of company, even the dog would have been better.

One of them stirred, sighed, leaned forward.

"Lucie?"

"Yes."

Like all the poor, they were ungrateful. Like all the ignorant, they were unconcerned with knowledge. Like all of the past, they were filled with danger. "Is Jérôme all right?" he finally said.

"He has just proved it," she said. "And he proved it all weekend. But nobody knows that I know." She sat back and looked out the window, away from both men, wishing them vanished, for the rest of their time together.

*1970–71*

## A NOTE ON THE AUTHOR

Mavis Gallant was born in Montreal in 1922 and worked as a journalist at the *Standard* before moving to Europe in 1950 to devote herself to writing fiction. After travelling extensively she settled in Paris, where she still lives. Her many short-story collections include *The Other Paris*, *The End of the World*, *Home Truths*, *In Transit* and *The Moslem Wife*. She is also author of the novels *Green Water, Green Sky* and *A Fairly Good Time*. She is a Fellow of the Royal Society of Literature in London and a Companion of the Order of Canada. *The Selected Stories of Mavis Gallant* are published by Bloomsbury.